Acclaim for Ian Slater

WORLD WAR III

"Superior to the Tom Clancy genre . . . and the military aspect far more realistic."
—*The Spectator*

MacARTHUR MUST DIE

"A most satisfying what-if thriller . . . The plot [is] a full-speed-ahead page-turner. . . . Flashy, fast fun."
—*New York Daily News*

"Searing suspense . . . [A] rousing, splendidly told adventure."
—*Los Angeles Times*

"Taughtly written, this novel is loaded with scenes that will have you grasping the book so tightly your knuckles will turn white. . . . The final scene is a climactic hair-raising thriller."
—*West Coast Review of Books*

Please turn the page
for more reviews. . . .

FIRESPILL
"In the right place at the right time with the right story."
—*MacLean's*

"A good, powerful, readable, terrifying, inescapable story."
—*Vancouver Sun*

"An excellent book . . . There's something for everyone in the plot."
—*Canadian Book Review Annual*

ORWELL: THE ROAD TO AIRSTRIP ONE
"It is doubtful that any book provides a better foundation for a full understanding of Orwell's unique and troubling vision."
—*The Washington Post*

"The best introduction I know of to the life and ideas of George Orwell, [written] with insight, intelligence, and imagination."
—PETER STANSKY
Author of *From William Morris to Sergeant Pepper: Studies in the Radical Domestic*

"Penetrating and illuminating—one of the few treatments of Orwell which is at once completely informed and freshly intelligent."
—ROBERT CONQUEST
Author of *Reflections of a Ravaged Century*

By Ian Slater

FIRESPILL
SEA GOLD
AIR GOLD RED
ORWELL: THE ROAD TO AIRSTRIP ONE
STORM
DEEP CHILL
FORBIDDEN ZONE*
MACARTHUR MUST DIE
WW III*
WW III: RAGE OF BATTLE*
WW III: ARCTIC FRONT*
WW III: WARSHOT*
WW III: ASIAN FRONT*
WW III: FORCE OF ARMS*
WW III: SOUTH CHINA SEA*
SHOWDOWN: USA vs. Militia*
BATTLE FRONT: USA vs. Militia*
MANHUNT: USA vs. Militia*
FORCE 10: USA vs. Milita*
KNOCKOUT: USA vs. Militia*

*Published by The Ballantine Publishing Group

KNOCKOUT

Ian Slater

BALLANTINE BOOKS • NEW YORK

A Ballantine Book
Published by The Ballantine Publishing Group
Copyright © 2001 by Bunyip Enterprises

www.ballantinebooks.com

ISBN 0-449-00559-3

Manufactured in the United States of America

First Edition: December 2001

10 9 8 7 6 5 4 3 2 1

For Marian, Serena, and Blair

ACKNOWLEDGMENTS

Once again, I would like to thank Mr. D. W. Reiley for his expertise regarding small arms and associated subjects, and my friend David Leask for his communication technology advice. As always, I would like to thank my wife, Marian, whose patience, typing, and grammatical skills continue to give me invaluable support in my work.

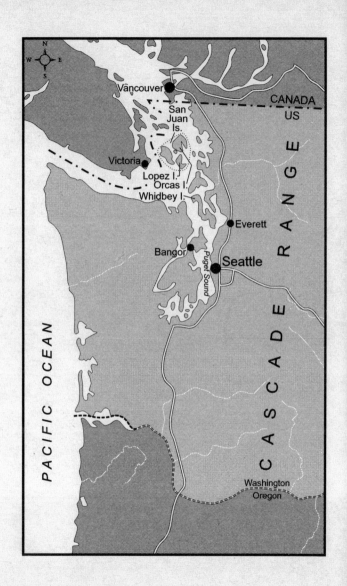

KNOCKOUT:
USA vs. Militia

PROLOGUE

THE MAN'S VOICE was calm, measured. "Is this the White House?"

"Yes, sir. How may I direct your call?"

"You'll do."

"Sir. How may I direct your call?"

The man shook his head. He was in a phone booth on the I-5 above Seattle, watching the line of traffic branching off toward Anacortes, the terminal for the ferry run to the San Juan Islands off Washington State.

"Sir, how may I direct your call?"

"To the President."

"Sir, I can't—"

"Now listen to me. You tell the son of a bitch that he's to release everyone at Camp Fairchild within twenty-four hours or the USMC is going to blow something up."

"Sir, could you repeat—"

Of course, NSA—No Such Agency—would now be taping him. He'd have to cut it short. Even so, he wasn't at all flustered. "The USMC," he told the receptionist, "is the United States Militia Corps, and that's twenty-four hours from *now*." He hung up and drove over to the mall at Burlington for a coffee and a sugar-soaked Cinabon roll. He prided himself on keeping in shape—everyone in his unit did—but he believed in rewards too, and he had been planning this for a long time,

1

ever since the government inquiry came out with what he considered whitewash hogwash about Waco, saying the Federals had done nothing wrong. Uh-huh, they only used *tanks* against women and kids before they incinerated them.

Twenty-four hours after the phone call, no one at Fairchild, where the Feds held all the militia who'd run afoul of the law, had been released. They probably thought he was a nut case.

CHAPTER ONE

Everett, Washington State

EVERYONE IN THE crowd of visitors, most of them American, was excited, impatient to start the tour of the Boeing plant. And why shouldn't they be? Since 1916, Boeing had made the biggest and the best, everything from the Model 40 which had carried the U.S. mail and two passengers—"load permitting"—to the ubiquitous B-52 bomber; the Saturn booster that had launched Armstrong to the moon; the ever popular Air Force One; the International Space Station in '98; and, for the millennium, the magical tilt-rotor Osprey, which performed either as a standard prop plane or helicopter. And sitting on the test runway, not far from the tour center, was one of the new generation of 737s, the world's largest digital state-of-the-art completely computer-designed twin jet airliner. A band struck up the national anthem of Thailand amid a cluster of suits, sunglasses, and ribbons as Boeing's latest effort was ceremoniously handed over to its new owners.

Mel Haley and Pete Rainor had bought tickets for the eleven A.M. tour. It was now ten-fifty and like most of the other tourists, they were biding their time looking at the exhibits in the tour center. Rainor stared at the big grainy black-and-white blowup of the massive Flying Boats Boeing had built just before the Second World War, when airfields were scarce, which quickly changed with the onset of war, dooming the flying palaces. "Every passenger," Rainor said, "had his own bed. Can you believe it?"

"What—oh, yeah," Mel said, wondering whether he had enough time to run across the parking lot to the washroom. Rainor had told him there were none on the tour. He heard a woman behind the ticket counter trying to explain to a group of Japanese that no one under four-foot-two or cameras were allowed on the tour. Rainor told Mel he'd better decide about the washroom because the eleven A.M. tour would soon be called to the theater for a ten minute time-lapse film of how a Boeing 737 was constructed. After that they'd board the bus and go to the Everett Building, which would be about another ten minutes. And then they'd go through the long tunnel to the big freight elevator capable of holding an entire busload of tourists at one time.

Rainor's attention was fixed on a photo of the Flying Boat's flight deck. "Enormous," he told Mel, but his companion was preoccupied with his bladder. It was the excitement, he guessed. He'd always wanted to go on a tour of the Boeing factory at Everett. Hell, just the building alone was worth seeing, the largest by volume in the world.

"How many football fields did you say it would hold?" Mel asked, trying to put the washroom out of mind.

"I didn't," Rainor said. "You must've read it somewhere."

Mel shrugged. He was more a soccer than a football fan anyway. "I'm gonna ask the guide how many soccer fields it covers."

"Don't you ask him anything," Rainor advised.

Mel nodded. Rainor had a point. It wasn't that Mel thought Rainor was inherently smarter, but he had done all the homework, and besides, Mel knew he was a relative newcomer. He hailed from the wet west side of the Olympic Peninsula, from down near La Push, where it rained fourteen feet a year. He'd tried to make a living as a fisherman, but had joined the militia because of the Supreme Court ruling that said he couldn't fish for salmon but the local Mi'kmaq Indians could, and that they could kill whales "for ceremonial reasons," when anyone else would have been jailed for doing the same thing. It was just like some soft-assed liberal judge in Washington, D.C., to side with the Indians, he thought, because they claimed they were the first inhabitants of North America and had been exploited. Who wasn't? he wondered. And anyway, he wanted them to bring that guy out from the vault in Oregon—the corpse that anthropologists said had Caucasian features and thereby predated the Indians' occupancy of the North American continent. But oh no, the Indians had made a big stink, and together with the soft-assed liberals, had made sure the guy was shoved away in a vault.

" 'Cause," Mel opined, "if it's proven the Indians weren't here first, there goes their claims for being First Nations and all that bullshit. An end to the federal handouts. Then the sons of bitches might have to live like the rest of us." His favorite No Trespassing sign against the Feds, Indians, and everybody else was one he'd seen on the Oregon side of the Columbia River that said simply: "Keep the Fuck Out!" A free man on his land, unafraid of the government. That's how it should be, and if you found any goddamn arrowheads on your property, you should throw them in the river before the goddamn gov-

ernment declared your place a midden—"a sacred site"—and
sent out some goddamn medicine man to help the Feds ex-
propriate it as a "heritage site."

Mel didn't take in much of the time-lapse film on the construction of the 737 because now that the tour—or rather,
the introduction to it—had begun, he was getting nervous.
There was a sense that there was no turning back. The only
thing he remembered about the movie was how fragile the
huge jumbo seemed when you saw it not as a finished, solid-
looking object, but as an arrangement of so many individual
pieces.

When the lights came back on, one of the guides, a snappily
dressed young blonde in her early twenties, gave a short spiel
about safety in the plant. "You'll be seeing a lot of signs saying
FOD—anyone know what that means? Yes, that's right, 'Foreign Objects Debris.' The planes you'll see cost millions of
dollars to make, and we don't want anything to get into these
planes that shouldn't be there. You might be flying on one of
them someday, and you don't want anything in there that
shouldn't be there. Right?" Ripple of laughter. "Which is why
Boeing doesn't permit any cameras or bags, etcetera, which
might accidentally fall down onto the assembly floor from the
viewing level."

"Yeah, right," said a paunchy, golf-shirted tourist in shorts
sitting next to Rainor. "Wouldn't be because they don't want
you taking photos, would it? Trade secrets?"

Pete smiled but said nothing. Now the pert blonde was di-
viding the theater audience of a hundred into two busloads
according to the color of their tickets. "Mind your step, and
when you return, remember the gift shop near the entrance to
the parking area."

"I'm gonna get a bunch of 'em Boeing pens with the
reading light at the tip," said a teenage boy next to Mel.
"They're cool, man."

"You be frugal," his mother said. "Got a ways to go yet."

"What's frugal mean?"

"It means," the golf shirt said, "be careful. Don't blow it all at once."

"Don't look at him," Rainor hissed at Mel. "Anonymous, remember. Stay focused."

"Watch your step, sir," the driver advised Rainor, who, following his own advice, kept his head down, looking at the step stool, not at the driver. Mel followed suit.

A middle-aged man took over as guide on the ten minute drive past security toward the Everett plant's main factory building. ". . . immense structure covers 98.3 acres . . . seventy-five football fields and 911 basketball courts, 2.33 miles of pedestrian tunnels. Now, when we alight from the bus we'll descend a flight of stairs then turn left into one of these tunnels. It's one-third of a mile long, or half a kilometer for some of you folks. Please keep to your right because other tour groups'll be coming out on your left. And don't be surprised if you see some strange characters in this tunnel—they're joggers. Boeing encourages its workers to stay fit—by the way, women earn the same pay as the men here." There was a smatter of applause. "And the tunnels are an ideal workout for joggers—particularly up here in the Northwest where, as you might have heard, it rains a little in the winter. Just stay well to the side of the tunnel, otherwise these joggers'll run right over you. Last year we lost about six tourists that way . . . no, just kidding, folks."

A sarcastic "Ha! Ha!" came from the frugal kid.

As the fifty of them walked along the eastern side of the north-south tunnel, Mel took a quick look at one of the three twelve-inch-diameter pipes that ran along the sides. The lowest of the three pipes was ringed with a green stripe for compressed air. The red-striped pipe identified it as the fire sprinkler feed. After they ascended several floors in the big, freight-sized elevator, they found themselves on the observation deck.

The first thing Mel saw when he exited the elevator was a huge, open-shark-mouthed cutaway section of a jumbo jet, showing its three levels. There was an excited babble of foreign tongues as people reacted to the height of the cutaway and the vastness of the production floor spread out beneath them. The guide exhorted everyone to move down and around the protective railings so they could get a better view of the 777s.

"Even given the cold winters of the Northwest, the building has no heating bill—or in the summer no air-conditioning bill," he said, "because there are so many lights that enough heat is generated to keep the place at a steady sixty-nine to seventy-one degrees Fahrenheit. If it gets too hot or too cold, why, we just slide open or shut one of the six big doors. Four of the doors measure three hundred feet long by eighty-seven feet wide, or, if you like, ninety-one meters by 265 meters."

"Ain't that big!" the kid said.

"Shut your mouth!" Mr. Paunch retorted. "Biggest goddamn doors you'll ever see!"

"Language, Henry!" his wife cautioned.

The guide was pointing to the forty-ton-load crane, an enormously wide I-bar that looked like part of the roof until it began moving, with its red housing attached halfway along and below it. Mel glanced nervously at his watch, then at Rainor, who, cool as always, was looking around and listening as if he'd never been on the tour before. Rainor's gaze moved from one of four blue explanatory diagram boards attached to the observation deck rail down to the production floor below.

The guide was saying something about how, when they painted each aircraft, it added over five hundred pounds to the weight of the plane. Someone asked how much fuel was in a jumbo's wing.

"Seventeen thousand gallons."

"Wow!" It was the kid again.

"Shut it!" his father told him.

Mel could feel his heart beating faster as they reentered the elevator and saw the big door close. He felt claustrophobic. The press of fifty people, plus his anger at the kid, combined with the knowledge of what he—or rather, Rainor—was about to do, gave him a pain in his throat. He felt as if he couldn't get enough air. And his bladder felt like it was going to burst.

They exited the elevator back into the tunnel as another tour group entered. Mel and Rainor fell back to the rear of the crowd. "Don't sweat it," Rainor told him. "It'll take less than thirty seconds. Timer's already set."

"You got the sponge?" Mel asked anxiously.

"Oh shit," Rainor said. "I forgot!"

Mel went white.

"Just kidding," Rainor told him. "Relax, for chrissake."

A jogger who had reached the southern end near the stairs leading up to the bus U-turned and ran back the other way.

"Damn, I need to pee," Mel said.

"Hang on."

Behind them they heard a thump as the elevator doors closed. The tunnel was empty.

"All clear?" Rainor asked, reaching in his jacket pocket for the two-inch-square sponge.

"All clear," Mel confirmed. "Go!"

Rainor bent down as if to tie his shoes, but instead reached quickly under the pipe with the green stripe, wiped for dust, slipped the sponge back into his pocket, and was taking out a hamburger-patty-sized slab of C-4 plastique with detonator and timer attached when Mel hissed, "Stop!" A cluster of Japanese tourists, having gone the wrong way after alighting the bus, came running along the tunnel toward the elevator.

The sudden noise in the tunnel unnerved Mel so much he almost wet himself. "Jesus Christ!"

Rainor nonchalantly placed the lump of C-4 by his shoe and pretended to do up his laces, his right hand blocking any view of the explosive. "Calm down," he told Mel, looking down at his shoes. "It's all right."

"I think one of 'em had a camera," Mel said.

"Camera's aren't allowed," Rainor reminded him.

Mel turned his head to watch the Japanese laughing, some of them panting as they reached the elevator, whose door soon closed. "It's clear now," he said, his shirt collar sodden with sweat.

Rainor slid his hand under the pipe, pressing the plastique to the surface nearest the wall. Mel, with a trembling hand, reached in his pocket and took out two six-inch strips of adhesive tape, which Rainor crisscrossed on the puttylike plastique. It had taken him less than ten seconds. "Can you see it?" he asked Mel as he used the small household sponge to wipe away a few dust particles on the floor that had fallen from the pipe.

"Negative," Mel said, which made Rainor smile.

"Ten-four," he said, chuckling as he got up and they began walking toward the stairs.

"What's so funny?" Mel asked.

"Negative," Rainor ribbed him.

Mel chuckled too, relief sweeping over him now that the charge had been placed. As they reached the stairs, Mel started taking them two at a time toward the sunlight.

"Slow down," Rainor cautioned him. "Lots of time."

There were still ten or so people waiting their turn to board the bus.

When they arrived back outside the tour center, Mel walked—Rainor told him not to run—straight from the bus to the washroom and then to Rainor's Chevy Tahoe. They headed back out to the I-5, and Rainor, noting the time and keeping a close eye on his speed, drove fourteen miles south to Lynwood. An hour and two tour groups later, he made a call—his second—to the White House.

"White House switchboard. How may I direct your call?"

"How you doin'? I'm from the USMC. I called you people yesterday about Camp Fairchild."

"Yes, sir. How may I direct your call?"

"You can tell the President there's gonna be an explosion in one minute at the Boeing plant in Everett, Washington, because he didn't do what I told him. And tell the son of a bitch if he doesn't want to lose the next election, he'll release those boys from Fairchild right now or there'll be more trouble."

"Ah, sir, could you—"

"And you boys at NSA," Rainor yelled, "have a nice day!"

"Sir?"

The line went dead.

The plastique detonated with a sharp crack, as its explosion tore through the tunnel like a tornado. Compressed air screamed out of the severed pipe, hurling a passing jogger and several members of a tour group across the tunnel like rag dolls, slamming them into the other side of the tunnel. Their screams were lost in the tunnel's feral roar of "wild air," as it was later described by investigators. Immediately, every air pressure tool in the production line went dead, at a staggering financial cost to Boeing. The tour center was abruptly closed, but no one was allowed out of it or its parking area until checked by both Boeing security and the Snohomish County Sheriff's Office.

News of the sabotage was being broadcast by King TV within two minutes, and on CNN, via the King feed, three minutes later. The President and aides were watching it in the West Wing's National Security Advisor's office, kitty corner to the Oval Office, where they'd been discussing—some said later by pure coincidence—the Emergency Response Team's estimate of the greatest potential threat to the United States in the twenty-first century, "Domestic Terrorism."

National Security Advisor Michael Brownlee turned to his assistant. "Was it the same man who made the call yesterday?"

"Secret Service people think it is. Same voice print."

"Then it *is* the same man," Brownlee said irritably.

"Yes, sir."

"Location is different, I suppose," Brownlee said.

"Yes. NSA had one tagged at a call box at Burlington, Washington State. The other—about ten minutes ago, just before the explosion—was forty-five miles south of Burlington on the Washington-Oregon interstate."

"Same demand?"

"Yes, sir. Everyone in Camp Fairchild to be—"

"Shh," the President cut in. "Turn up the sound."

CNN was interviewing a group from the Militia of Michigan. Veteran correspondent Marte Price, quoting from the *National Post* of August 12, 2000, noted that MOM had been founded by preacher and gun dealer Norm Olson and had grown from twenty-eight members in 1994 to twelve thousand six years later. The militiamen said they were sorry for those hurt in the blast, "But hey," one of them was telling Marte Price, "the government has to be called to account. We're being taxed to death. *Real* criminals are getting off scot free. Illegal immigration from Mexico's out of control. We've got Mexican workers undercutting American workers, and the Bureau of Land Management's out of control. Something you folks back East don't understand: less than twenty percent of land in the eastern United States is owned by the Feds. In the west it's more than sixty percent. Can't spit out here 'less you got a special permit. An' meanwhile you're giving the Indians special privileges, their own police forces, own lands. Hell, the Founding Fathers meant there to be the same law for everyone. And then you've got all these know-nothing liberals and their gun registration. What they want to do is to disarm the American citizen. It's a clear violation of our Second Amendment rights!"

"I suppose it hasn't occurred to him that he's free to say what he's just said," the President commented, "that we haven't got him locked up."

"Maybe we should," Brownlee said.

The President smiled. "Well, I'm not going to yield to blackmail. You'd think they'd realize that." He paused, watching the pictures of the vast Boeing plant, idled by the explosion. "We're going to have to take the gloves off with these people before they do any more damage. How in hell were they able to get into the Boeing plant like that?"

"Free society, Mr. President," Brownlee answered.

"I don't need a civics lecture, Mike. I mean, wasn't there any damn security up there?"

"Not enough, apparently," Brownlee answered. "But you can bet there will be now. I wouldn't be surprised if that's the end of tours to the Boeing plant."

An excited aide burst in, his hair and bow tie askew. "We've got them!" He had everyone's attention.

"Well, go on!" Brownlee snapped.

"Japanese tourist. Didn't understand the tour guide, apparently, that people on the tour aren't supposed to take cameras. He had one of those palm-sized digitals. He was shooting in some tunnel that they say leads up to an observation deck. Anyway, he got these two guys in the frame—one of 'em kneeling down, looking like he was planting some device. The Jap heard—"

"Jap*anese*," the President corrected him. "Go on."

"The Japanese guy heard the news of the explosion, put one and one together, and contacted the police."

"So they've been arrested," Brownlee said.

"No. I mean they know who they are. I've seen it on the computer image they sent us. You can see the guy kneeling and—"

"Jesus Christ, Lawson!" Brownlee exploded at the aide. "You said they *had* them!"

The President raised his hand to quiet everyone down. "FBI'll pick them up without much trouble. Show their mugs on TV. Offer a reward." He turned to Brownlee. "Mike. These militia no-hopers in Fairchild, will they have heard about this?"

"No, sir. I've checked that one out already. No TV or radio allowed at Fairchild. Nada. Part of the price they pay for federal crimes."

"Good," the President said. "We don't want to encourage them, make them think they're getting out or anything." He turned to his aide, Lawson. "Raymond, let me know the moment we've got these two yokels behind bars."

"Yes, sir."

"Excuse me, Mr. President." It was Donna Fargo, a tall, striking blonde who was director of media relations. "The press are clamoring for a response."

"I don't respond to militia threats, Donna. That's my response." He grinned, looking around the room. "Especially when we're dealing with militia idiots who get caught on camera."

There was loud laughter as he exited, telling Donna, "Besides, this thing'll blow over as soon as the buffoons are arrested."

CHAPTER TWO

GENERAL WILLIAM C. Wilcox, Commandant of the United States Militia Corps, was furious. Rainor and Haley's caper hadn't been authorized by USMC HQ, and their failure to get anyone released from Fairchild made the militia look doubly stupid and inept in the eyes of both the Federals and the general public. Ironically, however, the dismal failure of the two militiamen's "cowboy antics," as the commandant angrily referred to them, had now made it imperative, for the sake of militia morale and continued recruitment in all states, that the Fairchild question be settled once and for all. What was needed, the commandant told his shift, was a knockout blow against the Feds, something so audacious it would make the whole country sit up and take notice.

"Who's going to do it?" was the question amongst the militia corps.

The answer was, "Lucky McBride."

"Who's he?" inquired a new recruit from MOM, the fourteen thousand Militia of Michigan contingent.

"A legend," said one of the old hands.

And it was true. Lucky McBride, a major in the militia corps, was as famous among the five million corpsmen throughout the country as his Federal nemesis, General Douglas Freeman, and he was ready to strike, selected for the job by the militia's chiefs of staff because he was the only one who had passed the test at their Idaho camp at Hayden Lake. There, the militia general, Wilcox, had given him a Colt .45 handgun, told him there was a traitor in the next room, and to go in and shoot him. McBride stepped into the room, saw it was his best friend, Gunner Brock, and fired twice. They were blanks, but McBride didn't know that. It shocked the hell out of Brock, but the message was unequivocal: McBride would stop at nothing in his war against the federal government. And Wilcox decided there and then that McBride was unquestionably the man for the most dangerous mission the rebels had ever undertaken against the Federals.

"Are he and Brock still friends?" the MOM recruit asked.

"Sort of."

"Geez," the recruit said. "McBride must be tough."

Yes, they told him, but Freeman, commander of FEDFOR, the federal forces, was just as tough. Freeman's force, which included SpecWar types, had rounded up many of the more than two thousand militia who were now incarcerated in Camp Fairchild, one of the leftover camps from WW II, when the United States had over ninety thousand German and Italian POWs throughout the country. Fairchild held every kind of militiaman—rebels determined to battle the federal government over everything from mandatory gun control to taxes and getting prayers back into the schools. Some of the hard-core types even harbored a sneaking sympathy for the Oklahoma bombing, which they saw as payback for what they considered the "murder" of Randy Weaver's wife, their son, and baby, whom Mrs. Weaver was cradling in her arms when the federal marshals gunned her down. Others saw the Oklahoma bombing as payback for the "outrage" at Waco, where Federals had killed over eighty of David Koresh's followers, half of them women and children.

"What's so tough about Freeman?" the recruit pressed. "Anyone can put people in jail."

In response, the old hands told him how, during a showdown with the militia in the Northwest on the Oregon-Washington border, a militiaman had taken hostages in order to gain passage for himself and his comrades across a bridge held by FEDFOR. Afterward, the militiamen could have encircled and wiped out a FEDFOR platoon. Upon being informed of the situation, Freeman gave the order to "take the bridge." The FEDFOR officer on the spot, a brigadier, had hesitated, radioing Freeman that there were women and children on the bridge. Freeman repeated, "Take the bridge." And the brigadier did, his men killing several women and children in the process. Freeman, under questioning by the press, pointed out to CNN reporter Marte Price that in taking the bridge he'd saved the lives of a lot of his men, who, like the militia, also had wives and children. The message was unequivocal. There were going to be no compromises with the militia—no turning back. A fight to the finish.

"Freeman and McBride," one militiaman said, "were made for each other."

CHAPTER THREE

Camp Fairchild, Eastern Washington

THE GUARD SHOUTED for the prisoner to stop.

But the militiaman kept running, a wave of hope sweeping

through the dusty camp. The imprisoned militiamen poured out of the fifty huts, yelling, surging toward the eastern perimeter, the rolls of razor wire atop it linking each of the three guard towers—towers which the federal authorities called "observation posts," despite the fact that they bristled with machine guns and sensor arrays.

"Stop or I'll shoot!" the guard shouted, but the man in militia fatigues—a tall, craggy individual by the name of Sommers, whom everyone knew as "Lanky"—kept going. A machine gunner fired a long burst that kicked up dust before the trip wire. A crowd of militia prisoners slowed but continued to cheer wildly as Lanky reached the trip wire and jumped over it. Miraculously, he did not set off any of the antipersonnel mines seeded in the ten-foot-wide No Go zone. And without pausing—which everyone, including Militia Captain Jeremy Eleen, would remember—Lanky adroitly placed the tip of his homemade pole at the bottom of the twelve-foot wire fence and gracefully vaulted clear over, to the hysterical cheers of over a thousand prisoners. Dropping down gazellelike on the other side, Lanky began running again. There was another burst of M-60 machine-gun fire from the nearest tower, a cloud of desert dust rising about him, and he fell, his right leg twitching spasmodically. In the awful silence that followed, dust rose amid the clumps of sagebrush like smoke, then disappeared into the hard blue air, the body stilled.

"You bastard!" a militiaman shouted up at the tower, and for a moment the entire population of over a thousand militiamen moved as one toward the wire. Then a panicky guard fired a long burst that stitched the dry earth for a hundred yards along the trip wire, setting off antipersonnel mines in the No Go zone margin between the trip wire and the twelve-foot-high fence.

"Fucking murderer!" another militiaman yelled, and a

pandemonium of booing and jeering broke out. Some men picked up pebbles from the sun-baked earth and threw them in an ineffectual hail in the direction of the tower as the public address system, via the big loudspeakers on the towers, ordered the men back into the huts.

"This is a lockdown!" It was Commander Moorehead. "I *repeat*, this is a lockdown. Return to your barracks immediately."

No one moved, a deafening chorus of catcalls and whistles erupting.

"I repeat—"

"C'mon, boys. Go inside." It was the understanding but measured voice of a man who'd been standing perilously close to the trip wire, as if mesmerized by the sizzle of the electric-wired fence against Sommers's pole vault. It was Eleen, CO of the POWs. He had already spent two years in the camp near Fairchild Air Force Base in eastern Washington. The Federals, making no distinction between accommodations for officers and other ranks, had refused to acknowledge the military ranks adopted by the militia, designating all USMC members as "hostiles" to the United States government. Which was why Eleen was there with the men.

"C'mon, boys," Eleen repeated, moving slowly but purposefully through the throng of POWs, whose sullen retreat kicked up the earth that covered the camp in a talc-fine dust that rose from the sagebrush country, at times obscuring the guard towers. Because it meant they couldn't see the prisoners clearly, the dust made the guards increasingly nervous. For this reason, Moorehead wanted to clear the yard before any of the guards—some of whom were recruits and had never been in combat—became disorientated and panicked; letting off a burst could turn the already angry POWs into a barrack-wrecking mob. Not that it would have bothered Moorehead to let the POWs freeze in the desert night until new tent accommodations could be arranged, but he was a career soldier, and a riot among prisoners under your charge did nothing for your chances of promotion.

Two guards, ordered by the commandant to switch off the electricity and position a mobile arm outside the wire with which to retrieve the pole Sommers had used, stood by an Army ambulance, a Humvee, ready to make its way from the administration block outside the camp to pick up the body. But both the guard and ambulance held back until the dust cleared, as the POWs, always intent on inconveniencing their jailers, petulantly kicked up more dust as they sullenly returned to the barracks.

Moorehead couldn't see through the eye-itching clouds of dirt, but he was sure that Eleen must be as aware of the potential for unnecessary violence as he. And so, taking the PA's microphone, Moorehead announced, "Eleen! Get your men into barracks in five minutes—I'm starting the clock now—or I'll send in the dogs."

A low rumble of protest arose from the dust-shrouded POWs, but Moorehead was confident that increased movement toward the barracks was under way. The Federal commandant, a thickset, balding man, who always appeared taller than he was because of what the prisoners called his Nazi bearing, had seen brave men buckle at the knees when the Dobermans and pit bulls were sent in. The fierce snarls and barking of the K-9 squads worked even better, in Moorehead's opinion, than tear gas, for, like the dust cloud now blanketing the camp, gas and smoke, unless you had perfectly fitting masks, could incapacitate and confuse the guards as much as the enemy.

"Two minutes!" came the commandant's booming voice.

"Is that two minutes gone or two minutes to go or what?" asked a militiaman pedantically.

"Doesn't matter, just keep movin'," advised Militia Sergeant Mead, who had served under Captain Eleen at a now famous winter battle between the Federals and militia near Packwood in eastern Washington, during which they'd been captured. "They used a friggin' dog on us at Packwood. Sent 'im in with a miniature camera strapped to 'im—transmits pictures back to the Feds. Any K-9 mutt is bad news."

"I like dogs," replied his companion, coughing from the dust.

"Cats for me," Mead said.

"One minute!" Moorehead's booming voice warned.

"Screw you!" a POW shouted back, but there was a definite albeit reluctant increase in the POWs' pace as they cleared the parade ground, the dust now descending on an empty expanse. The only vegetation visible was the dusty sagebrush outside the camp's barbed wire, the red cross on the Federals' khaki ambulance streaked with the sandy loam kicked up by the POWs.

The ambulance driver inched forward, pumping the window-washing-fluid button with a finger, creating a slurry of mud on the glass before it cleared enough for him to see where he was going. The guards in the tower nearest the main gate and the two retrieving the pole cursed the vehicle for kicking up even more dust.

"Which way's the body?" the driver radioed the guard tower.

"Can't see because of all this shit in the air," the guard replied grumpily. "But I think it's about two o'clock from the tower—out about fifty yards or so."

"Two o'clock from which tower?"

"From my fucking tower, you dork!"

"Hey, knock it off, you two!" It was the duty officer back in the admin building cutting in on the frequency. "No cussing. Proper procedure. All right?"

"Yes, sir," the guard said.

There was silence for about thirty seconds, during which the duty officer could hear the monotonous howl of the ambulance.

"Sir . . ." came the driver's voice.

"What?"

"There's nothing out here."

"What do you mean?"

"I mean nothing out here. No body."

"You sure?"

The ambulance driver switched over to the guard tower frequency. "You see anything, Tower?"

Silence.

"Tower?"

"Ah—negative. He's gone."

"Gone!" It was the duty officer. "Jesus Christ!"

Some of the Parrots, the militia's nickname for their chain of militia lookouts throughout the camp, scampered to their peepholes in the huts' rafters now that the dust was clearing. "He's gone!" one of them confirmed joyously. "Sonofabitch faked it. He's gone!"

"Whaddayamean, *gone*?"

"Taken off! Sayonara! Arrivederci!"

"That magnificent fucker!" Mead shouted.

Eleen, uncharacteristically, wore a broad smile. A Mormon, he didn't approve of bad language, particularly taking the Lord's name in vain, but this was a spit in the Federal eye if ever there was one. Eleen said a quiet prayer that Sommers would make it.

"Oh shit!" said one of the lookouts. "They're sending out the dogs!"

Hidden by sagebrush atop a knoll two miles away, toward Spokane, Lucky McBride was watching the camp, his khaki-colored binoculars and Gulf War fatigues perfectly camouflaging him against the desert. When he saw the dogs picking up the scent of the POW he'd seen go over the wire, he withdrew to the Yamaha he'd secreted amid silver sage and balsam root bush.

Riding the 600cc motorcycle over the rough ground toward I-90, McBride, had nothing to do with the escape. He'd merely come out for a look-see as part of the Knockout plan, and grinned behind his goggles at the POW's audacity. The POW, lying still, playing dead, using the dust as a cover, was smart, and McBride figured that if the escapee could reach I-90 as darkness fell, he might just make it. Stranger things had happened.

McBride recalled when he and his buddy Gunner Brock and two other militiamen had been on a night mission in a force-ten gale off the Washington coast and their boat was shot out from under them by the Feds. Everyone had given them up for dead, but being in a trans-Pacific shipping lane, they'd lucked out. They were picked up by a Japanese whaler whose captain promised not to report the rescue to the U.S. Coast Guard if McBride and his fellow militiamen agreed not to report the Japanese whaler for harpooning humpbacks, which were on the endangered species list. McBride had again "lucked" out, which was why other militiamen liked to serve with him. Even the fundamentalist Christian militiamen, who eschewed the notion of omens and good luck charms, liked to be near McBride when the shooting started. They said it wasn't luck on McBride's part as much as good preparation and attention to detail—the kind of thoroughness and care that his Federal nemesis, General Freeman, was also noted for.

Others, however, said that some men were just born lucky, and that's all there was to it. Now, McBride glanced back over his shoulder for any sign of the escaped POW. He had no idea who the man was, but if he made it, he was the kind of militiaman McBride knew he wanted on his team. Someone with guts—someone who'd do the totally unexpected. A pole vault! It was beautiful, and the excitement of seeing the man's escape and the thrill he felt got his adrenaline pumping hard.

In Spokane he rode down by the river and stopped near a row of small, four-room stucco bungalows. Though it was dark, he sat on the Yamaha for several minutes, alert for any sign of trouble, his finger on the starter button. Satisfied it was safe, he parked the bike beneath a willow, went into the ill-kept yard of one of the bungalows. He lifted the rock in the wild rose garden, extracted the key, and unlocked the door. The moment he stepped inside he could smell her perfume and sweat, heavy in the musky, dank bedroom. There, all but invisible in the dark, she lay sleeping after her night shift at the sawmill. She started when he walked in, and murmured something. He didn't understand what she said, and he didn't care. Not bothering to undress, he unzipped and, seeing her more clearly now—she was lying on her stomach—flung the sheet aside, feeling for her.

"What are you doing?" she asked groggily.

"What do you think?"

"Can't you wait?"

He took her right hand, put it on him, and felt her squeeze his hardness.

"You'll split me apart," she told him, and began to roll onto her back.

"No," he said, pushing her facedown. "Like you are now." Her smell engulfed him, and cupping her breasts, he entered her slowly from behind, withdrew, and kept doing it until his throat was as dry as the desert. He heard the sound of the river somewhere beyond as her soft wetness sucked him into her until he felt a sweet, unstoppable rush.

After, as they disentwined, McBride still breathing hard, one arm shading his eyes despite the darkness, she asked cheekily, "Now you've done it to me, I suppose you're off to stick it to the Feds?"

"You betcha!" His voice had a dry, rasping tone. "Got anything to drink?"

She leaned over him to grab a pack of cigarettes from the bedside table. "Think there's a Bud—lite."

"No. No booze. I'm driving."

She laughed. "One won't hurt."

"No." He was adamant. "Shaves your concentration." He turned to her. "Even one drink."

"Well, I've got no juice. It'll have to be water."

"That'll do," he said, getting up and going out to the kitchen.

Just like him, she thought. So damned focused he wouldn't risk one beer. Then again, he'd risked seeing her. She lit a cigarette and smiled to herself in the darkness. She saw the bathroom light go on and heard the distinct sound of him putting the Beretta 9mm he always carried on the top of the porcelain toilet tank, where he said he could reach it quickly. She heard him lock the door and turn on the shower. Mirela smiled to herself again, buoyed by the fact that he'd made time to stop off and see her when everyone in town knew the militia were so preoccupied with the fallout from the Boeing thing they could think of nothing else. She exhaled a long stream of smoke.

Next thing she knew, she woke with a start, the sheet smoldering. "Holy shit! Lucky?"

He was gone.

He was on Highway 90, heading out of Spokane for the Idaho panhandle and Hayden Lake, home of the Aryan nation. He was going to pick up what the militia had code-named the "egg-breaker" and an eight-by-two-foot-wide piece of equipment wrapped in blue plastic, which McBride merely referred to as the ROE. At the border, he gassed up, checked the tires, and made a call, couched in innocuous-sounding language to HQ. He requested that two new men in his brigade, Ron Stanes and Art Maddin, check out "two quickies." He laughed and made "two quickies" sound lewd. Back on the Yamaha, eating up the center line as if it was tracer coming at him, he saw the light was fading fast now and hoped the escaped POW's luck would hold.

CHAPTER FOUR

SOMEONE WHOSE LUCK didn't hold was the woman with the plunging neckline at the glittering VIP dinner in Washington, D.C. Bedecked with diamonds that sparkled against her cream-smooth skin, she leaned forward to make a point to her host, the Chief of Naval Operations, at the far end of the dining room table. Standing behind her, ex-SEAL and SpecWar warrior "Aussie" Lewis took in her cleavage as he ladled turtle consommé from an ornately engraved silver tureen. It wasn't a job Lewis wanted. He hated it. But in the draconian downsizing of the U.S. Armed Forces that had followed the end of the Cold War, the Gulf War, and Kosovo, many such warriors had been discharged and had to take what they could get. For the Australian-born-and-raised American citizen, an ex-SEAL whose special missions for the legendary general, Douglas Freeman, had ranged from clandestine drops as far afield as Iraq and Siberia to fighting terrorists and outlaw militia groups in the U.S., retirement from active duty at age thirty-seven was anathema. In Aussie's case, it had also been a virtual "forced" retirement, because a military court-martial had found his terse explanation of what had happened to a militia terrorist he'd captured during a manhunt in the Southwest "singularly unconvincing."

Aussie Lewis had told Admiral Nevin, the convener of the court-martial, that his prisoner had "fallen off a cliff."

"What happened to the prisoner's civil rights?" the admiral had asked Lewis.

"Guess they fell off too—sir."

The cleavage of the woman he was serving was so deep and alluring that Aussie's concentration momentarily strayed, and he spilled the turtle consommé on the starched white tablecloth beside her. Another, haughty-looking woman from the State Department, draped in black silk, chided, "Oh, *do* be careful!" her accent decidedly more British than American.

Aussie paused. The memory of the injustices and arrogance the British upper class had heaped upon his colonial forebears surfaced, and he dropped the ladle into the tureen. "Get your own fuckin' soup!" Consommé splattered the haughty woman's bodice a moment before Lewis tore off his server's waistcoat, tossed it on the gladioli centerpiece, and stormed out of the room.

There was a stunned silence among the VIPs, broken only by the steady dripping of the consommé onto the polished hardwood floor. Finally, the woman declared, "What appalling behavior!"

"One of Freeman's savages," her tuxedoed host explained. "I should have known better. I'm sorry."

As Lewis entered the kitchen, the chef, crimson-faced with embarrassment and rage, confronted him. "What the hell's wrong with you?"

Lewis kept walking and talking. "I've fought all kinds of vermin so these bastards can *dine* in peace and comfort. I don't have to take that shit —Do be careful!' "

The chef, a much larger man, grasped Lewis's shoulder. "You'll take whatever—"

Aussie hit him with a left jab. It was a short punch, but with 160 pounds of wiry strength behind it, it did the job. The chef, reaching vainly for the counter, missed it, collapsing noisily onto the tiled floor beneath an avalanche of tossed salad and garlic croutons.

"Jimmy's getting angry!" Lewis said. It was one of his favorite expressions, from an old *Seinfeld* episode. "Don't touch Jimmy!"

"He's nuts," a sous-chef said, helping his winded boss to his feet.

"He's—He's fired!" the chef thundered, fighting for breath. "He'll never work in this business again."

He was right.

CHAPTER FIVE

IN EASTERN WASHINGTON State it was still daylight but the sun was falling fast. Lanky Sommers got up the moment he'd seen the dust cloud envelop him, hiding him from the camp, and ran across the dry sagebrush plain east of the camp for another hundred yards or so. Then he swung south along a dry coulee that coursed like a jagged trench through the ice-age-scoured landscape whose soil could only be brought to life by the giant, rotating arms and wheels of irrigation sprinklers. Nearing a huge circle of golden grain, the wide arms of an irrigation spray rotating overhead, Lanky paused to quench his thirst, but not enough to cramp his gut. Then he turned east northeast, having timed his breakout to occur near twilight, when the headlights of the highway would guide him. He knew the police would have been alerted by Moorehead, but Spokane was a good-sized city, and if you were lucky, you could use it to lose yourself. Plus, it was only eighteen miles from the Idaho border—which meant only thirty miles from one of the most powerful militia groups in the U.S., the Aryan nation, around Hayden Lake. The lake lay in the 140-mile-long north-south Idaho panhandle, the handle forty miles wide, the pan 120 miles across. Unlike the desert, it was an area of stunning scenery, where massive glaciers from Canada's ancient past had ground down from the north, creating a land of deep, ice-carved lakes and thick forests. The forests spilled out into the panhandle between the peaks of eastern Washington's savagely picturesque Selkirk Range and the bulk of western Montana's Cabinet Mountains.

He saw Spokane's streetlights come on in the near distance, twinkling in the arid desert air. Slowing to catch his breath, Lanky walked alongside an irrigation ditch where a copse of poplar and cottonwood trees took nourishment from the water, and where a run of silver sage along the rim of the ditch's embankment afforded him added camouflage in the twilight. He saw a chicken hawk hover before diving, disappearing below the rim momentarily, to emerge seconds later with something twitching in its talons. Then he heard the unmistakable barking of dogs, which he'd thrown off earlier by walking down the water ditch. He began running again in the ditch channel, the highway a quarter mile off, the civil airport north of him. The airport was an alternative escape route he'd thought of, should he encounter any patrols coming toward him from the city.

* * *

Lanky Sommers's daring escape had exhilarated his fellow militia POWs in Camp Fairchild, including Captain Jeremy Eleen. But Eleen's earlier buoyant mood was now undermined by anger as he sat on his bunk in hut 5A. Why hadn't Sommers confided his plan to him? he wondered. As senior Chief Escape Officer in Fairchild, he should have been advised of any escape plan in advance. One of the lessons Eleen and his escape committee had garnered from the wisdom of WWII veterans was that escapes needed to be coordinated. This was to prevent what Eleen, in one of his rare lighter moments, designated BOO—Break Out Overlap—or, as Sergeant Mead and other POWs called it, BOFU—Break Out Fuck Up—which was when two or more POWs tried to escape from camp on the same night. During several attempts in the early days of the camp, escapees had on occasion literally bumped into one another, using the same route. The resulting confusion had alerted the guards, with the result that the small, forlorn POW cemetery outside the camp's eastern gate contained the graves of eleven militiamen who'd tried to breach the razor wire.

"Sommers should have told the committee," Eleen insisted. "For all he knew, we might have had another breakout planned for tonight."

"Well, strictly speaking," Sergeant Mead responded, "Lanky didn't do his big vault at night. It's only really turning dark now, and—"

"Don't be pedantic!" Eleen shot back with uncharacteristic spleen. "No matter what time he—" Eleen abruptly stopped talking. Something had occurred to him. "Mead," he said, "get the rest of the escape committee here immediately, and alert the two parrots."

Within minutes the chain of over 250 "parrots," a minimum of four for each of the seventy huts, covering every possible approach by the "goons," were alerted by a series of hand signals and whistles to keep watch while the seven-man escape committee met, each of the seven representing a line of ten huts. When they arrived, Eleen, under the pressure of an impending curfew that would prevent movement from hut to hut, dispensed with the usual small talk and courtesies that normally preceded such gatherings.

"No time to lose," he told the other six reps. "We've got a chance for a breakout tonight. Moorehead's made a mistake." Without pausing to answer the puzzled looks on the other reps' faces, he asked, "How many escape kits have we got?"

"Two per hut," responded Wyse, who was in charge of the painstakingly assembled kits.

"Complete?" Eleen inquired.

"Everything. Maps, money, compass, forged social insurance and driver's licenses. We've even got the locations of bus stops marked for them on local area maps. There's a Greyhound stop at Hayford a few miles south of us, and one in—"

"Legends?" Eleen cut in. He meant cover stories prepared for potential escapees to obscure any possible connection with militia, should they be stopped and questioned by police or Feds.

"All set," Wyse assured him.

"Clothes?"

"Two guards' uniforms. Some civilian."

"Some?"

"About fifty-fifty," the "tailor" answered. "Civilian clothes are our least concern because the U.S. Army has sold so many surplus uniforms, all kinds of civilians go around in combat fatigues, caps, etcetera, looking just like our guys."

"The Y?" Eleen asked next.

"It's ready." The Y-shaped ladder was made of leftover lumber and materials, stolen and secreted away by the camp "scroungers" during the Federals' rush to build additional huts to hold more militia prisoners, most of whom had been captured by National Guard units, some as far away as the Florida Everglades. The two arms of the V in the Y were wrapped with a thick batten of old cloth remnants, some appropriated from the clothes of unsuccessful escapees before burial. The idea was that should the time come to use the ladder, the batten would protect each escapee's hands from the barbed wire as he steadied himself against the V before jumping over.

"Sir," interjected one of the reps, "you said Moorehead had made a mistake?"

"The dogs," Eleen said. "He's got them all out looking for Lanky. And the goons won't be expecting another escape attempt tonight. They'll figure we're all too shaken by the shooting from the tower. And they're right." He looked around at the others. "We all know how people tend to hold back after gunplay. After those bursts of M-60 fire from the gun towers, everyone'll be spooked for a while. Moorehead won't expect us to try, that's the thing. They won't *expect* a bust-out within twenty-four hours, let alone on the same day."

"How we gonna do it?" one of the reps pressed excitedly.

"Same way as Lanky," Eleen said. "Pole vault. Only we use the Y ladder."

"But he went straight over the wire," Mead objected. "I mean, he cleared it. We'll have to lean the Y against the wire. That'll set off the lights and sensors—"

"We have contingency plans to short out the circuit, haven't we?" Eleen asked calmly. "Or don't we have an electrician among a thousand militia?"

"Yeah," Mead said. "We can do that all right, but—"

"All right," Eleen said. "We have our blackout. Men in huts forty-nine and fifty'll start a diversion, draw the goons down there. We put our Y ladder up against the wire and get as many of our boys over as we can. Say at most we buy only five minutes' time, we could still get ten, maybe fifteen, over."

"But how about the buried antipersonnel pressure mines?" one of the excited but skeptical hut reps asked. "Moment you put the stem of the Y ladder in the No Go zone, you could set one off."

"I get it," another rep interrupted. "You mean we follow Lanky's footsteps *exactly* in the No Go zone—"

"No," Eleen said. "The dust obliterated them, and the guards have removed the pole. But ever since they discovered that Sommers pulled a fast one, they've been so busy going after him they haven't filled in those holes."

"Holes?"

"When that tower guard opened fire," Eleen explained, "with the M-60—"

"He detonated some mines in the No Go!" Mead cut in.

"Yes," Eleen said. "We'll use one of the holes as a safe base for the Y." Eleen glanced at his watch. "But we only have ten, fifteen minutes before the curfew."

"I hope it works," one of the men said.

"Really!" Eleen replied, with uncharacteristic sarcasm.

He'd been at Fairchild for two long years. He'd seen it all, since the first bitterly cold day he'd arrived, after a Federal helicopter his unit had commandeered crashed. He could still see Rubinski, a member of his militia squad, left behind in the snow as they boarded another helo, reaching out to him as the helo lifted off. Rubinski's cold face had been blue as he screamed for help, and Eleen's sergeant, holding Eleen back, yelled that it was too late. But had it been too late, Eleen wondered afterward, or had it been cowardice that held him back? The question still haunted him. A deeply religious man, Eleen believed in redemption, and now saw a chance of achieving it, atoning for Rubinski by helping as many of his men as possible to escape. For a moment the memory of Rubinski, and what might have become of him overwhelmed him, and he fell silent as the reps hurried out of 5A to get things moving.

"Sir?" Two of the reps had returned.

"Yes?"

"Johnny and I have been talking. It's time you and Mead had another go. Use the two guards' uniforms and take the fake M-16." It was an M-16 one of the POWs had hand carved—hidden with guard uniforms in hut 5A.

"Yes," the other rep added. "You've both earned it, Captain. I'll take over as CEO."

Eleen was touched, and he knew he'd put in more than enough time to qualify, but right now it was his responsibility to oversee the escape till the last man was out.

"Not now," he said, "but—" He turned to Mead. "—you should go, Wally."

"Not unless you go, Captain."

"We'll see," Eleen told the two reps, having no intention of taking up their offer but feeling guilty about holding Mead back. "Get back to your huts."

"We'll bring the two guards' uniforms anyway," one of the reps said. "In case you change your mind."

CHAPTER SIX

Washington State

DRIVING WEST ON 308 from Keyport, a small community on Port Orchard Bay, a westward arm of Puget Sound, militiamen Art Maddin and Ron Stanes, having just met as members assigned to McBride's brigade, were on their way to do what McBride had facetiously called "two quickies." Cresting a hill, Maddin driving though it was Stanes's truck, the pickup headed down to the T intersection where the highway approached the east gate of Washington State's remote, heavily forested, and highly classified submarine base at Bangor. On the eastern shore of the mile-and-a-half-wide Hood Canal, the base proper was obscured from view by miles of forest. Neither Stanes, from the northwest Washington detachment of the militia corps, nor Maddin, who hailed from eastern Washington, had been to the gate before, which was precisely why McBride had chosen them—neither man had any preconception of the level of security.

Stanes, a tall, sinewy, and normally affable man in his midtwenties, found himself thinking too hard about not looking at Maddin, a short, thickset man in his thirties, his face marred by the dark red stain of a tablespoon-shaped birthmark from high on his right cheek to below his bottom lip. The deep purplish color was accentuated by Maddin's futile attempt to hide it beneath a bushy, ginger-colored beard. In fact, it wasn't strictly speaking a birthmark, but a vascular discoloration, albeit a particularly vivid one that increased in intensity under stress. The medical distinction, however, meant nothing to school kids who had relentlessly tormented him through his childhood as "the guy with the birthmark" or as "Spoonface." Stanes kept looking at the road ahead.

Maddin slowed the pickup and slowly approached the high cyclone wire and security island that formed the cross piece of the T-shaped junction where the highway met the base's boundary. The gate's armed guard ran toward them, his right palm held high, as he yelled at them, his voice booming over a loudspeaker. "You in the blue pickup. Back behind the blue line. *Now!*"

"What?" Maddin said, startled by the sudden outburst.

"Behind the blue line. Now!"

"What the hell—what friggin' blue line?" Then, turning, Stanes saw it behind them: a narrow blue strip painted across the road about ten yards back from the gate. "Geez," he said, "I don't know how you're expected to see that in time to—"

"Behind the blue line!" the guard was bellowing, his hand on the holster. *"Now!"*

"Yeah, yeah," Maddin responded, clearly addled by the command that now seemed to be coming from the forest itself, beyond the cyclone fence. "I can't back up. There's traffic. Have to make a U-turn," he called out placatingly.

"Behind the blue line! *Now!*"

"There," Stanes advised coolly, pointing ahead at a gap in the median. "You can make a U-turn through there." But it meant going forward a few yards instead of immediately backing up behind the holy blue line.

"I dunno," Maddin began, flustered. The guard was approaching them, taking out his sidearm, the sign behind him proclaiming DEADLY FORCE AUTHORIZED.

"Go on," Stanes urged Maddin. "You'll be around before he gets here."

More in fright than conviction, Maddin took his foot off the brake, and the pickup shot forward into the U—the guard yelling furiously.

"Jesus Christ!" Maddin said, heading back along the highway. Soon all they could hear was the hum of the pickup's tires on the blacktop.

"You okay?" Stanes inquired after a few minutes.

"Yeah. Why?"

"Seemed a bit rattled back there."

"Rattled, shit! Just don't like being yelled at. Guy's hysterical. Last prick I saw carryin' on like that was a commie in Berlin. Guard at Checkpoint Charlie. Must be—I dunno—fifteen, twenty years ago. 'Fore the wall came down. Sonofabitch was waving his Kalashnikov around and screaming at me 'cause I took a goddamn picture of his guard tower. What's so goddamn sacred about a goddamn guard tower? I just took it as a, you know, keepsake. Went absolutely bananas! They're all the same, commies and Feds. Authoritarian bastards, yellin' at everyone. Power crazy!"

"You said it," Stanes agreed.

Maddin shifted the automatic into L. "Where to now, Hood Canal Bridge?"

"That's what the man told us." He meant McBride. "The second quickie."

"You think he can pull this off?" Maddin asked.

"Oh yeah," Stanes responded. "That's why they call him Lucky."

CHAPTER SEVEN

LANKY SOMMERS HEARD the dogs closing, saw the highway off to his right disappearing into Spokane's south-western suburbs, but they were still a mile off. Realizing he couldn't reach the outskirts in time, he veered out of the irrigation ditch and toward the highway. If it became necessary, he'd stand in the middle of it—force someone to stop. Ten yards from the irrigation ditch he spotted a dry, narrow gully he'd have to cross. He ran down into it, the dogs getting closer, and was clambering up the other side when the first one, a pit bull, brought him down, the cloud of dust rising from the gully looking strangely like steam staining the velvet twilight. On his back, his chest heaving in panic and exhaustion, Lanky froze, knowing better than to fight the pit bull, which he now recognized as Moorehead's.

"Call him off!" he shouted. "Call off your dog!"

Moorehead was covered in dust from the chase and per-spiring heavily, but his breathing wasn't as labored as the militiaman's, so when he drew his service issue 9mm, his hand was steady.

"I'm not armed!" Sommers said, holding up his hands, the pit bull slathering and snarling only inches from his face. Even so, Sommers's daring never left him. "You should clean that mutt's teeth!"

"Think you can make a monkey out of me?" Moorehead

said. "You militia shit." Moorehead shot him in the face, twice. Sommers's body flew back, still for a moment, then went into violent spasm. Moorehead quickly knelt down, took a snub-nosed .38 from his left pocket, and fired once behind him before placing the gun into Sommers's right hand just as a camp guard reached the edge of the gully.

Moorehead had straightened up before he heard a noise. Spinning around, he saw the guard. "Jesus! How long you been there?"

"Long enough," the guard said, cradling his pump-action twelve-gauge while catching his breath in the cool, sage-scented air.

There was a long silence, broken only by the sound of crickets in the darkness, before Moorehead spoke again. "What's that supposed to mean?"

The guard looked behind him, the other dogs closing by now. "Long enough to see you plant the gun."

"Then keep your mouth shut," Moorehead told him, "if you know what's good for you." He pointed down at the dead militiaman. "These bastards have to be made an example of."

"Yeah," the guard said. But his tone was noncommittal.

The other guards and their dogs were less than a hundred yards away.

"What's your name?" Moorehead inquired. *"Quickly, boy!"*

"Dillon."

Moorehead couldn't place him. "You new?"

"Transferred over from Fort Lewis." It was near Tacoma, on the coast.

"Uh-huh," Moorehead said, but by now two other guards were approaching the edge of the gully, their flashlights dancing about above the sagebrush.

"You got 'im?" one of them asked.

"Yeah," Dillon said. "Asshole took a shot at the boss."

"Shit—he was armed!"

"A .38," Dillon said. "Must've had it smuggled into the camp."

"Sonofabitch! You all right, Major?"

"Yeah," Moorehead said. "You boys carry him out to the highway. Put your flashlight on its green filter to let the other boys know we've got 'im. I'll get outta this hole, radio the highway patrol. Dillon, you come with me."

"You betcha."

As Moorehead called the Washington State Patrol and waited for a reply, he asked Dillon what he wanted.

"I don't like it up here," Dillon told him. "Hotter'n hell in the summer. Cold as sin in winter."

"What do you want?"

"Oh hell, I'm not fussy, but I tell you, Major, I've always had a hankerin' for southern California."

"I'll make a few calls," Moorehead said. "But you better keep your mouth shut."

"It's in the vault," Dillon said.

"In the *what*?" The commandant wasn't a TV fan.

"Won't say a word," Dillon assured him.

Moorehead grunted. "Better not, 'less you want to end up in Adak."

"Where's that?"

"Aleutian Islands. Most godforsaken posting on earth."

"I'd prefer California."

The state patrol came on the line then, and Moorehead gave them GPS coordinates for the pickup.

Two hundred miles to the east, Pete Rainor was worried. Mel Haley was in a blind panic. Photographs of them as "the Boeing Terrorists," Rainor in his Little League coaching uniform, and Haley, a shot taken from his wedding, were all over TV and in the newspapers, the media, including radio, giving out the license numbers of their vehicles. When Rainor rang the USMC HQ emergency help line, his voice was barely under control. HQ, in turn, called McBride insofar as he, being in charge of the hoped-for knockout against the federals, should be at once apprised of the two militamen's situation and be given the chance to advise HQ on how to respond. McBride's cell phone was difficult to hear above the roar of the Yamaha and the wind, and it took half a dozen rings before he was aware of HQ calling. Not being on a land line, HQ couched its question to him carefully despite the unlikelihood that NSA's computer-linked microwave sweep of cell phone frequencies would pick him up. McBride thought hard but fast, instructing HQ that the two militiamen should be told to go immediately to the "Redoubt." It was the militia's secret hideout in the Northwest—so secret that any militiaman who was even suspected of revealing its location was "eliminated," likewise the person to whom the location had been divulged.

CHAPTER EIGHT

"INCREDIBLE," ART MADDIN said, looking through the binoculars down Hood Canal from the boat ramp adjacent to the canal bridge. "I heard it was like this, but if I hadn't seen it myself I wouldn't have believed it."

Ron Stanes wasn't sure how to take Maddin's comment. He knew that from where Maddin came, eastern Washington, the scenery consisted largely of sagebrush desert, whereas here on the coast, before the rain clouds had the moisture sucked out of them after passing over the high mountains and rain forests of the Olympic Peninsula and the Cascade range, the scenery was lush. And around Hood Canal—a misnomer, since the canal was a natural phenomenon—the environment was especially luxuriant. The mile and a half long bridge that spanned the canal, on the other hand, was definitely man-made. A spectacular engineering feat, part of it, near the eastern shore, had been designed to retract into itself, rather than be raised or swung out like so many waterway crossings. Its retraction allowed passage of marine traffic, which included the nuclear subs coming up north out of Bangor before they turned westward into the Strait of Juan de Fuca and then to the Pacific.

"Beautiful isn't it?" Stanes said.

"What?" Maddin replied irritably, the "birthmark" taking on a brighter hue as he moved out of the shadow of the trees by the launch ramp into the sunlight. Lowering the binoculars, Maddin shifted his gaze to the traffic lining up along the bridge, waiting for a big launch to pass through the gap that would be cleared by the retractable section. "Looks like they even have a friggin' viewing platform where pedestrians can peer right down on it."

Stanes took a long drag on his cigarette and nodded in agreement, though Maddin's caustic tone annoyed him. "Well, I don't think it's really a viewing platform. It's where the pedestrians have to stop, I guess, when the retractable section is pulled back."

"It's a viewing platform!" Maddin said. "But hey, don't take me wrong. That's great. Goddamned ironic, that's all, don't you think? Feds spend a billion dollars on their most secret warship—won't let you near the base, all hush hush, screamin' at you to keep behind the fucking blue line—so what do they do when vehicles get to the bridge? They let 'em line up from both ends—right up to the retractable section—

so any Tom, Dick, or bitch can get out of their car and watch the sub inch its way through."

Stanes had to agree. It was ironic. Despite all the hullabaloo of tight security at the Bangor gate, he recalled Federal General Freeman telling the press that in the United States, base security was "more an assumption than a reality." It was a comment that militia leader Wilcox drove home to every one of his regional and state commanders, including those in Alaska and Hawaii.

Maddin raised the binoculars again, this time focusing on one of the two beige towers resembling blockhouses. They were involved in the telescoping of the retractable section of the bridge, and he could see several people standing by the stoplights on either side of the section. "Jesus Christ, they're fishing! You can get so close you could piss on it."

Stanes, looking across the boat ramp, saw the sheer, unmitigated meanness in Maddin's eyes, and realized that Maddin's driving force in joining the militia wasn't to hope for a better country, but just unequivocal hatred. It could have been an unmitigated thirst for revenge against God, the government, against anything and anybody—because of the horrific mark that marred his face.

"Yes sir," Maddin repeated. "You could piss on it."

"Well, we're not gonna piss on it, are we?" Stanes said.

"Nope!" Maddin replied. "They'd get you before you got off the fucking bridge. Nope, I think we're gonna go fishing."

Stanes said nothing, checking his license plate mount. It was a rectangular, four-sided box with only one side visible from the rear, like any normal plate. But it could be rotated on a quarter-inch-diameter axle by means of a switch he'd rigged up in the cigarette lighter socket. It would rotate the box, and a new license number would appear. He'd never had to use it, but now that he'd joined McBride's outfit, he figured he might need it, especially with Maddin along for the ride. He didn't like Maddin, but like the old Communists used to say, you can't make an omelet without breaking eggs. Guys like Maddin had their uses, and in the next twenty-four hours the militia planned to break the biggest egg the Federals had. Unless Eleen managed a breakout before then.

Leaving the Hood Canal Bridge they headed up to Port Townsend, at the northeastern tip of Olympic Peninsula. They booked into the Cove Motel, then went to its café for lunch. Their booth overlooked Indian Island and Admiralty Inlet. Gazing northeastward, beyond the deep cobalt blue of the ten-mile-wide inlet, Stanes, who always took pride in showing off the rugged vistas of the Northwest to new-comers, pointed beyond to the ice-cream-white dome of Mount Baker, the dormant volcano that rose over ten thousand feet out of the northern Cascades, its white summit reflecting sun. "Beautiful, isn't it?"

"What?" Maddin asked, perusing the menu.

"Mount Baker. Quite a sight."

"I hear it could blow any minute."

"You always so cheerful?"

A boy, about seven or eight, was staring at Maddin from the next booth.

"Well, the whole Northwest is shaking, isn't it?" Maddin proffered, glancing angrily at the kid, who was still staring at him.

"Yeah," Stanes conceded. "We're on the Juan de Fuca plate out here. Have tremors all the time. Guys at Washington State U say we average three or four earthquakes every week but they're so small you don't feel them."

"I wouldn't want to live out here," Maddin said morosely. "Worst thing I can think of is being trapped under a pile of rubble. Comes my time—" He saw the kid was still gawking at him. "—I want to go bang, just like that. In my sleep."

"You are a morbid son of a gun," Stanes commented.

"Yeah," Maddin answered.

"What's wrong?" Stanes pressed.

"Nothing," Maddin retorted sharply, looking around the restaurant. "What've you got to do to get some service 'round here?"

"They're busy. Have some water."

The boy, one hand in front of his mouth, was whispering animatedly to his mother, his eyes still fixed on Maddin.

"What?" the boy's mother asked irritably. "Andrew, I can't hear ya if ya mumble."

Then Stanes heard the boy say something about "on his chin," and the mother, her voice dropping low, said, "It's a birthmark. Don't stare."

Maddin was beet red with embarrassment—the big spoon-shaped splotch beneath the stubble of beard turning to an angry crimson, in striking contrast to the rest of his face. Stanes, not knowing quite what to do, called over to the waitress. "Could we order here, miss?"

"Comin' fast as I can," she called back.

"Yeah," Stanes said softly, smiling at Maddin. "So's Christmas."

Art Maddin didn't hear. All he could think of was smashing the kid's head in—all the humiliation he'd suffered as a child welling up in him, coagulating in a gut-knotting fury as he remembered all that had been done to him and his kind, the outcasts of America, dumped on by the establishment and its minions, shut out because they were different. The only antidote for the injustice he felt in the war between *us* and *them*, between the militia and *them*, was a violence that would even the score, a violence so stunning it would make them all sit up and take notice, make the bastards sorry for their smug indifference.

After they were served, Maddin, intent on leaving the café as soon as possible, began gulping his food so quickly that he was barely aware of what he was eating. In the strained silence, Stanes wanted to say something to break the tension, even though the woman and the boy had now left the booth, the woman paying at the register, the boy still gawking back at Maddin.

"So," Stanes said, "you have it all worked out?"

Maddin ripped a roll in half to mop up the gravy. "Got what all worked out?"

"You know," he said, lowering his voice. "The op."

"I worked it out this morning."

"I mean the diversion."

"Diversion?"

"Hey," Stanes said, in obvious annoyance. "Are we in an echo chamber here?"

Maddin swiped his plate clean of gravy.

"No, we're in a café, and if you had any damned sense you'd be quiet."

"I was only trying to make conversation, dammit," Stanes said archly, and before he could stop himself, added, "I wasn't the one staring at you."

CHAPTER NINE

"NAME?" THE UNEMPLOYMENT office clerk demanded imperiously, though Aussie Lewis had already slid his driver's license under the counter grill.

"Lewis. D. Lewis."

The clerk typed in the name on the computer.

Lewis hated the *clack clack clack* of computer keys—the bureaucracy locking him up in cyberspace, putting him in another box. And he'd had to take a number, wait on a goddamn bench for an hour.

"Social Security number?"

The clerk had an earring in his ear and a "Peace and Love" tattoo on his left wrist, neither of which Aussie Lewis liked any more than the computer.

The unemployment clerk didn't like Lewis either. It was evident in his condescending air toward the ex-SEAL. "It says here you left your last job voluntarily."

"Correct."

"You can't just go leaving jobs we've sent you to."

"It's a free country."

"That's got nothing to do with it."

"It's got everything to do with it. The job sucked."

"It was a job."

"Yeah, well, I'm not a toady."

"A *what*?"

"A toady. A fucking gofer."

"There's no need for bad language here."

"There's every need for bad language here. I served this country for—I dunno how many years, and you want me to be a fucking toady?"

The clerk turned to his supervisor. "Mr. Baylis—"

Baylis, middle-aged, balding, wore bifocals and peered over them first at the clerk, then at Lewis. "What's the problem?"

"This gentleman is unhappy about his job allocation," the clerk said. "He says his service record entitles him to something better."

Baylis, still holding a sheaf of papers, glanced down at

the computer screen. "CNO office requested . . . and you were assigned—" He moved closer to the screen, forehead furrowed in concentration. "—to a catering company as . . ." He touched the scroll button.

"As a toady," Lewis cut in. "Pouring soup for some stuck-up bitch from the State Department."

Baylis, turning from the screen, said to Lewis, "You assaulted the chef?"

"He grabbed me."

"You're lucky he didn't press charges. Before we assign you to any other job, I think it appropriate that you apologize personally to Mister—" He looked at the screen again. "—Mr. Suarez."

"Fuck Mr. Suarez!" Some people waiting on the benches looked up; others kept staring at worn magazines, sensing danger.

The supervisor ignored the obscenity. "You're too proud to be a waiter, is that it? A SEAL can kill people but he can't serve them soup, is that what you're saying?"

Aussie Lewis snatched up the application he'd completed and stormed out. "Fucking bureaucrats!"

"You tell 'em, bro," said a black man waiting on the benches. "They're all the same!"

"Ain't that the truth!" When Lewis hit the fresh air of the street he was already cursing himself. The supervisor had been right, goddammit. He *was* too proud to be a waiter. No, he didn't look down on waiters, but he'd been trained as a warrior, and you wouldn't send a waiter upcountry to do a shooter's job would you? But pride had its price, and except for a hundred and thirty bucks and change, any savings he and his wife Alexsandra had—which weren't much from a SpecWar man's payout—were gone. Of course there was the freelance market: a gun for hire to any bunch of terrorists who were looking for extra shooters, all the way from the

Middle East to the drug cartels of South America. But Lewis harbored the old-fashioned notion, still at large in America, that when you fought, it should be for something you believed in.

At loose ends, he called David Brentwood, his ex-SEAL buddy and Medal of Honor winner, in L.A. The phone was picked up on the second ring. "Brentwood Electronics."

"G'day, mate. You heard the one about the bullfight?"

"No," Brentwood answered, recognizing the Aussie twang.

"Well, these two guys in Spain go watch a bullfight, then go to a restaurant after and order dinner. One of 'em sees these big plate-sized disks of meat his buddy gets and says, 'What's that?'

" 'Ze bull's testicles,' says the waiter. 'They use all parts of ze bull. It's A-1 grade beef.'

" 'Oh, hell,' the guy says. 'I should've ordered that. I went and got the chicken.'

" 'Oh well,' his buddy says, 'there'll be another bullfight tomorrow. We'll eat here again and you can order them then.'

" 'Yeah,' the other guy says. 'I will.'

"So next night he orders testicles instead of chicken, and the waiter brings him these little disks of meat the size of a silver dollar. 'What the hell's this?' the guy asks the waiter. 'Last night my buddy here ordered testicles and he gets plate-sized ones. I order 'em tonight and get these itty bitty things. What's goin' on?' "

Brentwood cut in, " 'Well,' the waiter answers, 'sometimes ze bull wins.' "

"You dick!" Aussie charged. "You let me tell the whole friggin' joke then hijack the punch line."

"I'd've stolen it earlier," Brentwood responded good-naturedly, "but I figured I couldn't get a word in edgewise. How you doin', Aussie?"

"I'm broke. Need a job. Heard of anything?"

"I heard you told a woman at a State Department dinner to F off."

"Nah. Told her to pour her own fuckin' soup."

"I couldn't hire you, Aussie, even if I had work—which I don't. You're a loose cannon. Have to keep you chained up in the cellar."

"I can behave myself if I fuckin' have to."

There was silence on the line, then Brentwood asked, "Have you tried Sal?"

Sal was Salvini, another SEAL and SpecOps warrior.

"Yeah," Aussie Lewis answered, "but Sal's on the out and out too. Got some chickenshit job with a security outfit in New York. Think they use wad-cutter rounds instead of street load. Bunch of wankers. And I've lost contact with Choir. Last I heard, he was negotiating with a bunch of fucking wet-backs in L.A."

"For what?" Brentwood asked.

"Some PR job. Not my line of country."

"Uh-huh," Brentwood said noncommittally. "Look, Aussie, I'll ask around."

Hearing a frustrated expulsion of air on the other end, he added, "I'll get on the e-mail right now, buddy."

"What we need," Aussie said, "is a good war. Kick-start a few of those dormant DOD programs."

"Yeah," David said, laughing, but he could tell Aussie was dead serious. He was one of those men whom the peace people despised, but whom you sent in when things got out of hand with types like Saddam Hussein, Noriega, Milosevic, and the rest. He could strip any weapon you could name, from an M-16 to a Russian Makarov 9mm, in the dark, and reassemble it in record time. He had made over three hundred jumps, twenty-three of them in combat, and had participated in the Battle of Butcher's Ridge against the militia in the Northwest's harsh, unforgiving Cascade Mountains. He'd also survived fierce fighting, often hand-to-hand in the rat-infested tunnels of Southeast Asia.

But he couldn't handle peace.

CHAPTER TEN

DARKNESS HAD FALLEN at Hayden Lake in the Idaho Panhandle. Lights twinkled around the black water's edge as Lucky McBride and Gunner Brock, ringed by a platform of heavily armed militia, loaded the "egg-breaker" into the back of a Ford Windstar parked under cover of a heavy camouflage tarpaulin. It wasn't raining, didn't even look like it. The tarpaulin was intended to block the view of any of the infrared government surveillance satellites that could conceivably be photographing the area.

Preceded by outriders, and with five pickups in front, five guarding the rear, and jerry cans of extra gas in each vehicle, they would drive the Windstar in convoy over three hundred miles across the desert, over the Cascade Mountains, and down to the coast. And God help anyone who tried to stop them. There were six men in each of the ten four-wheel-drive pickups—a driver and five shooters. Three of the shooters in each truck were armed with everything from M-16s to full automatic drum shotguns; the other two shooters manned a swivel-mounted M-60 machine gun. Together with three outriders front and rear, sixty-eight men in all, they would travel east on Highway 2, or alternatively, on Highway 90 farther south. McBride had taken both roads many times, but nevertheless was careful to choose men from the ranks of the eastern Washington regiment, since they were intimately familiar with fifty-mile segments of each highway: the main bridges, side roads, and the pull-offs built exclusively for trucks whose brakes might fail on the steep curves of the Cascade Mountain range, as well as the byways hidden from the normal traveler by overgrown brush and forest. To ram home his concern, he had questioned each man closely.

"Does this side road cross Watson's Creek?" he asked one man, an eager twenty-five-year-old militiaman from Peshastin, three miles east of Leavenworth, where desert landscape would suddenly be blocked by the mountains.

"Ah—yes, sir, I believe so."

"You *believe* or you *know*?"

"Yes, sir, it does."

McBride didn't include the man in the convoy. There *was* no Watson's Creek. The man had assumed it was the name of one of the hundreds of snow-fed streams.

"No, sir," another candidate answered. "There's no Watson's Creek that I know of." The recruit pointed to the 1:12,000 scale map. "The road does cross Icicle Creek."

"Good," McBride said. "Draw ammo and rations. You're in vehicle six. Except for Neilson in the front truck, all of you will change positions en route. That is, you'll move up behind Neilson when the convoy enters your zone of expertise."

"Yes, sir. Thank you, sir," the recruit answered.

"You won't thank me if we run into Federals."

The man wasn't deterred—to have been on a "gig," as a militia mission was inappropriately called, with McBride gave you a certain cachet within militia ranks.

For McBride, only one more piece of the puzzle remained to be put in place as he flipped open his cell and called Ron

Stanes. He asked Stanes about the two "quickies," meaning the security situation at the Bangor gate and the canal. "Was I right?"

"Yep," Stanes answered. "Maximum at the first, minimum at the second."

"Good," McBride said. "One more thing. We need to know if the customers always leave the mall by the building's main door or if they sometimes go out through the basement?"

"I'm pretty sure they always use the main door."

"*Pretty* sure?" McBride pressed. "Does that mean you're certain?" There was a pause, and McBride seized its implication. "That's not good enough," he told Stanes.

"Maybe there's not enough room under the building?" Stanes said.

"No," McBride said, "there's plenty of room." Which meant he knew the "building,"—that is, Hood Canal—was deep enough to accommodate submerged traffic if the navy so wished.

Stanes saw that it raised a perfectly good question: Why *didn't* the subs go through submerged? "How would we find that out?" he asked. "Wouldn't want the neighbors to think we were, you know, snooping."

"Local watering hole," McBride said. "You're from the area. You must know where the construction workers hang out?"

"Sure," Stanes answered. "Wash—" He almost said, "Washington Avenue," where a lot of bars frequented by navy types and by dock workers were situated near the naval shipyards in Bremerton, a short ferry ride across from Seattle. "Yes, I know where they are."

"Well, see what you can find out," McBride told him. "I have to be certain."

"When do you need to know?"

"Yesterday."

* * *

Stanes slipped his cell into his pocket and walked back into the café.

"What's wrong?" Maddin asked.

"Nothing," Stanes said, glancing around, seeing that the nearest diners were out of earshot. "He wants to know whether they always open the bridge for them. Doesn't understand why they don't go under it. You know, submerged."

"Not deep enough," Maddin proffered.

"Apparently it is. He's checked that out too."

"Maybe he's got a point, then," Maddin said. "Why don't they go through submerged?"

Stanes nodded, realizing that if some of the submarines did pass under the bridge submerged, no one would have seen them, and so McBride was right to press the point. If anything went wrong and the situation became definitely and unreservedly FUBAR—fucked up beyond all recognition—as they said in the Army, the militia would have egg all over its face again, a double humiliation on the tail of Rainor and Haley's failure to get a single POW returned following the Boeing fiasco. And the Federals would have even more militia to imprison in Fairchild, rather than being forced to free Eleen and the other POWs.

"Guess that's why they call him 'Lucky,'" Maddin said. "He double-checks everything."

"Uh-huh," Stanes replied distractedly. McBride was right. It didn't make sense for the navy to expose the most complicated and deadly fighting machine the world had ever seen by having it pass through a gap in the bridge. Why wouldn't the subs submerge? "Feel like a drink?" he asked Maddin.

"Where?"

"Down by the *Turner Joy.*"

"What's that?"

"Destroyer, tied up in Bremerton navy yard off Washington Avenue. It was the ship that was fired on in the Gulf of Tonkin. Or so Lyndon Johnson said. Escalated the Vietnam War."

"Another federal fuck-up," Maddin said.

"You got it."

Stanes calculated that it would take them an hour to drive down to Bremerton, about sixty miles to the south.

They split the bill, cash, under strict orders from McBride never to use a credit card, and walked toward the blue pickup.

"Sorry I got snarky in there," Maddin said, looking morosely out the windshield at the ice-cream-white sailboats on the darkening slab of the inlet. "Can't stand people staring at me—ever since I was a kid."

Stanes nodded as he eased the pickup out of the parking lot. "I understand, but you know they can fix that."

Maddin looked nonplused. How in hell could you stop people being bone ignorant?

"Laser surgery," Stanes explained.

"Oh, that," Maddin said, his mind on the diversion he'd planned against the Feds.

Well hell, Stanes thought, if Maddin knew about it, why didn't he get it done? Or was he at heart one of those fundamentalists—God made you look like that, so that's the way you should stay? Maddin was one strange bird.

"I don't want to say much about the diversion," Maddin said, abruptly changing the subject.

Stanes said nothing.

"I mean," Maddin continued, "what if the Feds got you? Made you talk?"

"Christ, I already know the main plan, don't I? I drive, you handle the diversion."

"Yeah, but you don't know exactly how I'm gonna do it. We should all operate on a need-to-know basis, right?"

So that was it. Maddin was nuts about security, like so many other militia guys—an A-1, one-hundred-percent certifiable "wacko." The word reminded Stanes of Waco, and he thought that maybe it took a militia crazy like Maddin to deal with government crazies who, as Charlton Heston Moses said, were trying to deny their Second Amendment rights. Not all at once, but like McBride and Wilcox said, a registration law here, a longer background check there. Bit by bit. Feds had done the same thing with smokers. First you couldn't smoke in federal buildings, then on federal transport, then in parts of restaurants, then in restaurants period, then—

"Where we going in Bremerton? What bar?" Maddin asked.

"Don't think I should tell you. You know, what if we're picked up by the Feds and they make you talk?"

Maddin nodded morosely in agreement.

"Jesus," Stanes said. "It's a joke, Arthur. We're going to a bar called the Crow's Nest."

CHAPTER ELEVEN

AS ELEEN HAD instructed, the men in two of the huts began making a ruckus to divert the guards' attention from the camp's perimeter, particularly the No Go zone between the main fence and the inner trip wire. Beyond that point, a prisoner chasing one of their homemade baseballs or footballs couldn't go without risking either being shot or stepping on a mine.

In hut 5A, Eleen handed Sergeant Mead the two guards' uniforms a rep had brought him. "Put these away," he told Mead, then looked toward the escape party.

A hundred POWs from all over the camp had entered through the rear of 5A in the intervals between the search-light sweeps. It would never have worked if the dogs had been around the camp, but they had not yet returned from the search for Lanky Sommers. All the POWs, blindfolded to accustom themselves to darkness, were standing in line.

Eleen looked across at the hut's parrot. "Electrician ready?"

"Ready, sir."

"All right," Eleen told him. "Relay the message. Blackout now!"

Next, he turned to the two men who would carry the Y ladder. "Remember, it'll take ten minutes for the goons' emergency generator to kick in after we cut the current. The escape must stop at eight minutes sharp. Got it?"

"Yes, sir."

"And," Mead added, "don't jerk the twine we've rigged to the wire." He placed his hands on the shoulders of the two men who would carry the Y. "Remember, guys, there's some moonlight, but not much. The hole is five boot lengths from the wire. It's big, so you shouldn't have any trouble—"

"Yeah, we know. We saw it."

"Just reminding you."

"We know. And don't breaking the friggin' twine."

Eleen doubted they'd have time to get a hundred men over the Y ladder, but even a third of that number would throw the Federals in disarray and inject a much needed boost to camp morale, especially after the militia demand to the Feds to release everyone in Fairchild had backfired when the Boeing operation had gone awry. After that bit of unwelcome news, a long-timer in Sergeant Mead's old squad in hut 12, already severely depressed for months, had gone to the john and hung himself with the chain, a source of great amusement to Moorehead's guards.

Now, suddenly, the camp was plunged into darkness.

"Go!"

Eleen heard the rustle of the blindfolds slipping down, the men having been told not to waste precious seconds trying to lift them up over their heads or to untie the knots. The POWs filed quietly but quickly out of the door of 5A, the first two carrying the Y ladder. Within fifteen seconds the bottom of the Y ladder's stem was placed in the hole, two long pieces of torn blanket taking up the tension as the padded ladders came to rest against the barbed wire. In another twelve seconds the first escapee was atop the wire and jumped clear. He was down and running as a squad of flashlight-toting guards entered the far end of the camp, yelling at the rebels in huts 49 and 50 to shut up and turn in. They were met by a string of obscenities that goaded the guards further, several of them looking for the illegal moonshine they assumed must be intoxicating the unruly prisoners. The prisoners were so riotous that the duty officer, a young lieutenant, panicked. Drawing his standard issue Beretta 9mm, he fired into the air, and seconds later several of the guards followed suit. There was a brief lull before the POWs began the ruckus anew, louder than before, some of the long-timers intoxicated by their opportunity to defy authority. The clutch of guards, becoming frightened, glanced at the duty officer for guidance.

The young lieutenant had two choices: fire *into* the two huts or withdraw and leave them to it. He'd never shot a man before, however, and he knew that if he fired into the militia, some of his men might not make it to the gate in the dark. But if he did nothing, he'd lose face completely, not only with the POWs but with his own men. He pulled out his cell phone and called Moorehead. It was still a loss of face but not as bad as running for the gate. The POWs, sensing his indecision and alarm, grew even more boisterous and threatening.

"What?" Moorehead bellowed on being told of the blackout and the POWs' wild party. "You moron!" Moorehead berated him, the sound of the commandant's dogs barking in the background. "It's obviously a ploy. Which huts are involved? Their numbers? Quickly!"

"Ah—huts forty-nine and fifty sir," the rattled lieutenant answered.

"Get out of there, goddammit, and check the perimeter up near the first ten huts."

"Yes, sir."

The duty officer and his squad withdrew in the darkness under a barrage of catcalls and a shower of miscellaneous items flung out from the two huts.

Three minutes later the emergency generator kicked in. Lights flickered then came on to full power, the guard towers' searchlights sweeping the wire. Nothing. Everything looked fine—until the third sweep. A guard in the tower nearest hut 5A saw something he had at first thought was a snatch of wind-blown sage on the wire. It was a piece of cloth. Trembling, the duty officer called Moorehead, who ordered every light in the camp, inside as well as outside the huts, turned on and a full body count undertaken. "Now!"

"Yes, sir," the mortified duty officer answered.

"And Lieutenant . . ."

"Sir?"

"Every prisoner is to be touched during the count."

The duty officer didn't understand why but was too afraid to ask.

CHAPTER TWELVE

FROM THE NEWLY renovated Crow's Nest Bar on Washington Avenue, Stanes and Maddin looked out on Bremerton's floodlit slate-gray docks. The docks provided anchorage for six mothballed nuclear subs, a Nimitz class carrier, other assorted naval supply vessels, and the USS *Turner Joy*, its normally blue canvas rail panels stained black in a drizzle typical of the ever-changing weather in Puget Sound.

Stanes struck up a conversation with three sailors in dress whites who wore the coveted dolphin insignia on their chests. "So, you guys do come up for air?" he joshed.

"Occasionally," one of the submariners answered.

"Not me," Stanes said. "I'd rather be on one of the surface boats," and instantly regretted saying "boats" instead of "ships." It was not the way to pass himself off as one of the thousands of dock workers in Bremerton, who'd be familiar with the correct nautical terms.

"Uh-huh," the submariner responded, leaving the conversation suspended in midair.

Stanes knew submariners were trained that way. Even if they were garrulous types when they first joined the Silent Service, the men who manned the pig boats, as the subs were still called by some, were told to button up when it came to anyone talking to them about what they did. Small things counted, which was why in the nuclear navy submariners never even told their loved ones where they were going, or even where they'd been, lest it enable enemy operatives to "back-plot" patrol routes. And the truth was, as Stanes had told Maddin on the drive down, most people on a U.S. sub never knew where they were during patrol anyway—only the captain, navigator, and the officer who had the con needed to know.

"What do you guys do?" one of the submariners asked.

"Fishermen," Maddin said, draining his glass and surprising Stanes with his unexpected contribution.

"Fish*ers*," Stanes corrected him good-naturedly, or "fisher-*persons.*"

"Persons?" Maddin said dourly. "I don't go for that bullshit!"

The submariners laughed. "Know what you mean," said one of them, a young engineering lab technician from New York named Danny Gianelli. "All this feminist crap."

Stanes saw an opportunity to open up the conversation. "Yeah, I hear the Navy's thinking about putting women aboard subs."

"Well," Gianelli retorted, "they'd better think pretty hard."

"You can say that again," added one of the other two submariners, who, Stanes saw from the insignia below his black eagle, was a planesman.

"Know what you mean," Stanes continued sympathetically. "I was watching a documentary on subs the other night. Man, I thought you guys had a lot more room in those boats, you know, compared to the old pig boats, but they were showing how you 'hot bunk' it." He paused. "That's what you call it, right?"

"Yeah," the planesman answered, a short, wiry Californian, his hair cut so short he was almost bald. "Hot bunkin'."

"Because," Stanes continued before draining his glass of

beer, "one guy finishes sleeping, goes on watch, and the next guy bunks down. Mattress is still hot. You're packed in pretty close. Right?"

"Yeah."

" 'Course," Stanes joshed, getting the attention of the bartender and pointing to his glass for a refill, "I wouldn't mind bunking down close to a blonde—say like Pamela Anderson."

The planesman allowed himself a smile. "Me too, but man, you get a skirt down there and . . ." He shook his head.

"Bad for the concentration, eh?" It was Maddin, surprising Stanes again—damn, the grouch was doing all right. Knew just when to come in. Stanes only hoped Maddin's timing was as good when it came time for the two of them to run interference for McBride's main play.

"Tits on a sub's bad for everything, period," young Gianelli said. "Have a fight on your hands 'fore you left port."

Stanes couldn't believe his luck, and it had all opened up because Maddin, obviously out of his bad mood from the café, or at least hiding his bad temper for the moment, had struck a nerve with the submariners. "Yeah," Stanes continued, "they were talking about leaving port in this documentary, and there was something queer about it."

"Queer?" the ELT challenged. "What was *queer* about it?"

Stanes had to stop himself from smiling—nothing could get a sailor on the defensive quicker than an imagined slight upon his masculinity.

"Well," Stanes said, assuming a puzzled expression, "this sub was putting out to sea, passing through the Hood Canal Bridge and up through the Strait of Juan de Fuca—over a hundred miles—before it submerged. Like, you know, tellin' the Russians, Chinese, whoever, 'Here we are, boys.' Queer navy if you ask me. Stupid."

"Yeah, well," Gianelli interjected, "nobody's askin' you.

B'sides," he continued venomously, "any fool knows why we don't submerge on the way out. 'Cause of the salt."

Stanes's face creased with confusion until Maddin asked the submariner if he was talking about the Strategic Arms Limitation Treaty—SALT.

"Yeah," Gianelli said condescendingly. "What the fuck else would I mean? Salt an' pepper, for christsake? Under the treaty, neither side can dive till we reach the Continental Shelf. That way, no one can sneak out of port without the other one knowing."

"Oh," Stanes said, acting suitably chagrined. "Then it wasn't so queer after all?"

"No," Gianelli retorted angrily.

Stanes was flabbergasted. Of course he, Maddin, and most other people had heard about SALT at one time or other, on TV, in the papers, but how could the public be expected to know the fine print? Hell, he hadn't even read the fine print in his household insurance policy. And yet there it was, the explanation for why the subs didn't submerge until they reached the open sea. The answer to McBride's query. Public information—nothing that was classified.

"So," Stanes told Maddin as they left the warmth of the Crow's Nest to be met by a bracing wind off Puget Sound, "they'll be egressing on the surface."

"E-*what*?" Maddin asked, pulling up his collar.

"Egressing," Stanes repeated. "You know, heading out."

"Fancy word," Maddin charged.

Stanes had the choice of making a smart-ass reply or adopting a tone of conciliation. He thought about what they had to do tomorrow and decided that what he needed now, along with a good night's sleep back at the hotel, was cooperation. "You know," he told Maddin as they neared the pickup, "you were pretty sharp in there—drawing those guys out."

Maddin grunted, but Stanes could tell he was pleased, or at least as pleased as Maddin could get.

In the Crow's Nest, the planesman asked his ELT buddy Gianelli and the other submariner if they had change.

"What for?"

"I'm gonna call the base. Don't like the look of those two guys."

"So?" Gianelli said. "We never told 'em anything."

"You told 'em about SALT, Danny."

"Ain't classified," Gianelli said defensively, tossing him a dime and a quarter. "They could've found that out at the damn library."

"Yeah," chimed in the other submariner, one of the sub's missile technicians. "Or they could have found it on the Net."

"If they'd known where to look," the planesman said. "Anyway, that isn't the point. Point is *why* they want to know."

"Right," the MT agreed.

"Well shit!" Gianelli said. "What are you gonna tell base?"

"Don't worry, I'm not gonna put you in it. But you know what NIS says. If we suspect anyone of being too nosy we should notify 'em. Remember the *Coe*."

"NIS," Gianelli said, referring to the Naval Intelligence Service. "What are they gonna do?"

The planesman shrugged. "Check these guys out."

"How?" the MT asked derisively, now siding with Gianelli. "NIS couldn't find their dick. Worst intel outfit in the country."

"I watched those two guys walking back to their truck," the planesman said. "I got their license number."

Danny Gianelli made a face and looked at the missile technician while jerking his thumb toward the planesman. "We got a regular Sherlock Holmes aboard!"

The planesman grinned, went over to the phone cubicle by the south wall and called the Bangor base duty officer. He gave a good physical description of Stanes and Maddin, and told the DO that the two claimed to be fishermen and were driving a blue Ford pickup.

"Half the country's driving blue pickups," the duty officer riposted. The planesman had deliberately withheld the license number till now. He didn't like the DO, and it gave him pleasure to be able to read out, "Washington State plates XM4 387."

"I'll pass it on." He hung up.

"That prick!" the planesman told the other two submariners. "But I aced him with the license number."

"Huh," Gianelli said. "He's probably round-filed it."

"No," the planesman said. "If he throws that in the garbage bin, he's in deep doodah. He's gotta tell NIS."

"To cover his ass," the MT said.

"Exactly," the planesman replied while signaling the bartender for another beer.

"I think our two fisherpersons are in for a surprise. State patrol'll be looking for 'em in about ten minutes."

"If NIS tells 'em," Gianelli said, keen to deflate the other's air of self-congratulation.

"NIS might get 'em!" the missile technician proffered.

The planesman paid for his Bud Lite. "Thought you said NIS couldn't find their dick?"

"Any friggin' idiot can read a license plate."

"Whatever," the planesman said. "State patrol or NIS. Our nosy friends are gonna get pulled over and questioned."

"Well," the MT added, "I guess better safe than sorry, eh?"

CHAPTER THIRTEEN

HAVING ORDERED ALL arc lights in the camp switched on, as Moorehead had ordered him, the young lieutenant called out over a hundred guards in Camp Fairchild; every one, in fact, who wasn't out with Moorehead and the dogs. Even so, it was difficult to get the recalcitrant POWs to line up on the parade ground according to huts, the dust hanging in the floodlit air like smoke as the militiamen scuffed and dragged their feet, doing anything to confound the Federals' task, giving those who'd escaped more time.

"Captain Eleen!" the young lieutenant shouted, his left hand grasping a loud hailer, his right hand on his covered holster. "Tell your men to cooperate!"

"What was that?" Eleen asked, his hand cupping his ears.

"Get your men to cooperate!"

"They are."

"They're screwing around!" the lieutenant shouted. "Somebody's going to get hurt!"

Eleen's normally calm, almost baby-faced expression seemed to crinkle with concern, straining to hear again. "Who's going to get hurt?" Eleen saw the lieutenant unclip his holster, the young officer's face red with embarrassment, and he realized that someone, almost certainly a militia POW, *would* be hurt if he didn't back off. "Give me the hailer," Eleen told the lieutenant, who quickly obliged.

"All right, men," Eleen ordered, the metallic ring of his voice heard across the parade ground. "Fall in!"

The young lieutenant was open-mouthed at the sudden transition, the unruly rabble of a minute before now quickly forming themselves into platoon-sized blocks whose bearing would have done the Marine Corps proud. The hundreds of militiamen not only stood smartly at attention but, most astonishing to the young lieutenant and his fellow guards, silently.

"Ah, start the count!" the lieutenant ordered, and the guards began moving down the ranks of militiamen until an outburst of profanity, a scuffle between a guard and a POW, threatened to break up the platoons.

"Steady in the ranks!" Eleen shouted, telling the POW, as the lieutenant told his guard, to knock it off, several guards rushing to their comrades' aid, M-16s raised to club the militiaman.

"Hold off!" the lieutenant commanded. Reluctantly, they obeyed, but stood menacingly over the militiaman, barely giving him room to get up.

"What's going on here?" the lieutenant asked sharply, determined to at least act as confidently as Eleen.

The militiaman, pointing to one of the guards and trying to catch his breath, said, "I don't like being mauled by one of your goons."

"Mauled?"

The guard in question was dusting himself off beneath one of the arc lights. "You told us we had to touch each man, sir."

Eleen looked at the lieutenant. "Is that true?"

"Yes, sir. I—" The lieutenant stopped, humiliated that he had just addressed Eleen as "sir," in clear violation of federal policy that under no circumstances were militia to be accorded the respect normally given to enemy combatants. To do so, Washington had impressed upon all the federal employees, would be to accord the rebels a legitimacy

Washington was determined to withhold from them. Moorehead had pointed out to his guards that even the phrase "prisoner of *war*," which normally acknowledged military combatants, was a designation suborned by the militia, and not one accredited them by Washington.

"Who gave you the order to touch my men?" Eleen demanded, adding, "That's assault!" But as the lieutenant foundered, trying futilely to explain what even to him had seemed a weird order from Moorehead, Eleen already knew the answer. And, as much as he despised Moorehead and all the bully boy Federals like him, he had to admit the commandant was as smart as he was ruthless. Moorehead was obviously aware that talented POWs, with nothing but time on their hands, were capable of constructing mannequins, even providing them with a face convincing enough for a guard passing down the assembled platoons who was concentrating on not losing the count. Such dummies could buy valuable time for escapees. Despite the floodlit parade ground, at night, with so many shadows cast by the hundreds of men, it would be easy for a guard to walk right by a figure in militia fatigues and cap and think he'd checked off another prisoner in the count. In fact, at least seven mannequins were being used tonight, and that bothered Eleen.

After the touch count, the game was up. Five of the mannequins were discovered, unable to be smuggled back into the huts in time. With the discovery of each mannequin, the guards' earlier annoyance at having been called out for a night count gave way to increasing cockiness, their earlier reluctance to touch militiamen giving way to sharp jabs with rifle barrels in the gut—"This bag of shit is for real!"—and vicious blows to the prisoners' backs. By the time the count was finished, the militiamen were seething and it took all their composure not to strike back. Besides, during the "party" earlier at huts 49 and 50, there had been only a nine-man goon squad, but here on the parade ground, with over a hundred guards fully armed and wanting any excuse to open fire, guards indisputably held the upper hand.

"Don't move!" Eleen told his men. This only emboldened the guards further, and left the POWs beside themselves with rage, though they knew that Eleen was right. What had been the POWs' normal disdain—in some cases, hatred—of the Federals metamorphosed into a thirst for revenge.

By now Moorehead's dogs and their handlers were approaching the camp, returning from the outskirts of Spokane where Lanky Sommers had almost made it. Moorehead did not stay long in the camp, pausing only to have Sommers's bullet-riddled corpse dumped, faceup, into the compound for all to see. A crude sign, SPOKANE OR BUST! had been hung around his neck.

"How many are missing?" he asked the lieutenant curtly.

"Ah, thirty-two, sir."

Moorehead was covered in dust, the perspiration on his face sending rivulets down his cheeks. But far from looking exhausted, he was energized, ordering many of the guards who'd made the count to join him in the "hunt," as he called it, for the thirty-two rebels who had escaped. The dog handlers, tired from the chase for Sommers, wanted to rest, but no one complained except Dillon, the guard who'd seen Moorehead shoot Sommers in cold blood and whose silence had been bought with the promised transfer to sunny California. "Think I'll call it a day," he told Moorehead, who grunted his assent, before telling the handlers to pick up the scent of the escapees. He assumed, correctly, they would be headed west and southwest of Fairchild, away from the direction of Spokane, where everyone had seen the dogs take off after Sommers.

Eleen told Moorehead that he wanted to lodge an official complaint about the bullet-riddled body of Lanky Sommers.

Though Moorehead knew that Eleen had no official status as far as the Federals were concerned, he couldn't resist the opportunity to drive home his success in capturing Sommers.

"You got a problem?" he sneeringly asked.

"That man," Eleen said, indicating the corpse, "was unarmed. And that sign—"

"The hell he was unarmed. Sonofabitch was carrying a concealed weapon. Snub-nosed .38. 'Course, I suppose you wouldn't know anything about that."

"The man was unarmed!"

Moorehead's face was so close to Eleen—the young lieutenant and Eleen's sergeant, Mead, quickly stepping aside—that the militia commander could smell a foul combination of pizza and decaying teeth on the commandant's breath. "You tried to be a clever Trevor didn't you?" Moorehead charged. "Soon as I was gone with the dogs, you thought you'd take advantage of the situation here and pull a fast one. Well"—his right index finger stabbed Eleen's chest so hard it pushed the militiaman off balance—"I'm gonna find the rest of your rebel boys and they'll be back in here 'fore daybreak." He paused, smiling. "The ones that can still walk, that is."

"In the name of—" Eleen almost said "God," but even in this dire situation his Mormon background prevented him. Instead, Eleen demanded to know what Moorehead meant by "the ones that can still walk."

"It means," Moorehead retorted, a cloud of his spittle caught in the floodlight, "that whatever happens is on your head." With that, Moorehead turned away and started barking orders at the whey-faced lieutenant to call the state patrol for a chopper. "Land line only," he added, "no cell phone," to stress it was a matter of highest priority to keep any knowledge of the escape from the press, who often scanned cell frequencies. "We've got to stop the bastards reaching 90 or 2." He was referring to the two highways that led west toward the

Cascade Mountains and the coast. "And get the Hummer," he instructed the lieutenant. "We'll use it as well as the half-tracks. Load it with a box of flares and grenades."

"Grenades?" the lieutenant inquired. "Flash bangs?"

"No. I want to do more than stun the bastards. This isn't a domestic dispute we're up against, Lieutenant. It's a mass escape, goddammit! And I want a belt-fed MK-19 on one of those half-tracks." Mounted on a tripod, the M-19 was a weapon that from a distance might look like a medium machine gun, until you saw the shotgun-sized rounds that were in fact 40mm high explosive grenades. When they went off, as far out as five hundred meters, they would kill or incapacitate anyone within fifteen feet or more.

"You okay, sir?" Sergeant Mead asked Eleen as they made their way back despondently to hut 5A.

"Moorehead's right," he told Mead. "It *is* on my head. It was my bright idea to take advantage of Sommers's escape." He paused, looking out beyond the wire where two guards had been posted by the Y ladder. "I thought it would take them a lot longer to find Sommers. I should've known just how relentless Moorehead is." He paused again. "I'm sure he murdered Sommers, that Sommers was unarmed."

"Don't blame yourself, sir," Mead said, and tried to change the subject. "Anyway, it was a good idea using the Y. Heck, that's why we had it hidden away—for just such an opportunity. The men were going stir-crazy. Some of 'em have been locked up here since Freeman's outfit caught 'em at Butcher's Ridge."

Eleen was still looking beyond the Y ladder on the wire and the two guards, beyond the penumbra of the perimeter arc lights, into the darkness of the cold desert. "One of them," Eleen said, his voice taking on a strange, disembodied tone, "is a young kid from the Eugene militia down in Oregon. Marion Jubal. Hut 12."

"I know him," Mead said. "Guys were always taking the piss—taking the mickey out of him because his first name's Marion."

For the first time in a long while Mead saw the flicker of a smile on the captain's face. "Yes," Eleen said. "He told me his father called him that after John Wayne, whose real name was Marion something."

"Marion Morrison," Mead said, smiling. "The Duke!"

But any humor he might have detected in Eleen's tone was now gone. Eleen turned his attention toward the camp's squat administration building beyond the main gate, where Moorehead's Hummer was being loaded. The dogs, having been watered, were piling into the back of half-tracks, which were ideally suited for a "hunt" in the desert.

"He's been in here just over a year," Eleen said. "The day the Feds picked him up—just a few hours before it happened, he said—his wife told him she was pregnant. First child." Eleen turned to Mead. "You see, I thought he should go, see his child."

"Sir, you're worrying too much. Our boys got a good half hour start on 'em. Some of them are bound to make it."

"A half hour?" Eleen responded. "Against dogs and vehicles?"

"Some will've made it to the main roads," Mead said reassuringly. "They're not running naked," by which he meant the thirty-two escapees were equipped with legends, money, maps. "Ten-to-one some of 'em have already caught the evening bus out of Hayford, their feet up and watchin' the scenery slip by."

But no amount of levity could now bring Eleen out of his black mood. Out in the floodlit compound, the guards still hadn't removed Sommers's corpse, and the militia captain was visited by a horror story that sympathetic World War Two veterans had once told him: after the mass escape of seventy-six Allied POWs in 1944 from Stalag Luft III near Sagan, fifty of those recaptured had been murdered by the SS. And there was no doubt in Eleen's mind that Moorehead was every bit as brutal as the SS.

From hut 5A, Eleen heard, then saw, a half-track beyond the wire, noisily traveling around the perimeter, approaching the gate from the northeast corner. It stopped every now and then in a cloud of dust beneath the arc lights, picking up guards who had been stationed along the wire since the breakout, no doubt collecting them to join in Moorehead's hunt. But then, unexpectedly, instead of continuing south past the main gate, the half-track turned abruptly toward the main gate.

"Mead!" Eleen shouted to his militia sergeant, who was halfway down the hut.

"Sir?"

"Get into one of those guard uniforms. Quickly!"

One of the hut's off-duty parrots extracted one of the two uniforms that had been hidden inside a bunk's mattress and handed it to Mead, and as the sergeant stripped off his prison garb and got into the uniform, another member of the escape committee prepped him: "Maps and forty bucks top left pocket. Matchbox, compass, and matches, top right. Knife taped inside. Thin aluminum—so it won't take any torque. Straight in and out if you have to use it."

"Or slash," said another man, tossing him one of the fake wooden M-16s.

"Got it!" Mead said, noticing that Eleen had told the parrot to put the other uniform back in the mattress.

Eleen saw his sergeant's surprise, and anticipating an objection from Mead, told him quietly, "Do as I say, Mead. That's an order. I'm not going. If they're coming into the camp, it's most likely for me. Moorehead holds me responsible." Eleen paused as he saw the main gate open and the half-track kicking up more dust. "And as I said before, he's right."

"But sir—"

"Now listen. That half-track's creating a dust storm. And it's unlikely all those guards know one another. They've obviously been called out from different shifts. Half of them look like they're still asleep. So use the night and the dust cloud as cover and get aboard the half-track. It's worth a try."

Mead nodded, adding, "Wish you were coming with me, Captain."

"So do—" Eleen began.

The half-track had braked hard in a cloud of dust that ballooned in front of 5A. A squad of heavily armed guards, led by a hefty sergeant and backed by a .50 Browning mounted on the half-track, ran up the steps and ordered Eleen out. Eleen's men moved ominously toward the guards. Eleen restrained them. There was nothing to gain by resisting.

"Where are you taking him?" a hut rep demanded.

"Shut your mouth!" the sergeant said.

They cuffed Eleen, which produced a chorus of boos and obscenities, then pushed him out to the half-track. Surely, he thought, they weren't going to kill him—there were too many witnesses seeing him being taken away.

"There's gonna be a fire tonight," one of the guards taunted him. "Guess which hut?"

The sergeant, lighting up a cheap cigar, his teeth pearly white beneath the arc lights, said, "The *captain* here, he's gonna feel so responsible for everything that's gone wrong—well hell, he'll probably hang himself in solitary."

"Now how's he gonna do that?" asked a guard with a distinct southern accent. "They take everything from you in solitary—boot laces, belt, suspenders. How's he gonna do it?"

"We'll think of something, Leroi."

"Shit," Leroi said, "Ah bet you will. You old dog."

Amid the roar of the half-track, the stink of its exhaust, and the dust enveloping it, Eleen said a prayer, a simple but direct supplication not for himself but for the men who had escaped. If Moorehead's goons were so blatant as to take him away in front of many witnesses to kill him, he felt sick at what they might do to Jubal and the others if they caught them.

Above the rumbling of the half-track, the sergeant shouted, "Some guys in Leavenworth hung 'emselves with their jockey shorts."

"Bull*shit*!"

"I'm tellin' you the truth, Leroi. Took out the elastic band, used it as a noose, other end tied to a shirtsleeve, whatever, then wrapped that around one of the window bars, and bam! Jumped off the stool they'd put on top o' the shit bucket. 'Course they kicked awhile."

Leroi jabbed Eleen with his elbow. "What you say about that reb?"

A strange calm had come over Eleen, an acceptance of his fate, and he answered so quietly that had it not been for the half-track coming to a stop in front of the punishment block, the guard wouldn't have heard him ask, "You southerners were once rebs, weren't you, Leroi?"

"By God, he's got you there, Leroi," the sergeant said, the other half-dozen guards joining in the sergeant's laughter.

"You!" Leroi said, jabbing Eleen viciously again in the ribs. "Shut your mouth!"

Beyond his cell in the punishment block, Eleen could see Moorehead driving off fast in his bloodred Hummer, the two half-tracks following. Eleen had the unmistakable premonition of death.

CHAPTER FOURTEEN

MCBRIDE'S MILITIA CONVOY coming out of Idaho on I-90 had no idea as they crossed the border into Washington State that a breakout was in progress from Camp Fairchild. Though Moorehead had sought the help of a state patrol helo out of Spokane, no one in the media had as yet been alerted. Having stayed in mid-convoy from Hayden Lake to make sure the tarpaulin-covered egg-breaker was riding well, McBride's Windstar moved to the head of the eleven-vehicle, sixty-eight-man motorcade once it crossed the border and he'd had everyone, including the outriders, double-check their weapons. Most had M-16s or AK-47s, but McBride's selection of a weapon, apart from his 9mm Beretta handgun, was instructive to the half-dozen or so men who'd most recently joined the Idaho detachment. This was particularly so for three Canadians who had crossed the Canadian–U.S. border following their outrage at their government's "settlement" gift of over nine hundred square miles to the West Coast Tadish Indian band.

The Canadians, because of their government's strict gun laws—draconian by American standards—had only heard about but never seen the vaunted laser aimer SAR-21 5.56mm Bullpup up close. The state-of-the-art Bullpup integrated its receiver mechanism and butt stock into a single piece, giving its operator a full-sized rifle barrel in a much shorter polymer/steel assembly, its fire controls fully ambidextrous. McBride was especially drawn to the weapon because it combined laser accuracy with ruggedness, and above all could be field stripped without tools in fifteen seconds and, though old militia hands found it difficult to believe, it did not require zeroing in.

"Don't like the Bullpup," Gunner Brock had complained before making his way to the rear of the Windstar, squeezing past the covered-up egg-breaker and a box of extra motorcycle helmets to join the crew of the van's tarpaulin-shrouded M-60 machine gun. "Goddamn chamber's right on your cheek and—"

"It's well vented," McBride cut in testily. "Besides, the composite plate'll protect you from burn."

"Well, it's not for me!" Brock replied grumpily, leading McBride to believe his friend was still confounded by his unblinking execution of "the traitor" in the hut at Hayden Lake.

"Suit yourself," McBride said.

"I will." Everyone was tense, even the legendary McBride.

Neilson, McBride's co-driver, didn't like the exchange between the two old friends—or were they still old friends? He could understand Brock's trauma after McBride had fired two shots at his buddy. Neilson told himself he'd be mighty pissed too. What kind of friend was that? One tough son of a bitch militiaman, sure, but what kind of friend?

Right now, however, Neilson was more concerned about Brock's readiness to vacate the Windstar and man the M-60 they had ready in the back along with the egg-breaker and ROE. Through repeated practice, the pickup crews in the other ten vehicles had got the "whip-off" of the tarpaulin in the back of their vehicles, all pickups, down to four seconds. This included heaving two protective bales of hay that helped hide the guns, which were set far enough back on each pickup's flatbed for the M-60s to command a full 180-degree field of fire. McBride had also ordered all drivers and co-drivers in the ten armed pickups to carry earplugs. Though McBride considered it highly unlikely that there'd be any confrontation with Federals on the way, he prided himself on being well prepared. If it became necessary to open fire, he knew the noise of the 7.62mm rounds, along with the racket of the gun itself, could stun a person, temporarily deafening them to any orders he might have to issue over the two-way radios. And any momentary confusion could cause a horrendous pileup—end of mission, end of any hope of getting the Federals to shut down Fairchild and free a thousand militia comrades.

"Egg-breaker okay?" driver Neilson asked McBride.

The militia leader didn't even bother to look back at the package. "We could roll and it'd be intact. Styrofoamed and stowed. Better than FedEx."

"I hear it's not that heavy," Neilson said. "Fifty pounds?"

"Forty-nine point six," McBride answered. "And watch where you're driving."

"Yes, boss!" Neilson answered good-naturedly, struck once again by McBride's penchant for detail. Not fifty pounds—forty-nine point six! And when he'd organized the convoy, he hadn't put one outrider up front, but three—triple insurance against any contingency. McBride's attention to detail reminded Neilson of the stories he'd heard about General Douglas Freeman, another stickler for military minutiae. They said Freeman was nuts, believed in reincarnation, like his hero Patton, but had a reputation, like McBride, for being a meticulous planner.

"You believe in reincarnation?" Neilson queried McBride.

"No. Why?"

"I was just thinking that if—"

McBride's radio crackled to life. The front outrider had

spotted a highway patrol's chopper, or rather, its searchlight's beam, roiling with dust, skittering across the sage-dotted desert south of Camp Fairchild and just ahead of the militia convoy.

"Al here," came the outrider's voice. "Riley's rig is up ahead."

"Oh—how far?" McBride asked, his own voice as conversational as that of the outriders, lest anyone else was listening in on the band.

"About two clicks. You should see his taillights soon."

"Taillights" meant that the potential danger, whatever it was, was heading west. All the convoy's drivers would have similarly picked up the outrider's warning, waiting now for McBride to make a decision—stop, go, or turn back?

Neilson forgot all about reincarnation, his hands gripping the SUV's wheel that much tighter.

McBride glanced at his watch. To go back was out of the question—it would mean postponing the mission for at least another two weeks, requiring massive reorganization. To stop was an option, but that might look strange to the police chopper, eleven vehicles suddenly pulling off I-90. It was possible, McBride thought, that someone else had broken out of Camp Fairchild, like the man he'd seen the day before. If they only knew that right now he was in the process of trying to spring everyone from the camp . . . but apart from those directly involved, no one, including the POWs, knew of the mission.

Neilson too was wondering what the chopper was doing so close to Fairchild. "Maybe one of our guys made a break for it?" he said.

"So?" McBride replied calmly. "No reason for us to panic." He called the outrider, and could hear the throaty roar of the Yamaha threatening to drown him out. McBride was about to ask him, in their prearranged lingo, if there was any sign of a roadblock when the voice of another outrider invaded the Windstar's cabin, the name he gave identifying him as the last rider at the rear of the convoy. Ostensibly, he was sending out a jovial-sounding call to any fellow travelers on Highway 2 asking for info "on the nearest motel."

"Shit!" Neilson said. Now, as well as possible danger ahead, "motel" was the warning that there was some kind of trouble behind them. "Shit! Shit! Shit!"

"Be quiet!" McBride rebuked him. "Keep going." Trying to avoid undue chatter or tones of alarm on the convoy's intervehicle radios, McBride turned around to Gunner Brock. "Pass it on."

Brock used his flashlight to signal the pickup behind him, the procedure followed by each vehicle. In less than a minute the entire militia convoy, though on high alert, kept rolling westward.

The sight of a roiling white cone of light moving crazily over the desert created a surreal scene into which the militia convoy, headlights ablaze, was heading. Moorehead's red Hummer and two half-tracks were now less than a quarter mile from McBride's tail-end outrider. Suddenly, the beam disappeared, the only indication of the helo's position the faint blinking of its starboard green light arcing low in a parabola away from the convoy. Then just as suddenly it reappeared, swinging southward, and stopped, hovering a hundred feet above a clump of sage. A disembodied voice boomed down, commanding, "Don't move! Stay where you are!" Then Moorehead's Hummer, its driver oblivious to having gained on a militia convoy, swung off the highway, trailing a wake of fine pebbles and dust, followed by the two half-tracks, which unlike the Hummer tore over the road's shoulder. Dipping, they disappeared altogether, their headlight beams momentarily shooting skyward. The two vehicles were in sight seconds later, engines roaring, spewing exhaust, emerging from a coulee. They were running parallel to each other, ten yards apart and heading hell-bent for the base of the helo's beam, whose edges were atremble from the vibration of the chopper.

The militia convoy had kept moving, passing an irrigated field, their view of the half-tracks a quarter mile away veiled by moonlit spray from two of the enormous sprinkler arms. The militiamen in the last four pickups, however, saw something else: a clutch of five or six men emerging from a clump of sage, hands held high in abject surrender. Moorehead's guards in the half-tracks were shouting at them to "Get down!" as if, after Moorehead's report to his guards of his encounter with Lanky Sommers, the guards thought their captives might be armed.

"Must be some of our guys," one of the convoy militiaman said, "busting out of Fairchild."

"Yeah," said another. "Poor bastards!"

Now they could hear dogs barking, but were unsure whether the sounds had come from the red Hummer that had stopped or the half-tracks.

"We should give 'em a hand."

"Yeah, tell our driver to pull out, catch up with McBride. See what he says."

"We could call him on the radio."

"Too risky. We've got no lingo for this. 'Sides, the helo cops could be listening in."

"All right, tell Jake to pull out."

But Jake was equivocal about the idea. They'd all been told by McBride to maintain position in the convoy. Then again, this *was* clearly an unexpected emergency.

"C'mon, Jake!"

McBride's Ford Windstar was on the straightaway south of Hayford when Neilson saw a vehicle's headlights coming up fast behind them on the wrong side of the road. It wasn't till he saw its cabin light flicking on and off, another of McBride's ideas, that he knew it was one of theirs. As Jake drew parallel, he eased ahead, putting the machine gunner in the back, parallel to Neilson's window, pulling a fast one on the gunner, forcing him to do the talking.

"What's wrong?" Neilson shouted, McBride next to him looking intently at the gunner.

"Ah, looks like those guys the cops are on to. Damn—" He was thrown hard against one of the bales on either side of the M-60 as Jake, in the face of oncoming headlights, had to fall back, squeezing in behind Neilson until the oncoming car, a police cruiser doing at least 90 mph sped past. Its flashers, McBride noted, were turned off, probably so as not to alert any of the escaping POWs it had no doubt been called in to help capture. Then, coming from the direction of the half-tracks, they heard the unmistakable rip of a .50 caliber machine gun.

Jake swung out again, so violently the men in the back could hear the jerry cans sloshing. The gunner, his voice fighting the vehicle's slipstream, shouted out his request with renewed urgency.

"Get back in the convoy!" McBride shouted angrily. "Wind up your window!" he ordered Neilson, adding, "Goddamn idiot! We don't know they're our boys for sure. Even if they were, I wouldn't go back—risk the whole damn mission. Best we could do is maybe save a few and blow the chance to free a thousand. Is he nuts?"

"Guess he wanted to try all the same."

"Goddammit! For a man to break convoy like that—what was his name . . . ?"

"Sir?" Neilson queried.

"The idiot who broke convoy. What's his name?"

"Oh, Jake. Jake Carson."

"Where's he from?"

"From the Redoubt."

"I thought we had our *best* men there?"

"Well, not everyone's perfect," Neilson observed lightly, trying to joke McBride back into his old and more likable incarnation. "We sent Rainor and Haley there."

"I know," McBride replied archly. "Thank God they're not with the convoy." He fell silent, and all they could hear was the hum of tires. A minute or so later he commented, "Eleen should never had authorized a breakout like that. Certainly not tonight."

Neilson knew he was sticking his neck out, but felt obliged to respond. "Geez, Captain. How the heck would he know we'd be heading west tonight? Coincidence, that's all."

"I don't like coincidences. He's unwittingly jeopardizing the whole mission. Cops could be throwing up roadblocks further west." Neilson was feeling uncomfortable. They saw lights up ahead—the township of Sprague.

"I screwed a woman once in Sprague," Neilson announced. "One breast bigger'n the other."

"We'll stop at Ellensburg," McBride said. "Use the jerry cans to gas up, but not all in the same place. That'd be bound to raise suspicion."

"Fine. Just tell me when."

There was still something on Neilson's mind, but after McBride's display of ill temper, it took him ten minutes to bring it up. By that time they were well past Sprague.

"Captain?"

"Yes?"

"I know you've thought this all through, but d'you mind if I—"

"Say it, man!"

"I don't think it's a good idea for the convoy to leave you to do it by yourself. I mean, you're having the convoy running shotgun all the way to the coast. Why not have them hang around there in case there's trouble?"

"First," McBride said, his tone noticeably calmer, "I appreciate your concern. Second, there won't be trouble, and even if there was, I'm not going to risk having over sixty guys trapped. Look at the map of the Kitsap Peninsula. It's almost entirely surrounded by water. All the Feds have to do is close off the Canal Bridge, throw a roadblock up at Poulsbo twelve miles south, and they'd be caught like a rat in a trap."

"They could get off the peninsula by ferry," Neilson suggested weakly, and immediately realized the foolishness of the suggestion. But at least it got McBride laughing—for the first time in weeks.

"Oh, sure," McBride said. "Eleven vehicles all driving up to a ferry lineup—ticket agent peering into each one, making sure there are no extra bodies hiding under the tarpaulins. 'Oh—what's this, sir? Six adults, six jerry cans, and what's that long thing with the barrel and all those bullets hanging from it?' "

"That's my dick!" Neilson joshed, and both of them roared with laughter, the tension broken, McBride visibly relaxing. "You goddamn idiot!"

"All right, so I'm an idiot, but who's gonna look *after* we part company at the coast? You gonna carry the egg-breaker across on the ferry alone?"

"Coupla guys," McBride said easily. "They're gonna help me."

"Do I know 'em?"

"No. And you don't need to." McBride suspected there was a good chance that Neilson, also from the militia's Eastern Washington/Idaho Regiment, knew Maddin, but in the interest of security there was no point in mentioning his name.

"As long as you're not left alone."

"I won't be. Don't worry. All you have to be concerned

about is riding shotgun for me to the coast, leave the egg-breaker and ROE with me, then take the convoy back to Idaho."

"Okay, so long as these two minders of yours know the area."

"I've had them check it out. They'll do fine."

CHAPTER FIFTEEN

AT BANGOR, 220 miles due west of the convoy, the three submariners Stanes and Maddin had spoken to in the Crow's Nest were returning to base. Walking from Delta Pier across the gangway of the 560-foot-long USS *Maui*, an 18,000-ton Ohio class boomer, Danny Gianelli and his two comrades briskly snapped off two salutes, despite the alcohol coursing through their veins. One was to Old Glory, the other to the top-side watch, a submariner in sky-blue shirt and navy blue dungarees. His name was Meyers, and he was equipped with a two-way radio, ammo pouch belt, a 12-gauge pump-action shotgun, and a .45 caliber pistol. Meyers immediately recognized the three men, because along with six other submariners, they had been tossed overboard, as tradition demanded, upon qualifying for their dolphins, which were pinned on them by Captain Rosen. Gianelli and Meyers had gone through Groton together. Meyers, one of the *Maui*'s missile technicians, had the awesome responsibility of working amid the boomer's twenty-four Trident missiles, each capable of traveling four thousand nautical miles and topped with eight multiple independently targetable reentry vehicle warheads, each of the sub's 192 warheads containing more than forty times the power of the Hiroshima bomb. In addition, the *Maui* carried Advanced Capability MK48 torpedoes. It was, in short, the most powerful weapons platform in history. But there was no margin for error. Apart from the possibility of an Armageddon, should any of its weapons detonate aboard —as in the case of Russia's *Kursk*—any malfunction in the rest of the leviathan could drive it down to crush depth in seconds. After that, all that would be heard by enemy sonar or through the Sound Surveillance System—a vast network of underwater hydrophones—would be the buckling of the bulkheads as the doomed sub plummeted toward the sea floor under the enormous water pressure that had sent some subs in the ocean deeps screaming down, hitting the bottom at over a hundred miles per hour.

Once below, Gianelli and his three shipmates changed out of their liberty uniforms. Before climbing into their racks, they checked their navy blue "poopie suits," for leaving port in the morning. Out on the pier and in the sub, last minute work was still going on, but all major refits were completed. The huge, rust-red gantry was withdrawn and the last of the missiles were now in the boat. While Meyers stood the topside watch, his fellow MTs below secured the missile silos' eight-ton doors, sealing in the forty-two-foot-long Tridents. Each missile was capped with a blue plastic membrane which, in the event the President gave the order to fire, would break open like a segmented orange under the pressure of a waterproof nitrogen bubble that would shroud the seventy-thousand-pound missile on its way to the surface. The dry missile would burst out of the sea, falling back momentarily before its three-stage solid fuel rocket engine ignited, the missile then streaking into the stratosphere toward its targets.

As he drifted off to sleep, Danny Gianelli could hear the power lines from ashore being withdrawn, reactor startup already under way, and he was aware of a faint scrabbling noise against the pressure hull. He assumed, correctly, that it was the current coming down Hood Canal past Dabob Bay, pushing the plastic floats of *Maui*'s antipollution "necklace," or boom, against the starboard side of the eighteen-thousand-ton leviathan.

Up forward in *Maui*'s torpedo room, a hundred yards away from where Danny slept, a weapons officer checked the MK48 torpedoes. Two of the tubes' door handles were already draped with the sign:

WARNING

WARSHOT

LOADED

*   *   *

"Police behind us," Maddin said, and Stanes, left hand on the wheel, moved his right hand to what had been the cigarette lighter socket but was now the push-button control for the revolving license drum.

"Not now!" Maddin said, pushing Stanes's hand away. "They're right on our ass. Their headlights'll pick it up."

"Damn!" Stanes chided himself. "I should've rotated the drum when we left the Crow's Nest."

"Yeah," Maddin agreed, adding pointedly, "What's the good of all your fancy tricks if you forget to use 'em?"

"So they're behind us," Stanes said defensively. "It doesn't mean they're interested in us."

"No," Maddin conceded. "But I don't like cops anywhere—"

"Pull over!" boomed the voice from the cruiser's speaker.

"Jesus!" Stanes said, pumping the brake, easing the pickup

onto the road's shoulder. "Ten more minutes and we'd be back at the cove."

"McBride's depending on us," Maddin said, as if Stanes needed reminding.

"I know that," Stanes responded tartly.

"Only one trooper," Maddin observed, adding, "Keep your hands off the wheel, sit well back so he doesn't think you're about to take off."

"I'm not gonna take off!" Stanes replied angrily. "I've been pulled over by cops before, y'know."

"For speeding, maybe, but we haven't been speeding. One of those Navy guys must have blabbed."

"Just play it cool," Stanes told him.

"I will."

They could hear the trooper, boots crunching on the gravel, coming toward them. In the rearview mirror Stanes could see his right hand on his holster, and the cruiser's video camera unit, its pinpoint recording light on. Stanes wound down the window.

"Evening, sir," the trooper said.

"Evening, officer," and then Stanes heard the crash, a rush of hot air searing his face. His ears rang like the sound of a thousand cicadas, and the policeman's eyes protruded, mouth agape in shock, his hands flung out, a bloody hole between his eyes. He staggered backward into the glare of his own headlights, the stench of cordite from Maddin's 9mm filling the cabin.

"Go!" Maddin said.

Stanes, gasping, was staring out the window at the cop on the road, the dead man's face frozen and what looked like a dark pool of blood on the blacktop oozing out from beneath the back of his head.

"Go!" Maddin repeated.

Robotlike, Stanes released the hand brake and, the tires spinning in the gravel, pulled out without looking for traffic.

"Just as well it's dark," Maddin said excitedly, fishing around in the glove compartment for the packet of 9mm rounds. "Cruiser's video must have seen us, and it'll have transmitted our license number—so once we're up the road a bit, do your little trick."

It was a full minute before Stanes could speak. "Jesus! You killed him!"

Now it was Maddin's turn to be surprised. "You've never seen a dead man before?"

"No."

"Well, get used to it, bubba. It's only six hours to H hour, and McBride's not bringing flowers."

"If—if those Navy guys reported us, the Feds'll have a good description of us."

"Yeah," Maddin said, "but first they're looking for a license number. By then we'll be at the rendezvous."

"Even so, we should tell McBride. He won't want to use us now. By tomorrow midday the Feds'll be looking for a blue pickup."

"He's not gonna like it," Maddin said.

"He has to know," Stanes insisted. "We park this pickup anywhere near him, it'll put the whole operation in jeopardy."

"You chickening out?"

Stanes wouldn't answer.

"I've just done my bit," Maddin enjoined. "*You* tell 'im."

Ron Stanes's mind was racing, still stunned by the policeman's murder, still stunned by Maddin's decisiveness. But he had to admit, what choice did Maddin have? Everything was riding on the two of them being there tomorrow. What Stanes was discovering was that while he'd previously considered himself superior to Maddin, to the sullen man with the birthmark whom he thought had needed advice, right now it was he who needed to be told what to do.

"I'll have to think what to say," he told Maddin. "Need to couch it—you know, so anyone listening in can't—"

"That's up to you!" Maddin said sharply, his voice full of authority.

Killing the cop, Stanes realized, had given Maddin such a surge of adrenaline that suddenly he was the boss. "Don't call me bubba!" Stanes said.

"Make a U-turn," Maddin told him.

"Why?"

"Because the Feds'll be looking for us heading north from their cruiser's video. You change the license number yet?"

"Oh shit, I forgot."

"You were rattled," Maddin said patronizingly. "Do it now."

There was an electric whine.

"It's done," Stanes said. "Beautiful B.C."

"What?" Maddin asked.

"Beautiful British Columbia," Stanes explained. "You know—Canadian plates. RCV 625."

"Whatever. Pull the U-turn and head back to Bremerton. We'll still have time to rendezvous with McBride."

"All right, but why Bremerton?"

"I told you, we just came from there, headin' north. They won't expect us to be goin' south. Besides, I saw a Wal-Mart there and—" Two cruisers were coming toward them, flashers on. Rain began speckling the windshield, Stanes sitting forward, nervously clutching the wheel.

"They won't pull us over," Maddin said.

"They might."

"Why? Beautiful B.C., right?" Before Stanes could answer, Maddin, his disfigurement momentarily lit up by the headlights of the first cruiser, smiled malevolently. "If they do, they'll get the same treatment."

"There'll be more than one cop in each car," Stanes said.

"So?" Maddin said, watching the second cruiser. It appeared to be slowing. "There's more than one of us. Right?" Maddin unzipped his tote bag and pulled out a sawed-off 12-gauge shotgun.

"Jesus!" Stanes said. "Hold on—they're probably slowing because of the rain."

"Maybe."

"Jesus, Art, listen—I mean, don't you try to fire that thing past me like you did the Beretta. You'll take my head off."

"So when he comes to the window, put it in drive for a quick takeoff and slouch down a bit."

The cruiser sailed past them. Stanes exhaled with relief.

"How much cash you got?" Maddin asked.

"Sixty, seventy bucks."

Maddin nodded, figuring that together with the hundred he had, it should be enough so that when they got to the Wal-Mart he wouldn't have to use a credit card. Stanes switched on the radio, and within minutes KOMO out of Seattle was broadcasting what it referred to as "sketchy details" of the murder of a Kitsap County sheriff.

Maddin's bottom lip protruded in surprise. "A *sheriff*? Thought the fucker was just a deputy. Did you notice he was a sheriff?"

"I didn't have time."

Maddin started to laugh for the first time since Stanes had met him, and for Ron Stanes it solved a mystery—why McBride had paired two such different men as he and Maddin. He was the local who knew the area, but Maddin was a man who wouldn't hesitate to kill. In a bizarre way, Stanes realized, they made a perfect pair—at least for McBride's mission.

When they pulled in to Wal-Mart, Maddin told Stanes to keep the pickup running.

"What are you gonna get?" Stanes asked.

"Need to know," Maddin said, and Stanes couldn't tell from the other's tone whether it was meant as a joke or as a genuine concern for security.

"I could go in," Stanes said. "I need to take a leak."

"No," Maddin said. "That cruiser video didn't get any of me but it might have got a side shot of you talking to the cop. You can take a piss later." With that, Maddin was gone. Stanes mulled over the mercurial shift in his partner's mood—from the angry man in the café to cool executioner.

Sitting there alone in the parking lot, the pickup's V-8 shuddering beneath him, Stanes could still see the face of the murdered sheriff staring up at him, the blood pooling on the road.

Stanes was shaking his head, sobbing, nerves shot, wondering if he could go through with it now that he'd seen what the militia's abstraction of "Appropriate Action" really meant in practice. His hatred of the Federals hadn't waned, but was he hard enough to see it through? He looked uneasily at his watch. In less than ten hours he would know. McBride was counting on him and Maddin, the final link in the chain. Besides, if he reneged, he'd be unable to escape—at Hayden Lake, General Wilcox had very definite views on what to do with any of his militiamen who backed out. And Stanes knew Maddin, for one, wouldn't hesitate to mete out the punishment.

The shower passed over, and one sweep with the wipers cleared the windshield. He saw a man, about Maddin's build, come out of the Wal-Mart, pushing a grocery cart. He wore what looked like a black golf cap, its peak so low it almost touched his nose. The man was walking toward the pickup. Stanes's heart was thumping in panic until he realized it *was* Maddin, the cap having confused the issue. As well as pushing the cart, he was carrying several newspapers.

Stanes heard him unloading the cart into the back of the pickup, after which he climbed into the cabin, carrying a brown paper bag. "Anybody acting nosy?"

"No. You got a *cap*?"

"I like caps. And I don't wear 'em back to front. Every idiot who does that thinks they're cool, different. Soon everyone's so cool they all look the same. Sheep!"

Stanes couldn't figure him out—the man had just blown away a sheriff, and he was holding forth about *caps*?

"What's in the bag?" Stanes asked.

"Surprise," Maddin said. "Head north again. You know any side roads before Port Gamble?" The latter was several miles beyond the Hood Canal Bridge.

"Dozens," Stanes replied. "I've lived here for—"

"Fine," Maddin cut in, taking a packet of potato chips from the bag, tearing it open, offering it to Stanes. "Take a handful."

Stanes hesitated; his wife was always on him about his cholesterol count, which was almost twice normal.

"Go on," Maddin urged, shaking the bag. "Sea salt in these. Do you good."

Stanes was surprised how hungry he was as he reached over. And angry. For some reason he couldn't identify, he was obsessing over how rude the sheriff had sounded. Like all Feds. Like all those in authority—not "Would you pull over *please,*" just *"Pull over!"* Like that asshole at the gate: "Behind the blue line. *Now!*"

Maybe, Stanes thought, the anger he felt was a petty way of rationalizing the horror of the sheriff getting shot. Payback?

Maddin switched on the cabin light and studied the weather map on the back of a *USA Today*. "Says it's gonna be fine tomorrow, with possibility of showers. These weather guys—they're full of shit! Can't make up their minds."

"So why buy a paper? B'sides, the radio has weather reports every fifteen minutes."

Maddin switched off the light, wound down the window, and took in a deep breath of the surrounding forest air; as if, Stanes thought, he didn't have a care in the world. As if killing the cop was nothing. Cool as the proverbial cucumber.

CHAPTER SIXTEEN

PETE RAINOR WAS coming to terms with living in the Redoubt, the militia stronghold far removed from any metropolitan area, but Mel Haley missed his wife and two teenage sons, and not even the Redoubt's strict daily routine from sunup till lights out at 2100 hours could mitigate his homesickness. Photographs of them as the "Boeing Terrorists"—Rainor in his Little League coaching uniform, and Haley in a shot taken from his wedding picture—had been all over TV and in the newspapers. The radio had given out the license numbers of their vehicles.

When Rainor rang the USMC HQ emergency help line, his voice had barely been under control. HQ, in turn, called McBride, who was in charge of the Knockout campaign.

McBride had instructed HQ that the two militiamen should be told to go immediately to the Redoubt. It was the militia's

secret hideout in the Northwest—so secret that any militiaman even suspected of revealing its location was "eliminated," along with the person to whom the location had been
divulged.

The truth was that the duo's retreat to the Redoubt, necessi-
tated by the failure of their Boeing caper, had exacted more of
a psychological toll on Haley than on Rainor, who was by nature more adaptable to changing circumstances. Besides, he'd
made an unexpected discovery: there were more women in the
militia than he'd imagined. He had heard that, as in the hidden encampments of the French "maquis"—the battalions of
French resistance fighters in World War Two—the militia contained some female warriors, several of them the wives and
former companions of many of the militiamen who were now
prisoners in Camp Fairchild. It was said that federal law
enforcement officers in the Northwest, from Montana to
Oregon, and including British Columbia's Royal Canadian
Mounted Police, feared these militia "Amazons" more than
the militia*men* because North American law enforcement officers traditionally did not expect to be physically attacked by
women combatants, and so on occasion were taken completely by surprise. Then there were the usual horror stories,
endemic to any such society, of what women soldiers could do
to captive males. But in a society of warriors where the customary subtleties of social courtship had been brutalized by
the harsh demands of living outside normal society and the
law, Rainor found he was more than welcome. While there
were one or two women who felt the tug of loyalty to their incarcerated husbands and lovers in Fairchild, others were only
too happy to satiate their own lust with Rainor's. Their aggres-
siveness in some cases extended to these women literally
being atop him, stalks from a straw-stuffed palliasse—the
mattress of choice amongst some militia—poking him in the
backside as his uninhibited companion forced the pace.

"Why don't you use sleeping bags?" he asked one woman after a particularly vigorous encounter.

"You don't *know*?" the woman asked, incredulous at his naiveté.

"No."

The tousled female was then abruptly called out for sentry duty, so Rainor later put the question to Mel Haley.

"It's a ready made coffin," Haley answered. "If you get attacked in the middle of the night you'll be dead before you manage to get the thing unzipped." Looking about furtively to make sure no other militia were listening as they made their way back from the canvas-bag shower stalls, passing the camouflaged tents in the huge but carefully concealed militia encampment, Haley added plaintively, "I need to call my Colleen and the kids."

"Well, you can't call her," Rainor said. "Seems to me we've been over this before, Mel. Feds've got our mug shots and must have our home phones tapped—plus the phones of anyone who knows us. And No Such Agency's bound to have its satellites scouring cellular transmission. You want to risk the Feds finding out where we are? Risk the whole Redoubt?"

" 'Course not. It's just that—"

"I know. You're horny."

"I mean how long have we got to stay here?"

"Till we get amnesty. Right?"

"Think that'll happen?"

"The scuttlebutt," Rainor said, "is Wilcox has got Lucky McBride working on that too. And you know what McBride says? If you get 'em by the balls, their hearts and minds'll soon follow."

"McBride," Haley said, nodding approvingly. "All right!"

CHAPTER SEVENTEEN

"THIS FAR ENOUGH off the beaten track?" Stanes asked Maddin, pulling off Highway 3 on a side road that led deep into the wilds of Kitsap Peninsula. The road was obscured from the star-spangled night sky by fir and pine that had been bent over in a protective arc from the westerlies that blew eastward from the Pacific.

Reaching into the big Wal-Mart bag, Maddin extracted a snake-twist-handled flashlight and a roll of inch-wide masking tape. He tossed the tape to Stanes, explaining, "I'm going to put up a plastic sheet over the truck just in case we do get more showers. I want you to use the newspapers to mask the windows, windshield, headlights, and grill. Might as well cover the hubcaps too." With that, Maddin got out, grabbed the other bag from the back of the truck, and took out a two-quart paint can of white enamel. Next he took out a spray gun with a one-quart carafe tank attached.

Stanes refused to be surprised. "You'll need compressed air," he said.

Maddin was snaking the powerful flashlight around a low-hanging pine branch. "Nope," he replied, indicating the spray gun. "This is a Wagoner pulser, bubba. Runs straight off electricity." Then he reached into the Wal-Mart bag and took out a card-pack-size AC converter and jump cables. "Run 'er right off the battery. 'Course, it'll be better to keep the engine running." Maddin seemed like a different man.

But Stanes wasn't about to be outdone. "Well, we won't have all morning for it to dry."

"Don't need that long," Maddin assured him. "This enamel'll dry in two hours, once the sun's up. Besides, I brought along a little help."

"You got a hair dryer?" Stanes proffered.

"Nah," Maddin answered, opening the bag for Stanes to see. "*Two* dryers! Once I get this sheeting set up, we'll have this sucker repainted in an hour. That, plus your revolving license gizmo, will buy us at least a day. Maybe more."

Stanes unfolded the *USA Today* from the other newspapers Maddin had bought, and taped it to the windshield while Maddin unfurled the roll of green plastic. Maddin did it as quickly as possible, the crackly sound of the plastic making Stanes nervous, the noise eerily like that of a brush fire, Maddin's flashlight momentarily casting giant shadows across the plastic sheet canopy. Then Stanes heard another crackle. It could have been the plastic flexing in a phantom breeze. Or was it a wild animal passing through the brush?

"Shh!" he urged Maddin, who immediately turned off the flashlight and reached into the cabin for his 12-gauge.

In moonlight filtered by the pines and fir, Maddin saw two liquid eyes, the mule deer frozen, momentarily blinded by the beam from his wraparound flashlight, which illuminated the pickup beneath the plastic sheet. Maddin smacked the side of the pickup. The doe moved on, and Maddin, turning the flashlight back on, slid his shotgun back onto the pickup's seat. "Beautiful, aren't they?"

"Yes," Stanes said, surprised. Apparently, Maddin liked animals better than people. There were a lot of folks like that in the militia and beyond.

They worked a good hour with the hair dryers. Stanes's arms were aching, but he felt obliged to tell Maddin, "The right rear fender is still a bit wet. Sticky to touch."

"Who's gonna go 'round touching it?" Maddin asked. "All that matters is that this is now a white pickup—not blue—and we've got Canadian plates. That's gonna get us to the bridge and away with McBride to the Redoubt."

"You don't think we should dry it right out?" Stanes asked. "Wait a bit?"

"Rather be on the road. Out of the woods. Anyway, sun'll be up in a half hour. That'll do it. I don't want to risk being late. McBride'd have us court-martialed."

"True," Stanes conceded, untying the canopy, the crackling sound of the plastic like that of another creature walking the forest floor. It was the hunting season, and while the possibility that some errant deer stalker was at large wouldn't normally have bothered him, his nerves had been on edge ever since Maddin shot the sheriff. Besides, while the patrol car's video camera had no view of Maddin, Stanes was worried that it might have got his own face—at least the left profile. He'd been dwelling on it all the time Maddin was spraying the pickup, and now he was trying to recall the precise angle at which they had stopped on the road's shoulder vis-à-vis the angle of the sheriff's car. But try as he might, he couldn't remember. Everything had happened so fast.

He heard a footfall nearby. "Was that you?" he asked Maddin.

"What?" Maddin was kneeling down, packing up the spray gun. "I haven't moved."

"Something did."

"Relax, it's the deer."

"It moved off."

"So, it's another deer. Got the canopy wrapped?"

Picking up the paint gear in the dawn light, Maddin saw the glint of metal twenty feet away. A gun barrel. Again he snatched his 12-gauge from the seat. *Boom!* Stanes, falling onto the rolled-up plastic canopy, scrambled frantically under the pickup for cover. There was an agonized groan, a movement as if someone was crawling along the edge of the woods, then a third head-concussing *Boom!* as Maddin put an end to whoever it was he'd wounded with the first shot.

"C'mon!" Maddin shouted. "Check the left flank!"

Still stunned, embarrassed by his fear-induced scuttling, Stanes emerged from beneath the pickup, Maddin thrusting the military issue 9mm Beretta into his hand.

"I think he was alone," Maddin whispered, absurdly, given the horrendous sound of the shotgun only moments before. "But we'd better make sure no one else saw us."

As the two of them entered the deep woods, the pale wash of dawn cast a confusing light over the forest, turning deformed saplings and roots that thrust through the floor of thick needles into the figures of aggressors. But there was no one there, the forms Stanes was seeing mere projections of his frightened imagination. Maddin, on the other hand, was not imagining anything—a root was a root was a root, nothing more—as he moved cautiously but with more haste than Stanes, the reek of cordite from his shotgun blasts wafting from behind them into the woods in a cloud of smoke that hung suspended over moss-laden stumps.

Stanes, throat dry from the shock of it all, was no farther than twenty yards into the woods when he heard Maddin, twenty feet to his right but farther in, signal him over.

When he reached Maddin, Stanes saw him pointing down to the ground at a black soup-can-like object barely visible in the early light. Stanes saw they were near the edge of an open area about a hundred yards wide, surrounded by fir trees. How deep it went was difficult to tell, because while the area was devoid of trees, the two men's vision was obscured by the thicket of fir.

"You see it?" Maddin asked.

"What is it?" Stanes had no sooner asked the question than he noticed a faint length of fishing line attached to the black soup can and stretched taut between it and a sapling two yards away. "Booby trap?"

"You betcha!" Maddin answered, his voice lowered, eyes peering ahead into the forest-moated marijuana field. "Blow your goddamned foot off." His eyes flicked from one part of the field to another, and he nodded with approval. "Grow the best shit in the world up here—so they tell me."

"Should've known," Stanes said, since it was common knowledge that with the requisite rainfall, soil, and its vast, hidden forests, the Northwest was ideal for growing the weed, and just as important, provided relatively safe harvesting. More than one innocent hiker had lost his life by unintentionally stumbling onto just such a field.

"Let's get back to the truck," Stanes urged.

"Watch how you go," Maddin advised him. "There's bound to be more trip wires."

As they made their way back to the newly painted white pickup, the dawn light was stronger. In the pale light, Stanes glimpsed the man Maddin had shot, the *second* man Maddin had shot. The marijuana grower was—had been—in his late thirties, possibly early forties. He was clothed in military surplus fatigues, and there was a bloody cavity where his chest had been. The stink of his ordure and other fluids involuntarily released mixed with the whiff of cordite, snaking its way back accusingly through a copse of diseased spruce.

Resting his 12-gauge against a tree, Maddin strolled over to the corpse, whose face was now crawling with black flies, and began rifling the dead man's pockets.

"Oh hell," Stanes said disgustedly. "Don't do that, man!"

"Why?" Maddin asked, taking money from the dead man's wallet. "Won't do *him* any—" He heard a sound and reached for the shotgun, but it was only Stanes throwing up, both arms fully extended, pressing against the side of the pickup.

"Jesus," Maddin said. "Get off the paint! You'll leave a handprint."

Stanes did as he was told, wiping his mouth with his sleeve and glaring at Maddin, whose bloodred birthmark, even beneath his beard, was so vivid in the morning light that for a moment it seemed as if he had no beard at all.

"We'll take it nice and easy to the bridge," Maddin said. "Don't want to be pulled over for speeding. Besides, we have to pick up the rest of the gear."

Again Stanes was astonished at Maddin's calmness, given his earlier volatility, when he seemed little more than a bundle of nerves about to unravel. It was as if the violence of the past two hours had acted as a tranquilizer, rather than the adrenaline rush Stanes had sensed in him when he'd shot his first victim. Or was it his first? An ugly truth crept up on Ron Stanes. If Mad Maddin hadn't done what he did—hadn't taken out the two men—the mission might have been in serious jeopardy. Perversely, it seemed now as if Maddin's earlier irascibility, which might have imperiled the mission, had been calmed by the man's much deeper madness.

CHAPTER EIGHTEEN

THE COMBINATION OF moonlit desert, police helicopter, highway patrol cars, half-tracks, Moorehead's Hummer, and, most of all, the dogs, proved overwhelming to the thirty-two escapees from Fairchild. By midnight all but two had been recaptured and rudely returned to the camp, many of them suffering lacerations and multiple injuries, sustained, it was explained to the press, by prisoners "resisting arrest." Dillon, whom Moorehead had promised to transfer to California, came out of the administration block to watch the press scrum forming about Moorehead.

"The two missing convicts," as Moorehead described them, avoiding the phrase "prisoners of *war*," were identified as Marion Jubal—age, twenty-three; height, five feet eight inches; hair, brown; eyes, blue; distinguishing marks, bullet scar right thigh; home, Bellingham, Washington State—and John Mead—forty; five feet ten inches; brown hair; brown eyes; battle scars on his chest, back, and left calf.

Convict Mead's mug shot, Moorehead informed the press, had been identified by one of the guards who remembered seeing a man earlier who, at the time, he thought was a fellow guard, on one of the half-tracks. Convict Mead had disembarked from the half-track when it had become temporarily bogged in a coulee, presumably to join the other guards in pushing the vehicle, but was not seen thereafter.

"Major Moorehead?" It was Marte Price of CNN. "How does a half-track get bogged in a coulee, which by definition is dry?"

Moorhead forced a smile. Smart-assed bitch. "Ah, good question, Ms. Price. The answer is that apparently there was an irrigation overrun coming down the coulee. Turned sand into a bog."

"Oh? I though there were stringent water restrictions at night in this area?"

Bitch did her homework, he thought. "That's correct, but you'd have to take that up with the Bureau of Land Management. My job isn't to enforce the water restrictions, it's to guard over a thousand convicts. And I should add that convict Mead is armed and dangerous."

"Armed with what?" It was Marte Price again, her hourglass figure barely concealed beneath her parka.

"An M-16," Moorehead replied.

"How did he manage to get that?"

"Killed one of my guards. That's the sort of people we're dealing with."

"Name of the deceased, Major?" pressed a reporter from KING-TV in Seattle.

"I can't release that information," the commandant explained, "until next-of-kin have been notified."

"When will that be?" Marte Price asked.

"Can't say. It may be some time. His parents are apparently on vacation somewhere in Europe." Dillon was sure it was a lie, but Moorehead was as quick on his feet as he had been when killing Somers.

Marte Price looked skeptical, but he knew it would hold her awhile. Moorehead tried to fake civility, but he detested her. She had made a name for herself chronicling the militia uprisings, and, as in this case, had a knack for finding impending flash points that would pit the militia against Federals.

"Major Moorehead," Price said, "do you think this break-out was—"

"*Aborted* breakout," Moorehead corrected her.

Price ignored the distinction—after all, thirty-two men had breached the wall, even if all but two had been recaptured. "Do you think," she continued, "that the breakout was inspired by the attempt of the two militiamen at the Boeing factory in—"

"No way," Moorehead responded. "First of all, the militia's proven to be totally inept in any attempt to intimidate the government. Second, there is no way news of that *aborted* attempt influenced any of the convicts."

"How's that, Major?"

"Because, unlike some other facilities, Ms. Price, Camp Fairchild is a punishment camp—not Club Med. The convicts here aren't allowed access to TV, radio, etcetera. We keep a tight rein on the taxpayers' money."

"Bully for you," someone mumbled.

"But two men are still at large," Marte pointed out.

"I don't anticipate any problem there. We'll have Mead and Jubal back in custody within forty-eight hours."

"That a promise, Major?" Marte pressed.

Moorehead forced yet another a smile. "That's all, ladies and gentlemen. We've got work to do."

"Is militia leader Eleen in—" Marte began, but Moorehead was already striding back to the red Hummer with Dillon.

"Dillon, about that transfer to California."

"*Southern* California," Dillon said.

"How'd you like to make it Hawaii?"

"Depends. What do I have to do?"

"Bring me those two sons of bitches Jubal and Mead."

"Alive?"

"Whatever. Jubal's no doubt heading home to his little wife in Bellingham. He knocked her up before he was captured."

"How do you know that?"

"The cons are allowed one letter every three months. 'Course, we have to censor them. Quartermaster's office told me the last one from Jubal was full of lovey-dovey muck— how he wanted to see his little 'gift from God.' "

"But is he stupid enough to head straight for home?" Dillon asked. "He must know that's the first place that—"

"No, no, not straight for home," Moorehead said, starting the Hummer, "but in the area. Relatives, friends."

"How about Mead?"

"A hardass, that one. Militia veteran. Won't be easy, but we know he's wearing a guard's uniform. Get two of the handlers to take a dog to each of their bunks. Get the scent."

"Geez, if they got a lift on 90 or 2, they could be halfway to the mountains by now."

"That's right. You think Fort DeRussy comes cheap?"

"DeRussy?"

"Near Waikiki," Moorehead explained, starting the Hummer. "Don't worry, you've got help. Police have set up roadblocks on all three routes through the mountains. Check with them and the park ranger station along the way."

"They could just walk around a roadblock," Dillon pointed out.

"They could. But if someone picked 'em up and gave 'em a ride, they'd come onto the roadblock so quickly they wouldn't have time to let 'em out, if the police place the roadblocks where they should."

"Maybe Jubal and Mead haven't teamed up," Dillon suggested. "Each of 'em on his Molly Malone."

"On his *what*?"

"Molly Malone. Alone."

Moorehead grunted. "Well, either way, you have no time to lose. Take the other Hummer. Might even catch them hitching

a lift. Remember, we picked up most of the bastards within
five miles of the camp. These two pricks could still be 'round
here."

Dillon was assaulted by indecision. Should he spend time
here looking for them or head straight for the mountains over a
hundred miles to the west? He said as much to Moorehead. It
told the commandant that despite Dillon's initial cockiness—
doing a deal for a transfer—the man was no leader.

"Take a squad of six men," Moorehead told him. "Leave
four here with the dogs, you take two for the mountains."

Dillon nodded.

"And take your parka. It's damp up there. Lot of fog."

"Yeah," Dillon answered. "Fort DeRussy had better be
worth it."

Moorehead wasn't correct about the dogs finding Mead
within the hour, but he was more prescient when he'd predicted that if Mead had managed to get a lift, the vehicle's
driver would have no inkling of a roadblock until he was almost on top of it.

It was a farmer en route to Seattle, on a long drive from the
grizzly bear and bighorn sheep country around Metaline
Falls in the far northeast corner of the state, who spotted
Mead. The militiaman had thrown away the fake M-16 and
was hitching his way west on Highway 2.

While it was difficult for the police to spring surprise roadblocks in the wide open arid country of eastern Washington,
which in any event had been pretty well gone over by the police helicopters, it was a different matter in the mountains.
Here, the highway patrol set their trap fifteen miles west of
the Bavarian-style village of Leavensworth, amid the rugged
alpine country that marked the sudden and dramatic change
between the desert and the Cascades. The two police cars'
flashers were on, but visible only after a sharp fishhook turn

in the road east of the eight-thousand-foot-high Snowgrass Peak. Mead, however, was still alert, the danger and thrill of the escape still fueling him, and the instant he spied a strip of reflected yellow light atop the fishhook's culvert, he shouted at the farmer to brake, his left hand ramming the shift into park.

"What the—" the farmer began.

"Thanks!" Mead said. He opened the door and was gone into the mist. It wasn't until ten minutes later that the out-raged farmer realized his hitchhiker had stolen his .30 rifle from the passenger-side rack.

McBride's front outrider, upon seeing the roadblock, had reported it to McBride's convoy, which immediately made a U-turn, heading back through Leavenworth. swinging south onto the 97 connector to Highway 90, heading toward Liberty and then to South Cle Elum, eighty-one miles east of the coast.

"You figure they won't bother putting a roadblock on Highway 90 'cause it's further south?" Neilson asked.

McBride shrugged. "There's two ways to handle it if they have."

The militia convoy, with McBride back in midstream, was heading east in the darkness on I-90 not long afterward, fol-lowing the course of the Yakima River into the high country past South Cle Elum and Roslyn. There, Neilson, indicating the lights of the town, commented, "That's where the TV people made that show *Northern Exposure.*" McBride told him that if he had his way, half the stuff on TV would be canned, specifically snotty-nosed fashion shows where scowl-ing teens got ten grand an hour while old people were forced to sleep under bridges. The militia was going to change that, he said.

Thirty seconds later McBride and every other vehicle had

received the front outrider's warning, "RBA—10M—VsS."
Roadblock ahead—ten miles—vehicles staggered.

"Pull off," McBride instructed Neilson, telling the remainder of the convoy to continue at a reduced speed, with orders for Gunner Brock to transfer from McBride's Windstar to the convoy's lead pickup.

Remaining behind, McBride and Neilson dragged out the long, relatively narrow three-hundred-pound ROE, Neilson wondering whether the egg-breaker, still tied down by one of the Windstar's fold-down passenger seats, would be too bulky a load. All he knew about the ROE that McBride was assembling was that it was Navy surplus and it was noisy. As to where the egg-breaker had come from, he had no idea. McBride told him to pass him the motorcycle helmet and check its straps, as one might request the salt and pepper at table. Apart from the odd crackle of the Windstar's engine cooling, all Neilson and McBride could hear was the river, no more than fifteen feet below, as it rushed down from Snoqualmie Pass toward Yakima Canyon. Neilson felt abandoned with the convoy gone.

"Too bad you have to use the ROE."

"Thank God we've got it as a backup."

"Guess so. Long as you feel comfortable with it."

"I've rehearsed it at Hayden Lake at least a dozen times," McBride retorted, walking down to a clearing, "including in a heavy rainstorm."

"How about the noise?" Neilson persisted. "Feds might hear it, even above the noise of the river."

"Not if the convoy does its job," McBride replied, busily inserting the ROE's quick-release pins. "Now get on the cell and make sure my pickup from the Redoubt is waiting on the other side of that roadblock and that he's brought a worktable. Light—nothing heavy."

"Yes, sir." Neilson was tempted to ask why McBride hadn't

put this evasive plan into operation back on Highway 2, until he remembered that the roadblock here was "vehicles—staggered," which meant that the Feds, instead of having parked their cars nose-to-nose, which you might be able to bust through, had parked so that after they'd searched each vehicle for the two missing POWs, every driver would be forced to slow to a crawl, going through a tortuous S-turn.

McBride glanced at his watch. "Our convoy should be approaching the roadblock in five minutes."

The militia convoy's three advance outriders, their headlight beams piercing the mountains' predawn darkness, had no problem with the roadblock, politely giving the Federals their driver's licenses, none of the three motorcyclists' photos matching either of the mug shots an efficient Moorehead had e-mailed to every police detachment in Washington State.

"Where you boys headed?" the most senior of the four cops asked. One of the militia outriders was sorely tempted to tell him that under the law the fuzz had no right to ask anyone where they were going or where they'd come from. In the militiaman's view, the cop's question was another example of how a compliant citizenry had obsequiously surrendered their God-given right to go and come as they please without having to answer to the government.

"Goin' to Seattle," the outrider told the cop. "Gonna watch the Mariners whip Oakland's butt!"

The cop laughed. "That won't be hard!" he said, and handed back the license. "You boys not carryin' any firearms are ya?"

"No, sir."

"See you got binoculars there," the cop commented.

"Yeah," said the lead outrider, grinning. "See the girls clear across the field."

The cop, his name patch reading DORMAN, smiled and

waved the three motorcycles through. "Enjoy the game, boys."

"You betcha!"

A hundred yards on around a bend the three pulled their motorcycles over, engines still rumbling, and turned off their headlights, the dawn light not yet above the mountains. They kicked out their stands, got off the bikes, and all three fished out a hand grenade from their respective gas tanks. Each grenade's release lever was strapped tightly to the grenade with wire. Back on the bikes, they made a U-turn and slowly advanced to the bend from where they would be able to see their convoy, still several miles behind them, approach the roadblock.

They saw headlights approaching, and moved off around the bend, their lights still off. But there was no message coming through on their radios from the convoy. Then the three outriders saw something they didn't expect: a vehicle, its outline hidden in the glare of the police cars' lights, coming to a halt at the roadblock from the same direction as the convoy. Where the hell had it come from? Through his binoculars, the front rider saw it was an Oregon license plate.

"Any of our plates in the convoy from Oregon?" he asked his two colleagues.

It appeared to be an SUV. Or perhaps someone had driven down onto the highway from a side road between here and the convoy? Immediately, the outrider sent out his warning for the ten-vehicle convoy coming that way to slow down and wait for the vehicle in question to clear the roadblock. McBride's insistence on having outriders had paid off in spades.

From a different angle, through his binoculars, one of the other two outriders could now see that it was definitely an SUV at the roadblock, and some brouhaha was developing. Dorman, the cop who had let the three outriders through, had drawn his sidearm, pointing it at the SUV. The driver complied, though obviously voiced strong objections.

"Road rage," the second outrider commented.

"Go on!" said the first, watching the angry driver through the Zeiss lenses. "Do as he tells you, dork!" Normally, the outrider, like all militia, loved to see Feds challenged, but soon the dawn's early light would penetrate the deep clefts through which the highway had been cut, making it that much more difficult for McBride to move.

CHAPTER NINETEEN

MCBRIDE, HAVING ASSEMBLED everything in the clearing down by the river, was keen to go, his normally contained demeanor before an op being sorely tested, a situation not helped by Neilson's anxiety seeking release in a pestering stream of questions about McBride's equipment. "How long's it been out?" he asked.

"What?" McBride asked irritably. "Egg-breaker or the ROE?"

"The ROE?"

"Nineteen fifty-seven."

"Man!" Neilson whistled. "I wasn't even born then. Still, how come I never heard about it?"

Neilson's nervousness reminded McBride of his own early days in the corps, and he lightened up. "Well, there were quite a few of them around in the Korean War. Manufacturer called Hiller came up with the prototype. The Navy went for it—needed something collapsible that could be dropped to downed pilots in a streamlined container like this. Something you could assemble in five minutes, no screwing around, because soon as one of our sky jockeys bailed out, the ChiCom troops'd try to get him. So he needed something he could hop on and get out of Dodge." McBride tapped the seven-foot-long insectlike tripod he'd extracted from the Windstar. "No tools needed, just thirteen quick-release pins and that's that. To show how good the ROE was, a guy called Dick Peck—" McBride smiled, but it was forced humor. "—with a name like that, you can imagine the kind of ribbing the guy must have gotten."

Neilson said nothing.

"Well, anyway," McBride continued, "to promote the ROE, the company had Peck take one through the European Alps in 'fifty-eight. Impressed the hell out of everyone. West Germans bought the rights to produce it over there."

Neilson shook his head in admiration. "Man, there's nothin' to it really, a gas tank, little two-stroke. How fast is it?"

"Seventy miles an hour, but with the egg-breaker attached, it'll drop to around fifty, maybe forty, depending on the currents."

"How long's it take to assemble?"

"Three minutes. Remember, a downed pilot had to be able to 'assemble and go' in less than ten. Otherwise he'd be captured by the Chinese infantry."

"Three minutes!" Neilson was impressed.

"Took me longer at first, but I spent hours with it up at the lake because I knew it might have to haul the egg-breaker as well as me. It's all right, though. Maximum load is 256 pounds."

"Good job you're not overweight," Neilson joshed.

"No sweat. Even with the egg-breaker I've still got thirty

pounds to—" The message came through to the Windstar. There was a "NONCON V at RB."

"Nonconvoy vehicle at the roadblock," Neilson said. "What the hell's going on?"

"You've got no right," the man against the Durango SUV was berating Dorman.

The cop replied, "Shut your face, buddy. You're in enough trouble already. This hunting license expired a week ago and you've got a pronghorn in the back which is on the endangered species list."

"Fuck!" the hunter retorted. "We're the endangered species. Can't take a piss without a permit."

Dorman's partner, in the other cruiser, was writing up the citation.

"Need to feed my family," the hunter said.

"Uh-huh. Antelope a regular on your menu, is it?" Dorman quipped.

"Or," the other cop put in, "do you flog it to one of those upscale restaurants in Seattle? That it?"

"And," put in Dorman, shifting the weight of his considerable bulk, placing one foot on the Durango's runner, "looks like you're using illegal ammo. Black rhino?"

"Hey—gimme a break."

"Might have if you hadn't been so lippy," Dorman said. "You guys always know your rights, 'cept you don't know when to be quiet and show a little respect."

"*Respect?* For what? You assholes just like bossing people around."

"Okay, that does it, buddy." Dorman called to the other cop, who'd finished writing up the ticket, "Cuff him, Ralph. Read him his rights."

The convoy's lead pickup had now reached the roadblock, Gunner Brock watching the arrest, seeing Dorman snap his charge book shut, get into the Durango, and start backing it up onto the gravel shoulder.

"Ready to go!" Brock ordered. "Crescent!" It meant to make as much noise as possible to distract the cops as well as cover the sound of the ROE carrying the egg-breaker past the roadblock. McBride could have just gone over the mountain, since the ROE had the almost unbelievable ceiling of thirteen thousand feet. But, despite its small size, that would immediately have put him on NORAD radar screens from Washington State to Omaha.

The ROE looked like little more than a big aluminum tube tripod, devoid of all but gas tank and small two-stroke, 45hp engine attached to the tripod's central aluminum alloy column—its folding rotor spar now sticking straight out, behind like an extended tripod handle. Along with a simple two-inch-diameter overhead cyclic-stick control that came down in front of the pilot's torso, the craft was maneuvered by means of a cable and two wheelchairlike pedals cum rudder controls attached to one of the tripod's legs, one of which had a tachometer and small fuel gauge attached. The deceptively skeletal-looking one-man helo had a range of 160 miles on eighty-six pounds of fuel, and could lift McBride's weight of 148 pounds, plus the egg-breaker and the egg-breaker's packing, 204 pounds in all. The moment he heard Brock's "Ready to go," McBride started the engine.

The tachometer's needle spun to 1,800 rpm and the ROE rose in a gut-dropping lurch above the clearing by the river and followed the defile of the highway carved, adjacent to the river's course, through the mountains. No one said the ROE would be quiet, and despite the muffling effect of his helmet, McBride found it too noisy. And when he felt the pull of the egg-breaker load suspended directly beneath his seat, the engine noise rose even higher as the two-bladed antitorque rotor took up the strain and he tilted the rotor forward. Glancing up at a high, jagged ridge between two peaks, he saw a gold braid of sunlight, and twisted the throttle control till his wrist hurt. A tailwind assist pushed him from an expected fifty mph, which he had achieved most times during practice at Hayden Lake, to 58 mph, which meant he'd be at the roadblock in less than four minutes.

Gunner Brock's lead vehicle was traveling slowly west, only thirty feet from the roadblock, when Brock saw the Bradley, heading east, also approaching the roadblock. Despite all the contingency preparedness of Lucky McBride's plan, Murphy's Law had struck: now Brock saw a second Bradley. They were both M-3s—cavalry versions. He'd seen numbers of the armored Fighting Vehicles before; Fort Lewis Army Base twenty miles south of Seattle had been a major staging area for the Gulf War and was an ongoing center for the Army's new Intermediate Response Brigade, the desert area east of the Cascades a perfect training terrain for AFVs. But *here*!

The Bradleys had taken the convoy utterly by surprise. Still, Brock had no choice, his orders clear: to provide covering fire for McBride's all-important flight over any roadblock or other impediment that might present itself. Brock ordered the convoy, to the perplexity of the two cops, to form a tight crescent in front of the two police cruisers. "Open fire!"

The deafening and for the policemen utterly unexpected cacophony of the convoy's M-60s and M-16s alone would have smothered the sound of the Rotorcycle's rotor, besides which the attention of each of the three-man Bradley crews and their two scouts was completely focused on the enfilade of fire erupting from the militia convoy at virtually point-blank range. One of the police cars in front of the Bradleys was already engulfed in flame.

Inside the cruiser, Officer Dorman's colleague was being

incinerated, and the other car, with the handcuffed hunter inside, was starting to burn. Dorman, caught behind the wheel of the hunter's Durango in the process of backing it off onto the road's shoulder, was cut to pieces by the convoy's first M-60 bursts. The handcuffed hunter, who'd thrown himself to the floor of the locked cruiser in self-protection, was frantically kicking the rear of the burning cruiser, screaming for deliverance. M-16 and 7.62mm rounds zipped overhead toward the two Bradleys, which by now had pulled abreast of each other.

In each Bradley, the commander right of the gunner instructed the two scouts in the rear compartment to stay put for the moment, then gave the order to fire. The gunners sighted their targets and fired. The Bradleys' 25mm rounds tore into the militia convoy at a combined rate of ten a second. Meanwhile, the sun rose above the high, gold-singed ridges, giving off a freakish mirrorlike flash of light that whited out the thermal sight of one of the Bradley gunners, temporarily blinding him. His commander immediately went to override, gripping his joystick control, aiming and firing the 25mm chain gun. Together with the gun on the other Bradley, it riddled the convoy so full of holes that the morning sun showed through in hundreds of inch-diameter rays.

Fifty militiamen were blown apart by the Bradley's armor-piercing rounds. The golden sunbeams and flames from one of the burning vehicles, cast against the background of green forest, had a macabre beauty, as gunpowder rose like mist above the ribbon of highway.

Now all that could be heard were the sounds of the convoy burning and the frantic drumming and shouting of the hunter. Having thrown himself to the police cruiser's floor and survived the deadly cross fire because the convoy's guns had turned so quickly from the police cars to the ten-foot-high Bradleys, he was now in danger of being roasted alive. One of the Bradleys' hydraulic rear ramp doors opened, and its two scouts, armed with M-16s, took up defensive positions on either side of the rear hatch. While the Bradley's M-60 opened up, sweeping across the chopped-up convoy, the two scouts dashed toward the flaming cruiser, yelled for the hunter to keep down, and fired three-round bursts that shattered the rear window. The hunter got off the floor, thrusting his head through the opening, and the two soldiers dragged him well away from the vehicle, his hair crackling, it was so dry and brittle from the radiant heat. He collapsed on the roadway, gasping for air. The pain not yet fully upon him, the hunter surveyed his ruined Durango, its paint bubbling in huge blisters, its interior splattered by Dorman's bloodied remains. In front of him he saw the rubbish heap that had been the convoy, blood dripping and, in some places running out in rivulets from the bullet-ridden doors of the pickups.

"Jesus!" he said, face contorted as the pain started to cut through the euphoria of his rescue.

Whoomp! It was the other cruiser's gas tank exploding, spewing a rain of flames down over the highway.

"Jesus Christ!" the hunter screamed. "I'm hurting like hell!"

"We've called an ambulance," one of the scouts assured him.

"Haven't you got something?" he pleaded.

The Bradley's commander, though he'd seen Iraqis who refused to surrender buried alive by the Army's bulldozers, had never seen so many dead men in one battle. He'd sent out a request for as many ambulances as possible, and soon the quietude of the mountains was riven with the wailing of sirens. But it was all for nothing. All they could do, as news of the bloodbath hit the airwaves, was pull out what few bodies were still intact, hosing out the rest.

CHAPTER TWENTY

HAVING PASSED OVER the din in the shadows of the mountains, McBride briefly glimpsed the disaster that had befallen his convoy. But with that singleness of purpose that separates the easily dissuaded from those who will see it through, no matter what, he shoved the horror of what he'd seen out of his mind, devoting all his energy to the task at hand—to Knockout, for which he had so assiduously trained himself during the past months at Hayden Lake.

With the fifty-six pound load slung beneath the ROE, his feet, given the bare bones construction of the rotorcycle, felt surprisingly comfortable on the foot controls that stuck out in front of him from a single spar. The ROE proved easier to handle than during many of his training flights at Hayden Lake. Indeed, the only part of his body that felt tired was his right hand, which gripped the overhead control stick that arced down from the rotor head directly above him, his fingers keeping the wrist-twist grip at full throttle. He followed the lines and curves of the highway, spotting two or three cars traveling in the early morning, the drivers glimpsing the ROE passing overhead like some huge stick insect, the blur of its antitorque rotor appearing saucerlike to at least one of the observers, who called the nearest 911 in Ellensburg. In the Northwest, however, an area second only to Area 51 in the American Southwest for UFO sightings, Ellensburg received at least four such reports a month. Which was why the deputy who took the call was less than interested until he realized it was in the area reported by Highway 20 Emergency Services as the site of a massacre.

"How high up was this thing, ma'am?"

"Can't say for sure—maybe a hundred, five hundred feet."

The deputy shook his head as he checked that the call was being properly recorded. *One* hundred or *five* hundred feet, he mused. That was always the problem—people had no idea of height or distance, giving you wildly different guesstimates you could do little with.

"Uh-huh. What color was it?"

"Kind of black and gold." The deputy heard the woman talking to a companion. "Yeah, a kind of gold top ... What? ... Oh yes, and a sort of pole underneath—you know, like those things we used to play with as kids—you pulled out an elastic cord and the round part would take off up in the air."

"Like a helicopter," a man's voice cut in, "with some sort of thing flying beneath it."

"Could it have been a police chopper?" the deputy asked.

"None like I've ever seen," the man cut in, asking his companion, "You ever seen a helo like that, Darlene?"

"No no," she said irritably. "It wasn't a helicopter. It was something else. Like a gold disk with black sticks beneath."

"Thought you said one stick?"

"Yes, well, it went by real fast. Only saw it for a second, then we were around a curve."

"Uh-huh." There was a static-filled pause, and for a moment the deputy thought the call had been lost to the mountains.

"We haven't been drinking!" It was the woman's voice, defensively angry.

"What? Oh no, I didn't think you had, ma'am. If you see anything else, you let us know. Appreciate the call.

"Darn it," the deputy said to himself afterward. He should have warned them about the massacre they'd be coming across a few miles on, unless the ambulances had cleared everything, which from the initial reports he very much doubted. He made a note of the sighting for the sheriff but remained convinced that what the couple had glimpsed was a police chopper, maybe sent up from Yakima.

By the time the deputy finished typing out the memo on the computer, doing a spell check so he wouldn't look stupid, Lucky McBride, seeing the signal lamp of his waiting pickup vehicle farther east, was in the process of preparing to land.

He lowered the egg-breaker beneath him before adroitly setting the ROE down in a big patch of river grass he was sure would accommodate the eight-foot-four-inch-diameter landing circle. The ROE came to rest a mere six feet from the egg-breaker, both of which he disassembled with the help of Malcolm Cope, of Cope's Plumbing, Inc., who was waiting in a '99 Ford Excursion. Quickly, with a lot of sweating but without panic, McBride collapsed the ROE's rotors and telescopic spars, which folded in like the spars of a huge beach umbrella. Then, with Cope's help, he lifted them into the SUV.

Cope was a thin, wiry man in his late twenties, in first-rate condition. But as he manhandled the ROE past the aluminum table he'd brought, he complained, "She's a bitch to lift, Major."

It was the first time in a long while anyone had addressed McBride by his militia rank. "Exercise'll do you good," McBride said. He was already lifting the egg-breaker aboard by himself, its Styrofoam casing squeaking as he pushed it inside.

"How are we for time?" Cope asked.

"You know the schedule," McBride replied, immediately giving Cope a share of the responsibility for the mission, and gave him the calm, confident look that had inspired so many young militiamen. "I assume," he told Cope, while waving away one of the biggest and ugliest blowflies he'd ever seen, "you've heard from the boys at the other end?" He meant Ron Stanes and Art Maddin.

Cope nodded solemnly. "They're in trouble."

McBride was too good a leader to show alarm, but if Cope hadn't been standing behind him as he secured the fifty-six-pound load, he would have seen his jaw muscles tighten. "What kind of trouble?" McBride inquired calmly.

"Don't know all of it, but KING- and KOMO-TV have been giving a description of their pickup and license number. They say it's the biggest manhunt in a long while."

"But you've heard from them?"

"Yeah, all systems are go."

"Fine," McBride said. "Then they must have taken care of it."

Cope looked puzzled.

"They must have evaded the police."

"Yeah," Cope conceded, "but for how long?"

"Long enough to get the job done."

"Then what?" Cope pressed apprehensively.

"The Redoubt," McBride said, looking at Cope. "Listen, I chose you because your unit commander in Kitsap County said you knew the area and you're strong. I took that to mean mentally as well." McBride's tone was a question as much as an explanation, and before Cope could reply, McBride concluded, "But if you haven't got the balls for this, I'll have one of them assist me. I don't have to have both of them to provide a diversion."

"No," Cope said quickly. "You know, I was just wondering—"

"You're wondering," McBride cut in, "if we'll get away with it. It's only natural, but I don't want you with me, son, if I can't count on you one hundred percent." He paused. "You've driven the route, right?"

"I won't let you down, Major."

"Good." McBride's hand shot out and captured the blow-fly, fingering it against the Excursion, dead. Cope looked startled. "Never slap an insect," McBride told him. "Makes too much noise. Lost a buddy in Granada who did that."

Driving over the spine of the Cascades down through the three-thousand-foot-high Snoqualmie Pass toward Bandera, they saw ambulances, police cars, fire trucks—lights flashing—wailing past them as dark, bruised cumulonimbus clouds sucked down by the jagged saw-toothed peaks shut out the sun. Rain ensued, torrential in its ferocity, the wipers at one point so overwhelmed that McBride told Cope to slow down. A bullying, uninhabited gloom pressed in on either side from the enormous expanse of Snoqualmie National Forest. In an hour or so everything would change, the vast forest giving way to the verdant but heavily populated coastal plain on the western edge of Puget Sound. And then once they crossed the sound on the ferry, north of Boeing Field, they would be on Kitsap Peninsula, which, though well-populated in places, was for the most part as heavily forested and as lonely as the mountain fastness of Snoqualmie. Which is precisely why McBride had chosen it.

"I don't like it up here," Cope said, indicating the gloomy terrain. "Gives me the willies."

"You believe in omens, then?" McBride said.

"Don't you?"

"No," McBride replied. "Beliefs in omens are psychological weaknesses, Cope. Excuses for failure. Knew a guy in the Gulf—always looking for omens. So busy looking for them he stepped on a land mine. Doesn't have to worry about omens anymore."

He's a hard bastard, Cope thought. But then, hard bastards

were what was needed against the Federals. The boys said that the Fairchild commandant was a hard bastard too. And the Federal, General Freeman. The world was hard.

CHAPTER TWENTY-ONE

Bangor

HER REACTOR STARTUP complete, brow rolled ashore, lines cast off, tugs at the ready, the SSBN *Maui* passed through the massive tin shed, or degaussing station, where her magnetic fields were wiped clean to prevent the triggering of underwater mines during her six-month patrol. After this, the 560-foot-long *Maui*, over eighty percent of her hidden underwater even though she was surfaced, her twenty-four Trident ICBMs in place, steamed north from the isolated base at Bangor up the Hood Canal, pushing a constant bulge of water ahead of her sail.

Two lookouts and her executive officer, Lieutenant Commander Richard O'Malley, orange-glo safety harnesses attached, stood in the sail's cockpit, taking in the salty air twenty-one feet above the boomer's deck. Immediately behind them stood a thicket of radio antenna masts, attack periscopes, satellite receiver, snorkel induction and radar masts. Above them the Stars and Stripes flapped noisily in the breeze, for not until they were out of the canal and clear of the Strait of Juan de Fuca would the officer of the deck order the two lookouts to strike the colors and clear the bridge.

Passing by Dabob Bay on their port side, they saw the morose gray waters of the canal suddenly turn a stunning cobalt blue, the sun streaming through a gap in the clouds. In the cramped space forward of the gray-spotted, camouflaged attack and search periscopes, one of the lookouts, engineering lab technician Danny Gianelli, while checking for any surface traffic, focused his binoculars on the road that ran parallel with them up the eastern side of the two-mile-wide canal. Through occasional breaks in the forest he caught sight of the usual stream of vehicles heading out from the base, as families and loved ones of the *Maui*'s sixteen officers and 156 enlisted men drove up toward the Hood Canal Bridge. From there they traditionally watched the nineteen-thousand-ton leviathan egress until it was a mere dot on the horizon, continuing its journey beyond Kitsap, past the southern half of Whidbey Island on its right, before turning westward to the Strait of Juan de Fuca and through to the open sea.

Likewise, on the port side of the sail's cockpit, the other lookout, a missile technician, Ernie Prescott, scanned the wide stretch of blue sea left of the boomer, also scanning for surface traffic. He noted a small pleasure craft three points off the port bow, about a mile away. Accordingly, he informed the officer of the deck, XO O'Malley, who raised his binoculars, checking to see whether the twenty-foot vessel was moving, anchored, or simply holding its position. O'Malley saw that a lone figure, well rugged up, was fishing from the craft's stern.

Beneath *Maui*'s sail in the belly of the boomer, men were waking up from the night shift, only the fact that the sub was "white"-lighted instead of "red" telling them it was day instead of night. The oily showroom smell of the sub was permeated now by odors from the galley, where noise, as in the rest of the warship, was kept to a minimum, the sound and vibrations of the sub's six-thousand-horsepower engine deadened by thousands of rubber mountings that helped *Maui* stay undetected by the enemy.

High above the pressure hull, Gianelli, turning around in the sail to search forward, almost struck O'Malley with his binoculars. "Sorry, sir."

"Paying me back for that lesson, are you?" O'Malley said good-naturedly.

Danny grinned. O'Malley had been the one who, at the beginning of every enlisted sailor's bid to complete their qualifications cards, helped allay any fears the newcomer might have about the nuclear reactor aboard. O'Malley drove home the fact that basically the sub was still driven by a steam engine, the radioactive fuel rods for the reactor merely being a substitute for either oil or coal to fire up the steam engine.

"What about the missiles' warheads?" Danny had asked during the newcomers' tour, referring to the eight warheads housed in the reentry vehicles atop each of the sub's twenty-four Trident D5s, which gave *Maui* the capacity to hit 192 independent targets from over four thousand miles away.

"Warheads aren't your job," O'Malley had replied. "That's the MT's worry."

Now, Danny Gianelli glanced over at Ernie Prescott, wondering how the little New Englander would respond if push came to shove and the *Maui* had to "engage." Danny didn't envy his companion one little bit.

By now O'Malley, as OOD, had noted that the pleasure craft had moved away farther to port, heading, it seemed, toward the Hood Canal Bridge and the Shine Tidelands beyond. At least it was far enough away for O'Malley not to have to worry about the risk of collision, as had happened in 2000, when one of the myriad pleasure craft plying the Northwest waters had collided with one of the big Canadian ferries, despite all regulatory warning signals. Having been running parallel with the ferry, the craft had, for some inexplicable reason, suddenly tacked hard to the left under the ferry's bow. Dragged the full length of the big ship, it had resurfaced in pieces, one of the two aboard the pleasure craft dead at the scene, the other dying a few hours later in hospital. In O'Malley's view, all such pleasure craft were a damned nuisance, and when Margaret and Rick Junior, his seventeen-year-old twins, had insisted on joining Washington State U's sailing club, he'd made them promise—literally made them put their hand on the Bible and swear—that they would "never ever" go aboard any water craft without wearing a life jacket.

"How 'bout when we're in a rubber tube, Dad?" Rick Junior had teased.

"Very funny."

"Can't we just keep it nearby?" his daughter asked. "I mean, you don't actually want us to wear it all the time, do you?"

"Yes."

Margaret made a face. "*Dad!* We'll look like total idiots!"

"Listen," O'Malley warned them, "a sudden gust hits you when you're broaching, the boom swings across, clobbers you on the head. Before you know it you're ass over T in the drink *and* you're unconscious. Remember cousin—"

"But Dad, it looks so dorky."

"Hey, I'd rather you look dorky than dead. You've no idea," he went on, "how quickly things happen at sea. One second everything's hunky-dory, the next—" He snapped his fingers. "Just like that!"

At 0910 hours, in *Maui*'s control center directly beneath him, the electronics officer tapped out an address on his computer and watched the screen as the Internet picture, portraying what was going on above him, showed the eastern half of the Hood Canal Bridge starting to open, *Maui*'s navigating officer having timed the sub's arrival at the bridge after peak hour morning traffic had crossed.

Through his binoculars atop the sub's sail, O'Malley could see the circular wooden bulge two miles away that served as the bridge's fishing pontoon. The anomalous bulge was all that remained of the western half of the mile and a half bridge that had been washed away in the great storm of '79 when wind gusts reached 120 miles per hour. Once the two sections of the massive, hydraulically operated draw-span section were withdrawn, a 550-foot-wide gap would result, allowing the *Maui* to steam on northward up past the Shine Tidelands on the sub's port side.

By now the small pleasure craft O'Malley had seen earlier was nothing more than a dot, disappearing well north of the bridge behind the heavily forested hump of Hood Head, which, though it looked like an island, was in fact connected to the mainland by a sandy spit at low tide.

Turning left off the highway and driving onto the bridge from its eastern end, Stanes and Maddin, in their newly painted white pickup, saw an orange-striped cement barrier to their right, and several white-striped orange-glo plastic barrel markers delineating a pull-off work area. Here, several Washington State highway trucks were parked near what looked like a tall green gravel hopper, probably used for road repairs in the area. Ahead of them was the gradual downslope of the two-lane bridge, the dark wooden bulge the fishing pontoon that Maddin had seen the day before from the boat ramp at the opposite, western end of the bridge. The bridge was starting to retract, vehicles having been stopped twenty feet from either end of the retractable section, several fishermen casting lines.

Maddin drove the white pickup over to the shoulder near the orange-striped cement barrier. This way he or Stanes

could back up along the soft margin to the intersection of the
highway and bridge turnoff instead of being trapped in the
line of halted bridge traffic. As they got out of the pickup,
Maddin asked Stanes, "What would they get here?"

Stanes looked blankly at him.

"What kind of *fish*?" Maddin explained, rummaging
around in his brand new tackle box as they continued toward
the ever-widening gap. "Salmon? Perch?"

"Yeah, salmon, perch," Stanes answered robotically.

"You all right?"

"Yeah."

"The shit you are. Don't beat the whistle, bubba. Remember, make it look as if you're baiting your hook. Nobody
watches that. It's only when you reel something in anyone's
interested. Everyone likes a winner. Right?"

"I'm all right."

"You look like shit."

McBride and Cope, having also parked their vehicles,
were already in the recreational area known as Salsbury Park,
several hundred yards to the right of the bridge and about the
same distance away from the retracting section of the bridge
as was the *Maui*, a half mile off. The weather, despite the tem-
porary break in the clouds, was moody, the western half of
the bridge in shadow, the water beneath it as gray as the low,
somber clouds that were moving down the sound. Ironically,
the bridge's eastern half was still bathed in the sunlight that
had broken through the cumulonimbus and turned the water
around the sub a deep blue, the latter increasingly wrinkled
in a tug-of-war between the incoming tide and a brisk wind
that was blowing down from Canada and over the San Juan
Islands.

"We could use one of the picnic tables," Cope suggested.
"No one here."

"No," McBride said. The weather was so unpredictable in Puget Sound that McBride hadn't anticipated being able to use a picnic table, for fear that if the weather this side had turned sunny and hot, some RV type might be tempted to pull off into the park. Besides which, a picnic table hereabouts could be eaten through, weakened by termites. Instead, with characteristic caution, he had decided to park near the bushy perimeter of the small park, carry the egg-breaker through the narrow bush trail down to the water's edge, and use the lightweight worktable upon which he now set the egg-breaker after quickly removing its green Styrofoam packing.

Cope had never seen it in the flesh, as it were. "Why do you call it an egg-breaker?" he asked.

"Because," McBride said, speaking softly, one eye southward on the *Maui*, "a sub's bow is egg-shaped."

"Is it new?" asked Cope, who'd been surprised earlier by the somewhat ancient though admittedly effective ROE.

"State of the art," McBride replied, checking his handheld Magellan GPS and the nine-pound Command Launch Unit, electing to use its integrated four-power magnification day sight rather than the thermal imaging employed in reduced visibility conditions and at night. Next, with Cope standing watch, McBride checked out the weapon's lithium battery, then attached the nine-pound CLU to the two-foot-long, 5.6-inch-diameter disposable launch tube. The Javelin missile, already inside, was armed with two shaped charges in tandem capable of penetrating over two feet of the most advanced, superhardened armor in the world from a distance of two miles. The stand-alone, man-portable Javelin, issued first to the Marine Corps in 2000 then to the 101st Airborne, was the most revolutionary shoulder-fired antiarmor missile system ever made. Unlike all before it, its tank-killer guidance system depended on neither fiber wire nor laser beam but was pure "fire and forget," guiding itself to the target the nanosecond it was launched, leaving its operator to either reload—seventeen seconds—or run. Shoot and scoot!

Cope, hearing movement in the bushes, spun about, slipping on the wet grass, and fell heavily close to a pile of empty beer cans and other litter left by a picnic table. McBride, his glance of disgust saying it all, realigned his eye with the CLU's eyepiece display, saw it was dirty, licked a Kleenex, wiped away the dust, then gave the CLU its Lock On Before Launch command. Next, resting his elbows on the aluminum table, he switched the attack mode from Direct to Top Attack Flight Path. This meant that instead of having to eyeball a specific point *on* the moving target, the missile's warhead, once over the target, should dive down at a forty-five-degree angle for a downward blast over the sub's sail, where the *Maui*'s "lid," as it were, would be thinner than the sub's three-inch-thick hull, made of high tensile steel that formed the all-important pressure hull or "egg." Placing the cursor box sight over the image of the oncoming boomer, McBride estimated he would have to wait another eight minutes until the sail of the 560-foot-long sub had all but cleared the gap in the bridge. If he fired it any earlier, the homing round might explode prematurely over the bridge's metal pontoons instead of the metal of the sub.

On the bridge's wooden fishing platform, whose convex sides bulged out from the two-lane bridge like some dark aneurysm on an otherwise healthy artery, Stanes and Maddin knelt down by their tackle box, ostensibly sorting through sinkers, line, and other paraphernalia essential to the art.

Waiting.

When McBride squeezed the trigger grip, he felt the relatively soft recoil, heard the backblast, the missile's tenth-of-a-second kick motor having already ejected the Javelin clear of the tube, its eight steering vanes deployed, the missile streaking toward the sub at over 1,800 feet a second.

Atop the sub's sail, O'Malley, Prescott, and Gianelli saw the wink that was the missile's second stage igniting at the same time the radar operator below saw it on his screen. An instant later the Javelin exploded above the sail. What had been O'Malley and the other two lookouts was now pink mist, the massive explosion reverberating throughout the sub. Intuitively, the captain wanted to dive the boat, but instead ordered maximum reverse thrust, knowing a crash dive could invite catastrophic flooding had the pressure hull been penetrated by the explosion above, whatever it was. The twenty-one-year-old helmsman controlled the *Maui*'s tail rudder, quickly responding to a whirlpool of current that had pushed hard against the port bow. Despite his training, however, he had become momentarily unnerved by the tremendous explosion above him, and he overcompensated. It caused the starboard side's horizontal stabilizer, which stuck out aft from the pressure hull, to smash hard into the bridge's eastern pontoon. This in turn buckled the stabilizer's end plate and sheared off the vertical plate to which it was attached.

The second after, as Stanes and Maddin, having pulled the pins on the six smoke grenades in their tackle box, walked back along the bridge, a seventy-foot-long section on the starboard side of the boat could be heard scraping, dragged by the current along the rusted edge of the pontoon. The pontoon tore into the sound-absorbing anechoic coating, the ear-grating sound that resulted convincing the crew that the sub was being ripped asunder.

An off-duty Electronics Warfare Officer, who had been on his daily jog around the twenty-four missiles of "Sherwood Forest," was knocked down so hard on the waxed decking he was certain that thousands of tons of water would soon be cascading into the boat, driving the 18,000-ton leviathan to the bottom, her bulkheads collapsing, images of the stricken *Kursk* flashing through his mind. While the pressure hull's integrity wasn't breached, over sixty feet of vitally important hydrophone arrays were lost as a steel maintenance boom, arcing out from one of the retracting section's pontoons, gutted the seam along *Maui*'s side where the hydrophones' long tubular housing had been welded to the hull. On the fourth, or bottom, level of Sherwood Forest, the missile compartment's "Rover"—the man whose job it was to check for any fire hazard, security access door violations, and leaks—also thought the end had come as he felt the sub roll hard right. In Sherwood Forest, the lights above the eight groups of missiles flickered ominously, *Maui* righting herself, but not before over six million dollars worth of damage had been done to the billion-dollar sub and the three men in the sail's cockpit killed. It left one of the most powerful nuclear weapons platforms in the world essentially unsteerable when she had barely left port.

McBride, grabbing the Javelin's nine-pound CLU, followed Cope, scurrying up the slippery path through blackberry bushes, vine maple, and fir saplings to the Excursion. They drove east for a mile on the 104, through Port Gamble, then south and east again to the Kingston ferry, waiting for the twenty-minute crossing from the Kitsap Peninsula to Edmonds and the safety of the never-ending traffic stream on Interstate 5.

On the bridge itself, confusion and panic reigned, smoke pouring up from the fishing pontoon. Stanes and Maddin were now running toward their vehicle, Maddin with a cloth over his mouth, shouting, "Gas! Poison gas!"

Panic turned to hysteria as men and women, screaming at children to follow them, vacated the line of waiting vehicles, fleeing back along the bridge as the clouds of dense smoke enveloped them. One man screamed into his cell phone that a submarine had "exploded," releasing a deadly cloud of radiation. Another, who'd likewise dialed 911 on the run, reported that a "bomb or something" had exploded and that the sub was on fire, spewing toxic fumes "from its sail."

"Sail?" the 911 operator asked. "There's a sailboat involved?"

"What?"

"Is there a sailboat involved?"

"No, goddamn it! A *submarine*!" the man shouted as he kept running, glancing back through the dense white smoke that was now laced with acrid black clouds of fumes buffeted by the breeze coming down from the San Juans.

An elderly woman, falling in the melee and glancing back to the sub, saw something she would never forget: a splattering of blood against the periscope and radar masts, and brownish streaks bubbling and running down the sail, dripping like fat onto the sail's starboard diving plane, a sweetish burnt smell momentarily permeating the sour air. And then there was more ear-screeching noise, the sub's port side again being scraped by the barnacle-encrusted pontoon.

CHAPTER TWENTY-TWO

Camp Fairchild HQ

"THAT'S THE MILITIA," Moorehead proclaimed, on hearing the news from Seattle's KING radio about an explosion on the nuclear sub.

"Coulda been something on board," proffered Leroi, who'd taken Eleen to solitary.

"No," the commandant said. "It's got militia written all over it. I knew the bastards would get back at us after the Boeing fiasco."

Leroi jabbed his thumb in the direction of the mug shots of HQ's notice board. "You think it's those two again?"

"Rainor and Haley?" Moorehead harrumphed. "Those two idiots couldn't start a fire with gasoline and matches. Besides, everybody's on the lookout for them. No, this is someone else. The timing—just as the sub is at its most vulnerable, inching its way through the gap in the bridge. When it had no room to maneuver."

"Should've been submerged," another guard suggested.

"Through a gap like that?" another countered. "You couldn't see where the fuck you were going."

Moorehead leaned forward in his overstuffed recliner, extracting a corncob pipe and tobacco tin from the Naugahyde's side pocket. "Well," he said, "the new attorney general's gonna get her tits in a knot over this one. Biggest confrontation we've had since Waco."

"Huh," Leroi put in. "She'd better handle it better than Reno did Waco."

"Amen to that," Moorehead agreed. "Reno didn't handle it. She screwed it up."

"Isn't that the truth?"

The phone jangled on the duty officer's desk. He picked up the receiver and slid a Post-it pad toward him. "How long ago? . . . Yeah . . . Two sets? . . . Uh-huh. Yep, I'll get right to it."

By now Moorehead had packed his pipe and was sucking the lazy yellow flame of his Bic lighter into the corncob's bowl, simultaneously expelling thick, grayish-blue clouds of smoke through his tobacco-stained teeth. "Who was that?" he asked the DO.

"Dillon," the duty officer replied. "Head of the squad you sent to look for that Mead and Jubal."

"*I* know who I sent," Moorehead growled. "What'd he say?"

"He's up in the mountains. Stevens Pass. Got a tip from one of the park rangers. Said there was a snowfall—light but cold. Ranger spotted a set of tracks heading west off Highway 2, south of Lake Valhalla."

"Hell," Leroi interjected, "don't mean a hill o' beans. All kinds of yuppies go up there for the weekend, cross-country skiing and—"

"Unplug your ears," Moorehead cut in. "The ranger said it was a *light* fall of snow. Besides, Leroi—it isn't the weekend."

"Besides which," Sampson, the duty officer, added, "the ranger said two guys in Army fatigues had been spotted not far back in Berne."

"Well hell," Leroi said, "that's different, then."

Moorehead, drawing hard on his pipe, was thinking aloud. "But only *one* set of tracks." He looked over at Sampson. "That right? *One* set?"

"Yes, sir."

Moorehead turned back to Leroi. "Could be a hiker."

Well geez, Leroi thought, that's what I said in the first place.

"Still," Moorehead continued, the rich, pungent smell of the dark Erinmore tobacco wafting up the HQ hut's ceiling, where it flattened then rolled out, curling at the edges in a bluish gray tsunami, "they could have bypassed a roadblock, got a lift to the pass, then split up."

"You want me to send up dogs?" the DO asked the commandant. "Dillon is waiting for me to call back."

Moorehead mulled over his options. To send dogs up

would undoubtedly draw the attention of the locals in the smattering of tiny towns in the area, such as Berne. It would be the biggest thing to happen up there since the horror avalanche of 1910 that had swept down, derailing two trains and killing ninety-six people. It might also draw the attention of the press hounds in Seattle only sixty miles to the east. And sooner rather than later, that would mean Marte Price, and if she got a chance to talk to either Mead or Jubal—before he, Moorehead, got to them—she'd discover a few discrepancies in what he'd said about the POWs being "killers on the run." Which in turn might open an inquiry into his behavior. Especially if the CNN bitch got the opportunity to grill Dillon about Lanky Sommers's death. Not that Dillon would intentionally scuttle his transfer from Fairchild to sunnier climes, but Moorehead knew that Marte Price was wily.

On the other hand, Moorehead mused, blowing out smoke, if Mead and Jubal managed to evade capture, how would he look, having boasted how he'd soon run the two "convicts" to ground? He would have egg on his face, and Price would replay his boast on CNN. He stabbed his pipe stem at Sampson. "Tell Dillon we'll bring a coupla dogs up but we'll have to try to be circumspect about it."

Moorehead saw Leroi was puzzled by "circumspect."

"Play it close to the chest," the commandant explained.

"Huh," Leroi responded, embarrassed by his ignorance, determined to regain his pride. "Don't see how you can play it close to the chest. Damn dogs'll yap their damned heads off."

Moorehead knew Leroi was right. If it was Mead who had made the footprints in the snow, he'd likely be armed, put up one hell of a fight. Then Moorehead saw the answer. "Go get Eleen," he told Leroi.

"Why me?" Leroi demanded, his questioning of an order by the commandant something the latter wouldn't have brooked in or outside the HQ except in the casual atmosphere he always permitted after a "good hunt." Moorehead was smoking up a storm again, his yellow-stained teeth clamped tight on the pipe's stem. "I want you to go fetch him, Leroi, because we all know how much you like Mormons."

This got a laugh from DO Sampson and the other guards, who knew the southerner hated the Mormons more than he did any other POW because he couldn't stand the thought of polygamy among the Mormons—the possibility that some men were getting it off with a "har*eem*," as he called it, of nubile young wives. Even so, Leroi was mollified by Moorehead's obvious plan to let the guards use Eleen as a bargaining chip to take the fight out of Mead. If it *was* Mead. It was just as possible, of course, that the set of tracks the park ranger had seen were Marion Jubal's. And equally possible that the tracks belonged to two locals—with a penchant for military surplus clothing.

Moorehead got up to study the map of the Northwest on the wall of the HQ hut.

"Sampson," he said to the DO, "get on the Net and bring up a one-to-24,000 detail of the Stevens Pass area. Run it off in segments and staple 'em."

"Will do," the DO said. "I know what you're thinking."

"Do you, now?"

"He's heading for the Cascade Tunnel."

"If memory serves me right," Moorehead said, "tunnel's *south* of the highway, Sampson. The tracks the ranger saw were heading *north*."

"Well, maybe it's just some damn hiker—like Leroi said?"

"You got that map yet?"

"No, takes forever for this server to log on. We need a new computer. *And* a new printer. The contour lines are so faint."

Moorehead strapped on his holster while he waited. He had a gut feeling it was Mead.

CHAPTER TWENTY-THREE

THE PRESIDENT, CONFERRING in the West Wing with National Security Advisor Michael Brownlee and other aides, was trying not to overreact, lest he panic Wall Street, while at the same time wanting to act quickly and decisively and with sufficient force to "run these bastards down."

"Can't use the Army," Brownlee advised.

General Alan Rogers, Chairman of the Joint Chiefs of Staff, agreed. "It would make the U.S. look like a banana republic, sending soldiers into the streets." Especially, Brownlee noted, after the Bush-Gore election fiasco a few years ago, when even America's most steadfast allies couldn't help smiling behind Washington's back at the banana-republic-like atmosphere occasioned by the six million voters of "Flori*duh*."

"Besides," Brownlee continued, "constitutionally, we're hamstrung when it comes to using any of the armed forces in domestic matters. To do that *would* make us look like a banana republic. And we certainly can't bomb them. Not after Waco. The American public would never—"

"Well dammit!" the President said. "Our police aren't having any success. And it was some of our Army boys who stopped that militia convoy in the—"

"Cascade Mountains," Brownlee said.

"Yes, Mr. President," Rogers conceded, "but those two Bradleys were en route to Spokane. Merely serendipitous."

"Can't we send in the National Guard at least? Say they're on maneuvers? That's not the same as sending in the regular army."

General Rogers nodded sagely. "We could, sir. That might overcome the constitutional constraints, but *where* are the people who attacked the sub? Without knowing that—"

"FBI report!" It was Brownlee, taking a sheet from his fax. "The Bureau's convinced the militia convoy in the Cascades and the attack on the *Maui* are connected."

"Of course they're connected," the President said irritably. "And wasn't a cop murdered in the area?"

General Rogers kept silent as he read the full text of the two-page report. He'd seen too many tactical and strategic blunders made by commanders who automatically assumed that because two events happened within twenty-four hours of each other they were necessarily connected. In Salsbury Park the FBI had found an expendable launch tube, which experts from Fort Lewis confirmed was a launch tube assembly for Javelin, America's preeminent antitank weapon. The tube, said the report, "was found at the southern end of the park, which itself is situated just north of the eastern end of the Hood Canal Bridge." Leading up from the launch site there was a narrow path through a brush of blackberry bushes and vine maple to the highway, where a vehicle had obviously been parked. The report also noted that the smoke that had temporarily obscured the eastern end of the bridge hadn't been poison gas after all. Along with the launch tube, the FBI agents had found a half-dozen crushed beer cans—Budweiser, an empty McDonald's apple pie box, some crumpled Kleenex, dog excrement, and Styrofoam packing. The agent in charge who signed off on the report noted that all this information had been shared with local authorities.

"Do they know what kind of dogshit it is?" the President inquired dryly.

"Well, they did get up from Seattle pretty quickly," Brownlee said, in the FBI's defense. "Hopefully, forensics will tell us more."

"I know," the President conceded. "It's just that I'm damn sure it's the militia. I mean how in hell would a terrorist smuggle one of these antitank missiles into the country? We've tightened up all the border crossings coming down from Canada, haven't we? Ever since that mad Muslim tried to get through a few years ago. Where was it, Port Angeles?"

"Yes," the general said. "Unfortunately, it's a two-way street in that regard. We share a border over four thousand miles long with Canada. There are hundreds of places in the Pacific Northwest's forests alone where drug smugglers and anyone else can slip through."

"By now," the President said, in words that unnerved Brownlee, "the perpetrators, whoever they are, are probably up there. The CNO tells me that sub base at Bangor is only eighty miles south of the border."

"Well, wherever they are," Brownlee opined, "I think that when we do get a sure lead on them, we should send in USFs."

"English, Michael. English."

"Sorry, sir—undercover special forces. A team not on our active list. This way we'd sidestep the constitutional constraints and we wouldn't waste time butting heads with Congress."

The President frowned, not in anger but from concentrating, recalling how another head of state, Margaret Thatcher, had sent her secret Special Air Services into Gibraltar after the IRA terrorists who'd launched a mortar attack on her at 10 Downing Street. They were all shot while trying to "evade arrest."

"All right," the President said. "Is there anyone you can suggest?"

Before Brownlee or anyone else in the room could respond, the President hurriedly added, "But if anyone mentions Freeman and his—his *gang* of cutthroats—I'll have his guts for garters!"

The office fell silent, save for the noticeably loud ticking of Brownlee's pendulum clock, his Civil War treasure passed down from a Walter G. Brownlee, who'd fought in the Battle of Bull Run during America's *first* civil war.

Finally, the President spoke. "We need someone, as you say, Michael, who's not on the active list." He looked at Rogers, but the general remained silent, mulling over Brownlee's suggestion. This was hardly the time, Rogers thought, to remind his commander in chief that, like most of those in the upper echelons of the Armed Services, he had little time for "cowboys," a derogatory phrase that encompassed all so-called elite units: the Navy's SEAL, the Army's Delta Force, Freeman's now defunct Sea, Air, Land Emergency Response Team, and the Green Berets. In the view of generals and admirals used to moving masses of men and matériel in the great battles from D-Day to Desert Storm, the comparatively small commando forces received publicity out of all proportion to their contribution. Nevertheless, given the political considerations involved—in this case, domestic terrorism and the need to maintain overseas investor confidence in American stability—Rogers realized that a small, highly trained, low-profile elite force might be the answer to the problem, once the White House knew exactly who and where the saboteurs were.

"General?" the President said. "You have anyone in mind?"

"Yes, sir."

"Who?"

"A man who punched out a chef."

Brownlee and his fellow aides looked inquiringly at one another, but clearly no one knew what the general was talking about.

Rogers wasn't a toady, nor was he a fool, and he worked his

way into it by saying that what they'd need to run down crazies who'd knocked the most powerful warship in the world
out of commission were other crazies, equally motivated men
who, he told the President, "loved to fight."

The President shifted uncomfortably. Though he was commander in chief, at heart he was a politician, a man who got
where he was by more often than not glossing over the less
savory aspects of the human condition. And even if he called
himself a "realist," he was reluctant to confront the harsh
truth Rogers had just alluded to—namely, that while most
men did not live to fight, and that generals in particular were
obliged to say, "I *hate* war," there were those who did like to
fight, and at certain times in a nation's history you had to
open that closet and let them out. As Maggie Thatcher had, he
thought, to get the job done.

"By God," the President said to Rogers, "you want to bring
in George C. Scott. I can see it in your eyes."

Now, Brownlee realized they were talking about retired
General Douglas Freeman, who bore an uncanny resemblance to the actor who'd played Patton in the movie.

"So it was one of his *gang*," the President angrily charged,
"who KO'd that chef at State?"

"He's the one," Rogers confirmed, looking for support
from Brownlee and receiving none. Brownlee knew General
Rogers had won the Silver Star in Iraq, but it struck the aide
that Rogers's suggesting Freeman for this operation was infinitely braver. The President loathed Freeman, who, despite
all the combat honors bestowed upon him, had once lam-
basted Washington, D.C., as "a haven of political whores
who'd bend over for any Chinese commie with campaign
cash," by which he had meant President Clinton. And at a Veterans of Foreign Wars dinner he had referred to "turtle-soup-
sucking mandarins" in the State Department as "the most
lamentable collection of fuckwits this side of Hanoi," and

called the "dark wall" of the Vietnamese monument a "national disgrace," one that "should have been raised high for our youth to see and not hidden away like a thing of shame." His remarks had gone over well with the veterans but not the government or in the Pentagon, where defense budgets depended on the goodwill of the government.

"Do you know what he called me?" the President challenged Rogers.

"No, sir," the general lied, "but he called me a 'time server and a place seeker—a gofer for a government who won't stand up to terrorists.' But he's the man for this job, Mr. President. He's swift and he's ruthless. He knows a lot about conventional and unconventional warfare, and this attack on the *Maui* sure as hell was unconventional."

"He's too old," the President retorted. "Must be sixty if he's a day."

"He works out. Ran the New York Marathon."

"Huh, so did fifty thousand others. Did he finish?"

"Top of the senior division."

"I'll bet. How many old ladies did he run down?"

"Actually, the ladies say he's quite the gentleman. Southern roots. Like his hero Patton."

"Another egomaniac!"

"Mr. President," Brownlee cut in. "Can I have a word?"

The two of them walked into the Vice President's office next door. "What is it?" the President asked gruffly.

"Sir, this is unbecoming of you. If the Chairman of the Joint Chiefs of Staff can bury the hatchet—at least for as long as this takes—I think you should too."

The President glared at his aide. "I'm not allowed any payback at *all*?"

"No, sir. You're the President of the United States."

"Michael, Freeman wanted Clinton to launch Tomahawk

missiles against terrorist camps in the Middle East—one for
every American killed on the *Coe*. He's a loose cannon."

"Patton wanted to rearm the Germans he'd beaten and attack Russia," Brownlee responded. "But we kept him on a
leash. Besides, once we find where the bastards are hiding
out, it should be a short, hard hit. Over in a matter of hours.
Then we can send Freeman back to his war room."

The President visibly relaxed. "*Our* war room," the President corrected.

"No, *his*. In Monterey. Apparently he has one set up in his
basement—for contingency planning."

The President shook his head.

"I'm serious," Brownlee said, noting that the President
was no longer so uptight, starting perhaps to accept Rogers's
idea. "Patton did the same. On holiday in France in 1913 he
toured the Loire Valley, going over all the old battlefields.
He was sure there'd be a war and wanted to be ready in case
he got the call. He did—four years later."

"You're not telling me Freeman foresaw this—the attack
on the sub?"

"No, sir. I doubt he's clairvoyant. But he is prescient."

"All right, Mike. Call him. Have him get a team on
standby."

"Yes, sir."

"Of course the police, FBI, might have it all locked up in
the next few hours. If so, the question of Freeman and his . . ."

"Cutthroats?"

"Yes, the question of using him and his cutthroats will be
purely academic."

"How long do you want to give the police?" Brownlee
pressed. "Every hour that passes, we're getting more flak
from the press."

"Another twenty-four hours," the President said as they returned to Brownlee's office. "We haven't got the FBI's forensic

report yet. The things they can do now in their labs—it's astounding."

Brownlee nodded but said nothing.

"I don't suppose," the President said, "you have General Patton's number by any chance?"

"I'm sure it's on file, sir. Ah, would you like to make the call?"

"Certainly not. You do it. And tell him it's strictly on standby at this point. Nothing more. Quite frankly, I don't think we'll need him."

CHAPTER TWENTY-FOUR

"FREEMAN HERE." THERE was a lot of noise on the line, as if Freeman was jogging or, Brownlee joked in an aside to one of his aides, "having it off with some woman," though Freeman was reputedly a man of probity.

"General, this is Mike Brownlee from Washington, D.C. Can you hear me?"

"Yes, go ahead."

"We have a situation here—"

"You people should've called me earlier, Brownlee," the general cut in, his labored breathing unabated. "Not that it matters. I've got a team ready."

Brownlee was taken aback. "Team?" he challenged Freeman. "Ready for what?"

"To go in and sort out these militia bastards. You people can't allow this kind of nonsense—attacking our submarines. Whole world's watching, dammit! Makes Washington look like a nest of ninnies. You tell me where these militia sons of bitches are holed up and we'll go in and kick ass!"

"I thought you would have already figured out where they were," Brownlee said pointedly, "seeing as you're so sure it's the militia involved."

More heavy breathing. " 'Course it's the militia. Cunning sons of bitches, though. Have a lot of ex-Special War people among 'em."

"Some of *your* old people, perhaps?"

"Possibly," Freeman replied archly. "They're certainly giving—" There was a fumbling sound. "—giving you people the runaround."

"You people!" Brownlee challenged. "I thought you were on our side, General?"

"I am, but I understand militia frustration even if I don't agree with them. That's why my team is the best suited to deal with them."

"When you know where they are," Brownlee said.

"Did you call me for help, Brownlee, or to get my goat?"

"My apologies, General. We'd like you to be on standby in the event federal law enforcement agencies can't—"

"That submarine was attacked by a missile. Correct?"

"That's our information, yes—"

"How many of your law enforcement agencies are equipped to deal with missile attacks?"

"I take your point, General, but we might—" The general was grunting. "You all right, General?"

"Yes yes. Go on."

"Point is, we might be able to nab the perpetrators before they return to their hideout—wherever that is."

Surprisingly, Freeman conceded the point. "Well, I didn't

say our law enforcement agencies weren't brave, Michael. They might— Goddammit!"

"General, if this is an inconvenient time I won't—"

"No no, go on."

"If on the other hand they don't nab them," Brownlee continued, "the President's authorized General Rogers to give you the go ahead. But our law enforcement people might get them. Remember, some of our police officers are ex-Special Forces also."

"My God!" Freeman said. "You're right."

It was the one thing Brownlee liked about the general. He might be profane, occasionally obnoxious, but when someone alerted him to something, some fact he hadn't considered, which wasn't very often, he was quick to concede it. Then Brownlee heard a loud slap, as if an open hand had smacked someone on the backside. Brownlee's aide, hearing it on open speaker, quickly scribbled a note to Brownlee: *Ask the general if she's blond or brunette.*

Brownlee almost did, but courage failed him. Still, he compromised by asking, with just the right amount of innuendo disguised as genuine concern, "Are you all right, General? That sounded like a gunshot." Brownlee's agent doubled up.

"Gunshot?" Freeman said, his breathing noticeably easier, calmer now. "Wasn't a damn gunshot, man. My—" It sounded like "shoot opening."

"Your what?" Brownlee's aide had to leave the room.

"My *parachute*!" Freeman shouted. "Been in HALO for the last ten minutes."

"Halo?"

"High altitude, low opening," Freeman said, his tone that of an English teacher discovering a pupil had never heard of Shakespeare.

"A parachute jump?" Brownlee said, clearly chagrined by

his earlier assumptions of what the retired general had been up to.

"Yes," Freeman confirmed. "Out at twenty thousand. Free fall for two and a half minutes, then you open your steerable at two and a half thousand. Guess that's the noise you heard. Initial lift-up, then come down behind the bastards, wherever you want—if you've done it enough. And I have—sorry, there's a bad cross wind. Gotta go!"

"The eagle has landed!" Brownlee said aloud, replacing the phone in its cradle, not expecting Freeman to call back.

But a half hour later the general did. "Brownlee."

"Yes, General?"

"I've been thinking. The White House is under enormous public pressure to do something about that massacre in the Cascades. Correct?"

"General, *we*—that is, the two Bradleys from Fort Lewis—massacred *them*."

"Yes yes," Freeman agreed impatiently, "but there's widespread fear about the source of that convoy. Correct? Where the hell it came from? Will there be more?"

Brownlee shifted uneasily in his seat. The general had zoomed in on what Brownlee and others in the White House staff knew was a growing threat to the presidency, a public perception of impotency, one that could turn out to be every bit as deadly as the Iran hostage crisis had become for Jimmy Carter.

"I'm right, aren't I?" Freeman pressed.

"Yes, General, but at the moment we're trying to run down the attackers of the sub."

"It'd be one hell of a diversion," Freeman offered, "to score a knockout against the source of that convoy. And one hell of a plus for the President. Lord knows he needs it."

Typical Freeman, Brownlee thought, itching for a fight. He also happened to be right. It would be a diversion, but again, not one in which the President would want to use regular troops, for fear of coming across as the head of a banana republic. Especially if it failed.

"Minor point, General," Brownlee said wryly. "Where *did* the militia convoy originate?"

"Hell," Freeman responded, "that's the easy part. Ruby Lake."

Brownlee had never heard of it.

"Idaho," Freeman continued. "White supremacist country. Attracts racists like flies."

"How do you know—"

"The Net," Freeman answered. "Every militia group in the country is online. The congratulations are all swirling around the Hayden Lake Web site. But Ruby Lake is actually the HQ. Right now it's raining up there like a cow peeing on a hard rock. Forecast is for the low to hang around for the next two weeks. So, no jumps. We'd have to use an Osprey."

"How many men would you take in?" Brownlee asked.

"Twenty men max."

Brownlee was incredulous. "*Twenty?* General, there might be—I don't know—a hundred militia there."

"Only a *hundred*?"

"Cyrano de Bergerac," Brownlee said, not expecting Freeman to know of the great swordsman's reply to the warning that he'd be greatly outnumbered.

"I'm not de Bergerac," Freeman replied. "For one, I don't have a long nose. I never lie."

"Hmm. That's Pinocchio, General. Anyway, twenty men . . . Is that realistic, really?"

"Damn right. You know your theater, Brownlee, but do you know your Bonaparte?" Brownlee didn't, but in any case, before he could answer, Freeman raced on. "One, 'surprise.' Two, 'the army which remains behind its fortified positions will always be defeated.' And three, 'speed.' Given enough velocity, Bonaparte said, he could drive a tallow candle through a steel plate. And he was right. A small, compact, highly trained elite force. We'll have them on the ropes within ten minutes—twenty at the outside—and it'll all be over. A knockout punch."

"Well maybe, General, but I hear we've had some technological improvements since Napoleon's day, and the militia may have—"

"Principle's the same, Brownlee. Hit 'em fast, hit 'em hard, before they know it. It's an unbeatable combination. Plus—"

"I'll speak to the President."

"Now?"

Brownlee shook his head. The general's impatience, like Patton's, once he got the bit in his mouth, was well known, and a pain in the neck for those around him. "I'll speak to him, General."

"I'll hold."

"General, it'll take at least an hour."

"Very well. I'll call in a few old IOUs, get myself and the boys up to McChord."

Brownlee was becoming irritated, but because he didn't know where McChord was and didn't want to admit as much to Freeman, he merely said, "Might all be for nothing, General."

"Don't see the old man has a choice."

"Oh, really," Brownlee said, "you might be surprised, General."

"McChord Air Force Base," Freeman said, "is adjacent to Fort Lewis, that's just south of Tacoma. Near Seattle."

"I know *that*," Brownlee answered. At least, he knew where Seattle was.

"Two hundred and seventy miles from Ruby Lake," Freeman informed him. "Osprey'd get us there in forty-five minutes. Less if there's a tailwind."

"Not if the President says no."

"I'm confident he'll agree," Freeman said.

"I'm not."

CHAPTER TWENTY-FIVE

AT THE SUN-DRENCHED Kingston Ferry terminal, the air heavy with the exhaust of waiting cars, the ticket agent was shaking his head disgustedly at the radio above him in the booth. "You hear the news?" he asked Cope, who had wound down the driver's side window of the Excursion just far enough to pay.

"What's up?" Cope asked dutifully, squinting in the sunlight that was in imminent danger of being eclipsed by a massive sheet of stratus cloud.

"Some terrorist blew up one of our subs."

"Where?" McBride asked.

"Up at Port Gamble. Hood Canal Bridge. Some kinda bomb."

"Like that guy up at Port Angeles," McBride said, his suggestion, though the ticket agent couldn't see him, immediately striking a responsive chord.

"Yeah," the ticket agent said, not looking up, busy with the change. "I remember, back in 2000. That Muslim trying to smuggle explosives in from Canada. You ask me, the Canucks are too darn soft. Let anybody in." The agent gave Cope the change. "Washington should get tough with those Canucks."

"They won't," McBride said. "Bunch of old women in Washington."

The agent lifted a plastic cup to take a sip. "Isn't that the—"

"Hey, buddy!" shouted the driver of a Lincoln Town Car behind Cope and McBride. "You selling tickets or what?"

The agent glowered back at the Lincoln, waving Cope on.

Cope eased the Excursion forward. "Thought you said we should keep a low profile," he challenged McBride.

"It engaged him," McBride countered. "Last thing he was thinking of was looking in the back of the van. Besides, he couldn't see me clearly past you."

McBride was an enigma to Cope, who thought the militia commander would be more nervous now than before the attack, what with the whole weight of the government brought to bear on whoever had dared to immobilize America's most powerful weapons platform, a vital link in America's first line of defense.

McBride allowed himself a smile, and Cope could tell McBride knew what he was thinking. "They don't know who did it," McBride assured him.

"But after the Boeing plant—"

"Oh sure. They might think it's the militia. But like that ticket agent, they might also think it's terrorists. They'll have to narrow the field. By then we'll be safe in the Redoubt. Only one more ferry to catch."

"But the government *does* see us as terrorists," Cope pointed out.

For the first time since Cope had met McBride, he saw the famed militia commander nonplused, the notion that he might be viewed by other Americans as a terrorist having never been seriously entertained by him. He'd always considered himself a patriot, a man who in his youth had fought America's enemies abroad and who now fought against her enemies at home, a government out of control.

"Sir!"

"Jesus!" Cope started. It was the ticket agent, eyes hidden behind mirrored shades. "Your left taillight's smashed."

Cope was so taken aback he couldn't answer.

"Thanks," McBride said. "Hadn't noticed."

"You're welcome," the agent said, smiling.

McBride figured he had deliberately left his station to piss off the driver of the Lincoln, making him wait a little longer. It was working. As the adjacent line continued on through, the Lincoln was going nowhere, its driver having a bad case of ferry rage, thumping the steering wheel, shouting at the agent.

"He'll be lucky if he's out of here by midnight," McBride said wryly.

"They've got us on camera, you know," Cope said, as if McBride wasn't taking it seriously enough.

"They've got everybody on camera," McBride said. "God-damn government's watching us all the time. Big Brother's everywhere, my friend. Have access to everything you buy, from condoms to cars. Got cameras in the hotels. I don't mean the foyers—they're in bedrooms as well." McBride checked the rearview mirror before continuing. "With a lens no bigger than a pinhead they can see everything at the push of a button, from who's playing with themselves to who's screwing who." He thought of Mirela in Spokane—how they could hear the river from her bedroom, how she'd told him, "You'll split me apart." It seemed so long ago.

"You're kidding," Cope said.

"Seriously," McBride assured him. "FBI wants something on everybody—gives them leverage. They show a video to a guy humping some skirt in a motel and say, 'Is that your wife?' The guy's terrified, so the FBI says, 'Okay, now here's what we want you to do.' "

"Blackmail."

"Listen . . ." McBride began, pausing to watch the side mirror. The driver of the Lincoln had given a credit card to the ticket agent, the agent examining it like it might be counterfeit.

"You started to say something?" Cope said.

"I did?" McBride was in a quiet revelry. What in hell could the Feds do? Refuse to release all militia prisoners, and he'd hit 'em somewhere else. "Yeah, I was going to ask you how you thought the FBI and all the other Federals solve their cases? From *investigation*?" He made it sound ridiculous. "No, they do it mainly from informants and video. Spying on everyone. Everything goes on computer." Their lane started to move toward the ferry ramp.

"Uh-oh," Cope said, distracted by the show going on in his rearview mirror. "Mr. Lincoln's getting out of his car. They've pulled him aside."

"Well then," McBride said, "he's literally missed the boat. Should've kept his yap shut."

Now they saw a police car entering the terminal, which surprised McBride. He thought every available cruiser would have been converging up north around the bridge. Besides, didn't the Washington State ferries have their own security people?

Their lane had stopped dead three vehicles short of the ramp, and they heard the sound of an engine trying to start on a sick battery.

"Shit!" Cope said. "It's that blue pickup up ahead. God-damn thing's a crock." McBride looked out to see if they could pull out of the lane, but there was no room, everyone in tight. Horns started blaring, the blue pickup coughing and wheezing as if it were having an asthma attack, the driver immediately in front of the Excursion throwing up his hands in frustration.

McBride could tell that Cope was taking it as an omen. "Murphy's Law," he told Cope, an expression that Cope took as incontrovertible evidence that Lucky McBride, despite his earlier denial, believed in omens as much as anybody else. In the side mirror Cope saw a cop walking past the Lincoln.

"Maybe," Cope said, "he's gonna tell us to get the taillight fixed?"

"Stay calm," McBride said quietly.

"*You* stay calm," Cope retorted.

"You told me you had the balls for this?"

The policeman walking past the Lincoln continued on down lane four and stopped by the stalled blue pickup, two vehicles in front of Cope and McBride's SUV, as exhaust fumes from the lineup continued to choke the air.

"You see," McBride told Cope, "there was no need to panic. That blue pickup's the same model as our two smoke grenade boys were driving when they whacked that sheriff. That's probably why the cop's checking it out."

"Christ!" Cope said. "Maybe it's them!"

"It's not them. Relax."

"But the cop's checking their registration papers," Cope said, adding, "Bad enough the poor bastards are stalled."

"Fed's given their papers back," McBride pointed out, "and they're hooking up jump cables. They'll be fine."

Cope heard the pickup's motor roaring back to life, the cop waving at the ferry's load master to resume boarding, then walking back up the line past Cope's SUV toward his colleague, who by now had the driver of the Lincoln assuming the position against the car.

"Man," Cope groused, "I'll be glad when we're on the I-5 and headed nor—"

The cop had stopped. Pausing by the rear of their SUV, he was speaking into his walkie-talkie. A few seconds later lane four was halted again.

"Jesus Murphy!" Cope exclaimed.

"What's he looking at?" McBride asked, Cope's arm on the steering wheel blocking the SUV's driver side mirror.

"Got me beat," Cope answered.

"Jesus!" McBride said. "Don't tell me you didn't switch plates on this thing?"

"I'm not stupid, Major."

"Then don't call me major around here, goddammit!" There was a tone of alarm in McBride's voice that Cope hadn't heard before, and he saw McBride's right hand momentarily reach inside his jacket. "Doors unlocked?" McBride asked tersely, his eyes fixed on the rearview mirror.

"No."

"Then unlock 'em," McBride commanded, his brain racing. There was a click as Cope pushed the button, and McBride was out of the SUV, walking quickly toward the rear of the vehicle, smiling. "There a problem, officer?"

"What's that doing there?" the cop asked, pointing down at the rear bumper at a short trail of russet-red vine maple leaves.

"Oh that," McBride said easily. "We've been hunting. Must've caught something when I closed the door."

"You've been huntin'?"

"Yes."

"Uh-huh. Whereabouts?"

"Down the peninsula."

"Where, exactly?"

"Near Wodeen."

"Never heard of that."

It happened so fast, McBride's gun against his stomach,

that the cop was wide-eyed. "Get in the van," McBride ordered. "Now!"

McBride heard a woman yelling for police, but by now Cope, though terrified, had opened the slide panel, and McBride, close up against the cop, pushed him into the van, holding the Beretta's barrel hard up under his chin. "On the floor!" he said, yelling so loudly Cope squirmed.

"Oh shit! Man, what—"

"Shut up!" McBride told him. He shifted his gun hard against the cop's neck, unclipped the man's walkie-talkie from his belt and said: "Tell your buddy no one leaves the terminal. Next, I want a helo—fast. One pilot—no one else aboard. I don't like flying, so I want three chutes, just in case anything goes wrong. *And* I want it here in *ten* minutes or I'll blow your fucking head off." McBride jabbed the barrel farther into his hostage's neck. "You got that?"

The cop gave a mumbled yes.

"What happened?" Cope asked, his voice so strained it was a gasp.

"Bastard must've made me when he walked past us," McBride answered.

"Through tinted glass?" Cope asked skeptically, but McBride wasn't listening.

"Then he saw some vine maple stuck in our bumper."

"There was vine maple in the park!" Cope said.

"What?"

"There was vine maple in the park. All over the place."

Only now did it hit McBride why the cop had lucked out.

The cop asked if he could sit up.

"No. Make the call." Already they could hear sirens converging on the Kingston terminal.

"You won't get away with—" the cop began.

McBride lifted the gun, brought it down hard on the man's left cheek and heard bone crack. "Make the fucking call!"

Cope, whom McBride told to get down low, opened the glove compartment and took out his Colt .45, his hand shaking. He was whey-faced with fear. Had the legendary commander blundered? Maybe if he'd just followed his own advice and stayed calm, he might have bluffed his way out of the vine maple crap. But then the cop probably would have asked to open the rear door, and there was the Javelin's CLU and the ROE, not something your average motorist carried onto the ferry. What worried Cope now, however, was how they were going to get to the chopper helo, if it came. One man with a hostage—it could be done, had been done hundreds, maybe thousands, of times—but two men moving with one hostage? A federal sharpshooter could pick one of them off easily, and McBride had the advantage of being the one with the hostage. What would a sniper have to lose by taking him out? Cope wondered. And besides, maybe McBride didn't care about him? After all, he'd built a reputation for being a hard bastard. And who was more important to the movement?

With Whidbey Island Naval Air Station so close to the Kingston ferry, the Chief of Naval Operations was called in for advice. He was adamant. "No deal, Mr. President. Don't give them a chopper. Shoot them."

"And risk killing the police officer? You know I can't do that, Admiral."

"Mr. President," the CNO countered, "do you know how much this attack on the *Maui* has cost us? Not only the three men killed, but in terms of our international prestige? The most powerful national defense instrument of the most powerful nation on earth knocked out of the ring before it even got to open water. The Chinese, the Russians, the North Koreans—not to mention the goddamned towel heads from Saudi to Yemen, and every two-bit terrorist from Hezbollah to Japan's Aum Shinri Kyo—have suddenly been shown a window of opportunity that they never dreamed of—"

"I understand, Admiral. I'm as mad as you are about it, but I can't put an innocent law officer's life at risk at this juncture. Can you imagine what that would do to the morale of every law enforcement agency in the country, and just when we need all the help they can give us? No, we'll give them the chopper from . . ."

"Whidbey Island Naval Air Station," Brownlee prompted.

"Yes, from Whidbey," the President continued, "which as I understand it is about thirty or forty miles north of this ferry terminal."

"We can't track it below the radar screen, Mr. President," the admiral warned. "And visual sighting'll be impossible. There's a low pressure system coming in from the North Pacific, and Whidbey itself'll be socked in soon."

"Admiral, I will not risk that police officer's life. It's early in the game. Time's on our side."

"Not if they do a D.B. Cooper, Mr. President. A lot of the terrain up there is incredibly rugged."

"Who in hell's D.B. Cooper?"

"Hijacked a commercial jet," the admiral answered. "In Portland—sticks of dynamite strapped to his chest, or so the police believed. He demanded two parachutes and a lot of money. Dropped out in pitch-blackness somewhere over the Cascades. Never found him. He's legendary in the Northwest. And what we don't need now, sir, is another legend, a poster boy for any would-be terrorist."

"I agree, but for the moment they have us over a barrel. You'll have to go along with me on this, Admiral. At least for the time being."

"Yes, sir." The CNO paused. "I didn't mean to be disrespectful, sir."

"You weren't, Admiral. You're quite right to object. There's no denying it—we've taken a body blow on this one. But at least the officer will be able to give us a good description of these two after. That's another reason why we shouldn't risk losing him. In any event, we should get a good look at them as they head for the helo."

"Not if they move fast," the admiral said.

"Bear with me, Admiral. As soon as we feel we can, we'll exact our vengeance. I'll let you know the minute we've identified the perpetrators, and I'll seek your advice on how we should proceed. Rest assured of that."

"Very well, Mr. President."

Thirty seconds later the CNO was on the phone to the CO of Naval Air Station Whidbey and asking to be patched through to the chopper pilot.

"Chopper's already left, Admiral," the Whidbey CO told him.

"Well, I hope to God you didn't send the pilot in naked."

"No, sir. We didn't. Pilot's armed."

"Good."

In the White House the President buzzed Brownlee. "Michael, call Freeman. Have him hit Ruby Lake. I've taken enough crap for one day. Tell him to kick ass."

CHAPTER TWENTY-SIX

WITH LEROI DRIVING the red Hummer, Moorehead in the passenger seat, and four guards, including Sampson, in the back, Eleen was forced to sit on the floor. He was handcuffed to the rear of the driver's seat frame, hard up against the massive ribbed drive-train housing. Moorehead used his side of the housing as a table, studying the 1:24,000 scale map— better than an inch to a quarter mile—of the Stevens Pass area. Despite the poor quality of the copy, Moorehead could faintly make out sections of the famed 2,638-mile-long Pacific Coast Trail, which passed through twenty-four national forests and seven national parks, including Yosemite and Crater Lake, all the way from Mexico to the U.S.–Canada border and into British Columbia. On the Stevens Pass section, Moorehead saw that the PCT would offer escapees a route through what would otherwise have been the impenetrable barrier of Henry Jackson Wilderness and the cold, stream-veined high country of Chelan and Snohomish counties.

"Maybe he's heading for Canada," Leroi said, watching Moorehead marking the trail with pink highlighter.

"Maybe we'll end up in a ditch if you don't watch the goddamned road," the commandant retorted.

Sampson looked back through the mist rolling down from the high peaks around the Stevens Pass ski slopes and glimpsed the headlights of the Desert Storm Hummer that was carrying the two dogs. Turning back, he kicked Eleen hard in the ribs. "What do you think, moron? You think it's your Sergeant Mead we've run to ground or that Ju-Ju-Jubal? Eh?"

Eleen didn't respond, nor did Sampson expect him to. The militia leader had too much pride for that. Or, Sampson mused, was Eleen's silence the quietude of resignation, the high-profile POW steeling himself for what he must know was in the offing should they corner Mead or the young, homesick Jubal? A deal as old as warfare itself: "Give yourself up or we'll kill your comrade!"

In fact, for the moment at least, Eleen believed God was on his side, the poor quality of the 1:24,000 map an example of divine intervention—much of the Internet map's fine detail all but lost. Or was it simply the usual incompetence of the federal bureaucracy: spend a small fortune on mines and sensors for Fairchild, but don't update the HQ's printer?

As they crossed the bridge over Stevens Creek, the red Hummer's radio crackled. The driver of the second Hummer, the sound of the two dogs audible in the background, was informing Moorehead that the commandant's Hummer had gone right past the park ranger and Dillon, who had been standing by the road five hundred yards back near the branch-off to the Stevens Pass gravel pit.

"Must've been the fog," Leroi explained sheepishly to the other driver. "We'll head on back."

As the southerner slowed to make the U-turn, Moorehead glared up from his map at the rearview mirror. "Nice going, boys. With lookouts like you, we'll be lucky if the son of a bitch doesn't take *us* prisoner!"

"Windows are all misted up, sir," Sampson replied.

"Look, I know you're all beat from rounding up those scumbags, but whoever it is, Mead or Jubal, will have no intention of making it easy for us. They're gonna do everything possible to evade capture. Thanks to this A-hole we've got chained up here," Moorehead continued, unconsciously fingering his covered holster, "we've already got egg on our face from the mass outbreak he engineered. If we don't catch these two shitbags, we're gonna have omelet on our faces. And a few of you are going to end up in Adak. If you don't know where that is, ask Dillon."

"I know where it is," Sampson said.

"All right, then. Let's stay on the ball!"

Five minutes later, the damp forest air redolent with the smell of pine, the two dogs baying excitedly, Dillon and the park ranger led them to where the tracks began.

"Tracks go in for about a quarter mile," Dillon apprised Moorehead, his nose running from the cold, his tan leather boots stained dark from water. "Then they peter out down by the creek. We crossed, went up and down the bank a ways, but there was nothing."

"The dogs'll pick up the scent," Moorehead assured him.

The ranger elected to return to his station with Dillon's exhausted squad, leaving eight guards from the camp under Moorehead's command. The first two went ahead with the two dogs, followed by Moorehead and Dillon abreast, the remaining four following up the rear. The last of these, Leroi, was handcuffed to Eleen, ostensibly so the prisoner couldn't free himself, but in part, Leroi suspected, because he hadn't paid close enough attention to the road, missing the park ranger and Dillon in the fog.

"What makes you so sure that's it's one of the POWs?" Dillon asked Moorehead.

"Because if they were picked up, or stopped someone on the highway near the camp within a half hour of escaping, this is about where they'd be—in the middle of the Cascades. They sure as hell wouldn't have stayed in the desert with choppers and God knows what else buzzing overhead unless they were stupid. And Eleen back there doesn't train his scumbags to be stupid."

"But they could have headed east, toward Idaho," Dillon said.

"Uh-huh," Moorehead allowed, unclipping the safety strap on his holster, making sure the 9mm moved easily. "Why'd you think I let 'em see Sommers lying in the yard?" Dillon remembered the crude sign hung about the dead POW's neck, but only now realized it had been put there on Moorehead's orders. "To let those scumbags see what happens when you head east," Moorehead continued. "To show 'em we had Spokane locked up tighter'n a drum. That's how I know they're in these mountains, alone or—" He slowed, watching one of the dogs, the pit bull, splashing eagerly across the creek. "You develop an intuition in this job," he boasted to Dillon. "You know what I do before I go to sleep?"

Dillon thought of an answer, but knew it would take him straight to Adak.

"I lie there imagining how *I'd* bust out of Fairchild." He looked across at Dillon. "That surprise you? Thinking how to bust out of my own camp?"

"Well—no, sir. I mean, er—"

"Know one of the things you must never do as a warden, Dillon?"

"What's that, sir?" Dillon wasn't really interested. His face was freezing and he yearned to get out of the mist-shrouded high country back to the warmth of the eastern desert.

"The thing you must never do," Moorehead went on, "is fall into the trap of routine. Now don't misunderstand me. Routine's good for discipline, but it's a God-sent opportunity for convicts. That's why so many of our POWs got away from the Germans. The krauts were suckers for routine. Everything strictly by the clock, on the hour, half hour, or whatever. Get it?"

"Yes, sir."

"What you do," Moorehead explained, clenching his fist for emphasis, "is take your cons by surprise. Send in a search squad at 0312 hours, get what I mean? Odd times. Catch 'em off balance."

Dillon was tempted to add, "Like Eleen's boys caught you off balance." Instead he responded dutifully, "Yes, I see, sir."

"Another thing, you should never—Hello!"

The black-and-white pit bull, the ugliest dog Dillon had ever seen, had picked up the scent.

"Which one?" Moorehead called out.

"Jubal!" shouted the handler.

"I'll be . . ." Moorehead's face flushed with excitement and surprise. "It's our 'little bundle of joy.' Well, *good* for him! Full marks, eh, Dillon?"

"Yes, sir," Dillon said, and wondered whether this was Moorehead's admiration for Jubal or Moorehead congratulating himself on having predicted the POW's escape route.

Everybody, except Eleen, was energized by the pit bull straining forward on the long, retractable leash, sniffing eagerly above the crust of light snow.

Then just as suddenly the dog seemed confused, running aimlessly in circles around the moss-dappled trunk of a Douglas fir.

"Stupid dog!" Moorehead harrumphed, pulling the string tight on the hood of his parka, which, given his barrel-chested build, had the effect of giving him a comical roly-poly appearance.

Leroi yanked impatiently on the chain that bound him to Eleen, while yelling at the dog handler, "Look up the tree, you dork! Dog might've treed a fucking bear!"

"Watch your language!" Moorehead snapped.

"Sorry, sir."

"Give me that map!" Moorehead demanded.

Eleen prayed that his enemy wouldn't look too closely at the map, or that if he did, he would not see why the pit bull had become confused.

Leroi elbowed Eleen hard in the ribs. "We oughta sic the dogs onto you. Let 'em tear your dick off!"

Eleen, in a reversal of his determination to keep still and not draw attention to himself, saw a way of distracting Moorehead from a closer examination of the poorly printed map. Stopping suddenly, he asked Leroi. "Are you jealous you don't get as much tail as Mormons?"

Leroi was astonished. He'd rarely heard the Mormon say anything, let alone use a vulgar word such as "tail."

Eleen continued, "You know, Leroi, it wouldn't matter if you *were* a Mormon. You wouldn't get any. You're too damned ugly!"

The guards in front were equally startled, and waited for Leroi's response. It came with another vicious jab to Eleen's ribs, and a right cross that smashed into Eleen's jaw, knocking him down, but the handcuffs dragged Leroi down with him as well.

"What the hell?" Moorehead thrust the map at an open-mouthed Dillon and strode back to the prisoner and his guard, who were thrashing about in the sugarlike snow, Leroi's free hand pounding the militiaman. "Get up, you two! By God! Here!" he yelled at the other guards. "Help me for Christsake. He's gone berserk!"

CHAPTER TWENTY-SEVEN

AMID THE ROAR of its two big Allison turbos, the Osprey-22's sudden change from vertical to horizontal flight was different from anything most of Freeman's assembled twenty-man ALERT troop had experienced, the nose of the aircraft not dipping, as was often the case in a helo. But these men had been selected not only for their air, land, and sea fighting expertise, but also for their ability to adapt quickly to any situation, and they did so now. Faces streaked with camouflage paint, they were about to go into action again, and it was for action they lived, none more so than Freeman, who headed the line.

Behind him were David Brentwood, Aussie Lewis on the right side of the aircraft, Sal Salvini, Andy Shear, and Welshman Choir Williams. The latter had never lost his accent, despite his ten years residence in the U.S. and having graduated—like Brentwood, Aussie, and Sal—from the torture otherwise known as the SEAL training school at Corando. The remaining fourteen men of Freeman's twenty Fritz-helmeted special force consisted of seven ex-Rangers and seven ex-Delta men, Freeman having deliberately chosen seven from each cadre of retired commandos to infuse the "stick" of twenty with a sense of fierce, if friendly, competition. Brentwood, Lewis, Williams, and Salvini, however, needed no such incentive to hone their cutting edge. Having been on so many missions together, they had developed the kind of sixth sense an elite team often achieves after performing in a host of different wartime situations. Their guiding motto was Freeman's *"L'audace, I'audace, toujours l'audace!"* Audacity, audacity, always audacity. Though fit, Freeman, now that he was getting older, had also adopted a football coach's telling observation about the inimitable Walter Payton—that Payton was there for every practice when he felt like it and when he didn't feel like it, a daily training schedule tougher than that of the U.S. Marines.

The Osprey encountered a bumpy ride up to the Cascades, something Salvini had never gotten used to, despite all the times he'd been flown into an op. "How long now, General?" he asked Freeman.

"Thirty-two minutes, Sal. You going to bring up your lunch?"

"I'll be fine, sir," he replied, wiping his mouth on the sleeve of his green and khaki mountain smock and adjusting his Kevlar vest.

"Like something to eat, Sal?" Aussie Lewis asked, winking across at Choir Williams and the Delta men. "Side o' bacon? Fried eggs?"

Sal, the New Yorker from the Bronx, responded, to chortles of laughter, with his middle finger. "You Aussie prick! I'll—"

"All right, boys," Freeman cut in, "let's go over it once more. Brentwood, Aussie, Choir, Sal, Shear, and I will lead. Delta left flank, Rangers right . . ."

Using a laser clip-pen pointer, Freeman indicated the three three-sided cement buildings that formed a triangle atop a ten-foot-high rise, twenty yards between each of the buildings, the sides of which seemed to be about thirty feet long. The forested location had clearly been chosen, Freeman noted, to keep the buildings well out of sight, and was atop a rise for the best possible defense against any intruder.

"Remember," he said, shouting above the noise of the engines and the vibration of the Osprey's four stretchers at the rear of the aircraft, "it's raining buckets at the foot of the mountains, so though it's daylight, we'll have very little light. But that, gentlemen, is precisely why the last thing on these idiots' minds will be an attack, especially an attack from the air, in heavy rain to boot. Now, once again—we go in low across Ruby Lake, pilot'll bring us down on this small beach. Use this isolated jetty near this four-wheel-drive dirt road that leads through the woods to the compound. But *we do not* use the road—we go in through the woods. SATPIX contours suggest a one-in-twenty incline. My team will go for the building at the apex of the triangle. But remember, before we five hit it, we'll wait thirty seconds, maximum sixty, until you two teams on our left and right flank reach your respective targets. Above all, remember, *do not* use the road. Go through the woods. SATPIX tells us that using the road would allow you to be seen from the apex building, if not from the other two left and right behind it."

It was pedantic—they all knew what to do—but Freeman was known for his meticulous preparation. It saved attack lives.

"Sir?" Ranger leader Rick Logan said. "Do we have confirmation of surveillance—"

The Osprey suddenly fell for over two hundred feet, a gut-wrenching shear that had everyone, including the plane's four medics, grabbing for the overhead hold-ons, despite the fact that everyone was already secured by shoulder harness and seat belt. Sal, throwing up, had one hand on the hold-on, his other grasping a Ziploc bag.

"Can't take him anywhere!" Aussie quipped to young Andy Shear.

"We do not have confirmation," came Freeman's shouted answer to the Ranger leader. "But we must assume the worst case, Rick—that they do have the entire road under surveillance cameras. Which is why I've instructed the pilot to land on the lakeshore, well away from the road. Last SATPIX we have, before this torrent swept down from the Rockies, also shows six vehicles, all four-by-fours, pickups and SUVs. I want two men from Rangers, two from Delta, to immobilize these six vehicles."

A phalanx of hands shot up.

Freeman grinned. "I abrogate my responsibility at this point. I'll leave Ranger and Delta leaders to select your two fire teams for this plum assignment."

"*Immobilize* them, General?" Logan shouted. "Or blow the bastards up?"

The general joined the laughter. They all knew they were going to win. Might be sticky moments—there always were—but they'd win. "The latter, Rick," Freeman responded. "Blow the bastards up!" The plane dropped again and the general waited till the turbulence wasn't so violent. "I will now quote a poem by George Patton, apropos to our mission. Are you ready?"

"Ready!" came the roar of eighteen commandos, Sal busy barfing once more.

Freeman assumed his oratorical stance. "It was written, gentlemen, after the battle for the German town of Houffalize.

"Oh little town of Houffalize,
    How still we see thee lie;
    Above thy steep and battered streets
    The aeroplanes sail by.
    Yet in thy dark streets shineth
    Not any goddamned light;
    The hopes and fears of all thy years,
    Were blown to hell last night."

A roar of laughter surged through the Osprey, even Salvini managing a weak smile.

The aircraft, now beyond the Cascades, headed over the rolling hills and the great expanse of the Columbia River basin toward Spokane and the militia stronghold in the dense forests that spilled down from the Cabinet Mountains. There, the rugged beauty of the Rockies and the deep, glacier-gouged lakes gave birth to Idaho's appeal as the "way the rest of America used to be," the panhandle's forests, receiving up to sixty inches of rain a year, still the home of cougar, moose, and grizzly bear.

"Thank God for that!" Salvini said as the Osprey passed out of the Cascades-induced turbulence. The New Yorker laid his head back, eyes closed, his face still a chalky pallor, his voice audible only to Aussie Lewis and Choir Williams.

"Get some water in ya, mate," Aussie Lewis advised. "Reckon you must've lost a quart. You can throw up again when we hit the Rockies!"

"You're gonna get it!" Salvini told him. He said it good-naturedly, which was just as well—otherwise, the Delta and Ranger men nearby might have regarded Lewis as a singularly mean character. Nothing, however, could have been further from the truth, his seemingly perverse comments an inverse measure of his affection for Salvini and the other members of his team. All six ALERT, which included Freeman himself, bore the wounds of war, and their verbal repartee was as well known to each of them as were their moves in combat.

"So," Sal said, feeling decidedly better, "Alex let you come, Aussie?" He meant Aussie's strikingly beautiful, dark-eyed wife, Alexsandra, whom Aussie had met during the U.N.–U.S. mission to Siberia. Sal's suggestion that Aussie was under his wife's thumb was an anathema to the macho Lewis.

"Yeah," Aussie retorted. "She let me *come*." He winked at Choir and Andy Shear. "Anywhere I want. Usually in bed!"

"Filthy bastard!" came Sal's return serve.

"Drink your water, you bloody dago!"

Sal grinned. "Think I will," he said, nonchalantly unclipping his S4 canteen. Selected and purchased off the shelf by Freeman at his own cost, the S4 contained a combination filtration/disinfection unit and was way ahead of what the regular forces had. It was only now being studied by the DOD for possible use by the U.S. armed forces in the future.

The pilot's voice crackled in the speaker above the Ranger and Delta teams. "Sorry for the rough ride, guys, but we should have a reasonably even flight to your target area. Maybe a little choppy around the lake, some lightning, but other than that it should be okay."

Aussie raised his eyebrows at Sal, who was chugging at his S4. "Hear that, Sal? *Lightning!*"

Twenty minutes later, however, twenty-four miles from target, the jokes and ribbing died, each of the twenty commandos rechecking weapons and equipment. Freeman, ever conscious of the smallest detail, told Sal to top up his canteen from the medic's distilled water tank aft of the plane, since the sloshing of a half-empty canteen could give a man away as surely as any loose buckle or strap on what was supposed to be a silent approach. The noise of the rain on the fuselage was so loud now that it sounded, as Aussie noted, like they were going through "a bloody car wash."

"Don't worry, boyo," Choir told Aussie. "It'll help muffle the noise of the engines."

"I'm not worried, you Welsh wanker," Aussie retorted, testing the new transparent magazine Freeman had issued him for his Heckler & Koch submachine gun.

"What a terribly vulgar man you are," said Choir, his soft, lilting voice more that of a tenor than of a veteran of Britain's Special Air Service, where he'd first met Aussie Lewis, Sal, and David Brentwood on the U.K.–U.S. exchange program.

The red light pulsed to life above Freeman. For a HALO jump, this would be the signal for the stick of twenty commandos to stand, readying themselves for the door; but in the Osprey, all would remain seated until both the critical horizontal to vertical shift and vertical landing had been completed.

"Sure our driver knows where it is?" Rick Logan joshed.

"Yeah," Aussie joined in. "I don't fancy a swim with all this gear."

"Don't sweat it," David Brentwood said. The Medal of Honor winner had been silent for almost the entire flight. "With all that hot air, Aussie, you'd float."

"Cheeky prick!"

Suddenly, the pitch of the Osprey's two six-thousand-horsepower Allisons seemed to rise, or was it merely their change from horizontal to the vertical position? One of the Delta commandos, unused to the Osprey's noise, and more comfortable in what he called "proper" helos, betrayed a momentary anxiety above and beyond that normally felt by any soldier about to engage the enemy. Freeman spotted it immediately, announcing to everyone, "Don't sweat the racket, boys. Osprey's new baffles make it one of the quietest birds we've got. You hear a lot of stuff inside, but outside, and in this rain, it'll be barely detectable to anyone on the lake."

"We're not landing on the fucking lake," a Delta commando, Perez, told his comrade.

"Well, you're a wetback," said his comrade, a black Delta they called Ali.

"Fuck you, gringo!" Perez said.

"Anyway," Ali continued, the noise now directly overhead—and much louder, in his opinion, than the Hueys they were used to deplaning from. "The old man is the first out. Only goddamn general that is."

The water was now streaming down the windows, the heat

from the engines and the twin props' downblast turning the rain into a wildly swirling mist.

"Can't see a friggin' thing," Perez said.

"I see a boat," Ali said.

"Very funny."

"No, man," Ali said. "I see a boat. A rowboat. Over there!" He was tapping the water-streaked perspex, Perez straining his neck. Now Perez saw it, a faintly discernible blur as the Osprey began its descent. "Yeah—it's tied up to a jetty," he said with obvious relief, the small strip of beach now coming into view, dark green forest behind it.

"Never said it wasn't," Ali replied with a grin, giving Perez a friendly jab in the ribs. "All I said was it's a boat, man."

CHAPTER TWENTY-EIGHT

THERE WAS A soft thump beneath them and a green light came on. *"L'audace!"* said Freeman, and they all rose, led by Freeman, Brentwood, Aussie, Choir Williams, Sal, and young Andy Shear. Then came Rick Logan and his seven Rangers. Then the seven Deltas, including Ali and Perez, who'd been assigned the task of "immobilizing" the six vehicles parked haphazardly within the triangle formed by the three double-storied cement buildings. Right now, however, no buildings were in sight, only the three-hundred-yard-long crescent of sandy beach.

As the Osprey's muffled engines died, its rotors sent a shudder across Ruby Lake, the ever-widening ripples invading the steady hiss of the rain that was pockmarking the hitherto gray slatelike calm of water. The twenty commandos ran out in column, the latter broken only by a gap between the ALERTs, the seven Rangers and seven Deltas, their exit remarkably quiet due to noiseless kit and Vibram-soled combat boots. They smelled the pine and fir trees, the rain unabated, and heard a roll of thunder like approaching artillery coming down from Cedar Mountain, the monolith itself obscured by the unceasing downpour.

A hundred yards up the beach, the small jetty jutted out into the lake, and now they could smell wood smoke wafting toward them. Running at the head of the column, Freeman was the first to see what looked like an old man at the end of the jetty.

"He's fishing," Brentwood whispered into his throat mike.

"Check him out!" Freeman ordered. "Take Aussie with you. Two minutes max."

While the commando stick, appearing from the Osprey pilot's vantage point like a khaki snake, moved quickly along the beach for another twenty yards, it then wheeled to the left, heading for the beach-forest interface, the column breaking up into its three squads.

Aussie and Brentwood reached the lone figure bundled up against the wild weather. It was testimony to the Osprey's noise-damping engineering and the commandos' training, Aussie thought, that the figure on the jetty hadn't moved, presumably not having heard the commandos running up the beach behind him.

The two ALERT were five yards away when the solitary bundle came alive, a green toque popping up, revealing a young, pimpled teenager of indeterminate sex. A moment later the frightened voice revealed it was a girl, perhaps fifteen or sixteen, startled by the sudden appearance of the armed soldiers. Aussie held his beloved Heckler & Koch at the ready, while Brentwood quickly rummaged through the wicker tackle basket he saw by her side, not expecting to find anything dangerous but remembering from Freeman's pre-op intel briefing that it had apparently been a tackle basket that had been used to carry smoke grenades down to the Hood Canal Bridge, the smoke terrifying people, sending everyone stampeding off the bridge when the *Maui* was hit because they thought it was poisonous gas.

There was a pack of Winston cigarettes, a leftover salami sandwich in foil, a screw glass jar of live worms, and a hapless six-inch trout. Brentwood felt it. Stiff and cold. She'd been here a while. "Should've thrown that back!" he told her.

"Are you guys militia?"

"No," Aussie said. He was sure she wasn't a plant—a lookout—and he didn't like to be gruff with kids, but in younger days he'd seen buddies overseas killed by children. Once bitten, twice gruff. "Where's your lighter?" he asked her, indicating the cigarettes. Smallest detail! Freeman had always told them.

"Don't use a lighter," she told him, obviously feeling more comfortable now. "Are you guys Federals, then?"

"That your rowboat tied up?"

"Yeah."

"You live on the lake?"

"Uh-huh, down there 'bout half a mile—"

"You hop in and go home," Brentwood told her. "Okay?" Brentwood had a kind face, clear blue eyes. And he was holding a machine gun.

"Okay," she said easily, and began untying the boat. By the time Aussie Lewis and Brentwood rejoined Freeman a minute later, the girl was already thirty yards or so offshore.

"Kid fishing," Brentwood told Freeman. "No problem."

Freeman nodded and, checking on either side to make sure Delta and the Rangers were set, he spoke softly into his throat mike, "Let's do it."

The seven-six-seven line moved into the sodden forest that spilled down from Cedar Mountain to the lake. The sound of the rain, though muted by the forest's canopy, was nevertheless loud enough to dampen the noise of the commandos as they made their way through the thick woods, any sound they inadvertently made reduced also by the thick, wet carpet of pine needles. Fifty yards in, Freeman quickly ordered a halt, and though he no longer had the seven Delta or seven Rangers in sight, he knew that all the commandos would be listening for the slightest telltale sound, and straining their eyes for any trip wires or signs of other booby traps. Which is why he'd had the three groups pause at the beach-forest interface, each man adjusting to the sudden change in light intensity from the Osprey's artificially lit interior to the dreary light of the rain-streaked daylight.

Despite the close proximity of his troops, no one could hear anyone else breathing, every man in top physical condition. Not even the sprint from the plane, a hundred yards or so down the beach through wet sand, had winded them.

"Proceed," Freeman ordered softly into his throat mike, adjusting the volume on his earpiece.

"Roger that," came the replies from the Rangers' Rick Logan and Delta leader Norm Assmeir, a six-footer and holder of the Special Forces heavyweight belt. A drunk in the sergeants' mess had once asked Assmeir why he didn't change his name. Norm Assmeir had placed his glass down carefully on the bar and, speaking as softly as he was now, asked his questioner, "Do you have a dental plan?"

Everybody had gotten the message.

It was Assmeir, though still undercover, who was the first to see the foot of the rise where the forest abruptly ended, giving way to a sharp, untreed incline that looked almost vertical. It was covered only in broad-bladed grass that had obviously been mowed, the gradient impossible to climb even for the most rugged four-by-four. Assmeir waited till he glimpsed the rest of his Delta team, ready to break out of the forest, up the incline.

He heard Freeman's voice, a whisper in his earpiece. "You ready, Delta?"

"Delta's ready."

"Logan?"

"Rangers ready," Logan said, glancing quickly twenty yards to his right beyond the last man in his team, toward the only break the SATPIX had shown in the sharp rise: a ten-foot-wide culvert where the dirt road from the beach passed through. The smell of wood smoke was very strong now.

"Go!" Freeman commanded quietly, and the commandos broke from the forest, weapons "waisted" with one hand, the other clawing the wet-slicked grass, the downpour heavier now, the rain drumming on their helmets. The daylight was suddenly brighter, not just because they were out of the forest, but because spotlights in the trees all around the rise had come on, immediately followed by the sound, an ear-piercing, unbroken alarm.

"Sensors!" someone in Assmeir's team called, but no one answered, everyone too busy surmounting the rise. There was an explosion, a scream, spumes of sand-streaked black soil shooting skyward. A Ranger was dead. Another explosion, more earth erupting, and a man's arm—it was young Andy Shear who'd been hit, his severed limb spinning high in the air, blood everywhere. Shear's face was chalk-white, Choir Williams pulling him down.

Freeman was shouting, "Stop! Minefield!" his voice almost blowing the men's earpieces off. "Pull back! We'll go up the road. Follow me!"

Choir, with Shear, scrambled back down the incline, Shear still too much in shock to believe what had happened. Freeman ordered the Osprey's medics up to the jetty and designated Aussie and Sal to cover Choir as the Welshman tried to get Andy to the beach. Now they all heard the feral barking of dogs, the enraged animals obviously being held back, but just as clearly on the verge of being set loose if the commandos reached the three buildings.

In a rough V formation—Freeman and Brentwood leading, Assmeir and his five remaining Delta to the left, Logan and his other six Rangers to his right—the remaining commandos ran through the culvert toward the three triangular-shaped buildings.

Choir, cradling his carbine, stopped halfway down the road to the beach, tightening the tourniquet around what remained of Andy Shear's upper arm. Aussie and Sal were crouching low, Aussie's HK on automatic, Sal's USA5 shotgun, equipped with a twenty-round drum mag, ready to cut down any Jap, as the ex-Special Forces traditionally referred to their enemies, who tried to thwart the four men's dash to the beach.

As Freeman's fifteen broke up into three assault teams of five apiece for the other two triangular buildings, Freeman was the first to reach the door on the ground floor of the first building. Immediately seeing that there was no way of breaking in the door with a body rush, he yelled, "Semtex!" stepping aside as Brentwood quickly pushed the puttylike charge against the lock, setting its five-second detonator.

"Clear!" he shouted, the five of them taking cover behind the adjoining sides of the triangular building.

Glancing up, Freeman glimpsed a bearded face through a double glazed window and fired his HK as the *whoomp* of the Semtex imploded the heavy door, the window spiderwebbed from his burst of 5.56mm but not penetrated. Bulletproof.

The bastards were ready too, he thought, and clearly dug in tight.

First into the smoke-laced unlit ground floor living room/kitchen, Freeman fired an "insurance" burst up the stairwell, the bullets ricocheting off metal steps slotted into the building's cement walls. He tried the light switch by the door. Nothing. There was a wine-red sofa, a coffee table strewn with newspapers, spilled coffee mugs, and a big screen TV still on but without sound. Through the bitter taste coming from the Semtex's residual smoke, Freeman, Brentwood, and the three Rangers in his team could detect the odor of fried onions and freshly brewed coffee. Brentwood and the three Rangers approached the other four doors on the ground floor. As Freeman advanced toward the stairway, Brentwood and the other three commandos on the ground floor shot out the four doors, which collapsed inward. The rooms were empty.

Brentwood pulled his throat mike closer. "Careful, General." He'd no sooner warned Freeman, who was now approaching the second floor, than the general saw two small metal rings poking out from the dim hallway atop the stairs, the two metal rings constituting the business end of a double-barreled shotgun. Snatching a flash-bang from his vest load, he pulled the pin, tossing the grenade into the hallway. There was a tremendous flash of light, a shiver passing through the metal stairwell from the head-dunning noise. The next instant Freeman was in the hallway, the militiaman in a daze but still holding the double-barreled 12-gauge. Before he could pull either of the twin triggers, Freeman unleashed a burst that punched the man back along the hallway, one of his shotgun barrels belching orange-white flame. The buckshot hit Freeman full in the chest, knocking him down even as he unleashed a long six-round burst that all but decapitated the militiaman. The blood bubbled from the man's throat, dark in the hallway, the only illumination coming from a small skylight in one of the four rooms whose door, unlike the other three along the hallway, was open.

Freeman, his Kevlar having taken the impact of the buckshot, nevertheless lay winded, and knew he'd been badly bruised. By now the other four commandos, Brentwood at their head, were stepping over Freeman and the body, making for the closed doors. In the near distance they could hear the gut-punching thumps of Semtex, flash-bangs, and HE grenades going off as the other ten commandos went about clearing the remaining two buildings and destroying the militia vehicles. With each of his three companions ready, Brentwood gave the signal, and after their short but intense combined automatic fire, the last three doors gave way. Empty.

Freeman, using his HK as a prop, hauled himself grumpily to his feet, adjusting his radio earpiece, which had come loose during his fall. "Take that 12-gauge away from him!" he told Brentwood. "Bastard goes into spasm, his goddamn finger'll pull the other trigger. Blow my legs off!" A surge of static invaded his ear as he adjusted the volume control, regaining contact with Logan and Assmeir.

"Empty?" Freeman asked.

"Yes, sir," Logan confirmed. "Same with you, General?"

"It's the same here," Assmeir cut in. "Gone. Vanished."

"What the—" Freeman began. "Those dogs barking?"

"All bullshit, General. From speakers. My boys found all the gear in Apex 2."

Brentwood had carefully removed the dead militiaman's fingers from the inside of the trigger guard, and for the first time noticed that he was an old man. "In his seventies, if he's a day," Brentwood said. "I'd say he was the caretaker."

"What?"

"Caretaker. Too old to run. Others have flown the coop?"

Freeman remembered the smell of freshly brewed coffee, onions, and— "Must've missed 'em by what, fifteen, twenty minutes?" In the near silence of the cement buildings, all that the commandos could hear was the steady drumming of the rain and overflowing downspouts.

After the body of the Delta commando killed by the mine had been retrieved, Freeman led his men down the dirt road to the forlorn-looking beach, from which the two medics had quickly taken Andy Shear to the Osprey. They boarded the plane solemnly and no one spoke as the aircraft rose from the beach in a giant billow of yellow wet sand, the noise of the twin Allisons muffled by the incessant rain, the commandos' silence mute testimony to the dismal failure of their mission. "It was that damned kid!" Aussie said.

"How?" David Brentwood asked. "I frisked her."

"We didn't check the boat," Aussie replied. "Could've been in the damned boat when we were positioning overhead. Cell phone—whatever—in the boat. *I* should have checked the damn boat."

David Brentwood, a pang in his gut for all his toughness, suddenly remembered, "I didn't check her toque. Could've had a cell under there."

Freeman put an end to the others' self-recriminations. "I fucked up. Should've known there were mines."

"No way you could know that, General."

Freeman switched on the SATPIX map, its fluorescent backlight giving his face a sickly pallor, despite the greenish brown splotches of camouflage paint. He was staring at the SATPIX of the Ruby Lake compound. "I screwed up."

Despite the noise of the rain and engines, the commandos could hear the distinct *burr* of a body bag's zipper, assuming it was the Delta man killed by the mine. But it was Andy Shear's body, the Delta man's corpse already bagged before the plane had taken off.

Even among the hardened survivors of the futile raid, the news that young Andy Shear hadn't made it was a jolt.

Everyone, including the medics, had thought that despite the horrific amputation, Shear should have survived. But he'd gone into a particularly severe shock. And, together with what the medic's report would describe as an "extraordinary exsanguination," or rate of blood loss, it had done him in.

Two fatalities—ten percent of his force—an unacceptable rate of loss for any commander. And for what? Nothing. His sole achievement had been the death of a militia caretaker, Freeman thought, facing the final ignominy of discovering that the old man had a prosthetic leg. All they had discovered was what a lone policeman on a bicycle could have found out: the militia from Ruby Lake had gone.

He called Brownlee, one of the most difficult calls he'd ever made. He didn't dress it up, didn't blame the kid fishing from the jetty who might have tipped them off, and simply conceded he'd blown it.

"Not quite what you'd call a knockout," Brownlee responded. It was mean but it was true. "Besides," Brownlee told the President later, "while he did kill one militiaman, a pensioner by all accounts, he lost two of his own. For squat. I told him to disband his *team* and go home."

The President agreed and, though clearly disappointed by the failure of the clandestine mission to give him a win, or at least to divert the American public's attention from the attack on the *Maui*, the Chief Executive of the United States could not help enjoying the thought that the once-renowned general had fallen flat on his face.

CHAPTER TWENTY-NINE

THE SOLE PILOT of the November "Rescue" Huey made one pass over Kingston Ferry Terminal, the lines of vehicles stretched out beneath him like so many micro toys in the process of being vacuumed up by the white-and-green-striped ferry. A half-dozen police cars flanked lane four, the flashers blinking weakly beneath the metallic sky as the low-pressure front on Washington State's west coast edged down Puget Sound. Gyrating with the turn of the "Rescue" painted chopper, the blacktop apron of the ferry terminal appeared as a man-made island bordered east of Kingston by the shark-colored water of the sound and to the west by the dense, greenish-black forests of upper Kitsap Peninsula, which spread westward for ten miles to the very edge of Hood Canal.

On the second pass the pilot sighted a landing zone the police had marked off with yellow crime-scene tape.

McBride, still holding his gun against the cop's head, hadn't heard the *wokka wokka* sound of the chopper until it was directly overhead, a phenomenon that had puzzled him since 'Nam. His fellow militiamen up at the lake had remarked on the same thing with the ROE—that despite the noise of the whirlybirds, they were almost on top of you before you knew it.

"They're gonna see us!" Cope shouted above the roar of the descending chopper. "They're gonna see our faces!"

"Listen to me!" McBride said sharply, meeting panic with authority. If he didn't calm Cope down, he knew it would be an unmitigated disaster.

"We haven't got anything!" Cope continued frantically, meaning they didn't have anything they could use as masks.

"Wind down the passenger side window an inch or two," McBride ordered, "but no more. C'mon, hurry up!" His gun in one hand, McBride took hold of the federal's collar with the other. "You tell your buddy I want two pairs of panty hose brought down here. Quickly. Tell him he's to stand away from the vehicle and slide 'em through over the top of the passenger side window. Anyone tries to push something else through, like a Taser, and you're a dead man. Got it?"

"Got it!" the policeman shouted, frightening Cope who hadn't expected such a robust reply from a federal on the floor with a 9mm against his temple. Now the federal was giving his buddy instructions over the roar of the Huey's downblast, gravel and dust peppering the SUV like grape shot amid a rush of aviation gas fumes. "The federal's buddy said it'd take a while to get goddamn stockings."

"He's got three minutes!" McBride shouted.

"He wants *what*?" another cop at the ticket booth asked.

"Stockings. Reckon the prick's gonna use 'em as masks. He's given us two minutes."

"Fuck 'im! We'll take all the time we need. Tell 'im we don't carry hosiery in—"

"Get them!" cut in the Kitsap sheriff in charge. "No point in antagonizing him. We've got women and kids around here. I don't want a goddamn shoot-out." The sheriff himself approached a well-dressed woman in lane five and asked her.

"Certainly not!"

"Ma'am," the sheriff said, holding his hat against the Huey's rotorblast. "We've got a situation here."

"He's going to kill your man anyway, isn't he?" she retorted archly.

"We don't know that, ma'am. We're just trying—"

"No. Your man's seen them. He can identify them. They're going to kill him."

The sheriff was flabbergasted. She was probably right, but if he refused to meet the terrorists' demands and it was a bloodbath, as the sheriff in charge he'd be responsible.

He asked another woman, and, red-faced, asking him to avert his glance, she obliged.

When McBride got the two panty hose, which the sheriff himself pushed gingerly through the narrow slit above the tinted window, he told Cope to cut them into three sections. Three masks.

Next, McBride told his hostage to take off his boots, shirt, and hat. Cope, who a minute ago, amid the roaring of the chopper, spurts of static from the walkie-talkie, and the maelstrom of objects kicked up by the rotors, had been in near panic, began to laugh. McBride, veteran though he was, was unsure whether Cope was cracking up or just in a rush of nervous release.

"Man!" Cope shouted above the noise that now included a baby's scream, "You're always one step ahead, Major. Yessirree, Bob, they ain't gonna know which of us is which!"

"First," McBride said, "we get them to load the ROE and the CLU aboard the Huey."

"Won't that be too heavy?"

Lucky McBride, for the first time in the mission, was stymied. Was Cope really that stupid or was he trying to be the joker? Ease the tension maybe?

"Jesus, Cope, a Huey can carry ten men—fully armed!"

"I've never been in a chopper."

McBride's voice, like Cope's, sounded nasal coming through the mask. "Don't worry about it. When we take off there'll be a lurch, you'll think your gut's jumped to your throat, then it's all right. Now listen . . ." It was impossible for McBride to tell by Cope's distorted appearance whether he was listening or not.

"Yeah yeah," Cope assured him.

"All right, give me the Magellan from the glove box."

Cope passed him the handheld GPS.

"Good, now when we move to the chopper, we keep in a tight clutch, left hand on one another's belt." He jabbed the cop. "You hear that?"

"Yeah."

"They won't know who to shoot at anyway," Cope said. And it was true. When the three sheriff's deputies detailed to load the ROE and the CLU tried to ID who was who, two of them thought they knew which one was the hostage, but all three facial features were distorted by the nylon masks, the deputies' visual check further compounded by items of clothing switched around among the three men inside the van.

As the clutch of three men moved quickly toward the Huey, the Kitsap Country sheriff could see that all three men had handguns. But which one was loaded and whose had been swapped around?—everything made more complicated by the veil of face-stinging debris kicked up by the chopper. Which one was their colleague? Of course all the armchair quarterbacks at home watching the TV newscast said they'd known which one was the cop. But they weren't there, and the federals and Kitsap sheriff who were didn't have the luxury of time to run back videotape of the news footage until *after* the Huey had lifted off and disappeared into the sea of gray stratus.

Out of that rain-laden sky came McBride's flagrant demand to the White House. In essence, it was the same demand as Pete Rainor and Mel Haley had made before the Boeing fiasco: Release all POWs from Fairchild—or else.

But this time with the *Maui* crippled, three submariners dead, and the unspoken terror of what would have happened if *Maui*'s Sherwood Forest had gone up, the militia had shown the federals just how much damage they could inflict.

Millions of militiamen, all the way from the big units, such as MOM, to the smaller sabotage groups in the Hawaiian Islands pressing for independence from the contiguous forty-eight states, were electrified by the news of the "shoot and scoot," or, as old-timers called it, "hit and run," attack that had knocked out the federals' leviathan. Not even *Maui*'s billions of dollars worth of UKY series computers and other electronic wizardry or the awesome destructive power of her twenty-four multiple warhead Tridents could compensate for the simple, yet hugely humiliating, fact that the most complicated machine on earth—indeed more complicated than anything yet sent to outer space—was now ignominiously under tow down Puget Sound en route to the Bremerton Naval Shipyard. The navy's CNO on Larry King, and naval spin doctors on every TV and radio talk show available, tried valiantly to limit the damage to the navy's prestige, making much of the fact that the *Maui*'s reactor was never in danger, and that in any event the sub had a "bring-home" diesel engine capability in the event of reactor shutdown at sea. Also, there was also a small secreted "backup screw" that could be deployed to propel the sub home.

"Yes, I've heard about that, Admiral," Larry King responded, "but my sources tell me—and I don't believe this is classified information—that this backup prop can produce a maximum speed of only five mph. Is that correct?"

"Yes," a very stern CNO conceded. "However, that would only be used in emergency situations."

"It's not being used now, though, is it?" King pressed. "Why's that?"

"Ah, the boat has some maneuverability problems."

"You can't steer it?"

"No."

"So in effect," King concluded, "it's dead in the water."

The CNO and his fellow spokesmen tried to split hairs, but the more they talked, the more obvious it became that they had suffered a PR catastrophe, or, as the New York *Daily News* put it, MAUI SUB MAULED—PENTAGON PANICS.

Amid the press scrum, Chairman of the Joint Chiefs General Rogers kept his cool. "Of course not. There is absolutely no panic in the Pentagon. As for the rumor that the White House has received some kind of militia demand, that could be a crank call. As you know, we get these all the time. They're as common as bomb threats during college finals. Several groups have already claimed responsibility. No," he informed Marte Price, "there are no plans to bring any of our armed forces into this. We're not some banana republic that has to send troops out into the streets and the countryside after its wrongdoers. As with the USS *Coe* incident in 2000, we've turned this over to the appropriate law enforcement agencies, including the FBI."

A particularly aggressive ABC reporter shouted, "Have we any idea who the militia perpetrators are, General?"

"Not at this moment. As I've already said, we can't say yet whether it is or is not militia related."

"Yeah, right," murmured the ABC reporter to Marte Price. "Maybe it was the Boy Scouts?"

Marte Price, foregoing her cell, used a secure land line to call General Freeman. "General? Marte Price here."

"Hello, Marte. I thought someone had shot you."

"General, you owe me. I've given you more headlines than—"

"Not all of 'em have been good."

"General, have you been contacted by Washington vis-à-vis this militia business?"

"Visa *what*? Too big a word for me, Marte."

"Vis-à-vis the militia attack on *Maui*."

"The militias have attacked *Hawaii*?"

Which meant, Marte told herself, that the general had been muzzled, afraid to lose what little clout he had left in the capital. "I'll get back to you, General."

"Always glad to hear from the press."

"They tell me you've put on weight? Couldn't lead a team?"

"That's a damn lie."

"Oh, perhaps it's a bulletproof vest? *Extra large*."

"By God, you're—"

"The bitch who's given you some damned good headlines, Douglas. Be nice."

She was struck by the fact that for a man who was presently on the down and out, the general refused to stay down.

Since McBride had made his demand for the release of all Fairchild's POWs, fourteen more calls had come into the White House claiming responsibility for having crippled the *Maui*. Because McBride's demand for the release of all militia POWs had been transmitted by Robin Frieth, the helo's pilot, through Whidbey's Naval Air Station, there was no doubt at the White House that it was the militia that had struck. Nevertheless, politically it remained in the White House's interest to deny that the sub attack had been carried out by elements within the U.S. As serious as external threats were, internal threats of such magnitude were infinitely more disturbing to the American public—and Wall Street—and did not augur well for a President's reelection.

"How about the people at the ferry terminal?" Brownlee

pressed Washington's FBI chief. "Someone must have sold them a ticket?"

"The Kitsap sheriff checked that out, but a ticket agent sees hundreds of people in a single shift. He did give a rough description of the driver, but it doesn't fit anyone on file."

"How about the other guy?" Brownlee pressed, turning down the sound on his TV, watching the close captioning instead.

"Nothing," the Bureau chief replied. "Sheriff up there says the SUV's window was only wound down a fraction, and the glass on the SUV's—"

"Is tinted," Brownlee put in. "I suppose the vehicle was stolen. Plates switched?"

"Yes, sir."

"Have you got *anything* to go on?"

"Forensics are going over the miscellaneous items found at the site."

"Such as?"

"Prints on some beer cans we found, and—"

"They'd hardly be drinking!" Brownlee cut in.

"I agree. Best thing so far is a Kleenex. Saliva trace on it."

"DNA?"

"Yes, fresh, the lab says. There's a good chance it belongs to one of the perpetrators."

"But do you have anything you can match it up with?"

"No. I doubt whether these guys are registered blood donors."

"All right. What's the state of play with the chopper?"

"It took off eleven minutes ago. Disappeared into cloud cover."

"God isn't on our side."

"Not today. But I'm confident something'll break."

On CNN's *Money Talk*, Brownlee saw the Dow and the NASDAQ had tumbled as investors lost confidence in the federal government's ability to get a handle on the *Maui* incident.

In the chopper, McBride smashed the Huey's GPS, electing to be the navigator, and ordered Robin Frieth to turn off the Huey's transponder, reducing chances of radar surveillance. He then cuffed his hostage to the roll bar in the back, letting him take off the hot nylon mask. Cope and McBride kept theirs on even though the Huey's heater blasting forth made it uncomfortably hot, the fine nylon mesh clinging to their faces.

"Where to exactly?" asked Frieth, who Cope only now realized was a woman. Cope was terrified by the violent buffeting during the ascent into the swirling, gray world of zero visibility, not realizing that though Frieth was flying the chopper on instrumentation alone, she was aided by the November class's advanced avionics and Doppler navigation equipment.

"Where to exactly?" Robin repeated.

"You're doing fine," McBride told her. "Keep climbing. See if we can get above this."

"You're the boss." High enough, she thought, and they'd be on NORAD's radar screen. "Right!"

It didn't matter that McBride's adrenaline was pumping, that he had a dozen things on his mind, or that some of his comrades-in-arms, in moments of high danger like this, had said they were so scared that sex was the last damn thing they could think of. Like some carrier pilots he'd known who, under the intense g force of being catapulted from a carrier deck, involuntarily ejaculated, McBride's aphrodisiac was danger. And no matter the unisex helmet and uniform Robin Frieth was wearing, she couldn't hide a bustline and a face that made the highly disciplined militia commander want to jump her. He forced his mind back to the matter at hand. Perhaps the Federals had thought he'd be so preoccupied during his getaway, panicked even, that he'd miss a trick or two. But after all the planning and training that had gone into knocking out one of their boomers, he felt as focused as ever, Ms. Frieth notwithstanding.

The helo was still socked in by swirling stratus.

"All right," he told Robin, the nylon mask sticking annoyingly to his mouth. "One, take her back down below Whidbey's radar screen. Two, tell me where your ELB is."

"But I've turned off the transponder!" she told him. "It's not sending any signal out to—"

"Hey, you're still on radar. You think I'm an idiot?" He didn't give her a chance to reply. "Where's your ELB?"

Robin decided it was better tactically not to play dumb. He seemed to know what he was about. "Tail boom," she said.

McBride walked back past the cop, ROE, CLU, and the three chutes he'd ordered, until he saw the orange, car-radio-sized Emergency Locator Beacon, and moved the toggle switch from Armed through On to the Off position. Now that signal too was dead.

"I don't like this," Cope said, his body slumped forward, pea-soup-thick stratus roiling about the chopper, undoing his sense of balance. "Feel sick."

McBride ignored him, looking across at Robin instead. "Where are the others?"

"What do you mean?" she asked.

"The emergency locators you've planted in the chutes."

"*What?* Are you—"

"Hey!" McBride's voice was so loud it startled Cope upright, spittle drooling through his mask.

"I don't know about any such thing, mister!" she shouted back.

"They thought sending a skirt would throw me off, is that it?" McBride countered, swinging his 9mm toward the hostage. "You listen to me. Tell me where they are or I'm going to waste him—first his knee, then his—"

She was glaring at him, lips tight white, a wisp of blond hair peeking out from the helmet. "Now you listen to *me*, buddy. I don't know—"

McBride fired, the policeman yelling, "Jesus Christ! Jesus—"

"Holy shit!" Cope yelled. "McBride, what are you—"

"Shut your face!" McBride shouted, his gaze still on Robin Frieth.

"All right, all right," she said. "They're in the harness. The locators are in the harnesses!"

"And your chute," McBride demanded, the smoking gun still pointed at the cop.

"Mine too," she confessed. "In the harness as well."

"*Where* in the harness?"

"Disguised as one of the metal clips."

"Now, where's your weapon?"

She was still shaken from the shot. "Look, you can shoot . . . shoot all you want, but I'm telling you I don't have a weapon. The police wanted one planted, but my CO nixed the idea. And that's God's truth. Shoot if you want, but—"

"Okay," McBride said, his throat bone dry from all the shouting, and the smell of the Avgas, which he loathed, had given him a throbbing headache.

The police officer was amazed. Convinced that he'd been hit, even feeling pain, he now realized that McBride had fired wide, a ragged-edged hole in the fuselage instead.

"Christ, it's stifling in here," McBride complained. "Open the door," he told Cope.

"You'll freeze," Robin warned him, not that she particularly cared.

"Only for a second."

Cope, crouching and moving nervously as if he might fall out, opened the door a few inches.

"That's enough!" McBride said, relieved by the cold air, which had routed the stink of the gas, if only temporarily.

CHAPTER THIRTY

KNOWING HOW MUCH Leroi hated the Mormons, and Eleen in particular, Moorehead held the southerner totally responsible for the sudden brouhaha with Eleen.

"He started abusin' *me*!" Leroi countered petulantly, but his voice was barely audible over the noise the pit bull was making beneath the Douglas fir, and Moorehead returned to the head of the hunt, ignoring the southerner's protestations.

As for Eleen, he hoped he had bought some time for Jubal—any delay was useful, Eleen knowing only too well from having been captured by Freeman's men over two years before that a minute here or there could mean the difference between being free and being incarcerated in Moorehead's desert wasteland. But whether he'd succeeded in buying time for Jubal, he hadn't succeeded in entirely distracting Moorehead from the map, the federal commandant now returning to it, squinting down at the smudged contours.

Still smarting from being unjustly charged with taunting Eleen into a fight, Leroi seized the opportunity for payback under the guise of being helpful. "Lose your reading glasses again, sir? Need some help?"

Sampson winked at one of the dog handlers—everyone enjoyed sticking it to Moorehead when it was safe enough, and all of them knew that the commandant's vanity would make him go to almost any lengths rather than admit he needed readers.

Moorehead, however, rather than give Leroi the satisfaction, thrust the map at Sampson. "I think you *do* need a new printer. A goddamn owl couldn't distinguish one contour line from another. Can you make anything out?"

Peering over Moorehead's shoulder, Sampson pointed to a curving black line in the bottom of the lower right-hand quadrant. "That's the highway."

"I *know* that. The Pacific Coast Trail must be nearby. That's where he's headed."

"Huh," Sampson said, "looks like the trail runs onto another track here, another dotted line like the one that marks the PCT. No, wait a second . . ."

"What?" Moorehead pressed, stamping his feet impatiently in the cold. In a few hours it would be dark.

"This line the PCT runs into, where we are now, it doesn't look like a single line—more like a dotted line. It's faint, but there's a—"

"Shut those dogs up!" Moorehead shouted. "Can't hear myself think." He turned back to Sampson. "Go on."

"There's some printing here. Cas—I think it must be 'Cascade.' "

"No no," Moorehead said irritably. "Cascade Tunnel is a good mile south of the highway. We're north of it."

"You sure, sir?"

"I can read a map, Sampson. That's the highway, and we're on this side of it, and the top of a map is north, right? Always. Unless the Geological Survey have all gone bonkers."

Now that the dogs were quiet momentarily, the pit bull still snuffling at the base of the big fir, the other handler could overhear the conversation between Moorehead and Sampson. "Sir, there's another Cascade tunnel. This side of the highway."

Eleen felt an ice-cold stab of pain at the base of his spine.

"*Another* tunnel?" Moorehead inquired.

"Yes, sir. The old Cascade Tunnel. Believe it's abandoned."

"There's no one up this tree!" cut in the pit bull's handler.

And suddenly everything, as Eleen had feared, jelled for the commandant. It was here that the Pacific Coast Trail met an abandoned railway tunnel, Jubal's scent lost by the dog because the young militiaman—or "lovey-dovey," as Leroi called Jubal—had obviously climbed the tree to do what cons called the "monkey swing"—the tricky but highly effective method where an escapee, moving from tree to tree, throws off the dogs, then comes to ground farther on.

"Abandoned tunnel!" Moorehead growled. "Why in hell didn't you tell me this earlier?"

The bloodhound handler blurted, "I—I thought you knew, sir. It's about four miles long."

"I'm supposed to know every railway tunnel in the United States? Where's the entrance?"

"Ah, should be northwest of us—not far, as I recall."

"Dammit!" Moorehead said. "That's why the ranger saw tracks *north* of the highway, not south to the present-day tunnel. All right," he continued, reinvigorated by the new information. "Move out to your right. We're looking for the entrance to an abandoned tunnel. Jubal's in there or my mother's not Irish."

"Well, whaddya know?" Leroi taunted Eleen, jerking him forward. "Looks like lovey-dovey's in the tunnel!"

Moorehead stopped, sending the pit bull handler and three other guards on through the mist-shrouded woods to find the tunnel entrance.

"You," he said to the other dog handler. "Do you know where this abandoned tunnel comes out?"

"Yes, sir. Down about—"

"All right," Moorehead cut in. "We haven't time to waste. Take your hound and two men with you and come through the tunnel from that end. We'll catch him in a squeeze play."

"If he's not through already," the bloodhound's wrangler opined.

"Don't think so. You said the tunnel's about four miles long. From the way that pit bull was jumping around, the scent's pretty recent. In any case, your hound should be able to pick up the scent at the other end if he's passed through."

"Oh, Daisy'll pick it up all right," the guard said, affectionately scratching the bloodhound's head.

"Then get moving. Use the Desert Storm Hummer. Radio or phone communication might be a bit hairy in the tunnel, so if you find him, blink your flashlight on green filter. We'll do the same."

"You want us to wait for you if we get him?"

"Hell, no. Go back to your Hummer. Call Fairchild and the highway patrol. See if they've had any tips coming in on Mead, though I'll bet dollars to doughnuts he and Jubal are in the same neck o' the woods. Remember, the park ranger said he spotted two guys in military fatigues."

"What'll we do with this moron?" Leroi asked, yanking Eleen's chain.

"Bring him along," Moorehead commanded, who was walking fast to catch up with Dillon and the other guard, who in turn were following the pit bull handler through the soaking wet bush.

Within five minutes they'd found the entrance to the abandoned tunnel.

Leroi, bringing up the rear, jerked hard again on the chain.

"Better watch your step in there," he warned malevolently. "You could trip."

Eleen was watching his step, the ground uneven, a rain-soaked run of fern and moss-covered logs.

"I'm gonna get you for what happened back there," Leroi hissed, his breath momentarily visible before being absorbed into the mist like secondhand smoke.

Eleen saw the black horseshoe-shaped outline of the tunnel's entrance.

"When we get lovey-dovey," Leroi taunted him, "you think he's gonna make it back to camp? Think *you're* gonna make it back? Who the fuck knows where you are 'cept us boys? You escaped solitary didn't you?" Leroi jerked the chain. "Get what I mean?"

"With you talking so much," Eleen said evenly, "you aren't going to catch Jubal or anyone else. Might as well hire the town crier. Sloppiest search operation I've ever seen. Get what I mean?"

"Yeah, well, the dogs are louder than us, scumbag. Besides, all the noise spooks runaways—they break cover."

"Do they?"

"Yeah," Leroi said confidently, and Eleen knew Leroi was right. The noise *did* spook you, especially if you were someone as young and inexperienced as Jubal—worried about your wife, impatient to see your firstborn. It would take an older hand, like Mead, to stay cool enough to remain in place, to resist the temptation to bolt upon hearing dogs so close. It was always a gamble—like life itself. Were they on to you, or was it all lather and bluff, like beaters coming through the tiger grass, hoping you'd panic and break cover?

The pit bull's barking became frantic, the sound echoing as the dog charged into the blackness. Moorehead's flashlight's

beam roiled in the cold mist that poured in the tunnel like tendrils of dry ice. Moorehead stopped abruptly, and Eleen saw
rats scampering away along the dank, slimy west wall, disappearing into one of the tunnel's anterooms. The handler
holding hard onto the leash and flashlight cast an enormous
shadow.

At first Eleen had thought the pit bull had been barking at
the rats, but to his dismay he saw that the dog, at the edge of
Moorehead's flashlight beam, was straining ahead, showing
no interest whatsoever in the rodents. Instead, his dark eyes,
glinting marblelike, were drawn to a pile of grapefruit-sized
rubble, made up of broken glass from what presumably used
to be the tunnel's emergency overhead lighting, and including
lumps of cement that had fallen from the ceiling and walls
through years of neglect.

By the time Eleen and Leroi drew adjacent to it, Eleen's
shoes—the laces, as per regulation, having been taken from
him in solitary—were inundated with tiny fragments of the
fallen concrete. "I have to empty my shoes," he told Leroi,
who, though tiring of the rough going himself, felt obliged to
tell his prisoner to hurry up. By now the others, twenty or
thirty yards farther on, and barely outlined in the penumbra
from their flashlight beams, were encountering more rubble,
which seemingly had buried the splintered remains of old rot-
ting wooden sleepers.

In the darkness, Eleen, unsteady on his left foot as he replaced the right shoe, wobbled against Leroi, who rudely
shoved him away. "Sorry," Eleen said out of habit, Leroi
saying nothing, still refusing to shine his flashlight to the left
lest it assist his prisoner. Which was fine by Eleen, whose left
hand brought the rock up out of the darkness, smashing it into
Leroi's head with such force, and so quickly that the only
sound the southerner made was to gasp as he lost consciousness, his body's fall broken by Eleen's right arm.

Eleen lowered him to the ground, retrieving the flashlight with his left arm, his right feeling for Leroi's holster. It was empty—Moorehead's precaution, no doubt, after he'd found the two of them fighting, though Eleen hadn't seen him take it from Leroi. But then, what did it matter? The gun was gone. Heart racing, he searched the guard's pockets for the handcuff key. Nothing. Leroi groaned.

Ten seconds later Moorehead, his advance party intent on keeping pace with the dog, glanced back and noticed Leroi's flashlight wasn't moving. "Leroi . . . ?"

By now a concussed Leroi was only too conscious of his situation, Eleen telling him, "Tell him you're taking a leak!" Whether or not it was the concussion, the southerner found it odd to hear the Mormon say "leak," the word somehow out of keeping with Eleen's reputation for propriety.

"Taking a leak," Leroi answered Moorehead.

The commandant said something, but it was drowned out by the barking of the pit bull.

"Where's the key?" Eleen demanded, jerking the handcuffs.

"I haven't got it," Leroi said.

"Where's the *key*?" Eleen had wrapped the handcuffs chain around Leroi's neck.

"Told you, I haven't got it."

"I'm warning you."

"Fuck you. What are ya gonna do? Kill me?"

It was a problem—the southerner showing more courage than Eleen had anticipated. Usually bullies gave way when they were on the receiving end. Not this one, and he had a point—a strangled Leroi would be dead weight, and pretty soon the others would be aware of the fact that something was wrong.

"All right," Eleen said, unintentionally signaling to Leroi that he was stymied. "Walk in front of me."

"Fuck you."

Eleen figured he had four, maybe five minutes at most before the others figured out what was going on.

CHAPTER THIRTY-ONE

MEL HALEY COULDN'T take it anymore. For a week now he'd been dreaming of his wife, Colleen, and "every single time we're just about to do it I wake up. It's driving me crazy."

In the fading light, Pete Rainor carefully measured out the amount of shaving cream he needed, his habit of conserving supplies something that had been ingrained in the militia by Lucky McBride. McBride's own use of shaving cream, in one particularly harrowing training session—to mark out an exit through a minefield when he had nothing else handy—was widely known through the corps by militiamen who had never seen him but had heard about him. Federals who'd gotten wind of the shaving cream ploy claimed, correctly, that McBride had gotten the idea from General Schwartzkopf. And they pointed out that when the militia had tried it in a real combat situation—a firefight near the mouth of the Columbia River—a strong ocean breeze had scattered the shaving foam all over, utterly confusing militia troops, trapping them in the minefield, where they were either blown to pieces by mines or cut down in the Federal onslaught. But this criticism, voiced petulantly now by Mel Haley because Rainor hadn't responded to him about his dream of Colleen, did nothing to puncture Rainor's admiration for McBride.

"You haven't said anything," Haley complained.

"What d'you want me to say, Mel? You think you're the only one in the Redoubt that wakes up with a hard-on?"

"It's all these militia women, that's the trouble."

"I thought," Rainor said, observing his reflection in the shaving mirror, his tongue pushing out his cheek to meet the safety razor, "that your problem is you miss your wife."

"It is. But I mean, seeing all these women walking through camp, well, it doesn't help."

"Then take a *Penthouse* and go in the woods."

"That's disgusting!"

Rainor said nothing and swished the blunt razor through the mess pan.

"Anyhow," Haley said, "lot of religious nuts in this outfit. More likely to find a motion sensor around here than a girlie mag."

It sounded to Rainor like "censor," but what Haley meant were the sensors that federal agencies sometimes dropped in what the FBI, the Bureau of Alcohol, Tobacco and Firearms, etcetera, called HIRAS, or high risk areas, such as the smuggling strips along the Canada–U.S. border.

"There aren't any sensors in the Redoubt," Rainor replied easily, the razor scraping against the stubble under his chin. "If there were sensors here, you and I and everybody else here would be in Fairchild behind barbed wire."

Mel Haley frowned. "They'd have to put the women somewhere else."

"I guess so," Rainor replied jocularly. "Otherwise you'd go nuts."

Haley was so strung out, Rainor's barb went right by him. "You think McBride'll pull it off?" Haley inquired. "I mean, getting us amnesty as well as freeing Fairchild?"

Rainor, still looking in the mirror, wiped his neck with a towel and took up the razor again, considering a touch-up beneath his lower lip. "Are you kidding? What choice do the Feds have? McBride's shown 'em that if we can cripple a Trident we can hit anything."

"What if they get him?"

"Well—" Rainor began.

"You guys heard?" It was a young, thirtyish, silvery-haired militiawoman, buzz cut and no makeup. "Federals are onto McBride."

"Where?" Rainor asked, razor frozen in midair.

"Down south. Kingston Ferry."

"Oh hell!" Haley said, his mind momentarily off Colleen. But no sooner had this happened than he was thinking of her again, because now he knew it was all but certain that McBride would be heading for the safety of the Redoubt, which meant security would be extraordinarily high and that a request to make any phone call out would be denied.

"I guess he's on his way here," Haley said morosely.

"Not necessarily," said Buzz Cut, walking away. "He won't come unless he's sure he's shaken them. He won't betray the Redoubt."

"Good," Haley said.

Rainor turned on him. "What's the matter with you? You wanted to close Boeing down as much as I did. Now all you can think of is your dick."

It was several seconds before Haley responded, his attention on the derriere of the silvery-haired woman as she made her way toward the heavily camouflaged supply area. "I don't know. I guess I've never been away from Colleen for this long." He looked like a whipped dog.

"Stop moping about," Pete Rainor chastised him. "There's

tons of stuff to do around here. Volunteer for the inventory check. You might get paired off with that buzz cut."

Mel's expression broke. "You think so?"

Rainor swirled the razor about in the pan. "No, just kiddin'. She'd eat you alive."

CHAPTER THIRTY-TWO

THE HUEY WAS still in dense cloud as McBride, fighting to be heard over the roar of the Huey's twin engines, told the cop again to put on the chute. The ice-cold slipstream raced past the partially open door.

"Hey!" McBride shouted. "You can go out with it or without it. You've got one minute!"

The policeman pulled on the harness. "I've never jumped before! Can't see a thing out there!"

McBride moved to help him with the harness. "Don't worry. You've got a locator signal attached to the—"

The policeman's hands went for the gun.

The shot was a sharp crack in the confined space, leaving a ragged 9mm hole in the fuselage, wind whistling through it, the blood from the back of the man's head a fine aerosol in the windblown cabin.

"Shit, shit, shit!" was all Cope could say.

The pilot, as surprised as Cope, had no time to gaze at the disaster. All her attention was needed to fight a series of vicious shears that caused the Huey to plunge in heart-grabbing falls that all but wrenched the chopper from her control.

It wasn't until at least a minute later, Cope dry retching as the Huey leveled out, that McBride braced himself with one hand against the cabin wall, slid the door open, and pushed the dead man out, tossing the other three chutes after him.

It seemed quite clear to Lieutenant Robin Frieth what had happened. The militiaman had murdered the policeman. It seemed equally obvious to her that both militiamen were near panic, and that if they could so callously dispense with their police hostage in cold blood, they certainly had no intention of leaving her to fly back and tell Whidbey control where they had either bailed out or where they'd forced her to land. As her feet exerted rudder control, she felt her right calf muscle flex against the small Ultra Carry .45, for "optimum personal urban protection," according to the salesman who'd sold it to her.

But when could she use it? Frieth wondered. The time wasn't now. At ten thousand feet, all her attention was on the Huey's instrument panel, with only her radar to guide her in the swirling pea soup that was an excuse for sky. The right time would come. Patience.

A scant three minutes later, the one who was obviously the militia leader checked his handheld GPS and abruptly ordered her to take the Huey down through the maelstrom of bad weather. "Level off at a thousand meters!"

Her palms sweating because of the zero visibility, she did as she was told, any thought of reaching for the Ultra Carry held in abeyance as she fought wind shear and low turbulence, battling to hold the chopper steady at three thousand feet.

"I said a thousand meters!" McBride barked. "Take her back up 250 feet!"

Her error rattled her momentarily, but she quickly regained

control of the yoke and took the Huey back up, noting that wherever they were, they were almost certainly not in mountainous terrain, unless they were in one of the Cascades' glacier-carved valleys. McBride was so busy now checking his GPS, the other militiaman still whey-faced from shock and air sickness, his sour body odor filling the chopper, that Robin was tempted to try her luck with the Ultra Carry, but with the Huey bucking in the turbulence at just over three thousand feet, she knew there'd be no margin for recovery, should she miss either of them. Besides, as her CO had impressed upon her, it wasn't her job to try to play heroine, but simply to do as they told her and leave the business of capturing them up to the special federal task force being assembled by the White House.

A tear in the stratus below revealed a rush of drab green forest and a fleeting slash of earth that looked like a firebreak or logging road, then cloud closed in again, long trails of condensation rushing at the cockpit. For a half hour they were in this netherworld, then McBride called out, "Take her down. There's a field directly below."

"You hope!" Robin Frieth countered.

At twelve hundred feet they broke the cloud cover and she saw the field, its sunless brown grass looking like a patch of mange in a mist-shrouded wood, two forlorn-looking soccer nets at either end of it, and the remains of what appeared to be an overgrown baseball diamond. At five hundred feet she selected a slight rise fifty yards or so from one of the rickety-looking soccer posts off to her right, the rise itself partially bald of grass. She pulled down her goggles as McBride slid open the door, a whirling cloud of dirt, straw-link grass, and assorted airborne debris swirling about in the wash of the props, and several pieces of rain-sodden candy wrappers swept high above the field as McBride told her to cut the engine.

She did as she was told, but wondered why he wanted the helo shut down. She'd delivered them, hadn't she? That was the deal?

Once the Twin-Pac's engines had shut down and the rotors stilled, the eerie silence of that mist-shrouded field and the silence of the two militiamen suddenly overwhelmed her. Inside her flight suit she broke out into a cold, sticky sweat, for as she saw the two men staring at her, the wet nylon about their mouths collapsing rhythmically as they breathed, she had time to think over what had happened, recalling how the frightened one had yelled out in panic as his companion had fired at the hapless policeman something about "What are you doing, Bride?" or was it McBride? Over the roar of the twin turbos it had been difficult to hear exactly, but it was definitely the other man's name she'd heard, Bride or McBride. But had this Bride or McBride heard it too? If he had, what did she have to lose with the Ultra? But right now the barrel of Bride's or McBride's 9mm was staring straight at her.

"I need to take a pee." It was all she could think of.

"Use your funnel."

"Geez," Cope interjected. "For Pete's sake, at least let 'er go outside."

"Use the funnel!"

"Can't I have a *little* privacy?"

"All right." McBride gestured with the Beretta. "But no further than the edge of the field! Over by that tree."

As she walked quickly to the edge of the forlorn field, she knew he was planning to kill her, he would never permit her to take his identity back to the authorities at Whidbey, wherever that was from here.

She heard the rustle of some small animal at the edge of the dilapidated soccer field, and a moment later the sound of an approaching four-by-four. Then she saw it, bristling with masked, armed militia, charging straight past a shot-up stop sign. Something struck her as odd about the grass-obscured stop sign, another letter on it—perhaps an A—but in the sudden noise of the four-by-four's arrival and her haste to zip up, she thought no more of it, heading back quickly toward the Huey. She avoided eye contact with any of the arriving militia, fully expecting to be wolf-whistled and harassed. Surprisingly, there was none of that, and she saw that several of the militia troops were women.

"Get her a blindfold!" McBride said.

"I can't fly blindfolded!" Robin retorted.

"You're not going to. You think we're stupid enough to let you go, let you flick on your emergency beacon and back vector our position?"

So they were going to shoot her.

"Our boys'll take you up on the I-5. Turn you loose there."

"And you get to keep the chopper." Why did she open her big mouth? She asked herself. They were about to let her go, and she had to be lippy.

"Yes," McBride said, "we get to keep the chopper. It belongs to us."

She looked confused.

"We're taxpayers, aren't we?" he said.

Cope walked up to McBride and said something.

"What? All right, if you want."

Cope hesitated.

"Well, go on!" McBride said impatiently.

Cope, still masked, took a candy bar and a bottle of water from one of the other militiamen and stuffed them into Robin's flight suit pocket.

"He thinks you're gonna starve," McBride joshed. "Maybe die of thirst."

It was an O'Henry bar and a bottle of Evian, and though she wondered how she could be expected to consume either with her hands tied behind her back, she nevertheless gave Cope a heartfelt "Thank you." He was a follower, one of those, she guessed, who could be on either side. Though visibly relieved, she was still hoping, indeed praying, that this Bride, or McBride, wouldn't remember that the other man had called out his name when he'd shoved the policeman out of the helo along with the chutes, no doubt a ploy to mislead searchers.

They blindfolded her, and as the militia's four-by-four drove away from the field, she could hear their commander giving orders to throw a net over the bird—the helo—and tow it over closer to the woods. She tried to look and listen for other telltale signs of where she'd been, but apart from the dilapidated soccer field, the woods around the field looked and smelled like all woods looked and smelled in the Northwest. But one thing she was pretty sure of: she hadn't been east of the Cascades—the helo hadn't gone that high. It had probably been in one of the Cascade Mountain valleys. But if she could pinpoint it, the authorities would be able to go round these hobos up.

She'd been driven for what she guessed had been about fifteen minutes when she asked, "How long till we reach the I-5?"

"Can't say."

After a few more moments of silence, she thought of what had happened to the policeman on the helo and shut up. The chloroform-soaked cloth, the restraining hands, came upon her so suddenly that though she tried to struggle, there was no hope.

Her disorientation was complete. The noises of traffic, the blindfold, her inability to remove the plastic snap cuffs that tied her hands, her brain in the grip of a headache the likes of which she had never imagined, the pulsating, vicelike pressure—all combined to render her incapable of any speculation as to where on the I-5, if it was the I-5, they might have left her. Dimly, slowly, the intensity of the pain—perhaps an allergic reaction to the chloroform—abated somewhat. She heard a car stop, a door close—it was unbearably loud—then footsteps.

"Lieutenant Frieth?"

Her mouth was so parched she couldn't speak.

"You okay, ma'am?"

"No."

They removed her blindfold, and instantly she recoiled from the light.

Ten minutes later, courtesy of the Snohomish deputy, she was in Burlington, fifty miles north of Seattle, where she was diagnosed and being treated for migraine—the first she'd ever had. The pain was receding, but not quickly, her head and neck resting on ice packs for the short flight southwest to Whidbey Island Naval Air Station.

Not surprisingly, she wasn't in the best shape for a debriefing. Her CO, and Washington, were desperate to unearth the militia's hideout.

"Any idea where you were forced to land?" the CO asked her.

She shook her head, her body slumped, enveloped by a deep upholstered chair

"No," she said. "He smashed my GPS unit not long after we took off."

"And you say they destroyed your locator beacons."

"Uh-huh. Well, *they* didn't. *He* did." Suddenly, through the brain-judding pain, she remembered his name. "Bride! The other one called him Bride or McBride—something like that—when he shoved the policeman out of the helo."

"Good job, Lieutenant! Anything else? Either of them give any hint of the landing zone location? If you can tell us that, we've got a home run."

She tried to recollect every detail, encouraged by having recalled the leader's name, which was now being forwarded to D.C. "It was the kind of field you'd find anywhere in the Northwest," she told her CO. "About 150 yards long—maybe a hundred wide."

She'd wandered off for a moment, the Tylenol and codeine making her drowsy, dreamy. She remembered all the fights she'd had with her ex about his obsession with Monday Night Football. It was the first of what her lawyer would explain to the judge were "irreconcilable differences."

"You don't like *football*?" the judge had asked her accusingly.

"Lieutenant?"

"Oh, sorry, sir. What?"

"Were there goalposts? Any kind of—I dunno—team logos left about or—"

"No. There weren't any football posts. There were a couple of soccer things—you know, frames."

"Soccer?"

"Yes."

It didn't signify anything, not in the Northwest, where the Canadian immigrants' passion for soccer had invaded Washington and Oregon, particularly after the galvanizing World Cup win by the U.S. women's team in 2000.

"And there was a baseball diamond," Robin told him. "The soccer stuff didn't look like it had been used in ages."

The DO intercepted to tell the Whidbey CO that a White House aide, "a guy called Brownlee, said the President wanted to extend a personal 'well done' to you and Lieutenant Frieth for giving Washington the perpetrator's name. Actually, they referred to him as something else."

"I'll bet they did," the CO said.

It was the first time Robin Frieth had managed a smile since the beginning of the debriefing, and she leaned back in the recliner, conscious of a soft warmth against her thigh. It was the O'Henry bar the militiaman had given her, the candy having turned gooey in her flying suit. As the CO kept questioning her, she extracted the chocolate mess with obvious distaste, the DO refraining from making a scatological remark. "Didn't realize I was that frightened!" she said self-deprecatingly, which at once elicited laughter from both the CO and DO, the latter snatching a handful of Kleenex and passing them to her as she mopped up the mess of melted chocolate stuck to the wrapper. As the DO took it from her to toss it into the garbage can, he noticed something odd about the printing on the wrapper. Below the phrase, "Best ever!" he saw *"Meilleur que jamais!"* Holding up the wrapper, he asked Robin and the CO, "This is French, right?"

Then Robin remembered what it was that had bothered her about the sign she'd seen in the grass at the edge of the field were she'd gone to relieve herself. In addition to having "Stop" printed on it, there had been something else—the letter A—not graffiti, but professional signage.

In Washington, these bits of information, together with McBride's name, were immediately e-mailed by Michael Brownlee to Douglas Freeman. Because of the general's past encounters with the militia, it was possible he would be able to make something of it. Freeman responded at once, having recalled a deep-winter "punch-up," as Aussie Lewis had called it, when one of Freeman's SALERTs had spotted a B.C. on one of the militia's snowmobiles plates: British Columbia.

Regarding the A in the stop sign the lieutenant had seen, Freeman informed Whidbey Island's CO on the conference call hookup with the White House that the A must have been the first letter of *Arret*, the French word for "stop," which, Freeman posited, "together with the bilingual O'Henry bar, tells us that you're looking for a militia hideout across the Washington State–B.C. line. In Canada!"

"All right," said Brownlee at the White House. "But we still don't know *where* across the line. Besides which, we can't go in without the Canadian government's say so."

"We could be in and out," Freeman countered. "Snatch the son of a bitch and be out before anyone knew."

"That's called invasion, General," Brownlee countered.

"Well, get their okay," Freeman replied. "Meantime, with the weather clearing, we can have NSA give us a SATPIX readout of the Washington State–B.C. border. Zero in on a twenty-mile strip on either side. Their redoubt's probably close to the line so they can hop back and forth from the legal protection of one jurisdiction to another. What I'm afraid of is, the longer we have to wait, the more time McBride has to build up his defenses."

And so, when the President personally called NSA, he explained that the border overflight was to be given top priority, that he wanted blowups of the Washington–B.C. line within the half hour. "And," the President added, "you might as well include the Idaho–B.C. Sector as well," despite the Whidbey Island CO doubting Robin Frieth's helo could have reached that far.

"How about the Montana–B.C. border, Mr. President?" the NSA director inquired.

"The B.C. border goes that far?"

"Yes, sir. It'll take us longer to do."

The President quickly consulted with General Rogers and Brownlee, who in turn consulted again with the Whidbey Island CO, who asked Robin Frieth to try to gauge the distance flown. Could she remember what the fuel gauge had read when she'd landed the helo on the soccer field? She tried, but things had been so hectic. Besides, she'd lost track of the time

during her blindfolded trip from unconsciousness to the I-5.
And they'd smashed her GPS.

"I'm guessing, sir," she confessed, "but I doubt we were as
far away as Montana."

"I'd forget about the Montana sector," the CO told
Brownlee.

After he'd hung up, however, the CO pressed Robin Frieth,
"You're a hundred percent sure of that—that the helo couldn't
have reached Montana?"

"No, I'm not sure," she replied truthfully. "Remember, he
smashed my GPS."

CHAPTER THIRTY-THREE

"Leroi?" Moorehead called out again, his bellow echoing off
the grime-streaked walls of the tunnel. "You okay?"

Eleen held the shard of glass against Leroi's throat, the
southerner still groggy but conscious of his peril. "Tell 'em,"
Eleen instructed him, "you had to take a dump, or as the Lord
is my witness I'll cut your—"

"Lord" told Leroi just how serious Eleen was.

"Had to take a dump!" Leroi called out.

The laughter of the commandant, Sampson, and the handler was drowned by a new burst of excited barking from the
pit bull, but it turned out that it was a skunk ahead of them
that captured the pit bull's attention. The handler jerked hard

on the leash, but not in time to stop the skunk. The white streak of his tail lifting was glimpsed in the flashlight beam, the eye- and nose-burning stench evoking a chorus of oaths from Moorehead's three-man party, the pit bull emitting a puppylike wail.

Eleen had immediately taken advantage of the skunk's defensive spray to force Leroi into one of the tunnel's coal-black antechambers, telling him to kill the flashlight. Moorehead's advance party was discombobulated by the skunk's attack, or rather, defense, trying futilely to filter out the stench through handkerchiefs and hastily uncrumpled Kleenex. It was at least five minutes before any of the three men looked back.

"Leroi?"

"Maybe," Sampson joked, his eyes still stinging from the skunk's smell, "he's taking another dump!"

"It'd be better than—" the handler began, when Moorehead told him to be quiet.

"Leroi?"

Back in the antechamber, Eleen, though his voice was low, jerked the southerner's manacled arm, demanding, "Where do you keep the keys?"

"You idiot!" Leroi sneered defiantly, though still unsteady on his feet from Eleen's blow, and his head still in the grip of the militiaman's armlock. "You think *I* have them? The commandant carries 'em. Regulations."

Eleen didn't believe him—a guard had to have the means of freeing himself from a prisoner in unforeseen circumstances.

"Give me the keys," Eleen hissed, "or I'll cut your throat!"

"So that'll get you the keys, will it?" Leroi said, defiant again.

Eleen hesitated, but for only a second. Perhaps two years ago, before he'd been recaptured by Federal troops and thrown back into Fairchild—before the long days and nights in the hole—he wouldn't have been tough enough, but right now, seeing his chance of liberty, to join Mead and Jubal in their dash for freedom, made him as hard as his captors. Pushing the glass shard under Leroi's chin, he began drawing it across the southerner's throat.

"Right boot!" Leroi spat out. "Flap pocket!"

"Kneel down!"

There was a surge of static—Leroi's cell phone, the tunnel obliterating the satellite bounce-off.

Then "Leroi!" It was the dog handler calling from the tunnel, and from the side chamber Eleen could see the beam of a flashlight moving along the tunnel's opposite wall, coming back toward them. "Leroi!"

Eleen, the blood-warmed glass shard in his left hand, his right hand feeling down the side of Leroi's boot, was convinced Leroi had lied to buy time, when his fingers found the Velcro flap of the boot's side pocket, which he hadn't noticed before, the trouser hem covering the pocket. He found the key and undid the cuffs.

"Leroi?" And now Eleen could hear a panting noise. Moorehead had sent back the pit bull.

Eleen never saw the dog, but heard it scrabbling on gravel in the darkness. It came crashing into his chest with the force of a heavyweight's punch, knocking him back. The dog's snarling, ugly black-and-white head and teeth were at Eleen's throat, caught in the madly dancing beam of the handler's flashlight. Leroi rose from the rubble nearby, one hand feeling warm blood on his throat, his right foot kicking at the downed militiaman with such vehemence the handler heard the crack of bone.

"That's enough!" the handler cautioned, flashlight in one hand, handgun in the other. "Leroi—that's enough!"

Leroi stopped, then started kicking with his left foot at

Eleen's head, the handler calling off the dog and screaming at Eleen to get up.

Then Moorehead and Sampson arrived, grabbing the incensed Leroi by the collar, hauling him off Eleen, the handler getting control of the dog, Eleen motionless.

A shot from the guard farther down the tunnel reverberated in the antechamber. Another shot, then a third, Moorehead yelling at the handler to give his gun to Leroi and come back down the tunnel with his dog.

"I want him alive!" Moorehead ordered as he ran off, the dog handler and pit bull in tow. Leroi, dazed, was unsure whether the commandant's "him" meant Jubal, Mead, or both. Holding the dog handler's gun and still shaking from his ordeal, Leroi picked up his flashlight and leaned back against the weeping wall of the antechamber to catch his breath, shining the beam down on Eleen's prostrate figure. The militiaman, despite the pit bull having knocked him down, looked remarkably unscathed. Leroi took a step closer and delivered a vicious kick to the militiaman's groin. Eleen groaned as his body curled into a fetal position, his hands cupping his genitals.

"Get up, you Mormon shit!"

In the distance they could hear the pit bull, and from the racket it was making, Leroi knew the dog had cornered something. He wiped more blood from his throat—thank God for the pit bull having arrived in time. "Get up, you Mormon shit! We'll miss out on all the fun."

The sound of Moorehead's men shouting, flashlight beams dancing wildly in the tunnel, the crunching sound of their boots running on gravel, and the echoing of the pit bull barking at whatever he'd cornered, created such confusion that one of the guards mistook the shape of a comrade who had stumbled after his flashlight failed for either Jubal or

Mead. Striking him hard with his handgun, he turned confusion into near mayhem, until Moorehead bellowed for everyone to keep quiet. By the time Eleen and Leroi had caught up to them, the guards realized that the cornered shape was the skunk.

"Get the dog away!" Moorehead commanded the handler, then shot the skunk point-blank. "C'mon. Spread out across the tunnel and check every antechamber."

In Moorehead's men's sudden charge, assorted wildlife had fled toward the opposite end of the tunnel, only to be confronted by the approaching flashlights of Dillon and his bloodhound party. The eyes of fleeing rodents and other tunnel creatures were momentarily caught in the beams, and then a human form, illuminated one second, lost the next.

"Over there!" Dillon shouted, sweeping his flashlight back along the wall, the trapped man instinctively turning his face from the light, Dillon close enough to correctly guess that it was Jubal.

"Don't shoot!" Jubal pleaded.

Cursing the fact that his cell phone wouldn't work in the tunnel, Dillon shouted at the distant bobbing lights of Moorehead and his guards. "We've got Jubal!"

With Dillon and his two comrades shining their flashlights on the POW, the bloodhound slobbering and straining to get at him, Dillon saw that Jubal was the worse for wear. His camp-made civilian clothes had been ripped by undergrowth and no doubt by what Moorehead, on his arrival, called the "monkey business" of Jubal having gone up into the trees in hopes of shaking off the dog.

"You know where Mead is?" Moorehead asked the cowering POW.

"Mead?"

"Yeah. Mead."

"I don't know—I mean I don't know any Mead."

For a moment Dillon was tempted to believe him—after all, there were a thousand men in Fairchild. It was quite possible that the two had never met.

Moorehead, still catching his breath, said nothing for the moment, noting the ragged condition of the escapee's fatigues and a rash on the right side of his face, probably caused by nettles in the undergrowth. Most telling of all, Jubal's right boot was split, the ankle itself badly swollen and bloodied, which, if he'd been with Mead, would undoubtedly have slowed the pair down. If so, which way had Mead gone?

"You don't know Sergeant Mead?" Moorehead said caustically, Dillon struck by the fact that it was the first time he'd heard the commandant refer to any militiaman by his rank. "Sergeant Mead?" Moorehead repeated. "Hut 5A? Eleen's right-hand man. That correct, Eleen?" Moorehead added, without turning to Eleen.

"If you say so," Eleen said wryly.

Moorehead's kick to Jubal's ankle brought a yell from Jubal, who slid down the grime-slicked tunnel wall. "Well, by now," Jubal gasped, "I'd say Mead's already taken your Hummer!"

For a moment, except for the steady drip of water somewhere in the darkness, there was silence among Moorehead and the guards. Then Dillon asked disingenuously, "What Hummer?"

"I dunno," Jubal replied. "One of the two we saw coming up the highway."

"So!" Moorehead said triumphantly, seizing on Jubal's implied companion. "You little bastard! You and Mead *were* together!"

He kicked Jubal's inflamed ankle once more, Jubal barely managing to stifle a cry of pain.

"Until," Moorehead continued, "you twisted your ankle and he left you, eh?"

"Or," Leroi put in, "maybe little lovey-dovey here played the hero—told the other scumbag to go ahead!"

"Either way," Dillon observed, "if he gets our Hummer—"

Moorehead swung on him. "You mean you didn't secure?" He was referring to the antitheft steel cable from the Hummer's dashboard, which could be padlocked to the steering wheel.

"I secured!" Dillon replied, his defensiveness riding a tone of outright defiance.

"Huh!" It was Jubal issuing a defiance of his own. "Ever heard of a hacksaw?"

Moorehead grabbed Jubal's hair, shoving his head hard against the tunnel wall. "Listen, scumbag, if you want to see your 'God's little gift' and your missus, you'd better not be jerking me around. Has Mead got a hacksaw?"

"Yes."

"How come *my* dog didn't pick up his scent?" the bloodhound's handler asked.

"I dunno," Jubal said, the rash on his face markedly worse. "Maybe your dog's stupid!"

"Or maybe it was the skunk?" Dillon suggested. "That'll obliterate anything."

"All right," Moorehead said, standing back from Jubal. "Let's move!"

The two handlers raced forward, encouraging their two dogs, who were still confused by the overpowering stench of the skunk.

Though it was overcast outside as they broke free of the tunnel, it was as if they'd suddenly emerged into an explosion of light. Then came Moorehead, Sampson with the limping Jubal, the two other guards and the handler. Dillon and Leroi in charge of Eleen were still back in the darkness, though nearing the end of the tunnel. Outside, Moorehead, Sampson, and the guards had paused on an open stony apron of ground. Shading their eyes from the glare, they looked up at the highway two hundred yards away for the Desert Storm Hummer, their only transport back to Moorehead's vehicle. It was still there.

The first rifle shot blew Sampson off his feet, the Fairchild duty officer dead before he hit the ground, a flock of starlings erupting skyward. Then the bloodhound's handler crashed sideways from the stony apron into the fringe of undergrowth, grabbing futilely at a sapling and breaking it, the bloodhound whinnying like a horse in fright. Moorehead and the others, pulling Jubal with them, had made a dash into a thicket of pine just off the apron, a much closer refuge than the tunnel, now fifty yards of open ground behind them. A fourth shot rang out, the pit bull handler's hand exploding in a cloud of blood and bone, his body stumbling drunkenly, then collapsing noisily on gravel spill only a few feet from the woods into which Moorehead and the remaining two guards, with Jubal in tow, had vanished.

"Jesus!" It was Leroi, nearing the tunnel's exit, with Dillon and Eleen. "Who the hell's that?"

"Mead, you fool," Dillon said. "And turn off that flashlight. You wanna be next?"

"But where'd he get the gun?"

"How the fuck do I know? He's been on the run since yesterday. Maybe he got it from some farmer. Lot o' those bastards support the militia. Maybe he stole it from someone. I don't give a shit, Leroi. All I know is, we step outta here we'll get our friggin' heads blown off."

"Maybe it isn't Mead?" Leroi said.

"Well, it's not fuckin' Santa Claus," Dillon told Leroi. "Whoever it is, he doesn't like Federals, does he?"

"We could use Eleen here as a shield," Leroi suggested. "Get to the Hummer that way?"

"Nah," Dillon said. "He's too good a shot, whoever he is. 'Sides, there's too much ground to cover between here and the highway. And we'd have to go through those thick woods. He could be a foot from us and we'd never—Jesus!" Dillon had just noticed the blood on Leroi's throat.

"This prick!" Leroi said, indicating Eleen before turning his attention back to the woods over fifty yards away. "How about using the dogs? Set 'em loose."

"After that skunk?" Dillon said. "It'll take 'em two days 'fore they can smell their own shit."

"No, I don't think that's right. Now they're out of the tunnel—"

"Well, I'm not gonna go get 'em. You go get 'em."

Leroi turned on Eleen. "You bastards are gonna pay for this."

"I feel sorry for the dogs," was all Eleen would say.

And he meant it.

"Hey, Leroi—you asshole!"

Leroi started with fright. Not because he recognized Mead's voice shouting from somewhere in the woods, but because Mead knew it was him, Leroi, in the tunnel. Which meant either Leroi's voice had echoed from the tunnel's mouth, which acted as a giant megaphone, or Mead had somehow worked his way so close to the tunnel that he could hear them.

"You better answer him," Dillon advised Leroi.

"Why should I?"

"Leroi?"

Moorehead and his two guards could hear it too, but were too shaken by the deaths of their comrades within the last five minutes to do anything. Besides which they were still catching their breath.

"You gonna answer me, Leroi, or am I gonna have to use my infrared?"

"Holy shit," Dillon said, flattening himself against the wall. "Talk to 'im, Leroi! Talk to 'im!"

A hundred yards away, one of Moorehead's guards whispered to the commandant, "If he's got a night sight we'd better get out of here, sir."

Back in the tunnel, Leroi hesitated. "He's bluffing."

"What do you want?" Dillon shouted. He wasn't up for playing hero against some damn militia fanatic. He wanted to lie in the sun at that Fort DePussy, or whatever Moorehead called it.

"I want you guys to release Jubal and I'll let you walk free to the highway. You can go, Moorehead, you asshole!"

The next voice was Jubal's: "They've got Captain Eleen here too!"

Now the only sound that could be heard was that of the wind, which had picked up and was groaning through the tunnel. It was a shock to Mead that his commanding officer was there, that Moorehead had brought him along for bait—and Mead felt an enormous sense of victory. Despite his elation, however, Mead also felt acutely embarrassed, something he thought couldn't happen under the life-and-death circumstances he was facing. But there it was, he was embarrassed at the language he'd been using in front of Eleen. *Son of a bitch!* Mead realized that Moorehead was now out of the tunnel and could use his cell phone. It was a remote area in the mountains, but still . . .

"You've got thirty seconds, Leroi, then I'm using the night sight. Against that, your flashlights are nothing. In fact, you use your flashlights and it'll save me time."

Moorehead was tempted to yell to Leroi that he should stay put, but he knew that would reveal his and the guards' approximate position, and with the sniper's scope, Mead had the distinct advantage. Moorehead stayed quiet and kept dialing 911.

"Fifteen seconds, Leroi! And bring Captain Eleen with you!"

"I'll go if you go," Dillon said to Leroi.

"Walk to the edge of the stones!" Mead said. "Get the key to the Hummer's padlock. There's a path right of the apron, through the woods, to the Hummer. I'll have you in my sights all the way. And take the cuffs off Captain Eleen. And you, Moorehead, let Jubal go!"

Leroi and Dillon did as they were told, and Jubal was already stumbling toward the Hummer. But Mead had lied, and instead of keeping them in his sights he moved quickly out of the woods, up the scrub-strewn incline, crouching low as he made his way around to the highway side of the Hummer so that he was already there when they arrived.

Motioning with his .30 rifle toward the cable and padlock on the Hummer's steering wheel, he told Leroi to unlock the cable, then asked Eleen, "You up to driving, Captain?"

"I think so."

"Fine. I'll be in the back with Jubal and friend Leroi." It began to rain as Mead cuffed Leroi's hands to the Hummer's overhead center bar before waving Dillon away, telling him it was his lucky day. As Dillon hightailed it to the bushes, Mead and Jubal climbed into the backseat.

Despite its brutish size, the fact that the Hummer's entire drive train was elevated so high into the cabin to provide for ground clearance and fording capability meant that the interior was surprisingly cramped. Even Eleen's driver's seat, though it had the most room, seemed too small for him, and he understood why Mead had let Dillon go. This way the sergeant and Jubal could cram into the back while he and Leroi rode up front. The vibrations given off by the *pock pock* noise of the big 6.5 liter turbo diesel massaging his tired limbs, the Hummer cruised at a comfortable sixty-five mph toward the Redoubt.

"They give you a rough time, sir?" Mead asked.

"For a while," Eleen said, slipping the Hummer into cruise control and accidentally hitting the horn as he did so.

"Yeah," Mead commented, studying the bloody wound on Leroi's throat, "but looks like you gave a little payback—unless Leroi here cut himself shaving?"

"Huh," Leroi responded roughly, taking the strain on his cuffed wrists as the Hummer took a tight turn. "You militia bastards are gonna pay big-time for this little caper. The Feds in Washington are gonna send Freeman and his boys in after you lot. Sort you fuckers out real quick."

"Shut your face, Leroi!" Mead warned.

Leroi ignored him, looking murderously across at Eleen. "You remember General Freeman, don't you, Captain? Whopped your ass up at Butcher's Ridge. Gave you and your buddies a one-way ticket to Fairchild. Oh, yeah, except that one poor bastard *you* deserted. You remember? The guy bleeding to death in the snow and you hightailing it to—"

The butt of Mead's .30 smacked the left side of Leroi's head.

"Leave him be, Sergeant!" Eleen ordered Mead.

Leroi cowered against the door. "You'll ... Jesus Christ, you'll be the first, Mead, you fuckhead! Ain't gonna be no prisoners, boy, not this time." He shouted, "You hear, boy? Jesus Christ, we're gonna—"

"Do you want him to hit you again?" Eleen asked coldly. "You blaspheme once more and I'll turn Sergeant Mead loose on you. Understand?" It was the same tone the militia captain had used in the tunnel, holding the broken glass against Leroi's throat. "Do you understand?"

"Yeah," Leroi said reluctantly, looking out at the dull green rush of forest passing by. "I understand."

"Good," Eleen said, and Leroi glanced skyward for any sign of a police chopper that Moorehead might have managed to contact.

Eleen was grimacing from the pain inflicted earlier by

Leroi in the tunnel. "When we reach the I-5," he told Jubal, "blindfold him."

A half hour later Leroi could hear the sharp *swish swish swish* of passing traffic. Obviously they were on the I-5. And then, another half hour later, he was guided, with surprising gentility, by one of the three—most likely Eleen, he thought—into a building. The blindfold removed, he saw it was an empty, disused grain elevator, its sides pierced with bullet holes. Mead cuffed him to a small gauge pipe. "You'll be picked up soon," Eleen told him, Leroi calling out obscenities in the gloom.

"*How* soon?" he yelled. "You mongrels. We'll get you!"

An hour later a police cruiser arrived. It was the second militia kidnap victim that day. The location had been phoned in anonymously, in the same way that the pilot, Robin Frieth, had been found. "These militia bastards are out of control," said the older of the two sheriff's deputies, uncuffing Leroi.

"Where are we?" Leroi demanded.

"Western Washington."

"I *guessed* that," Leroi spat out. "I haven't been blind-folded all the way from Fairchild."

"Hey, hold on there, pardner. No need to take that tone. We're on the same side."

"You're in Bellingham," said the other deputy.

The southerner hadn't heard of it. "What's the nearest big city?"

"Vancouver, 'bout forty miles north."

"*Vancouver?* That's in Canada."

"That's right."

"Where the hell's Seattle?" He said it as if the city had gone AWOL.

"Fifty, sixty miles south," the deputy answered.

"Can you guys patch me through to your HQ? This has to get to Washington."

"HQ? No problem."

CHAPTER THIRTY-FOUR

National Security Agency, Maryland

AT TWENTY-THREE, Nora Ames was a big girl, or fat, depending on which National Security Agency employee you were talking to. She knew that, and had tried everything from Weight Watchers to a diet that consisted almost exclusively of apples, which afterward made it impossible for her to look at another apple without experiencing nausea. Nothing had worked. Oh, she'd lose weight for a while, buy new clothes in bursts of victorious determination, but soon the weight would all be back, and so would her depression. She doubted she'd ever find a man—had tried the Internet once and been humiliated and hurt by the hate mail—believed she faced the future devoid of hope for any lasting happiness. One morning, on her way to work at the NSA, she heard a man call a talk show, refusing to believe the overwhelming evidence that in some cases obesity wasn't a matter of overeating but of metabolism.

All Nora was left with was her work, dreaming of the kind of fame gained in the intelligence community by Eleanor Carruthers, one of the worker bees of British Intelligence, the patient spinster who had scored one of the most important coups of the Second World War. Going over aerial recon photos of the Belgian and French coasts, she pondered the mystery of what looked like ski jumps where the topography was flat. Others had seen the photos but either hadn't noticed the ski-jump-like areas or hadn't known what to make of them. Because of Eleanor Carruthers's inquiring eye and persistence, the RAF was asked for closer aerial recon of the "ski jumps," and, if possible, for surveillance reports of the jumps from agents on the ground, dangerous as this would be. The ski jumps turned out to be the secret launching sites of the V-1 flying bombs, the Nazi prototypes of the Cruise missile.

And so, when Nora Ames and the other nine SATRECON interpreters in her NSA unit viewed the photos of the forty-mile-wide strip of the Canada-U.S. border stretching from Washington to the Idaho panhandle, and their computers failed to match Robin Frieth's description of the soccer field to anything on the SATRECON feed, Nora Ames decided to forego a coffee break with her colleagues and to run the recon strip again. And again no match-up. She then decided to pull in the old SATRECON still photos of the ninety-mile-long stretch of the Canadian–U.S. border that stretches east of the Idaho panhandle.

From the reports of the police who had been at the Kingston Ferry Terminal, and from Robin Frieth's debriefing, it seemed clear to the White House that the militia commander McBride was the man who'd launched the attack on the *Maui*, though no one had actually seen him do it. But that supposition was not hard evidence, and in the opinion of the legal team, certainly not enough to convict. He would have to be cross-examined first, at least.

"Yes, yes," the President agreed impatiently, "but before

we can arrest him we have to find him. To do that, we have to find their . . ."

"Redoubt," Michael Brownlee said.

"Yes," the President said, turning to Donna Fargo. "Anything yet from NSA?"

"They can't find it from Frieth's description," she told him.

"Great!" the President snapped. "How about the Bangor sub base? Are they taking precautions against any future attack?" Before Brownlee or anyone else could answer him, the President continued to vent his spleen. "Having our most sophisticated weapons platform required to squeeze through a gap like that every time it goes to sea—it's preposterous! I couldn't have devised such vulnerability if I'd tried." He turned to General Rogers "How about *your* photo intel? Anything on this mysterious place where this Lieutenant Frieth was forced to land?"

"No match-up yet, sir."

While the Redoubt bristled with weaponry, as usual, there was no sense of alarm. McBride had raised the state of preparedness to DEFCON 4, a designation, borrowed from the federal lexicon, which meant one step away from all-out war. But in essence it was merely precautionary, McBride and his followers confident that neither the U.S. military nor the police knew the location of the Redoubt.

"Well," Cope said, cocky with relief after his and McBride's helo caper, "we've given those bastards something to think about, eh?"

McBride, never one to rest on his laurels, was inspecting the Redoubt's defenses, but now he stopped and looked hard at Cope, whose cockiness annoyed him. "Given them what to think about?"

"Fairchild," Cope answered. "You know—release the POWs or—"

"You don't remember what you've given those bastards to think about, do you?" McBride, who could no longer contain his anger, demanded.

Cope's confidence was ebbing as he sensed that he had somehow fouled McBride's plan to have the POWs released. "What'd I do?" he asked defensively.

"You called me by name."

"What?"

"You called me McBride. I might as well not have had a mask on."

Cope was open-mouthed.

"Yes," McBride said. "In the helo—when I fired a shot near the cop, to get that skirt to tell us where they'd planted emergency locators in the chutes. You freaked, thought I was aiming to kill the cop. You lost it, shouted my name." He paused. "She heard it. You know what that means?"

Cope was licking his lips nervously.

"Now they know *whose* face was behind the sub attack. And because we had to make a break for it and take that helo, they'll be looking for the landing zone. The tables have turned on us. The whole Redoubt is in danger because you couldn't cope, *Cope!* You got it?"

Cope was stunned by the revelation that he'd addressed the major by name. He was playing it all back in his mind—the 9mm in McBride's hand, the short, fierce tussle with the cop, the shot, the fine red cloud of blood, McBride pushing the dead man out. Cope saw too how the Federals, because of his outburst against McBride, might be convinced McBride had murdered the policeman.

Cope's tongue was so dry it stuck to his palate as he tried to get the spittle to speak. "We—well, shit! Who left the vine maple and crap trailing from the back of the van?"

"What?" McBride shot back angrily.

"You know—you didn't check the vine maple and—"

McBride turned away in disgust, walking quickly toward the copse of poplars that had held their own against a ring of evergreen firs and red cedars that formed the perimeter of the soccer field. He didn't have time to listen to Cope whining, evading his responsibility, even if he did have a point—they were both responsible for not having checked the van out. They'd both been in one big hurry to exit Salsbury Park. But that was then, and now he had to make sure things were ready.

"Aw," Cope said, catching up, trying to retrieve his earlier confidence, "they won't figure out where we are. You were smart with the way you handled it."

"Maybe," McBride said, unsure whether he'd been successful or not.

If not, he and his Redoubt's three hundred militia would not simply be called upon to beat off an attack, but would be fighting for their lives. "A redoubt is kin to a castle." It was something a colleague from the Michigan militia had cautioned him about during a meeting near Hayden Lake. While a castle provided a wonderfully defensive position, it was, his colleague warned, "a bitch to get out of" once the enemy arrived.

McBride was checking the camouflage net over the Huey they'd kept. He saw a militiawoman, the tough-looking silvery-haired woman with the buzz cut, checking the 7.62mm Minigun. It was a strange name, McBride thought, for such a deadly weapon—one which he had great respect for. Used in the Air Force's AC-47 "Spooky" gunships, a Minigun in action over Pleiku in '69 had annihilated an entire North Vietnamese battalion—441 men wiped out by this *Mini*gun, he thought. Since then it had been improved further. Now, the gun could be loaded without having to turn any of its six barrels, each of which rapidly became flesh-burning hot, given the weapon's rate of fire.

McBride ran his hand along the gun's J-shaped pintle that,

unlike the older, much heavier mounts, was made of lighter chrome molybdenum steel. "You have any SLAP points?" he asked Buzz Cut, referring to the light-armor-piercing rounds whose denser bullet was carried in a metal shoe, or "sabot," that detached itself after leaving the barrel, affording the bullet greater velocity and penetrating power.

"Four boxes only," she answered, her ample bosom pressing against her fatigues as she helped boss one of the boxes into place.

"That's four to eight minutes max," McBride mused. He was momentarily distracted by the rushing water sound of wind in the trees, which reminded him of Mirela's bungalow by the Spokane River, where the roaring sound of the rapids filled the darkness.

McBride snapped out of his reverie and asked the militiamen working under the net, "Could you people make a platform for the gun? So we could move it quickly if we had to—into the helo?"

"If we had the right equipment," replied a short, stocky militiaman.

"Well, you don't," McBride said testily. "If you can't improvise, you shouldn't be here. That's one of the qualifications for Redoubt membership. Correct?"

"Yes, Major," Buzz Cut said. "We can do it."

"How long?"

"Three, four hours."

"It'd have to be something on standby only," McBride explained, "because once you moved it into the helo it'd limit your field of fire."

"Understood," Buzz Cut said.

McBride admired her as a comrade-in-arms, bosom and all, but the thought of bedding her intimidated him as much as it did the other men. He believed she was as tough as she looked, with a hard, unyielding mouth that the nine-man squad under her command said hadn't smiled since her husband had been killed in a shoot-out with feds down by Astoria.

"You think they'll find us, Major?" asked another militiaman, a swarthy man in his mid-twenties. He had a wad of gum in his mouth as he worked diligently and painstakingly with his other squad members on a train of beeper bombs—ordinary pagers attached to blocks of C4 and detonated by merely dialing the beepers' numbers on a cell phone.

"They won't ferret us out," McBride assured him, "if my lures work."

"They'll know where we are," another militiaman said, "if we use our cell phones to call these pagers."

"True," McBride conceded. "But if we have to use our cells, it'll mean we're already in a firefight."

The militiaman nodded, dourly continuing to embed the pagers into the plastique.

"Hey, Nor," one of Nora Ames's male colleagues called out to her. "We've got some Danish here. Take a break."

"No thanks," she answered, her huge, tentlike dress bent over her desk.

"Don't ask her," another man in the ten-person unit whispered. "She'll gobble up the whole lot."

"Lay off," said his buddy, who'd asked Nora once more to join them for an afternoon coffee break. "The Danishes aren't all yours!"

Pretending not to hear, Nora continued examining a pile of old SATPIX black-and-white prints that had not yet been put on the hard drive. They had lain undisturbed for years in a box of dusty, musty-smelling, buff-colored 8½-by-11 manila envelopes marked MONTANA–B.C. BORDER—WESTERN. She was so obese that she had to push the photos forward beyond her bosom's periphery in order to use the magnifying stand. Patiently, she examined each one of more than two hundred, her neck muscles taut, head throbbing. Occasionally she would look up, out the window, at the greenery beyond, to forestall the dizziness that for some photo interpreters became an occupational hazard. But only seconds later she was back at it.

"Wasting her time," the protector of the Danish opined, taking another pastry.

"Guess she wants to find the soccer field mentioned in that helo pilot's report. Make a name for herself."

"She already has," said Danish. "Big Butt!"

"Give her credit. I think she's trying to cut down. Work probably keeps her mind off food."

"Great," Danish declared. "More for me," and as he strolled back to his desk he called out to her, "Wasting your time, Nora. They don't play soccer in Montana. It's a capital offense!"

Nora was aware of the accompanying laughter from the others. But she took no offense because the comment about soccer had given her an idea. What was it Michael Douglas had said in *Traffic*? "Think outside of the box." Think outside the normal assumptions we make. In this case it was the assumption NSA had made about Robin Frieth's debriefing.

Heart pounding, Nora pushed the Montana–British Columbia pile abruptly aside and turned back to her computer. The soccer goalposts, like the bilingual O'Henry bar, could have been nothing more than props, lures, to suggest to searchers that the field was close to if not in Canada. She removed goalposts from the search mode. Now she was searching for the same shape of field but without soccer goalposts.

Nothing.

She put goalposts back into the list of search variables, as well as drawing on SATPIX archives, but not from the Washington to Idaho strip along the U.S.–Canadian border, as suggested by Lieutenant Frieth's report. Instead, she now examined a relatively narrow, fifty-mile-wide strip within Washington

State alone, north to the Canadian border, south to Oregon. And the flashing green icon, top right of her screen, told her she'd found it. Quickly, she killed the icon, lest Danish see it, and watched the zoom's pixels expanding on the screen. She elected to scribble down the lat/long rather than turn on the printer, which would draw the attention of Danish and the others. She pressed Save, then Close, and the screen saver— New York during winter—came up. Struggling from her seat with more than usual agility, but trying desperately to hide her excitement, Nora walked down the room past Danish.

"Back in five," she said.

As she reached the corridor, the glass door closing behind her, Danish collapsed in his chair, arms dangling gorillalike, imitating Nora's labored, audible breathing, announcing to the others in a high-pitched voice, *"Back in five!"*

She was back in ten, as long as it had taken her boss to first quickly confirm her finding on his computer—an apparent match-up of computer image to Robin Frieth's verbal description—and then to call NSA's director, who quickly informed the White House that General Freeman's assumptions about the Redoubt had been wrong.

"Remarkable tenacity, Ms. Ames," the NSA director told Nora. "And initiative." But he didn't stop there. Cutting through the normal red tape to demonstrate how promptly he rewarded such dedication and experience, the director promoted her on the spot to Head of Unit, accompanying her back to her "old" desk, as he jocularly put it, where he announced her promotion to the unit. Two or three people clapped, then the others joined in, Danish included, though he sat stone-faced.

The director had left before Nora realized it. Standing alone now, heart pounding with the exhilaration of her Eleanor Carruthers dream come true, she told herself that as

Head of Unit it would be childish to seek revenge on Danish for his persistent backstabbing and cruelty, that she could not allow herself to sink to his level.

That afternoon, she discovered the promotion wasn't all glory, besieged as she was by colleagues anxious to know if there'd be any change in their shift allocations. She gladly took on the task, however, knowing that "it comes with the territory," as the director had so succinctly put it. Suck-up time!

She asked Danish when he'd prefer to work.

"Same as usual," he answered perfunctorily, refusing to look up from his computer screen. "Monday to Friday. Eight to four-thirty."

She peered at her clipboard. "Oh, gee. Sorry. I've got you slated for Fridays to Tuesdays. Let's see now . . . yup. Fridays to Tuesdays."

"What?" He swung away from his screen. "I can't do that. I've got tickets to the Knicks game on Saturday! I've already booked the shuttle flight to New York!"

"I don't think so," she said, smiling down at him.

His face turned beet red from the neck up, eyes bulging with fury.

Nora kept smiling. "You'll like the weekend people," she told him. "They're nice." Ticking the roster as she ambled away, she added, "Anyway, you can always tape your soccer game."

"Soc—" She heard a crack, and glancing back, saw Danish had snapped one—no, two—pencils clean in half.

CHAPTER THIRTY-FIVE

Seattle

"IN THE SAN Juans?" Police Chief Ernst Cordell was as surprised as Brownlee had been before passing on the news. But while Brownlee's surprise had been caused by his ignorance of just where the San Juans were, the Seattle police chief's utterance was more the expression of a local suddenly realizing that the militia's legendary hideout was in his own backyard—if "backyard" was the appropriate description. It consisted of more than 450 islands sprawled over seven hundred square miles of sea between the southern end of Vancouver Island and the northwestern coast of Washington State. Sprinkled like emeralds in a cobalt-colored sea, except on rainy days, when they turned greenish-black, lost in gray mists, only a handful of them were inhabited, with over 230 yet to be named.

"They're the last place on earth I would have expected the militia to set up," Cordell said. "I mean, the only way in is by air or boat, and only a few of the 450 islands have any airstrip or docking facilities."

"Which is precisely why I guess the militia chose it," Brownlee replied. "Isolated. Difficult to get to. The sea is their moat."

"What island is it?" Cordell asked. The only map in his office was a 1:70,000 scale chart showing the main islands of Orcas, Lopez, San Juan itself, and a few others.

"It's one of the no-names," Brownlee answered. "Shaped like a figure six. NSA people have pinpointed it a couple of miles or so west southwest of Castle Island, north of an old military dumping site. Geological Survey told them the island was probably teardrop-shaped eons ago, top part of it eaten into by wind and wave—"

"All right," Cordell cut in, uninterested in anything that had happened more than a month ago. "Give me the lat and long. We'll take care of the militia."

"Get your men ready, by all means, Chief," Brownlee replied, "but don't move out until we have an SPV on the island."

"A what?" Cordell asked, quickly making notes on a Post-it pad that kept sliding away from him as he held the phone in one hand, trying to write with the other.

"SATPIX verification," Brownlee said. "I'll have NSA use thermal imaging to make sure it's not a setup. Like—" He almost said "Ruby Lake." "You know, to make sure it's not a Ptompkin village. Shouldn't take long."

"SATPIX verification! Won't that put us in the soup?" Cordell asked. "Overhead spying by the government on its own people? Violating Fourth Amendment rights? Invasion of privacy?"

Brownlee replied, "Fuck 'em, Chief. They used a *missile* against our sub. While I'm arranging the SATPIX, you gather your guys together. How many do you have available?"

"As many as we need, Mr. Brownlee." He liked this guy's spirit. "We don't like being made to look like fools up here. We want those Boeing clowns Rainor, Haley, *and* this prick McBride. Plus we've ID'd the two scumbags people saw on the bridge—Stanes and Maddin. You should've received e-mail pictures of them by now."

Brownlee had, but he'd been deluged with information on

the militia in the last forty-eight hours—mug shots of every wanted militiamen from Seattle to Key West. *"Maddin?"* he mused.

"Yeah, a.k.a. 'Spoonface'—red birthmark running down the side of his face. Evil-looking son of a bitch."

Brownlee recalled a nephew who suffered the same affliction, and felt duty-bound to state, "Not everybody with a birthmark is a son of a bitch."

"What—no no, not at all. But it's his eyes. Got that not-here stare." Before Brownlee could answer, Cordell continued, "We also believe several escapees from Fairchild are making their way to the Redoubt. All the rats in the same sewer. Once we—"

"Hold on a moment, Chief," Brownlee said, his junior aide informing him that the results of NSA's SATPIX over the six-shaped island, now designated Redoubt, were coming in over the fax, revealing multiple infrared warm clusters. Possibly, the NSA director had noted—in very bad handwriting—some of the clusters were animals: deer, bear, and such. But most clusters, the report suggested, indicated "possible human habitation."

"You still there, Chief?" Brownlee inquired.

"Yes, sir."

"Hold on. I'm calling NSA on the other line."

"Yessir."

When the NSA director came on, Brownlee pressed him, "Does this suggested 'possible human habitation' mean your interpreters think there are a *lot* of people on the island?"

"I think it's safe to assume—"

"Hey!" Brownlee said sharply. "I don't want a load of save-your-ass bureaucratic bullshit here. I want a definite opinion. How much 'suggested habitation' are we talking about? Ten people, fifty, a—"

"We figure around a hundred, maybe a hundred and fifty."

"Thank you!" Brownlee said, and returned to Cordell's line. "Chief, NSA says there are about two hundred militia on the island. You have enough men?"

"I'll call in everyone I can spare, together with SWAT teams."

Brownlee paused for a moment before telling Cordell, "I have to be frank with you, Chief. The President doesn't want to use the armed forces to bring these guys in. Looks very bad internationally. Besides, they're criminals on that Redoubt, and so it *should* be a police action. But we could give you a National Guard assist, as we've done for riot control, etcetera. That's not the same as the President sending in *regular* armed forces."

"Like some banana republic?" said Cordell. Before Brownlee could recover, Cordell continued congenially, "Sounds good to me. We have good liaison up here with the Guard. Colonel Rice. A hardass, but he's a good guy. We've worked in tandem before."

"Good. I admire your lack of ego, Chief."

"I've got my fair share, Mr. Brownlee. Rice won't get all the glory."

"Okay, fine. But let's keep the joint operation in bounds. I mean—"

"I know," Cordell cut in presciently. "If we ship a Guard battalion out there with APCs and all the rest of its gear, we're bound to arouse suspicion. I propose no more than two companies of Guards, infantry—two hundred max, and a hundred of my boys, including fifty of my SWAT team members. A big Coast Guard cutter for the Guards' two hundred, and the Coast Guard rescue hovercraft for the first fifty of my guys under Bill Pollock—who, by the way, will have to include that pain-in-the-ass Moorehead from Fairchild. That Nazi's so pissed over the escape from his precious camp that he's obsessed with revenge."

"Use him," Brownlee said, not caring one way or another. "Why not?"

"Okay, that's that. My second fifty'll go in on the helos, after the Guard." Before Brownlee could comment, Cordell, caught up in the excitement of his plan, raced on. "You know the beauty of the hovercraft?"

"I guess," Brownlee said. "It can go straight in and unload quickly. No docking facilities required."

"Uh-huh," Cordell said politely, but any fool knew that. "The beauty of it, Mr. Brownlee, is that you come up on an island into the wind and those damn rebels won't hear it till it's too damn late."

"Good enough, Chief, but in that case why don't you put the Guard on a hovercraft too?"

"Because, Mr. Brownlee, your appropriation guys in Washington, D.C., wouldn't let the Coast Guard up here have more than one hovercraft."

"In the whole Northwest?" Brownlee said incredulously. "That can't be—"

"Oh yes, we have a few smaller air cushions, but they can only hold half a dozen or so civilians and a few Beaufort drum life rafts. But for any major maritime disaster, we have only one big hovercraft—Navy Landing Craft with—"

"Navy?" There was sudden panic in the otherwise unflappable White House voice. "Chief, we can't use a Navy assault craft, for Chrissake. I've just finished telling you—it's politically unacceptable to use any of our regular armed forces—"

"Hang on, Mr. Brownlee," Cordell said. "I mean it's a Navy *design*, that's all. Coast Guard up here got it secondhand from the Navy."

"No Navy markings, I hope?"

"No, sir. Good old red and white."

"All right," said an audibly relieved Brownlee. "When do you estimate you can hit them?"

"Well, once the President gives the Guard authority, we can—"

"Start preparations now," Brownlee cut in. "ASAP. The Guard'll have authority in ten minutes—I've just had my aide fax you an NSA six-inch-to-the-mile blowup of this Redoubt Island."

"I suggest," Cordell said, "we code name it Rats' Nest."

"Sounds appropriate."

As Brownlee called the President, the junior aide asked, with some trepidation, "Why did you tell him NSA estimated there were two hundred militia on the island?"

"Covering my ass," Brownlee explained. "Better they prepare for more opposition than less."

In Seattle, Ernst Cordell, going back over his hurriedly scribbled notes, turned to his aide, Mark Aitken. "Brownlee said something about a Pa-tom . . ."

"Ptompkin village," Aitken explained. "A Russian noble called Ptompkin used to construct fake village fronts—like those facades on the movie lots. Czar would ride through, all he could see was what he thought were nicely painted new buildings and happy peasants, paid for by Ptompkin, cheering. Czar's conclusion: 'My, the peasants are doing well!' "

"So Washington thinks the Redoubt might be a fake?"

"Not now, after there's been that thermal imaging verification."

"All right. Now listen, Mark, I want you to handle liaison between our guys and the Guards. The way we should do it is have the two hundred Guardsmen and our first fifty on the island before our fifty SWAT guys go in on the helos. I don't want those militia bastards tipped off by the choppers' noise. Same kind of op we used last year on that big dope outfit in Snohomish County. Only here the choppers'll be landing on this 'soccer field.' I'd say only four Hueys—unless we want to risk collision. From Brownlee's fax, that soccer paddock doesn't look much bigger than a football field."

"Okay," Aitken said. "I'll tell the Guard we need four." He paused. "Will that be enough, though?"

Cordell mulled it over. "Our Hueys are 1-Ns, ten to fifteen men apiece. It'll be, what?" He eyeballed the 1:70,000 scale chart. "Only a twenty, twenty-five minute flight from Anacortes."

As he looked down at the figure six shape of the island, which lay just south of the San Juans' maritime boundary and so wasn't included on most charts, Cordell's forefinger stabbed at it. "We'll go in on this beach on the west side of Rats' Nest." From the fax, the island looked to be no more than two miles from north to south, its mile-long stem a half-mile wide, narrowing to a treeless isthmus of only a few hundred yards wide before broadening out to form the base of the figure six, roughly two miles in diameter—in all, just under four square miles. To balance his policemen's attack on Rats' Nest's west beach, Cordell suggested they have Colonel Rice's Guardsmen land on the eastern side of the island, where the six's only other beach formed a slight curve as the stem of the six met its circle. This east beach looked to be no more than eighty yards long, but it would be enough room, Cordell estimated, for the Guardsmen to land on, shortly after they disembarked from a Coast Guard cutter's Zodiac boats. "Cutter will only need to be a few hundred yards offshore."

"Won't the militia suspect a cutter?" Aitken asked.

"The militia suspects their grandmother. Incipient paranoia is a prerequisite for membership, Mark. But Coast Guard cutters are a common enough sight in these waters that it shouldn't cause any undue suspicion."

"Be better if it was a Washington State ferry," Aitken said. "They're much more common passing through the islands than Coast Guard cutters."

"Yes, if the Rats' Nest was on a ferry run!"

"But remote as it is," Aitken pointed out, "the coordinates Brownlee's given us put it only five miles off the Seattle–San Juan Island ferry run, Chief."

"I know *that*," Cordell replied tartly. "A lot of the islands are only a few miles from a ferry run, but they're not *on* a ferry run, are they? Might as well be in Latvia. There's barely a handful of terminals on the big islands—San Juan, Orcas, Lopez, let alone—"

"Yes, sir, but what I'm getting at is how about loading the two hundred Guardsmen on the regular San Juan Island–Seattle ferry run and having them—"

"I've already thought of that," Cordell said irritably. "Setting off a half-dozen big Zodiacs full of National Guard from the ferry. No way, José. Washington State ferries with armed Guardsmen among the *civilians* aboard? Civilians used as cover for the dropping off of two companies of Guardsmen, everyone of 'em loaded for bear? Governor'd go ape. And if I was him, so would I."

Mark Aitken was concerned about the haste with which he'd have to set up the operation with the National Guard's Colonel Rice, and Aitken had an obsessive streak. Which in this case demanded he get all the events that had taken place recently in strict chronological order—everything since the Boeing plant fiasco and the murder of the marijuana grower to the deadly attack on the *Maui* by militia major McBride and his cohorts. Aitken was still staring down at the ferries map. A Coast Guard, that is, a federal ship, suddenly appearing on the militia's radar? He was positive the rats'd have radar. If the militia could get a Javelin, they could get that.

"What about using one of the *private* ferries to transport the Guard?" he asked Cordell. "You know, one of those fast, twin-hulled jobs out of Anacortes? Lot smaller than the big two-thousand-passenger Washington State ferries, *and* we

wouldn't have to use running lights, take 'em closer in to the
beach. It could cut straight down the eastern side of Lopez
past Decatur, Watmough Head, then swing westward past—"

"I'm not sure about that," Cordell said, sliding his finger
beyond Lopez Island's Colville Point to Castle and Swirl islands, off Iceberg Point, Lopez Island's most southwesterly
promontory, and on to the relatively tiny six that was the
militia's Redoubt. "Dozens of hidden rocks and tidal islands
dot that coastline, Mark."

"Ferry captains know that coast like their prick. Besides,
Chief," Aitken added, "the private ferries have radar too. And
the weather's calm."

Cordell was nodding. "It wouldn't come cheap. We'd have
to give the skipper and crew one hell of a bonus and tell them
just enough, but not too much, in case they leak it."

"Washington's paying," Aitken said. "Security'll be fine.
Big bonus, but if anyone on the ferry opens their yap, they
don't work again."

"You're a hard bastard!" Cordell said.

Aitken shrugged. "I'm just saying we can do it."

"All right, but if the militia hears the ferry, or picks it up on
radar and sees no running lights, they *will* be suspicious. A
Coast Guard vessel en route to somebody in distress is ac-
ceptable, but not a darkened ferry."

"So have it lit up like a Christmas tree if you like," Aitken
said, "and it'll be identified by them as just another private
ferry transporting cargo, building materials, whatever, to one
of the scores of islands not served by the state ferries. There
are over four hundred islands, remember. When the ferry gets
near the east beach, we have it slow to near dead stop, deploy
the Zodiacs carrying the Guard."

"Then," Cordell added, "our first fifty go in on the hovercraft to the west-side beach, and our fifty SWAT guys aboard
the helos can—"

Aitken slammed his desk with such a thud it startled Cordell. "I've got it! Let's have the ferry carrying Rice's Guardsmen and the hovercraft carrying our boys set up radio chatter—you know, the ferry's hit one of the reefs, taking on water . . ."

"The Coast Guard hovercraft is on its way to assist! Beautiful, Mark. I love it! Call Rice. Let's see if we can arrange H hour for midnight." The police chief glanced at his watch. "Twelve hours from now. Hit 'em while they're in bed. That'll mean having the private ferry leave Anacortes no later than 2300." He looked up at Aitken. "That gives you twelve hours, Mark. Think you can do it?"

Mark Aitken was struck by how "we" had suddenly become "you."

Aitken, on the phone to Rice, asked the colonel if it was possible for him to have two hundred Guardsmen ready to attack the Redoubt in twelve hours.

Rice replied, "No, we'll be ready in four. At Anacortes!" which told Aitken that the colonel must have already been prepared for the request by Brownlee. "Need some helos?" Rice added cheekily.

"You must be psychic, Colonel," Aitken said.

Rice's laugh was full and gravelly, belying the fact that he was a small reed of a man who, they said, had just made the Guards' height requirement by pumping iron and all but working himself to death on a rowing machine. "I'm not psychic, Mr. Aitken. A little bird told me you might be requiring our services."

"I hope your men realize the absolute necessity for surprise on this operation," Aitken said. He recalled the old World War Two slogan from his great-grandfather's days: "Loose lips sink ships."

"Don't sweat it," Rice said. "I've made sure the security lid on this is watertight."

"Good."

Aitken had no sooner got off the phone than he received a call from a CNN correspondent asking if there was any truth to the rumor that there'd been some kind of action launched against "militia elements" in northern Idaho?

"Not to my knowledge," Aitken replied. "But why ask us here in Seattle? Call Boise."

"I have. They say they know nothing about it."

"Neither do I. Who told you this—some militia nut?"

"A reliable source."

"If you don't mind me saying so, ma'am, I think your *source* has been on the *sauce*."

"Very droll," she answered wryly. "Well, if you do hear anything, would you let me know. I'd appreciate it."

"No problem. Can you give me your cell and e-mail?"

He wrote it down, hung up, and passed the information to his clerk, who, glancing at it, commented, "Marte Price. Isn't she the one with the big—"

"Have you got hold of SWAT HQ yet?" Aitken cut in sharply.

"I was just about to."

"Then do it!"

The moment Aitken said it, he was mad at himself. Who was he to act so self-righteously in the face of the clerk's earthy comment about this Marte Price's anatomy? Good Lord, he was behaving like that militia guy, Elway—no, Eleen, the Mormon POW he'd heard about. The guards at Fairchild said he wouldn't tolerate the slightest off-color remark from his subordinates. It reminded Aitken to check on the status of the manhunt for Eleen and the other two escaped militiamen, Mead and Jubal, each of whom Commandant Moorehead, now in Seattle, said had murdered his men at the abandoned Cascade Tunnel. But nothing came up on the screen. Aitken assumed that all of the wanted militiamen, including the escaped prisoners, McBride, and his cohort who'd been aboard Robin Frieth's helo, had undoubtedly made their way to the safety of the Redoubt—by canoe, if necessary.

Colonel Rice called to liaise with Aitken further, determined that no screw-up occur because of any overlooked detail. "We're going to use two companies, Able and Bravo, sending them in on eight thirty-foot Zodiacs. Four Zodiacs per company. Twenty-five in each boat. It's a full load but it's relatively calm, and it'll only be a short run into the east beach—a quarter, half mile, at the most."

"Fine by me," Aiken told him. "But won't the outboards make a racket?"

"Twin Mercurys, Mr. Aitken. They say they're very quiet."

As Aitken hung up, his aide called out to say he had SWAT HQ on the line, adding, "There should be enough noise to cover them, sir."

"What?"

"The Zodiacs—the rigid inflatables. The noise of the surf, even if the waves are small, should muffle the outboards pretty good."

"Uh-huh. Okay. Sorry I was a bit fritzy back there—about that Marte Price. But a lot's riding on this." It was the understatement of the year. "We've got to take these bastards by surprise."

"I understand, sir. Ah, our SWAT commander did ask me if they're to go in with medics."

"I guess. Here, give me the phone. Oh, and one more thing—we'll be using school buses again to transport everyone, Guards and our guys, from Seattle to Anacortes. Just like we did on the monster drug bust. We'll be going up the I-5 in the dark, but even so, a line of Army trucks could tip off the press as well as any militia spies. And while I'm talking to

SWAT, I want you to call Rice and tell him to remind his boys—no helmets until the buses are on the ferry. What have you told the ferry company?"

"It's a marine biology field trip from Seattle schools. Overnight on the ferry to see plankton fluorescence and other nighttime sea creatures."

Mark Aitken nodded appreciatively. "Excellent—you after my job?"

"Absolutely!"

Aitken finally turned to the phone. "Sorry to keep you waiting, Lieutenant." The SWAT commander was one of those who in February 2001, along with the Coast Guard and Canadian Mounties, had made the biggest cocaine bust in West Coast history—over two tons—from a Canadian fishing boat in the Juan de Fuca Strait. "Lieutenant, your Hueys are almost sixty feet long and the rotor span is—"

"Forty-eight feet," the lieutenant said, impatience in his voice. Had this bureaucrat kept him on hold just to show off that he'd been doing his homework?

But in fact Aitken had been worried about the possibility of collision when the four Hueys crowded in above the soccer field, which as well as being almost dead center in the base of the six-shaped island, was also no bigger than a football field.

"We've done this before, Aitken. We'll be on night vision goggles."

"I know, just making sure."

"Right!"

After the call, the SWAT lieutenant walked outside his training hut to where several of his twelve-man assault teams, called Wolf Packs, were standing before the SATPIX blowup of the Redoubt. Going over the SATPIX's hot spots that were scattered about the soccer field, the "deuce" and "quad" elements of the twelve-man Wolf Packs were being assigned their areas of responsibility—setting a perimeter of fire, for one, beyond which they couldn't shoot for fear of "blue on blue," or hitting their own men. Each of Rice's two hundred Guardsmen and Cordell's two fifty-man teams would have telltale "friend" or "foe" armbands and helmet markers, which, though normally invisible, could be picked up by each other's night vision goggles. Even so, the SWAT lieutenant knew that no matter how detailed his Emergency Assault Plan, in the fog of war, battle noise and darkness could sow confusion among the best trained SWAT veterans, and in Cordell's contingent of fifty regular heavily armed entry/arrest teams.

"Should've had two days at least to set up this EAP," one of the men opined.

"Yeah, well," replied the SWAT lieutenant, who went by the nickname of "Tunny," as in the tons of cocaine he'd helped seize. "We don't have that luxury. We can always use more time. But Washington wants this place swept for militia— now!"

"Wouldn't have anything to do with politics, would it?"

"Not our business," Tunny said. "We do know it has a lot to do with those three guys who were killed on the *Maui* and the cop who was thrown out of that chopper. And that highway patrolman. That's good enough for me." He turned to face the Wolf Pack. "All right, pay attention: rules of engagement. Simple. We order anyone we see to assume the position. If, however, we are in any danger of being fired upon, I repeat, *any danger,* we fire first."

Tunny looked at a neatly bearded policeman whose area of responsibility was evacuation, which included getting prisoners out as well as any wounded Wolf Pack members. Except for absence of birthmark, the policeman bore a passing resemblance to Art Maddin, one of the most wanted militiamen. "Ray, chopper four'll be our Medevac," Tunny said.

"Chopper four Medevac. Got it."

CHAPTER THIRTY-SIX

THE SMALL EIGHT-MAN crew of *Kingfisher II*, the passenger-cum-cargo-ferry, were happy to be readying the vessel for its run to southern Lopez; at least, that's where their captain had told them it was headed, after his usual inspection of the big catamaran's twin fiberglass hulls that made it one of the fastest in the Northwest archipelago. Limited only by its carrying capacity of 320 passengers and no vehicles, except for tourists' mountain bikes—all other cargo requiring a jetty to unload its usual resupply loads of food and diesel fuel for the outlying islands—*Kingfisher II* was a favorite for quick unscheduled runs. This was particularly true when building contractors in Anacortes were in a race to deliver building materials before the islands were hit by storms, though the San Juans normally received only a quarter of the rainfall that fell on Seattle, seventy-five miles to the south.

It wasn't until the skipper asked for all cell phones to be handed into the wheelhouse, and a long line of school buses arrived, followed by the delivery at the dock of eight thirty-foot-long Zodiacs from a supermarket container truck, that the ferry's eight crewmen knew something unprecedented was taking place. This was confirmed when two squad cars swooped down on a hapless bum and two young backpackers who'd wandered too close to the dock, the police quickly whisking them away. As soon as Able and Bravo companies had finished boarding, the Vibram-soled boots of the two hundred Guardsmen making remarkably little noise, the *Kingfisher* cast off. The six thirty-man platoons, each with its lightweight mortar and squad automatic weapons in place, were free to stand and move about only after they were well beyond sight of a huge raft of towed logs passing Green Point and out of view of what the colonel called "snugglers."

"Smugglers?" a confused radioman asked.

"Snugglers!" Able company's captain told him. "You know, lovebirds. Parking at the point."

"Huh, they'd be too busy getting it on to see us."

"Maybe," the captain said, gazing overhead at the *Kingfisher*'s bridge, which resembled the carrying handle of a giant flower basket, arcing over the deck. It gave the skipper an unimpeded view all about him and allowed the deck to be free of any superstructure that would have reduced cargo space. Turning to the troops, he instructed everyone to keep a low profile. "Don't go hanging over the railing."

"The gunwales," the rifleman corrected the captain, with an ease that only reserve units of men who often worked together at the same civilian jobs could muster.

"Rail, gunwale, whatever, just keep your friggin' head down." He spotted one man checking his ammo box for a SAW, putting on his helmet. "Hey, are you deaf? You were told not to wear your Fritz—not until we disembark."

"Sorry."

"That's okay. Ten lashes with a wet noodle."

The SAW gunner, a black man from Tacoma, gave a broad smile, his teeth a flash of white against the darkness of the Rosario Strait as *Kingfisher* pulled farther away, the deep throb of its engines unusually loud on the calm sea. "Least you've got good camouflage," Able's captain told the black Guardsman. Colonel Rice overheard the remark and felt good—that kind of interracial banter augured well. Still, Rice wouldn't let himself become overconfident.

Clear of the lights about Green Point, they sailed into a darkness unrelieved by the moon, which was hidden for the moment behind a scud of nimbostratus that extended from fifty miles south of Mount Baker and eastward for a hundred miles over the spine of the Cascades.

"Hope the moon stays hidden," Able's captain told Rice, who lit up a cigarette.

"We'll see."

"Colonel, at the risk of a court-martial, I thought you were giving those up?"

Rice, silhouetted against the gunwale of one of the Zodiacs, studied the cigarette as if surprised by its sudden appearance. "It's coming along, Captain!"

"Ought to bust you to private." Able's captain saw several other men light up, the red pinpoints dancing against the black sea. Perhaps, he thought, it was as much the cigarettes' warm glow in the darkness as the nicotine that afforded the men comfort.

The diminutive colonel took a long drag and flicked the cigarette over the side. "Satisfied?" he asked Able's captain, who now felt he might have overstepped the mark.

Rice was no doubt anxious about the coming assault on Redoubt's west beach once the *Kingfisher* had completed its perpendicular-shaped course from Anacortes, down past Decatur and Lopez islands, before a short jog north to the west beach. Able's captain was on edge himself, as were most of his men—if they had any brains. He knew, however, that this wasn't necessarily a bad thing; everyone performed best when they were on their toes. "Too laid back," his dad always told him, "and you're on the mat!"

Suddenly, silver slashes of light invaded the night, then another and another, dolphins crisscrossing the bows of the twin hulls. Several men requested permission to go up to the net that had been strung between the twin bows, permitting tourists a better view of the abundant marine life in the nutrient-rich waters.

Colonel Rice refused permission, concerned that even on the virtually deserted coasts of Decatur or Lopez, someone might be watching.

"They'd need a Hubble telescope!" the black gunner complained.

"You never know," a comrade said. "The colonel's playing it safe."

In Bravo company there wasn't as much grumbling, their captain a man who'd lost an older brother in a fight with militia fishermen over the 1974 ruling by the federal district court that had allocated half the local annual salmon catch to the native Indians. For this Bravo officer it was payback time against the militia.

Gazing down below the ferry's sliding prow of running lights, a mortarman thought he saw a shark's fin.

"Bullshit," his squad leader said. "You saw a dolphin, man. Water's too friggin' cold in the Northwest for sharks."

"Bullshit!" the mortar crewman retorted. "They've caught warm water fish up here."

"I know. In a can!"

"Can, my ass!"

"Keep your ass."

"No, c'mon," his comrade said, lighting up a cigarette. "Don't you remember that marlin they caught off Seattle?"

"Gimme a look at that," his squad leader said, gently taking the cigarette from the mortarman's fingers, studying it.

"What's wrong?" the mortarman asked.

His squad leader held the cigarette close to his nose, musing, "Wondered if you were on the weed."

"Hey," the mortarman riposted. "Money talks, bullshit

walks. How much you willing to bet they've caught warm water fish up here?"

The squad leader was now receiving some good-natured ribbing, to put up or shut up. "All right," he said. "Ten bucks says there's no warm water fish up here." He paused. "So who's gonna be the judge?"

The mortarman looked around. "Get Woody. He's the fishing fanatic."

Woody was summoned. A sergeant in his late thirties, bald as a billiard ball, he made his way to the railing through the cursing crush of men who were curled up against their packs.

"Woody?" the mortarman called out. "Did they catch a marlin off Seattle?"

"Yeah. Late nineties."

There was a chorus of cheers.

"Wait a minute!" the squad leader said. "Hold it. How about sharks, Woody?"

"Oh yeah. Sharks too! Basking shark, white shark, blue shark, salmon shark—"

"Shit!" the squad leader cut in.

"I love you, Woody," the victorious mortarman said.

"Gonna kiss 'im?" the squad leader said.

"I'm gonna marry 'im."

Another chorus of cheers.

"Settle down!" It was the colonel, his tone interpreted by some as disapproval.

"Eleen!" the mortarman commented to his ammo bearer, the custom of invoking the well-known militia captain's name whenever anyone objected to bad language or sexual innuendo as widespread throughout the National Guard as it was in the police force.

"We'll be there in fifteen minutes," Colonel Rice explained, "and your voices carry a long way at night, especially across water."

The squad leader, who, like every other Guardsman, was forbidden to carry loose change into battle for fear of it clinking and giving away their position, and because small change could become deadly shrapnel should they be hit, told the mortarman he'd pay him the ten bucks when they got back. Upon which, the mortarman turned to Woody. "It was a *hundred* bucks, wasn't it?"

"And fuck you too," the squad leader said good-humoredly. "You want me to put you on point?"

"Colonel!" It was the *Kingfisher*'s first mate. "The hovercraft is heading for the east side of the island. We've started the 'rescue' chatter."

"Any problems?"

"No, sir. They're doing a great job. By the time the militia catch on—if they do—your two hundred and the cops'll be ashore."

"Outstanding," the colonel said, complimenting him.

"Outstanding?" Able company's captain said to Bravo's CO. "Never heard him say that before."

"I have. His old man was in the Marines. They say that when they go for a dump. *Outstanding!*" In the background, Bravo's CO heard the frying sound of static invading the wheelhouse, the hovercraft's captain advising his counterpart on *Kingfisher* to try for the nearest landfall and assuring him that meanwhile the hovercraft would try to reach the supposedly sinking ferry.

"Hurry!" *Kingfisher*'s skipper said quietly. "I don't know if the pumps can handle it."

"Sounds convincing," Able's CO told Bravo's leader.

"You mean we *aren't* sinking?" Bravo's captain said.

The moon broke through the scud of cloud, black sea turned to silver, and for some inexplicable reason the salty tang of the sea seemed more pronounced. The mortarman could see the outline of a big passenger jet, presumably heading south from Vancouver to Seattle, but he was unable to hear it because of the noise of the *Kingfisher*'s engines, their diesel exhaust washing over Rice's men as the ferry turned north toward the six-shaped island.

"Wind's picking up," Rice noted to *Kingfisher*'s skipper, the Able and Bravo commanders telling their men to go to their assigned Zodiacs. A line of twelve Guardsmen along each side of their thirty-foot Zodiac readied themselves to lift up the ribbed rubber boat and move in unison toward the ferry's stern ramp for disembarkation. The coxswain, the twenty-fifth man in each Zodiac, guided them.

"Can't see the beach," the mortarman said.

"Can't see the friggin' island," added his "tube" man, who would operate the mortar the moment the base plate was set.

"It's there," the squad leader assured them. "You can't see it now because of the glare from the ferry's lights."

One of Able company's men had put on his night vision goggles in hopes of picking up a shore light, but the illumination from the ferry caused the night vision goggles to "bloom," or white out, even on the NVGs' lowest setting.

On *Kingfisher*'s high bridge, however, the captain had spotted a few pinpoints of light along the Redoubt's dark shore, and Rice, now on the starboard side of the bridge, could see the beach, a thin sliver of sand in intermittent moonlight, the black bulk of the island behind. What surprised him, though he and his two company COs had carefully studied the map contours on the thickly wooded island, was how high the shoreline was at the base of the six. It was almost as if the island was made up of two quite different topographies: the lower, bush-covered stem that formed the northern part, and the high, bulbous base, or southern part of the island.

"Sheer cliffs!" the *Kingfisher*'s skipper said. "That sucker must be over a hundred feet high."

"You've never seen it before?" Rice asked, surprised.

"Colonel, I've spent over thirty years moving freight and folk throughout the San Juans, and I don't even know a quarter of the islands—probably only really set foot on a dozen or so." He turned the wheel to compensate for a surprisingly strong current. "I'm in, I'm out," he continued. "Fast as I can. Time's money. I'm no backpacking tourist."

Rice was looking at his map. "Well, where the stem of the six joins the base, it looks all right." He meant low enough, estimating that the planned run to the soccer field in the middle of the base was no more than a one-in-ten incline through the woods. It was only beyond the soccer field that the land rose more steeply to the southern cliffs, which he estimated constituted no more than a quarter mile arc. "Surprising how little we know about the archipelago," Rice said.

The skipper laughed. "Doesn't surprise me. Pentagon had as detailed a map as you'd want of Belgrade, friggin' satellites, the lot, and we still didn't know which was the Yugoslav headquarters. Took out the Chinese Embassy instead."

Rice recalled the monumental screw-up. Well, there weren't going to be any screw-ups with the Guard. "How long before we can disembark?"

"Ten minutes or so."

"You said that five minutes ago."

"Patience, Colonel. That was before we had this current. Don't want to let you guys off prematurely."

From the darkness of the deck immediately below, Rice's men could hear the urgent chatter between the *Kingfisher's* mate and the hovercraft, the harried tone of the exchange injecting the waiting Guardsmen with the anticipatory excitement of going in and hitting hard before the militia really knew what the hell was happening.

"Vessel approaching dead ahead." It was the port side lookout. "Looks like it's a small job."

"Dammit!" Rice said, and now they could hear another raspy voice cutting into the emergency channel. "*Kingfisher,* this is Mike Ramsey. I'm a beachcomber out of Lopez. Picked up your SOS to the Coast Guard hover. Dunno what I can do, but my runabout can carry—I dunno—six, maybe eight, of your crew back to Lopez. That any help? Over."

"Think he's legit?" Rice asked the *Kingfisher*'s mate.

"Could be. Lot o' guys make a good living scouting the islands' beaches for stray logs that've come loose from the big timber rafts. Tow 'em to the mills on the mainland."

"Tell him thanks but we'll be okay," Rice instructed the mate.

The small but fast boat, its radar signature on *Kingfisher*'s screen absorbed in the bigger blip of the island, was now less than two hundred yards from *Kingfisher*. "You sure?" the beachcomber asked. "Hate to leave you in the lurch."

Rice was shaking his head, worried. "If he's near the island he must know the militia's there."

"Not necessarily," the skipper replied. "These beachcombers just pull in, camp overnight on the beach, gone the next morning." The skipper took the radio mike, asking his mate, "What'd he say his name was?"

"Ramsey," the mate replied.

"Ramsey? *Kingfisher*'s skipper here. Hovercraft's on the way. Looks like our pumps've picked up. We'll be fine but thanks, bud. Really appreciate it."

"No problem, *Kingfisher*. Good luck."

And with that the boat swung sharply away, heading in the direction of Lopez. The lamp in his hand was an electric trigger-operated type, its small but intense bluish-white light blinkered from anyone behind, the light now stabbing the darkness, the lookout party on the west beach having no difficulty understanding its message: *Large contingent of Feds. Big Zodiacs at the stern. Disembarkation imminent.*

* * *

"Right," McBride told his beach party calmly, his voice on the base walkie-talkie as clear as if he was only yards, instead of half a mile, away at the soccer field. "Defensive positions."

"How 'bout Ramsey?" Ron Stanes asked.

"Don't worry about him, just do your jobs." As he looked about the moonlit soccer field to make sure his own defensive positions were ready, Cope came up beside him, smiling to himself.

"Trapped by their own SOS plan, eh, Major? I wonder whether this hovercraft is for real. Probably some tug tied up in port somewhere."

"We'll soon find out," McBride said, his voice having nothing of Cope's celebratory tone. Knowing an enemy was coming at you was one thing; defeating them was quite another. "Cope, I want you to wake up Eleen and—" For a second the other two names escaped him.

"Jubal," Cope said, "and Mead."

"Yes. Go below. Get them roused. They can go down to the east beach with our mortar crew, just in case that hovercraft is for real."

"What makes you so sure it'd go to the east beach?"

"I'm not," McBride answered. "I'm not even sure it's coming. But if it does, where's it going to land? There are only two beaches. Rest of the shoreline is strewn with boulders or sheer cliffs."

"Ah, even if there is a hovercraft," Cope said, "it'll probably be one of those little itsy-bitsy jobs."

McBride grabbed his M-203 combination rifle and grenade launcher and shook his head.

"What's wrong?"

"You better grab a cup of coffee and wake up, Cope. Don't you realize that if a hovercraft is involved in the Feds' attack, it's hardly gonna be one of those little piss pots?"

CHAPTER THIRTY-SEVEN

KINGFISHER'S EIGHT ZODIACS, having taken five minutes in the current to assemble in line of attack, were now less than two hundred yards from the silvery strand of beach, the crashing of the phosphorescent-white line of surf ahead. An intense white light suddenly appeared above them, illuminating the sea, the booming of the breakers having muffled not only the clap of the flare opening but also the first bursts of militia machine-gun fire. The gentle arcing of one-in-four tracers belied the violence of what in fact was a simultaneous firing of six M-60s, over a hundred AK-47s, thirty M-203 40mm grenade launchers, and ten 60mm 2.2-mile range mortars. The latter's rounds, armed with proximity fuses, exploded above the twenty-five-man rigid inflatables. Showering the Guardsmen with water-sizzling, red-hot shrapnel, the mortars' warheads were also fitted with ear-splitting Stuka screamers whose purpose was nothing less than to add another dimension of terror to the militia's barrage.

And terror is what they inspired, the hapless Guardsmen, their Zodiacs bucking in the turbulence of waves cresting near shore, trying futilely to return fire. But only two or three men in each of the inflatables could risk this maneuver without hitting their own men. And to turn the Zodiacs side on to the beach, so as to afford at least twelve of the twenty-five men on each raft a broadside firing platform, could only present a wider, bigger target to the dug-in militia behind the treeline.

Under Eleen's command, Sergeant Mead moving quickly from one machine-gun nest to the other, the militia's beach company quickly found the range, and the other six rafts began taking full bursts of tracer fire. The militia mortars missed altogether, at least during the initial enfilade, but their collective *whoomps* created huge spumes of boiling white water whose noise added to the frightening crack and zip of Kalashnikov and M-16 rounds. The weird hissing of white-hot tracer streaked through the cold, surf-churned air as banshee mortar screamers continued to sow such panic among the weekend soldiers that the coxswains themselves were screaming for everyone to lie down and shut up. But not before two Zodiacs, under the relentless glare of more flares and at virtually point-blank range, were convulsed and ripped asunder by the militia's savage and unrelenting onslaught. Several of the big boats were punctured within seconds, water cascading in. They sank almost immediately, leaving only a detritus of torn and black rubber floating amid the frenzied splashing of men in the water whose agony was protracted until drowned or dragged under by the sheer weight of weaponry and equipment. Colonel Rice had been killed outright in the first volley of machine-gun fire, and the Guards' two company commanders were screaming for the remaining six Zodiacs to come about and head back to the *Kingfisher*. By the time the coxswains heard the order, however, shrapnel from another rain of mortar rounds set another Zodiac aflame. Mead's concentrated M-60 machine-gun fire poured into it as if the raft was willingly attracting the tracer like some great black magnet. Trapped in the frenetic tug and surge of the surf, the inferno that only a few moments before had been the raft was starving the survivors of oxygen, while the roar of its flames simultaneously cooked off boxes of ammunition in the stricken raft, the belt feeds going off like firecrackers.

Within six minutes only four Zodiacs remained, then three, as the one nearest the beach was swamped by the surf, its Guardsmen struggling but failing to get ashore through a fierce undertow in neck-high water. Merciless militia fire continued to cut them down at the roiling water's edge, crimson streams of their blood turning black in the hard light of more phosphorus flares. Among those who died here were the black man who had joked with Able's commander; Woody, the expert fisherman who'd settled the bet between the squad leader and the mortarman; and the mortarman himself, who had drowned with the rest of his mortar squad. Able's company commander, having reached the beach, was struck in the back with a spray of "friendly" automatic fire that blew his head off, his torso stumbling grotesquely to the sea's edge before dropping. A coxswain in one of three remaining Zodiacs, not seeing Able's CO decapitated, immediately turned his boat around to go back to pick him up.

"Leave him!" someone shouted. "Get back to the ferry!"

The coxswain did as he was told, a streak of light passing him, its heat buffeting him and several of the other Guardsmen in the Zodiac. They saw the LAW's high explosive antitank round strike the *Kingfisher* on the stern quarter in a huge, curling, orange-black ball of fire. The concussion wave slammed into them a millisecond later, the antitank round leaving a ragged, two-foot-diameter hole in the ferry. Seawater surged into it so fast that within another two minutes the *Kingfisher* was in danger of capsizing, her pumps clearly unable to handle the flood. Now, as the three remaining Zodiacs were approaching her, *Kingfisher*'s call to the USCG's hovercraft was in earnest, a call the hovercraft's captain duly ignored.

"This is not a drill!" *Kingfisher*'s captain was shouting. "This is not a drill. We are sinking!"

On the hovercraft dubbed *Orca*, the crew of five were delighted by the *Kingfisher*'s performance. "Put that man down for an Oscar," the captain said.

"Roger that!" Cordell's police commander, Pollock, replied.

"I'll second that," chimed in Moorehead, as if he were an old friend of everyone aboard rather than a swaggering new boy whose presence was not appreciated by Pollock.

Forty seconds later *Kingfisher* was gone, the explosion of her fuel engulfing the nearest Zodiac, which left only two, their twin Mercurys straining against the current, clearing the surf zone. But even at a half mile out they were still well within range of the militia's weapons, Eleen's west beach contingent continuing to send up clusters of flares.

Approaching the east beach on the other side of the island, several of Pollock's fifty riot police aboard *Orca*, their view westward obstructed by the high, thickly wooded base of the six, saw a pulsating white cloud several miles beyond.

"What in hell's that?" one of Pollock's men shouted, his voice barely audible.

"Storm," Pollock shouted back confidently.

"But there's no thunder."

"Flares?" someone else suggested.

By now the huge, eighty-five-foot-long hovercraft could be seen but not heard by the militia, the massive air cushion beneath the 160-ton craft blowing out what looked like clouds of silent, yet ferocious, steam from beneath the cushion's four-foot-high rubber skirting. It was the first sign of *Orca*'s power, of how her four six-foot-diameter lift fans, in concert with her two even bigger twelve-foot-diameter propulsion fans, had sped her from her Whidbey Island Coast Guard Station toward the Redoubt at over 55 mph.

As the curved sliver of east beach came into view on her radar, *Orca*'s commander, Chief Petty Officer Stein, in the control room, reduced speed to a mere thirty miles per hour, still faster than almost any ship afloat. The navigator, engineer, and pilot, to CPO Stein's right, could detect the marked downshift in the noise of four gas turbines. The vibration level, however, merely went from what the crew traditionally call EBS, or eyeball shaking high, to BBN, bone breaking normal, the sustained roar of the four-thousand horsepower engine and unabated blasting of spray from beneath the air cushion even penetrating ear protectors.

Meanwhile, the savage yaw and pitch of the big machine came as a gut-wrenching surprise to those relatively few men in Pollock's fifty-man team, who up to now had not had the pleasure of riding the monster which civilians, gazing from ashore, so often and mistakenly assumed glided over everything from calm seas to gale-churned waters with the undisturbed grace of a flying carpet. Because of the noise, Pollock's men, strapped in with full racing driver harnesses in the passenger enclosure aft of the twin wheelhouses, found it all but impossible to communicate with each other save by shouting. And the constant rush of seawater about the *Orca*'s "hump"— the raised portion of deck designed to allow for proper drainage as waves broached the craft—was so thunderously noisy that it alone dissuaded concentration, other than what was absolutely necessary to the upcoming disembarkation. Most disconcerting for Pollock's men was the fact that while Chief Petty Officer Stein and the other members of the five-man crew could see the island, courtesy of their broom-sized window wipers, the fine spray blown all around gave them the sense of going in blind.

High overhead, a Qantas pilot en route to Hawaii, his plane emerging from stratus, saw red and white scratches on the ocean ten thousand feet below. Punching in his GPS coordinator, he saw that they were south of the main San Juan archipelago, over the part of Juan de Fuca Strait, which the small, dotted circle on his chart designated an old military dumping site.

"Better log it anyway," the captain told his copilot, "and report it to SEATAC—it's U.S. waters."

The message received by the Seattle-Tacoma tower seventy miles farther south was in turn relayed to the USCG and thence to *Orca* and *Kingfisher*, the latter not responding. Frantic radio messages had already been received by Police Chief Cordell and Mark Aitken at Anacortes that the intended landing at the east beach had been a debacle, a fact that Cordell dutifully reported to presidential aide Brownlee, in Washington, D.C.

Brownlee immediately woke the President with the dire news at five-fifteen A.M. Disheveled in a Notre Dame robe, coffee mug in hand, the Chief Executive made his way to Brownlee's office, eschewing use of the Oval Office lest it alert the press, which hadn't yet got wind of the operation, though it was reported by Mark Aitken that CNN's Marte Price was still snooping around in Seattle, loath to give up on the rumor about Ruby Lake. The only thing in their favor, Aitken told Brownlee, was that, like any other reporter, Price was keen to get an exclusive on any story and so would keep any lead to herself until she'd run it to ground.

"How many men are lost?" the President asked.

Brownlee said it was unclear as to the number of casualties, but if four Zodiacs had been lost, "Maybe a hundred men."

"Jesus Christ!" the President thundered. "That's—That's—Good God, we only lost seventeen in the entire Gulf War. Where's that hovercraft?"

Brownlee glanced at the wall clock. "Within about two

minutes of unloading the fifty riot cops on east beach, as scheduled. Apparently it did receive an SOS but thought it was the ferry or Coast Guard HQ giving the prearranged cover."

"An SOS cover? Whose bright idea was that?"

"Not sure," Brownlee truthfully answered, not knowing whether it had been Cordell's or Aitken's, though he knew that as of now one or both of their careers was over.

The President slid over the chart Brownlee had on his desk. "How long will it take to reach the survivors off this—what is it—west beach?"

"Ten, fifteen minutes," Brownlee said, "at the outside," though he held little hope for them.

"And the men in the remaining Zodiacs? What's their status?"

"Heading to the nearest land, one of the other islands, I guess."

The President was incredulous, putting his coffee cup down as if it was under remote control. "The nearest land? Why aren't they picking up their buddies in the water, for God's sake?"

"That's a little unclear, sir. I guess they were under heavy fire." Brownlee quickly added, "Besides, if we sent them back in, they'd be chopped to pieces by the militia—same as their buddies were."

The President was pacing as General Rogers arrived via the security tunnel to avoid the press. "You want to move in regular troops, Mr. President?" he asked.

"No," Brownlee cut in. "Pull out, Mr. President. Cut our losses."

Both the general and the President stared at him—it was the first time they'd seen Brownlee lose his nerve. Even so, it was Rogers who felt duty bound to agree, pointing out the decisive factor—that it would take hours even for a rapid deployment force to be assembled and dispatched.

"Besides, Mr. President, Pollock's fifty men can't be pulled out," Brownlee said, "they're probably landing as we speak."

"Who else is going in?" the President asked.

"Cordell's fifty-man SWAT team. By helo."

The terrible fact was, the White House was between a rock and a hard place, their force in too deep to pull out, two-thirds of it already gone.

"Of course," Rogers said, "we haven't thrown in the towel yet. What we're forgetting here is that the LCAC is a different kettle of fish." He went on to explain that the Landing Craft Air Cushion was the old Navy designation for the hovercraft. "It's a big mother."

"So?" the President said. "That means it's a much bigger target for the militia than the Zodiacs were, doesn't it?"

"Yes, bigger but infinitely more maneuverable, Mr. President. Can turn on a dime, and it has speed. Steers more like a plane than a boat. Plus it has a few more surprises. And"—he had a Strangelovian look—"we're assuming that the militia are at the east beach, but they probably think the attack on the west beach was the whole operation!"

In fact, McBride had been too careful to assume that the Zodiac assault was all there was to the attack. But CPO Stein, on the hovercraft, had been just as careful.

Assuming the militia might be on the beach, Stein eschewed a straight-in run, deciding instead to use *Orca's* "unconventional elements" to the full. Coming in on a fast "nonrepeating" weaving pattern, using his rotatable and powerful pair of bow thrusters and their aerodynamic rudders to slide and skid, he turned what was normally a problem for the hovercraft, with its penchant for sliding or sideslipping during a hard turn to his advantage. Stein's maneuver, while inducing violent motion sickness in some of Pollock's men, succeeded in utterly confusing the seventy-strong militia force assigned to the east beach, their target's range and angle of attack changing by the second.

To make matters worse for the seventy militia, the hovercraft, upon receiving the first few rounds of tracer from the shore, immediately replied with bursts of heavy machine-gun fire from the two forward pintle-mounted .50 Brownings which, though inaccurate, given *Orca*'s violent maneuvering, kept most militia heads down and shook the rebels' confidence in what they had thought would be a one-sided engagement.

Only Buzz Cut and several men on either side of her failed to duck, her spartan bravery shaming them from doing so. The moment her AK-47 was empty, she grabbed another of the banana-shaped mags, thrust it in, and continued firing at the craft on its wildly gyrating way into the beach. "Where's that fucking Javelin?" she demanded.

"We've only got one!" Pete Rainor replied. "And our other detachment's got it on the other beach with Eleen."

"Well, get it here!" she shouted.

"It's at the field!" Cope put in nervously. "McBride's got it."

"Get it here!" Buzz Cut shouted over the din of militia fire and the mounting noise of the craft, which was now between two and three hundred yards offshore.

"Won't be time!" hollered Mel Haley, who glimpsed an ineffectual splattering of enemy tracer rounds hitting the water, the hovercraft beyond illuminated in sudden moonlight like a square block of ice spinning on its own axis.

There was screaming and cursing to Buzz Cut's right, and the unmistakable thudding sound of .50s going into the trees behind the militia line. At least three or four men had been hit.

The militia's east beach commander had to make a choice. He could withdraw into the woods away from the beach, letting the hovercraft unload, thus buying time for the Javelin to take out the Federals' craft, stranding them to be picked off at will later. Or he could stay on the beach and take heavy casualties, but prevent the Federals from dispersing into the woods, where they'd be infinitely more difficult to track down and kill.

The radio crackled. It was McBride. The Javelin was on its way. "Two minutes max!" McBride promised the east beach CO.

Not long afterward, through the ear-dunning noise of the firefight, the smell of nose-clogging diesel exhaust and gunpowder, and the agonizing screams of men being hit, the east beach CO heard a high banshee noise that had always intensely annoyed him but was now the most welcome whine he'd ever heard. It was the sound of the dirt motorcycle bearing the Javelin along the one-man trail, the driver having opened the throttle as wide as his NVGs' night sight would allow.

For a moment it looked to the beach CO as if the big hovercraft had stopped, but it sideslipped two hundred yards off through what must have been another gut-churning turn for those aboard. How many would there be? the militiaman wondered, approaching the sandy strip. As *Orca* thundered through the shallow water, her twin Brownings raked the militia positions that CPO Stein never doubted had reasonably good views of *Orca* through NVGs, despite the curtains of spray that continued to billow up from the hovercraft's rubber skirt.

The militia CO watched the hovercraft approach, and guessed it would arrive in about forty-five seconds.

CHAPTER THIRTY-EIGHT

HEAD DOWN, ARMS straining to keep control of the dirt bike, McBride was racing down along the narrow path leading to the east beach with the Javelin's command launch unit and two missiles in its disposable launch tube, in all sixty-four pounds, looking like two map tubes lashed to an old-fashioned silent movie box camera. "All you need now," his old convoy buddy Neilson had once joked during a practice session, "is a black hood over your head and one of those powder flash sticks." But now nothing was funny anymore—Neilson was dead, along with all the others who had started out from the lake to protect McBride. And McBride knew he owed them.

Through his NVGs he saw something across the trail. He braked the bike, throttled down, felt himself going into a skid. Fighting desperately for control, he heard the rear tire slam against a fallen fir branch the thickness of a man's arm. It wasn't difficult to remove, but it cost him valuable seconds, and the temptation was to go even faster. There was a narrow hairpin turn coming up before he could reach the east beach, and should there be any other obstacle on the trail, he knew he wouldn't have time to brake. Nevertheless, he opened up the throttle, felt the bike leap forward, threatening to become airborne despite its rear load, and leaned forward, stomach almost on the gas tank. Dirt and pine needles rained down on him, the smell of damp earth buffeting his face, and he heard the angry staccato of AK-47s, M-16s, and the tarpaper-tearing noise of machine guns not far ahead. He made the turn and smelled the salty sea breeze laced with the pungent reek of cordite, the woods, now behind him, red and white with tracer. Crisscrossing the beach, he spit up sand like coarse sugar in the moonlight.

Farther down the beach, the white, steamlike spray that had shrouded the craftily angled hovercraft was disappearing, *Orca*'s skirt already deflated. Its forward ramp was down and a line of black Fritz-helmeted figures were moving onto the beach, deploying in the moonlight as if emerging from behind an enormous translucent shower curtain. From atop the twin deckhouses, the two Brownings were laying down a devastating swath of heavy fire on the militia positions, which were no more than two hundred yards south of the *Orca*. As McBride quickly set up the Javelin, he realized how clever the *Orca*'s CPO was. Against all common sense and approved procedure, the CPO had ordered the stern ramp lowered as well. Had the *Orca* come in, as per standard procedure, at a ninety-degree angle to the beach, the rear ramp wouldn't have been down. Instead the CPO had nosed the *Orca* in hard left at an acute angle, allowing his .50s atop the twin deckhouses to fire without the port side gunner blocking the starboard gunner's field of fire.

The sharp landing angle also prevented all but a squad or two of militia at the far southern end of the beach from seeing twenty-five of Pollock's men disembarking from the rear into knee-high water, Pollock's men using *Orca* itself as an armor-plated blind even as spouts of exploding two-inch mortar shells erupted about them.

McBride, under covering fire from Buzz Cut and four of her squad, smartly attached one of the two launch tubes to the CLU and selected Direct rather than Top Attack mode for the tandem-charged missile's flight. Kneeling, he fixed the CLU's cursor box over the image of the hovercraft, and using the infrared magnification, initiated the Lock Before Launch command to the missile.

He squeezed the pistol grip trigger at the same time an M-19 projected grenade, fired in haste by a felled militiaman, exploded four feet away. The grenade's concussion, knocking McBride off balance, altered the missile's fifteen-foot-long glide path before its second stage ignited and its fins deployed. As a result, the Javelin streaked south past the *Orca* across the small bay formed by the C of the east beach. It went beyond, into the thick, silver-hued woods at the island's southernmost end, the missile disintegrating in a spectacular crimson explosion like some distant supernova, setting fire to a knot of craggy pine.

Immediately, McBride got up, blowing sand off the CLU's lens.

"Major!" a militiaman shouted, his voice rising above the ferocious firefight and the *Whoomp! Whoomp!* of militia mortar. "Base camp says it has choppers on radar. Four of 'em!"

McBride was praying the CLU's optics hadn't come undone and that the lithium battery's connections were intact. He'd had more combat experience than any militiaman on the beach, but he knew he couldn't be in two places at once. Right now his job was to take out the hovercraft, nothing else. Besides, he had delegated authority to those at the soccer field base camp. The timing, a night attack by the Federals, had surprised him, but not the attack itself. That had been in the cards ever since things started going wrong at the ferry terminal with the damned vine maple. He'd hate those plants for the rest of his life—if he survived.

Glancing down to make sure the CLU was still on Direct Fire mode, he was momentary blinded by a flash of light, his face stinging in an eruption of sand. A moment later he saw the *Orca* being ripped apart by a succession of rumbling detonations, its fuel tanks going up, pieces of the doomed hovercraft whistling through the air, including man-sized pieces of its rubber skirting. The stench of the burning rubber and the diesel fuel was choking.

Eight militiamen on the beach and nearly all the Federals were killed in the blast, and at least a dozen militia farther down the beach were seriously wounded by the shrapnel, which was composed of everything from the hovercraft's massive windshield wipers to huge slabs of ceramic armor. The armor, while not shattering, had been blown off in toto, the enormous explosions of the fuel tanks and ammunition tearing the aluminum superstructure apart as if it was nothing more than tinfoil-sheathed scaffolding.

Only a handful of Pollock's fifty armed riot police survived, and these, except, ironically, for Moorehead, the least fit of all, were in no shape to continue battle. They staggered about the fire-strewn beach in such a state of shock that some militiamen began to laugh. It was the laughter of those in battle shock themselves, a release from the neck-stiffening tension of combat at the sea's edge where, without either side announcing as much, it was intuitively understood there'd be few prisoners. The militia knew that any Federal who managed to make it to the woods, only a matter of fifteen yards or so from the hovercraft, would pose a hazard to every militiaman or woman on the island. And so, Buzz Cut, who had somehow survived, led the remaining members of her squad to finish off the Federals. But now stratus clouds swallowed the moonlight, which was the only means of illumination now that the burning wreckage of the *Orca* sizzled into quiescence, doused by successive waves.

It was only because a militiaman's M-16 jammed that Moorehead, his hands thrown up in quick surrender, was taken away toward the soccer field. Fervently thanking God for his deliverance, but praying he would be spared the humiliation of having to face any of his former prisoners, his arrogance began to reassert itself as he made demands of his captors, confident with his secret knowledge that help was on the way.

But for the other Federals on the beach, there was no such respite in the offing, the rip of the militia squad's submachine guns louder in the relative silence of the body-strewn beach than during the earlier full-scale firefight. The dead Federals rolled to and fro in the wash of the sea in mute testimony to the violent if short-lived debacle, one which as yet was unknown to the incoming SWAT helos, whose pilots, maintaining strict radio silence, descended to five hundred feet with five miles to go to the soccer field. The *Orca* debris appeared on their thermal NVGs as no more than a sprinkle of irregularly shaped white lights.

In the lead Huey, Chief Cordell was impatiently, anxiously, fingering the safety catch on his M-4, a shortened version of the Army's M-16 A2 with a 40mm grenade launcher attached. The last time Cordell had been in a take-down anything like the imminent assault on the militia's Redoubt was the big drug bust a year before, which had gained him enough favorable publicity to assure his promotion to chief. But the public memory was short. What he and his SWAT team needed was another well-deserved burst of publicity. That was why, just prior to his departure, he hinted to CNN's Marte Price that it would be worth her while to engage a private air charter firm in Bellingham that could fly her into Friday Harbor, the "biggest town in the San Juans."

Without asking for details, she'd replied, "Will they fly at night?" roughly aware of how remote the islands were, and also mindful of the unforgiving and rapid changes of weather in the region.

"Of course they fly at night," Cordell assured her.

*   *   *

Landing that night by helo on the airstrip in Friday Harbor, the worldly Marte Price, who had been everywhere from New York to the Antipodes, was still capable of being surprised by nature's beauty, and looking west across the straits, she saw Mount Baker's volcanic cone bathed in moonlight and diaphanous cloud, and recalled the comment of an easterner upon seeing the scenery of the rugged Northwest for the first time: that it appeared too theatrical to be true, as if some set designers for some fantastical musical, such as *The Sound of Music*, had taken leave of their earthbound senses. In such a setting, how could Cordell be correct in his coy suggestion that some ugly conflict between federal authorities and the militia was under way? she wondered. But then she reminded herself that the idyllic landscape of the Italian Alps so often in history had been the background for the bloody real-life clash of opposing views.

"Anything happening on San Juan Island?" she queried the pilot vaguely as he throttled down, taxiing towards the small terminal.

"Tourists," the pilot said.

"Uh-huh. What's accommodation like?"

"Tight."

"You heard of any riff between militia and the Feds?"

"Riff?"

"Trouble. Fighting."

"No." The man was determinedly unsmiling.

"I thought everyone was friendly on San Juan," Marte said.

"I don't live on San Juan."

Marte unbuckled her seat belt. What really ticked her off was that the pilot, apart from making sure she was belted in before takeoff, as per FAA regulations, hadn't even glanced at her. She was no spring chicken, but hell, she could still turn heads most places she went.

"Thanks for the ride," she said.

He nodded.

"Chief?"

Cordell looked up at his second in command, the SWAT lieutenant who had also been in on the big drug bust. "Yeah, Tunny?"

"Thirty seconds till touchdown."

Cordell gave the thumbs-up to his SWAT team. They responded in kind, Tunny then feeling for the elasticized band around his helmet, not satisfied until, for the umpteenth time, his fingers touched the first-aid packets beneath the band. Cordell took comfort from Tunny's obsessive ritual, the continual quest for reassurance making Cordell not feel so foolish about his own equally obsessive fidgeting with the M-4's safety catch. Like students before finals, they all had their pre-battle jitters, each man with his own rites or compulsions, whether undertaken consciously or not, to appease the gods, to assure good fortune in the capricious world. They were not filled with fear—on the contrary, they were confident. They were well-armed, well-trained, and Kevlar sheathed. They had all seen action, from dealing with madmen to drug wars. They were, in fact, supremely confident that their quick surgical strike to the heart of the Redoubt would succeed. And there was a sound strategic reason for their confidence: with most of the militia having been deployed to meet the threats on east and west beaches, the defenders in and around the soccer field would surely be in the minority.

But as the evil corporal in Berlin had once observed, going to war is like stepping into a dark room. Anything could happen—for either side.

"Hold on!" the Huey's rigger shouted.

It was unnecessary advice, for all twelve men, like those in the other three helos, already had a firm grip, readying for the bump of touchdown. The island raced toward them, the helos busily discharging scores of brilliant orange sucker flares, lest the militia possess Stingers, or any other heat-seeking missiles. Cordell, watching the flares rain down toward the moonlit race of sea, through his NVGs could now see the flotsam of what had been the hovercraft. Further to his left, above the high cliffs that marked the southern end of the island, he saw a globule of light whose shape kept changing, probably because of the helo's angle of approach.

The militia's Minigun had barely opened up when a SWAT sharpshooter, ignoring Huey 1's impending touchdown, "scoped" the militia gunner, placing his crosshairs on the helmet. Looping his Colt Automatic Rifle sling, but without time to extend the CAR's retractable stock, the sniper fired a three-round burst, the .223 caliber copper-clad "ball" bullets thumping into the militia gunner and his belt feeder. As they landed, however, a militia round hit the sharpshooter full face, fragments of his NVGs and bone striking Cordell and several other men. Tunny, covered in the sharpshooter's blood, felt for his pulse, confirming he was dead, before following Cordell and the other ten men, Hueys 2 and 3 on their flanks, Huey 4 at the rear of the "diamond."

The forty-nine men streamed from the helos and spread out into their Wolf Packs, Cordell anticipating that once beyond the soccer field, all of them would quickly be engaged entering the Redoubt's barracks, whatever these consisted of. The first thing Tunny was aware of was the feel and smell underfoot of moist, soft earth as he moved out from the apron of grass that had been flattened by the helos' rotor blasts, the Hueys having already sunk an inch or two into the sandy soil. All he could hear was the rotors' sustained roar interspersed with what sounded like firecrackers going off, militia small arms fire coming from all directions about the perimeter.

"Get that Minigun!" Cordell shouted. He needn't have worried. After his sniper had taken out the gunner, the sniper's buddies had made a point of zeroing in on the machine gun, lobbing at least a half-dozen HE and smoke grenades at the position, which lay no more than a hundred yards away, the smoke grenades marking the Minigun position for further punishment. As it transpired, the grenades silenced the gun, and the Wolf Pack's point men's fire was so concentrated and unrelenting that none of the militia could regain the gun, the Wolf Packs pressing ever closer to the soccer field's defensive perimeter.

Uppermost in the minds of many of the SWAT members was a determination to avoid the mistakes of Waco. There, over a hundred fellow SWAT men were used, and had passed on valuable lessons from the deadly fiasco. One of the most salient of these was never to use CS tear gas in an assault on a stronghold. The gas effect at Waco had been badly diluted because of unexpected wind currents and some of the SWATS' "back-assed" tactic, as Tunny called it, of poking holes in the building's wall to insert the CS cartridges. All this did was create as many exits for the gas as entry points. This time Cordell had ordered OC pepper spray instead—faster-acting, less prone to "windage," and producing instantaneous respiratory panic and blindness. And where at WACO the Federals had used psyops, blasting rock music in hopes of flushing Koresh and his heavily armed followers out of their hideaway, as it had Noriega in Panama, this too had backfired. Cordell knew that the Davidians viewed the psyops attempt on them and their children inside the redoubt as proof that the Federals were an evil and sadistic force. This time Cordell was ready: no CS, no psyops. Only the tried and true tactics of the drug bust, without the need to waste time seizing evidence.

But just as Cordell's men readied to fire the first barrage of pepper spray canisters, three of their helos exploded, turning the soccer field into a screaming caldron of exploding parts and burning Avgas. The wet grass of moments before was now parchment dry and aflame, crackling with such intensity that it swallowed the noise of the firefight around the brilliantly lit perimeter, where those SWAT men not dismembered by splintered rotors, detached fuselage, tail skids, and drive shaft casings, dived into what little protection was afforded by berry bushes and worm-ridden timber. It wasn't until Huey 4 blew a minute later and Tunny saw the earth erupting that he realized there was no longer a firefight at the field's perimeter, McBride's militia obviously having withdrawn before the first of the timed antitank mines went off.

First to reach the edge of the woods, where outer trees seemed to flicker in the garish light of the inferno behind him, Tunny glimpsed the clearly printed warning: FRONT TOWARD ENEMY, and froze, yelling, "Claymore!" the brakeshoe-shaped antipersonnel and antivehicle mine one of the most ubiquitous and effective weapons in the militia's arsenal.

Tunny knew that if the C4 charge hadn't yet detonated, either he hadn't hit the trip wire or, God forbid, the mine was "wired up"—controlled by a militia triggerman who had not yet pressed the button or was away from it. "Claymore!" he shouted again, risking giving his location away but hoping whoever was left in his Wolf Pack would hear the warning above the sustained roaring of the fire behind, from which the SWAT survivors were fleeing.

"Claymore!" came another voice. It sounded like Cordell, but Tunny couldn't be sure and didn't care as he inched back from the mine, surrounded by the horrible screams of men dying of their burns, others frantically dragging themselves toward the shelter of the woods.

On McBride's orders, the fifty claymores, which had been hooked up in a series around the perimeter, were now detonated, each of the mines sending seven hundred steel balls whistling out in a sixty-degree fan to a height of six and a half feet, probably only half that number getting past the scattered debris. But the thousands of steel balls that did sweep through the survivors from the four Wolf Packs were more than enough, cutting men down like a scythe, pulverizing their bodies above and below their Kevlar vests, mashing faces to unrecognizable pulp. Only Cordell and ten others—half of these already wounded—survived, lucky enough, after Tunny's warning, to be able to find cover in time behind the fungi-covered logs at the edge of the field.

Cordell lay immobilized by fear and shock. The knowledge that he had led his men into a trap so complete wracked him with waves of nausea, and the stench of burning flesh, burning fuel, and the fumes of plastique overwhelmed him. The only command he could give was a feeble, "Stay where you are! Don't move!"

Only the repetitive, precoded "crash" signals from the helos' so-called black boxes told Whidbey and, in short order, Brownlee, that Operation Rats' Nest had been a disaster.

CHAPTER THIRTY-NINE

IN SEATTLE, HELPING prepare for the forthcoming funerals for Andy Shear and the Delta commando, Douglas Freeman heard the beeping of his voice mail. It was a message from one of his many contacts in and out of the armed forces.

"Uncle Frederick, Johnny here. I've checked with the Pest Control guy about that infestation in your cottage. He did his best but apparently they were too much for him. He said it's a complete write-off. Sorry."

The moment the general had heard his contact say, "Frederick," as in Frederick the Great, one of Freeman's heroes because of the Prussian leader's penchant for exhorting his generals to always think audaciously, Freeman knew the message would most likely be explosive. It was, telling him that the Rats' Nest "infestation" had overwhelmed the Federals' attempt to root it out.

He called Brownlee, whose voice had a disembodied timbre to it, the President's aide clearly exhausted, and with good cause. With the catastrophic failure of the Guard and police to overcome the militia, the administration now faced the prospect of a political hurricane once the press got hold of the Rats' Nest debacle. Had Brownlee realized that CNN's Marte Price had already been flown into San Juan Island's Friday Harbor, his despondency would have plummeted into an abyss. He had no doubt what Freeman was calling about. The general's contacts were known to be so numerous and well-placed that it was unlikely he hadn't been tipped off about the "crash" signals Whidbey had received—and what they meant.

Without waiting for Freeman to say any more than hello, Brownlee asked, "How could you possibly make a difference, General?"

"A difference?" Freeman replied with barely a pause. "Dammit, we could turn this thing around."

"Who's *we*?"

"Same boys who were with me at Ruby Lake." Before Brownlee could muster a response, Freeman raced on, "I know . . . we were sucker punched at that lake. Happens to all of us one time or another, Michael, no matter what our jobs. Right?"

Brownlee didn't reply. He was too tired.

"You watch football, Brownlee?"

"Yes," the President's aide answered desultorily.

"Then you know how many games can be won—have been won—in the last few seconds? The Immaculate Reception?"

"The *what*?"

"Divisional playoff game in seventy-two," Freeman said. "Between the Steelers and the Raiders. Terry Bradshaw, quarterback for the Steelers—the Steelers losing—seconds to go, and he throws a pass. It misses the intended receiver, bounces off a guy, is caught by a Steelers running back, Franco Harris, who makes a touchdown and wins the game!"

"This isn't—wasn't—a game, General. We lost over a hundred and sixty—"

"Michael," Freeman cut in, "I've seen more battle casualties than you've seen lobbyists in Gucci Gulch. I'm about to bury two men who were killed at Ruby Lake, including a young man who—Poor bastard bled to death. I know it isn't a *game*."

"All right," Brownlee said by way of apology. "But General, you've got a team of twenty—now eighteen—men. If we lost over a hundred and sixty men, maybe more, I don't know, against the militia—who, it appears, were very well dug in— how could you possibly hope to turn things around?"

"L'audace, l'audace, toujours l'audace," Freeman replied. "It's the last thing they expect. You've hit 'em with your one-two punch and they've driven your boys into the sea. Shit, all we've probably got left are electronic transmitters beeping away. Right?"

"How did you know that?" Brownlee asked.

"I didn't for sure, but this is my line of country. I heard it was a wipeout, and in wipeouts you don't have helos coming back. All you get is their ELT signals."

Brownlee had to admit Freeman knew a hell of a lot more about this than he did.

"And if all we're getting is ELT sigs, then I'll bet you ten-to-one McBride's bastards've been using mines—maybe 'jump-ups'—Russian-made jobs that once they sense a chopper coming down, fly up like a goddamn grasshopper. You know how many survivors?"

"No," Brownlee said, embarrassed by the fact. "Whidbey's picked up a couple of the Zodiacs. But are there any survivors on the Redoubt? I don't know." It only now occurred to Brownlee that the general might be making a reasonable assumption, namely that if he and his relatively fresh team did go in, it would be a surprise attack against a garrison of already badly mauled and certainly fatigued militia.

"Look," Freeman pressed, "what've you people got to lose? If we fail—which we won't—but if we fail, you don't have to acknowledge our presence. Hell, if we pull it off, you don't have to acknowledge our presence. The White House takes the credit for getting that bastard."

It appealed to Brownlee, Freeman and company's anonymity being insurance against any future charge that the President recklessly committed another eighteen men after having lost his main force.

"Hold the line," Brownlee told Freeman. "I'll see if I can reach the President." While waiting, Brownlee asked Freeman, "You have a specific plan?"

"I do," Freeman said.

"And the other seventeen men have agreed to go with you?"

"Yes, sir."

The President said, "All right, I'll give him twelve hours. But I want it understood, Michael, we never had this conversation."

"Understood, Mr. President."

"Tell him to take medics with him. I have a hunch that any of our boys who are still alive on that damned island will need them. Whidbey's CO is telling me that a Coast Guard cutter has picked up the Zodiac survivors and that some of them claim the militia were shooting men in the water. Could that be true?"

Brownlee told Freeman he'd have to take two medics.

"No problem."

"And no dog tags," Brownlee added. "The *man* wants to keep it hush-hush."

"No dog tags," Freeman agreed.

Brownlee shook his head. This guy would do anything for a fight. "Fine," Brownlee said. "I'll contact Whidbey. You need transport?"

"No, we've still got the Osprey. Same two volunteer pilots."

"Your ETD?"

"Sooner the better. We can be ready within the hour. Fly out of Everett, north of Seattle. Boeing Field. They have a particular stake in getting those two idiots, Rainor and . . ."

"Haley," Brownlee said.

"Right. Can you get the two volunteer medics here by 0430?"

"Yes," Brownlee said, his fatigue put on hold momentarily by the slim hope that Freeman might pull it off. "You said 0430. So you plan a dawn attack?"

"I do."

"Break a leg."

Freeman said nothing.

"It's a show business term, General. It means—"

"I know what it means. Who was in charge of the Rats' Nest op?"

"Ah . . . police contingent, Chief Cordell. Guard, Colonel Rice."

"They still alive?"

"Zodiac survivors say Colonel Rice is dead. Cordell? No idea."

CHAPTER FORTY

THE MOON WAS lost in stratus again, and through his NVGs McBride could see several of his militiamen were shivering from the chill of the fresh breeze from the south, the wind now rapidly cooling what only minutes before had been bodies lathered in sweat because of the intense heat radiating from the wreckage of the Federals' helos. The flames were subsiding but still strong enough to cast enormous shadows over the soccer field, where a squad of militiamen—Stanes and Maddin among them—stood tensely, still wound up from the battle and escorting the eleven remaining SWAT team members, including Cordell. The chief had led their surrender in an ignominious moment in which the only white object he had to hold aloft on the end of his rifle barrel was a bunch of Kleenex, which with shaking hands he had to flatten out from the tight white ball they'd formed in his pocket.

As these defeated SWAT prisoners walked forward, Maddin, his birthmark a vivid crimson in the dying fires' light, called out, "Wolf Packs? Gimme a break. Bunch o' fuckin' girls!"

"Hey!" It was Buzz Cut.

"Aw," Maddin retorted, "you know what I mean."

"Yeah, I do," she said, and walked away.

"Keep quiet!" McBride told Maddin, before turning to Pete Rainor, who'd "volunteered" to give the situation report.

Rainor glanced down somberly at his scribbled notes. "Thirty-eight militia dead, fourteen wounded, unfit for duty. Another twenty-two wounded but still usable."

McBride was seldom surprised by anything, but to have more dead than wounded was not the way it usually went—until he thought of the hovercraft's two .50 Brownings that had got their licks in so early. What might be a wound if inflicted by most other small arms rounds quickly became a kill if you were hit anywhere with a big 13mm round from a .50, and on east beach the Federals on the hovercraft had been firing at not much more than point-blank range.

"Least we whipped 'em," Rainor said, looking around the killing field that was once the "soccer field." It was littered with blackened metal and bodies burned beyond recognition, limbs here and there curled, now stilled in grotesque shapes. "They must've lost ninety percent of their force. What—about a hundred and fifty, maybe two hundred? By the time they think about coming back here, we'll be gone."

McBride pushed his NVGs up, massaging his eyes for a moment. It looked as if he was crying—in shock. He wasn't, but nearby, Mel Haley was, and quickly moved away from the group, lest they hear his blubbering. But McBride heard him. "You all right?"

"I don't like the shooting."

McBride nodded. "Neither do I."

Stumbling through a copse of alder, his tears rendering his NVGs useless, Haley entered a patch of salmonberry canes

that gave off a bone-dry rattle despite the moist canopy of
trees above. He tripped over a body—Federal or militia, he
couldn't tell. It spooked him even more, heightening his
battle shock, and he began sobbing uncontrollably.

"You all right?"

He started, his fright arresting his crying but causing him
to shake even more. It was Buzz Cut, her voice resonant with
authority as usual, but also possessing something that neither
Haley nor any other militia had sensed in her before—a
mothering tone. She was sweating too, from the battle, but
she smelled different from the men.

Before he could say anything, she'd put her arms about
him. "It's okay," she said. "Leyland was the same. It was the
noise, he said, that used to get to him."

Though Haley had never heard the name before, he knew
intuitively that Leyland must have been her late husband, the
man they said the Federals had shot down in cold blood.

"He just couldn't stand it," she continued.

Haley unashamedly let himself fall into her embrace, her
breasts, incredibly soft, warm against him, rising and falling
with every breath she took. She placed her Kalashnikov
against a nearby alder and sat down on a log, sweet-smelling
with decay and surrounded by waist-high sword ferns.
Though he could hear voices back toward the killing field, he
felt as if he was a million miles away, kneeling in front of her,
arms about her waist, nuzzling into her. Without breaking his
embrace she began slowly lowering herself from the log, but
came down more abruptly than she'd intended, sabotaged by
a patch of slippery moss. She laughed, and he responded. He
realized then that no one had ever heard her laugh. It broke
the tension, but not his rising excitement.

"Is that a gun?" she asked flirtatiously, squeezing him and
hearing the soft rustle of her fatigues being undone. It wasn't
unknown after battle, senses at their peak, the exhilarated

rush of having cheated death evicting exhaustion, muscles relaxing, and the unstoppable urge for release. He thought of
Colleen, of the children, but restraint was beyond him.

"What's your name?" she asked.

At the savaged "soccer field," McBride had been so busy
overseeing the containment of the wreckage fire that when
Pete Rainor passed on reports that there was another fire
menacing the south end of the island, he had simply ordered
Rainor to "Keep an eye on it and report back as needed."

"D'you think the Feds'll try again?" Eleen asked, happy to
have McBride calling the shots in this butcher shop.

"Not right away," an obviously exhausted McBride replied. "Rainor's right. They'll lick their wounds like we are,
but unlike us, they'll need to rethink their whole strategy.
They sure as hell didn't expect the whipping we gave 'em."
McBride indicated a line of cumulonimbus coming down
from the mile-wide "slot" of Georgia Strait between Vancouver Island and the Canadian mainland. "God's on our
side, Captain. Those clouds'll give us good cover for our
escape."

"Praise His name."

"What—oh yes. I want you and Stanes," McBride called
out to Pete Rainor, "to check the boats and the personnel
allocations."

"We checked them a half hour ago, Major. We hid 'em
well. A couple were hit, but only superficial damage. We
could make a run for it before daybreak."

"No. They'll have spotter planes everywhere come daylight. Buzz Cut has lived in these parts for years, and she's
predicting that low-pressure front coming down the slot'll
give us lots of rain as well. Best cover we could ask for."

"Sure we can pull it off?" pressed Rainor, who, perhaps
more than most militia, except Eleen, Mead, and Jubal,

feared capture, given that his and Haley's mug shots had been posted in every police station in the country.

"I think we'll be all right," McBride said. "Everyone here has always known this was a possibility. Only thing I'm concerned about is that a lot of our boatmasters are KIAs or too badly wounded to operate their assigned boats."

"Hell, what's there to know?" Haley chimed in. He sounded like a new man. "You turn on the ignition, cast off and steer. Each boat's designated port stays the same. Same for Anacortes, Whidbey—"

"Not in rough weather," McBride cut in. "You need guys who know what they're doing."

"We've got enough guys who can handle a boat," Rainor said. "Remember, most of 'em are from the Northwest."

"You've been over the list?"

"When we checked the boats. It was a good idea of yours to keep most of them on the northern half—away from the beaches."

Obviously pleased, McBride slapped Pete Rainor on the back, asking good-humoredly, "You bucking for promotion?"

"What are the perks?"

"Less sleep, more worry."

"Think I'll pass." It was the only lighthearted moment Pete Rainor and McBride had had since the Feds' attack, and it didn't last long. Rainor knew that wherever he was, from now on he, McBride, and Mel Haley, all three of whom had been positively identified, would be men on the run.

"Haley," McBride ordered, "go monitor that fire at the south end. My guess is it'll probably burn itself out, but better safe than sorry."

CHAPTER FORTY-ONE

"LOW AS YOU can," Freeman told the Osprey pilot.

"Don't worry, General. We're already under the Whidbey screen."

"Well, son, never mind Whidbey. Maybe those militia sons of bitches have a radar on the beach."

The Osprey pilot complied, taking the Osprey down, black sea racing beneath them like an endless black desert, wrinkled intermittently by errant streaks of white, the wind picking up strength. The copilot saw an amber, tadpole-shaped blip appear on their radar. "There it is, General. ETA twelve minutes."

"Twelve minutes," Freeman confirmed, returning to the cabin where his seventeen fellow ALERTs, two volunteer medics, and two riggers sat waiting for the red. Someone was throwing up.

"For crying out loud, Sal!" Aussie joshed. "It's as flat as the bloody outback. Not a skerrick of turbulence."

Wiping his mouth, Salvini replied, "It's the damn Avgas. Billion dollar plane and they can't keep the damn fumes out."

"Can't smell gas," Aussie said, taking his Fritz off, sniffing. "Except Brentwood. He smells nice. Think it's Calvin Klein for Cutie Pies."

Brentwood's wry smile, like Aussie's comment, was lost to most of the ALERTs in the darkened, noisy cabin who, despite their usual high morale, were more reserved than usual, the embarrassment and the loss of two of their number at Ruby Lake riding with them. No one resented Aussie Lewis's antics—it was his way of dealing with the fear or, as he was fond of saying, "different strokes for different folks." Besides, they all knew that despite his ribbing of Salvini, Aussie invariably stuck close to the New Yorker upon deplaning until Sal found his legs. And more than once Sal, as Aussie was quick to acknowledge in more reflective moments, had "saved my bloody hide."

"It's not the Avgas he smells, Aussie," Choir Williams advised. "It's the jelly," the latter being the name the ALERTs gave to the mixture in the four forty-four-gallon drums aft.

"I know that, you daft Welshman," Aussie replied. "I'm just taking the piss out of him."

"What was it your people were transported from England for?" Choir asked in a calculated non sequitur. "Thievery, was it?"

"No," Sal cut in. "For talking too much."

"Oh, I get it," Aussie riposted. "It's a bloody conspiracy. The Welsh wart and the Bronx—"

"Listen up!" Freeman said, his voice booming above the noise of the twin Allisons. "We're going to stick with the original plan. We'll go in on two SPIEs"—he pronounced it "Spees," pointing at the fourteen-by-twenty-inch blowup of the Redoubt—"then the two riggers'll do their thing and will close, one SPIE moving from the east side of the stem, one SPIE from the west. Island's stem is only a quarter mile wide, so we should join up, fifteen minutes max." He paused, running down his checklist. "Snakes?" he asked the riggers, who answered in the affirmative by pointing to two large spools of what looked like common garden hose. "Thermal ID beacons?" he asked the commandos.

Everyone except the two riggers held up their hands.

"Good. Remember it's the last thing they'll expect after the whopping our side's already taken. *L'audace,* gentlemen. *Toujours l'audace.*" He then turned to the Guards' volunteer two medics, one of whom vouched for the fact that after the attack on the east beach, several Zodiac survivors had said they'd seen some kind of missile hitting the southern end of the island.

Freeman made his way back to the pilot's cabin. "You picked up anything on the southern end yet?"

The pilot indicated the radar. "Nothing."

Suddenly the Osprey's automatic wipers started up. "What the hell—"

"Sea spray, General. You wanted low."

"Huh. Well, let me know the moment you see it." With that, Freeman returned to his men, glancing at his watch on the under, less visible side of his wrist. ETA was seven minutes.

Richard Logan felt a sharp dig in his ribs. It was Assmeir, the Delta commando.

"What's up?" Logan asked.

"*Toujours l'audace.* Isn't that what he said goin' into Ruby Lake?"

"Yeah," Logan confirmed. "It's his mantra."

"Uh-huh. We were gonna take 'em by surprise at Ruby Lake, weren't we?"

Rick Logan had his eyes shut, pretending he hadn't heard the question in the roar of the plane.

"Don hoods," Freeman ordered, and the commandos, removing their Fritz helmets, pulled on licorice-green fire retardant flash hoods equipped with single-tube NVGs and respirator, the respirator's twin black filter drums situated below and on either side of the NVG to complete the alien look of modern commandos. But despite the NVGs' magic of boosting available moon- or starlight into a dual display, and the millennium's wizardry evident in their weapons' night-time infrared aiming light—its helium-neon laser and "death dot" invisible except on the commandos' NVGs—the fact was, Freeman hadn't had time to rustle up everything he wanted for this night operation. Most of all he had wanted four time-delay pencils in which a thin wire ran alongside a glass ampoule that was filled with acid, the wire restraining a spring-loaded firing pin two-thirds of the way down the pencil. When the ampoule was crushed, the acid leaked out of the broken ampoule and dissolved the thin wire, which, no longer restraining the firing pin, released it, which in turn hit the percussion cap.

Instead, Freeman once again exhibited his flair for initiative by ordering the riggers to duct-tape an HE grenade against each of the forty-four-gallon drums at the rear of the Osprey.

"You sure the screw tops on those drums are closed tight?" he called out.

"Tighter'n a virgin's pussy, sir."

"All right, but remember, not until the driver gives you the word," *driver* being an ongoing joke between commandos and air crew.

"Yes, sir."

"And use the junkyard count."

It was another example of Freeman's obsession with details.

"Junkyard count. Yes, sir."

The Special Purpose Insertion and Extraction rig—known by all who'd seen but not tried it, and by some of those who had, as the Specially Perverse Individual Extermination rig—consisted of a squad of anywhere from three to ten men lowered quickly on a helo's single rope, in this case a single line descent from the Osprey, a particularly hazardous enterprise because of the presence of the Osprey's two enormous vertical/tilt props. Should either of these de-icing booted props be thrown off kilter by ground-hugging thermals, the props would slice through rope and men like a bayonet through cream. A number of Marines had been killed in just such accidents, which in every case had also caused each $45 million plane to crash and burn. The outstanding advantage of the SPIE, however—at least, for Freeman—was that each man, being attached to the rope in web harness, had his hands free to use his weapon against ground targets on the way down. It was something their airborne forebears on D-Day and at Arnhem were unable to do, with the result that many were dead before they landed. Even so, as Choir Williams cautioned Aussie, it was a dicey proposition to be shooting from the rope, "easy to blow the man below you to pieces."

"Cheery bastard!" Aussie responded as he hooked up to the line. The last thing Aussie said, his voice muffled by the flash hood and respirator beneath his Fritz, was to Salvini. "You throw up on me, you Bronx bastard, and I'll blow your head off."

Sal's equally friendly reply, of which all Brentwood heard was ". . . your balls off!" was lost to the high whine of the Osprey going into the precarious twelve-second vertical-to-horizontal maneuver a hundred feet above the narrowest part of the six's stem, the Osprey now morphing into a state-of-the-art helo.

The first SPIE rope of eight commandos was down in twenty seconds. In the next six seconds, all had unclipped their harnesses from the rungs that had been spliced into the rope. The Osprey, already taking small arms fire from the south, where the virtually treeless stem of the island joined the thickly wooded base, shot half across the narrow-necked isthmus like a dragonfly, hovered and executed its second SPIE. This one, led by Rick Logan, was slower. One of the two volunteer medics, his kit caught up on the harness, took an agonizing twenty-eight seconds to unhook, the Osprey under an increasing crackle of small arms fire in the distance. Then, reaching the western side of the quarter-mile-wide stem, they unloaded the Delta leader, Assmeir, Ali, and his buddy Perez, the squad taking forty-eight seconds from descent to "harness free." The Osprey, buffeted by increasing wind from the storm, came down the slot.

In the Osprey, the pilot eased the thumb wheel forward, his flat, multifunction screen display confirming the two massive Allisons were beginning the first of the series of three-degree downward-rotation arcs. Passing from full horizontal to full vertical, checking his thrust control lever to his left, he turned the yoke hard right, the plane veering quickly eastward, away from the island, its decreased weight allowing it to climb fast. Its two riggers fought gravity as they laboriously made their way aft, having secured the door following the third and final SPIE insertion. At three thousand feet, the Osprey passed through the leading edge of anvil-shaped cumulonimbus. At five thousand, six miles out from the island, the Osprey, well beyond sight of even the most sophisticated NVGs the militia might have, began a slow left turn until the aircraft was once again on a westward heading. The plane's moving map display, slaved to the aircraft's inertial navigation system, showed a remarkably clear three-dimensional image of the six-shaped island, the pilot adjusting course west southwest, heading for the island's base, part of it now a whitish, boil-like image against the grayish background of the Osprey's high-powered forward-looking infrared screen.

"How come these militia goons picked a six-shaped island?" the copilot inquired.

The pilot didn't understand the question, or rather, its implications. "Why not a six?"

" 'Cause there're a lot of religious nuts in the militia. The figure six—Book of Revelations, man. It's the number of the devil. Bad medicine."

"Depends how you look at it," the pilot said. "Flying north to south, the island looks like a nine."

"Thank you, professor!"

"You ready, riggers?" the pilot asked.

"Not yet," the senior rigger answered.

"Get a move on, fellas. The man wants us to go in four minutes exactly."

"Four minutes. Got it."

"Remember, he wants you to use the junkyard count."

In his earpiece the pilot could hear the riggers huffing and puffing with the effort. "Those two," he told the copilot, "would never make Freeman's SpecWar team."

"Neither would we," the pilot answered.

"True. Guess the training's pretty rough."

"Brutal," the copilot said. "Aussie Lewis, Salvini—that crowd. Ex-SEALs, apparently. During their hell week the poor bastards are only allowed twenty minutes sleep a day. The shit they have to go through, man, I'd be banging their quitting bell 'fore lunch."

"All set back here, Cap'n!" came the voice of the senior rigger.

"Everything at the door? Cradle—"

"Yessir. Just waitin' for the light."

"On approach vector now. Three minutes approx. Remember, Freeman wants junkyard count."

The older rigger of the two, a sergeant, his once-immaculate overalls now streaked with dirt from the barrels they'd had to manhandle to the door, shook his head at his fellow rigger and switched off his mouthpiece. "If anyone else tells me we're on friggin' junkyard count I'll throw *them* out."

"Where the hell did Freeman get that junkyard business from?"

"*Junkyard Wars.* Limey TV show on PBS. It's a good program. They put two teams o' guys in a junkyard and give 'em so many hours to make something—a cannon, amphibious vehicle, whatever. It's amazing what they—"

"No," the other rigger said. "I mean what's the junkyard *count*?"

"Oh, one of the referees who started the countdown for the cannon's blast was from a Brit artillery regiment. When they count down from ten, they call ten, nine, eight, seven, six, four—don't say 'five' 'cause sometimes the gunners are so charged up, the second they hear 'fi—' they think it's 'fire'—when there's still another four seconds to—"

The red light was on, and while the senior rigger pulled down his goggles and opened the door, the Arctic-born wind blasting them in the face, the two men's overalls suddenly inflated, fluttering as fiercely as Old Glory.

The ruby red bulb changed to green. "Away!" the pilot commanded.

The young rigger pulled the pin from each drum's duct-taped grenade, the sergeant lifting the cradle's restraining gate, each of the forty-four-gallon drums rolling down the cradle's forty-five-degree incline like depth charges plunging from a destroyer's stern. The Osprey's load computer immediately registered the decrease in the plane's weight, the pilot beginning the hard-over right turn away from the base of the island, knowing that if Freeman's ad hoc taped-grenade fuses worked, he would have a very credible fuel-air explosive. The fuel would become a giant aerosol once the drums hit and burst, the sprayed fuel ignited a second later by the grenades' explosions. It wouldn't meet the precise timing requirements of the original FAE's napalm, but even if only half effective, it would do the job.

"Jesus!" It was the copilot's voice as through his NVGs he saw enormous white fireballs racing across the island's base in the vicinity of the high cliffs. The shock waves were visible in a terrifyingly fast ripple effect of white on white, so bright that his NVGs bloomed out.

Removing his NVGs, he now saw the black-streaked orange waves expanding sideways to both shores, the wind from the approaching front already whipping up a firestorm that he knew would be unstoppable by the militia or anyone else as, having nowhere else to run itself out, it continued to devour the island. Without warning, save possibly the very rapid rise in the air temp reading on the flat screen display, the Osprey was slammed by the first of the vertical shock waves.

The only thing more powerful ounce for ounce than a fuel-air explosive being a nuclear explosion, Freeman knew that the superheated blast from the hundreds of pounds of FAE in the four drums would be so severe that its overpressure would not only trigger all antipersonnel and antitank mines in the area, but also penetrate any surface or subterranean positions that were not completely airtight. It was the latter effect of the FAE, however, that was the major reason Freeman had decided to hastily construct his homemade FAE. He believed that the NSA's reports of 100 to 150 men on the island didn't jibe with the Guard's experience on the west beach, or the hammering Cordell's policemen had taken on the island's east side. There had to be tunnels, he concluded, an old post-'Nam obsession in the military academies of America.

He was wrong. The NSA's infrared SATPIX had simply underestimated, given wind and cloud temperature variations, how many people constituted one "hot spot."

In any event, the FAE's residual heat was felt even by the three SPIE teams of commandos now manning the thin waist of the island's stem, the full force of superheated air from the blast having scorched scores of McBride's remaining militia. On the rock-littered shores of the far southern half of the island, a half-dozen of McBride's escape boats burst into flame as the fire, spilling down from the cliffs, ate away their camouflage nets.

The militia survivors, 116 in all, had only one way to move—northward to the stem. But here, in a Quixotic shift of wind created by the fire itself, flying sparks descended on the bushy but virtually treeless narrow neck. Very soon it became unbearably hot for Freeman's commandos in their carbon-impregnated combat uniforms, the commandos knowing, however, that to remove their flash hoods would render them immediately vulnerable should the militia possess chemical or biological weaponry. Even so, several Rangers in Rick Logan's SPIE removed their black twin-filter "Darth Vader" masks to cool their faces with water from their canteens.

A tremendous explosion rocked the island, one of the Redoubt's two munitions dumps blowing up beneath enormous fingers of flame. The FAE-spawned fires, having encountered the unintended firebreak caused by the burned-out soccer field—a crematorium for dead Federals and militia alike— now raced around its edges like some creature not to be denied. Consuming volatile underbrush of swordfern and salmonberry canes, the flames quickly evaporated any moisture that had penetrated the woods' canopy, the fierce crackling heard by Freeman's three SPIE squads, though they were almost a mile to the north. Simultaneously, the multicolored pyrotechnics launched from the exploding ammunition dump provided a stunningly beautiful contrast against the night sky, streams of tracer and flares graphically reflected against the advancing front.

Meanwhile, the rising winds generated by the front swept most of the smoke southward, except for denser pockets that were held captive in the thick trees immediately north of the soccer field, where Mel Haley and Buzz Cut, hidden in their refuge of sword fern, had lain for a few blissful minutes, hand in hand, exhausted and oblivious to the madness all about them. Now they, like the remaining militia that had not perished in the firestorm, were forced to collect what weaponry and ammunition they could and, under McBride's leadership, try to make their way away from the fire toward the narrow neck, their main body preceded by two "short" platoons of twenty-five men each to "waste" the Federals before they had a chance to dig in across the narrow neck and block the escape route to the northern tip of the island. It was there that most of the small, fast boats had been hidden well away from the obvious combat zones of the two beaches.

What puzzled McBride, as they moved, was how the Federal commander, whoever he was, could possibly think the fire he'd started would spare him and his commandos.

CHAPTER FORTY-TWO

"I THOUGHT THE general didn't defend positions," one of Assmeir's Delta men said. "It's always attack, attack, attack."

"No," Logan said softly on his intercell lip mike. "Not when the enemy's coming to you. What d'you want to do, Assy? Go through the high grass into the woods an' let 'em pick you off?"

"No," Assmeir replied, "but I thought we could send Ali in—no one'd see him, provided he doesn't smile."

"Hey, Assy," the black man replied, "why don't you take your seventy-seven and stick it right up your—"

Looking south through his NVGs, watching the "neck," where the woods of the southern half of the island thinned out to become an all but treeless stem, Logan thought he saw something move over in what would be Assmeir's cone of fire.

"Bogey one o'clock!" Logan warned. "Hundred yards!"

"Ali," Assmeir said, and the black man, readying himself, switched the safety off his Heckler & Koch G36, his weapon of choice, given its ambidextrous cocking lever, which also served as a forward assist lever.

Ali initiated the laser beam, invisible even to Perez, who was right next to him. He saw something emerge from a cluster of foamflower and salmonberry bushes into the high grass, and checked for glowworm spots of light. Had he seen any, he would have known they were coming from the friend-or-foe thermal sleeve beacons worn by all of Freeman's commandos. Not seeing any, however, he was confident that whoever had moved wasn't one of the other two SPIE squads laying Freeman's snakes. Seeing movement again, he brought the laser's pulsating death dot to bear, and saw it was a deer, the terrified animal's fits and starts testimony to the fire-induced panic that was spawning an exodus of fauna from the south of the island.

"Holy shit!" It was Aussie, a hundred yards to Ali's left, astonished by what he saw in his NVGs. It was like a crazy Noah's ark, everything from deer to raccoons coming toward him and his comrades who, now that the three SPIEs were joining up, formed a line across the narrow neck of land that was the natural bridge to the north of the island. Rushing, spraying skunks engulfed Freeman's men with a stink so vile that not even the industrial strength filters of their donned respirator hoods could protect them. The worst afflicted were those, like Choir Williams, who had removed their flash hoods and NVGs moments before in anticipation of a cool sea breeze. They now found their eyes watering as never before, the assault of skunk and wood smoke temporarily blinding them.

Freeman was furious, incredulous that his commandos had violated a fundamental tenet by removing the hoods. He had every reason to be upset, for within the first few minutes of the stampede—the scores of rats shooting past him showing up as white blurs in his NVGs—he could see other warm spots invading his night goggles' field of view. These were the first of McBride's militia breaking cover, laying down heavy fire. Their shooting, however, as Freeman had anticipated, was decidedly wild, as would have been the case if his own men had been fleeing the wrath of nature's most destructive force. Many of the militia were out of breath before they'd reached the neck.

McBride, meanwhile, still couldn't figure it out. Did the Federals only a few hundred yards in front of him really think they were going to escape the fire? Then he saw and felt the Feds' answer as Freeman's two snakes—parallel three-hundred-yard-long, two-inch-diameter hoses filled with explosive—went up. They threw a wall of sandy loam soil ten to twelve feet high across the width of the narrow neck. Most of the force was directed sideways, as designed, into the high grass. The resulting rain of hot, loamy earth caused all of the forward militia's NVGs to bloom with heat overload, the soil falling on the rebels' steel helmets like showers of rice. A fire-break at least fifteen feet wide was cleared across the narrow neck—a moat of earth, in effect, protecting Freeman's commandos from the oncoming fire and slamming the gate on the militia.

But if Freeman was a legend among the SpecWar Feds, McBride had equal status amongst the militia and reckoned he was as quick on his feet. Besides, it was true that discretion was sometimes the better part of valor—to live so that you might fight another day. He gave his order to Rainor.

There was no response, Rainor lying inert on the ground.

Racing against time, the firefight growing more intense as the last of the trapped militia reached the narrow neck, the inferno gaining on them, McBride, glancing around for help, saw that Stanes was also dead. A burst of automatic fire had all but decapitated him. And Cope, hit in the shoulder, was writhing in agony. A moment later McBride glimpsed Maddin and Eleen's sergeant, Mead. Having heard McBride's order, Mead was emerging from a dense cloud of smoke with the string of seven captured policemen, Cordell at their head, and Moorehead—all of them handcuffed together, and Mead holding the keys along with his M-16.

"Keep 'em there!" McBride ordered Mead through the cacophony of the fighting and the roar of the insatiable fire. Falling prostrate by Rainor's corpse, McBride drew his K-bar and cut a snatch of cloth from his T-shirt, draping it over his M-16's barrel. Then, as Cordell had done before him, he thrust the barrel high and yelled for his men to cease firing.

For a second or two, errant clouds of hot, throat-burning wood smoke hid McBride from Freeman's men, but then Salvini spotted it. "White flag!"

Then, despite a few bursts from the western side of the Federal line—Logan, Ali, Perez, and company the last to see the white flag through the smoke—the firing stopped. There was no silence, however; indeed, the sense of danger among McBride's militia was suddenly heightened, the noise of Freeman's man-made forest fire startlingly louder. Cinders and sparks in a sudden shift of wind streamed over them, the bulk of the sparks, to add insult to the militia's injury, dying before reaching the Federal line beyond the firebreak.

"What do you want?" Freeman shouted. "Hurry up or you'll be barbecued!"

It was the first time McBride realized it was his old nemesis who was leading the attack. "Freeman!"

"Thought that prick was retired," a militiaman hidden in the high grass to McBride's left said.

"We have Commandant Moorehead, Police Chief Cordell, and six of his police officers prisoners!" McBride shouted. "We want safe passage to our boats—otherwise the cops are history!" McBride could feel the radiant heat from the fire, which was now flaring up again, aided by wind turbulence.

Logan and his Rangers, along with the Delta squad who were between him and Freeman's squad, awaited the general's response. Everyone in the line, except the two volunteer medics, swept their field of fire with lasers, hoping to find a militia target not camouflaged by the grass. Simultaneously, a few militia snipers, hurriedly assembling at the edge of the disappearing woods, their concentration sorely tested by the roar of the fire, tried to "reverse vector" the Federals' laser beams when the latter became momentarily visible in the smoke.

"Five seconds!" McBride demanded. "Or we'll shoot them!" He indicated the line of handcuffed policemen. "Or would you rather watch them die with us in the fire?"

With that, Freeman flicked up his lip mike, plugged into his line of commandos. "Target the prisoners' NLRs. Repeat, NLRs! Choir and Sal only—head shot for the Guard."

"Got it," Sal confirmed. "Head shot, Guard." Freeman could hear Aussie and Brentwood changing mags.

McBride, knowing everything was lost if he wasn't prepared to follow through on his threat, turned around and called out to Mead, "Anyone'll do!"

Mead gave the thumbs-up, the fire's light so strong now that he and the seven hostages were clearly silhouetted. Behind them gigantic flames licked the night sky, wildly gyrating columns of sparks swirling upward. In the near distance there were the sounds of trees exploding, bark shrapnel flying through the inferno with amazing speed, the air saturated with the smell of the burning wood, gunpowder, and the pungent, sweet odor rising from the cremated carcasses of animals. The fleeing creatures were so terrorized, disorientated by the wild orchestration of battle, fire, and rolling thunder, that many had run back into the fire.

Mead indicated Moorehead, and Maddin immediately un-shackled the commandant from Cordell and the other seven SWAT prisoners.

"Where do you think this'll get you?" Moorehead asked.

"Off the island!" Mead said, not a skerrick of pity in his parched throat. "Besides, it's time you faced your maker, you bastard!"

"Amen to that," added Maddin, who now told the other prisoners to move away as Mead chambered a round in his M-16 and waited for McBride. Would he call Freeman's bluff?

"Sergeant!" It was Eleen's voice, the militia captain having dropped behind, helping the militia's wounded, his hair singed, the right arm of his Fairchild fatigues soaked in blood. "Don't shoot them!" he ordered

"Are you kidding?" Maddin shouted. "These assholes wouldn't hesitate to—"

"Do it!" McBride shouted.

"No," Eleen shouted, reaching for Mead's rifle, upon which Maddin put his handgun to Moorehead's temple and pulled the trigger. The commandant staggered a foot or two, then buckled at the knees, blood jetting from the flickering wound. Cordell reeled from the sight triggering a boyhood memory of viewing TV news footage of the mayor of Saigon executing a Communist in exactly the same manner.

The next second, a coordinated death dot on every target, a volley of subsonic fire whistled across the firebreak, Mead and his string of prisoners hit and flung back like rag dolls, Mead dead even before he fell.

"Run for a boat!" McBride yelled, seeing his hopes of a hostage-shielded free passage to the boats collapse with the SWAT prisoners; felled by Freeman's ruthless decision to fire on his fellow Federals rather than yield to the militia's demands. "Any boat you can find!"

McBride and his militia followers, firing smoke grenades to add to the fire's smoke in a desperate attempt to give themselves cover, scattered left and right toward the cliffs on either side of the narrow neck, down to what few boats might remain in their half of the island. McBride had hoped to leave these exclusively for Eleen's slowly moving wounded, and they were now threatened with imminent destruction from the fire. As Eleen exhorted his charges to move in as fast as they could, Maddin was unable to move, a breath-snatching pain in his chest growing worse, the fire so close he could see individual pine and fir exploding.

Even now, Maddin didn't realize that he and the would-be hostages had been hit by rubber-jacketed nonlethal rounds, whose impact is so severe that, though designed not to kill unless they strike their victim in the head, as they had Mead—on Freeman's specific instruction to Choir and Aussie—they temporarily incapacitate as well as inflict serious pain and enormous purple bruises that would last for weeks. By the time Maddin managed to stagger to his feet, the SWAT men were rousing themselves under Cordell's ferocious language to get the handcuff keys from Mead.

It was too late to reverse the militia's rout, as men and women scrambled frantically down from the rocky heights above the surf-battered shore, some falling to their death. Frantically tearing off camouflage nets, the sputter of oxygen-starved engines in the small coves barely audible in the din from above, Freeman's commandos, their blood up, having lost two Delta men fatally hit in the firefight, split into two squads at either end of the firebreak, pursuing the militia down to the water's edge. Their NLR mags ejected, the commandos were now firing armor-piercing and incendiary tracer rounds, the latter appearing as segmented white arcs in the commandos' NVGs. Splinters of light flew up at the end of the arcs as boats the militia were climbing into were hit by an assortment of 5.6mm and 7.6mm rounds. The distance between militia and Federals, however, was still beyond the effective range of Freeman's AS-12 drum mag shotgun.

Despite unit discipline collapsing all about him, McBride regained his self-control after the initial shock he'd experienced at Freeman's apparently callous "clear the bridge" disregard for the lives of Cordell and the other prisoners. He was now vigorously organizing what rearguard action he could to provide covering fire for his withdrawing comrades. The latter now numbered between sixty and eighty, around twenty of these badly wounded. McBride ordered them, under Maddin's and Stanes's command, to wait for the last two of six small interisland boats, the only vessels as yet not gutted by the fire that had now all but consumed the base of the island.

Stanes, his left shin shattered, was shaking uncontrollably. But he was told, like Maddin, who'd barely made it down to the shore, to stand his ground behind a cluster of honeycombed volcanic rock at the shore's edge. McBride was now operating with the tough-minded rationale of first getting out the men still fit enough to fight another day—a basic tenet of militia doctrine.

Freeman's force was down to fourteen, his dead including one of the two volunteer medics, who was cut down by a burst from Maddin's M-16, the medic's red cross insignia either not visible to or disregarded by the militiaman. Maddin, despite his injury, was now no more than sixty yards away from the rapidly moving commando line as it broke to left and right flank. He'd also knocked down Salvini, the Bronx man saved by his bulletproof vest, but not before Maddin's rounds had punched holes through several layers of the Kevlar weave.

Through the smoke, Aussie Lewis saw another militiaman bearing down on Salvini and unleashed his HK burst from the hip. The militiaman's hands were flung out from his side, Aussie's rounds slamming into the man's head, the cloud of blood like an explosion of milk on Aussie's NVGs. The militiaman's last uncontrolled burst took out two of his own in a squad of militia as they hastily traversed a jumble of stones en route to a small rock-embraced cove on the neck's west side.

"*You* coming, Major?" someone in the last boat called out to McBride through a pall of smoke.

McBride sensed someone coming up behind him, whirled about, and saw it was Maddin. "Get to the boat!" he ordered him, realizing that while Maddin had looked badly wounded earlier, he now seemed battle fit.

In the fierce glow of the fire, consuming all the vegetation along the clifftop, Maddin shouted, "We were had!" Then, obediently following McBride's order, he waded out toward the remaining boats, two having capsized in the increasingly rough surf due either to panic-fueled overload, fire from Freeman's men, or both.

"Been *had*?" McBride shouted after Maddin, while dodging behind the rocks and grabbing another mag, his last one for the M-16. "What d'you mean, *had*?"

"Freeman used nonlethals on the SWAT!" Maddin shouted back. "Thought I was a goner too till I saw there was no blood. My canteen was leaking."

Under the strain and the all-but-unbearable heat, smoke,

and noise, the vascular stain in Maddin's face momentarily infuriated the normally sanguine McBride. It became for him an irrational focus for everything that had gone wrong, Maddin's face that of the unwanted messenger who had just revealed to the legendary militia leader that he had been duped into making a colossal mistake, ordering his people to run for their lives precisely when he should have regrouped. "Shit!"

"C'mon!" Maddin shouted, urging McBride to withdraw. Maddin was now wading through bodies and flotsam up to his waist, until he was roughly hauled aboard. Two more militiamen were hit as McBride delayed his decision on the shore.

"You go!" McBride replied. "Leave me some ammo."

Maddin and two other men tossed vest packs from the stern of their boat—a smoky bluish exhaust spewing out as the cream-colored fourteen-footer smacked into the waves, away from the wreckage of men and matériel.

"Get outta here," Stanes shouted to McBride. "You have to follow your own orders. Go—kick their ass on the mainland!"

"C'mon!" men in the last two boats were calling.

"Go!" someone else shouted. "For God's sake, Major!" In the confusion and noise, it was difficult to hear, but McBride thought he heard someone shouting, "Goes on the *Cloud*! On the *Cloud*!"—the *Cloud* being one of the four overloaded boats now leaving the island.

The boats were hidden by a fortuitous smoke-laden shift in the wind that provided them with ideal cover from the commandos. What's more, Freeman's men, though rushing to close with the remaining militia, were sweating so profusely that their NVGs were steaming up. By the time the general and his men had removed their NVGs, more smoke had poured down from the cliffs, further obscuring the boats.

Swimming toward the *Cloud*, McBride felt the cold that had temporarily rallied him now stiffening his muscles, his earlier fatigue returning with a vengeance. For all his resolve in following agreed-upon policy that able-bodied fighters, including himself, not be wasted in futile attempts to stay behind with the wounded, rather than leave a combat area to save themselves to carry on the fight, he was nevertheless sickened by the necessity. It gave him little comfort to recall how Eleen once had had to do the same thing, in his case leaving a wounded man in the snow while Eleen escaped in a captured Federal helo. He felt like a deserter, the overwhelming temptation in him to stay behind for honor's sake as much an impediment to him reaching the *Cloud* as the freezing sea. He reached toward what he thought was a helping hand from the boat, but it was the hand of a dead body floating facedown in the wind-whipped swells. It was the body of Mel Haley, the Boeing "idiot," momentarily illuminated by what McBride thought was lightning but which in fact was a slowly descending phosphorus flare lighting the fire's smoke, looking now like a billowing fog creeping over the sea.

CHAPTER FORTY-THREE

FREEMAN, LIKE ANY Federal who had had dealings with the militia, and who knew militia General Wilcox's policy of requiring all able-bodied militia to avoid capture if at all possible, was nevertheless determined to prevent his enemies from escaping the island.

David Brentwood, as tired as all of the others, asked, "Why worry, General? So a few of them might make it to the mainland. The point is, we've beaten them."

"The point is, David," Freeman retorted, "we haven't got McBride. He's the head of the snake. He's the legend. If he gets away, my God—they'll make him a goddamned saint!"

"Which means," Choir quietly told Aussie off mike, "he'll get more press than the old man."

"I agree with the boss," Aussie said. "McBride'll be a hero from here to Chechnya if he slips through our noose. Hero against Uncle Sam."

"Och," Choir said, checking his mag, "you like a fight you do."

"Oh, why are you here? To sing in the eisteddfod?"

"You're a troublemaker, that's what you are."

"Bet your ass!"

"We have to get a boat!" Freeman said.

"Ten o'clock!" Brentwood warned, unleashing a long burst from his Heckler & Koch. It was a black-tailed deer, its legs now thrashing in its death throes.

Freeman wasn't happy. It was the kind of misidentification that Brentwood rarely made—a sure sign of fatigue setting in. "You're ALERTs!" he chastised them. "Stay alert!"

Picking up the pace, Freeman led his men north of the firebreak.

"Old man can run!" Sal put in.

"A ladies' man too," Choir added. "They say he had a fling with that CNN—"

"See anything, Choir?" Freeman called.

"Not yet, General."

Freeman's men found two militia boats hidden along the first quarter mile of the northern shore, one equipped with two outboards, the other an inboard, the general selecting the inboard, since it looked like the more powerful and reliable of the two craft. Next, Freeman selected his old team of Aussie, Brentwood, Salvini, and Choir Williams, in addition to Ali, to accompany him, while Logan and his six commandos would keep the militia bottled up on the shore.

"They've got one hell of a start on us, General," Ali remarked skeptically.

"Their boats are loaded down with bodies, son," Freeman replied as he pushed the starter button, Aussie and Sal casting off. "We're traveling light."

"Problem is," Ali pressed, "which boat is McBride in—if he's in any of them?"

"Live and learn, Ali," Freeman said, checking his Glock 17's mag. "Bastard's in the last boat. Apart from militia policy, *any* commander worth his salt takes the last boat out, not the first. That McBride's a son of a bitch but he's a brave son of a bitch. Why do you think he's held in such esteem?" His voice was drowned out by the sky split open by an electric blue fork of lightning and a roll of thunder they felt in the pit of their stomachs.

Within five minutes of leaving the island, Sal was hanging over the starboard gunwale, Ali offering him a Gravol from his first-aid blister pack, which Salvini refused. It might cure his nausea, but it would make him sleepy, and sleepy wasn't what you wanted when closing on battle-hardened rebels. Sleepy could get you killed.

When McBride grasped the friendly end of an otherwise mean-looking grappling hook and was dragged aboard, waves already broaching the *Cloud*, he heard snatches of voices: ". . . Major . . . you're okay . . ."

Shivering uncontrollably, McBride looked up and saw it was Eleen talking to him. Next, he could feel someone draping blankets around his shoulders, another handing him a warm

mug of watery hot chocolate. "From our emergency supplies," the militiaman told him, trying to adopt a hopeful
tone, then exclaiming, "Oh, shit—" as the boat wallowed in a
heavy swell, McBride spilling most of the hot chocolate.

"Give 'im air!" someone said.

"Air?" another replied. "For chrissake, we're in the middle
of the friggin' ocean!"

The first speaker elbowed the second. "Eleen!"

"What?"

"Watch your language," the first man cautioned again.
"Eleen's right next to—"

"Fuck Eleen. We're in a situation here."

Eleen didn't like the blasphemy, of course, but more worrying to him was that the man's disrespect signaled a general
breakdown in discipline that had begun during the retreat.

Eleen urged McBride to go below to warm up in the
Cloud's small galley, but the militia leader, already getting a
whiff of the diesel exhaust, elected instead to go to the
Cloud's wheelhouse. Up till now, Eleen had taken McBride's
silence as evidence of the major's reluctance to obey the
militia policy that it was the duty of every able-bodied
militiaman to escape to the mainland to fight the Federals
another day. In McBride's case it would be a chance to
lead the militia once again, after his brilliant defense of
the Redoubt and stunning headline-grabbing attack on the
Maui, showing the whole world just how vulnerable the Federals were.

"I know what's troubling you, Major," Eleen told him. "Believe me, I've been through it. It sounds egotistical, I know,
but you're more valuable to the movement than any of us."

Coming from a man who'd engineered one of the great escapes from Fairchild, this was an unabashed compliment.
Still, McBride, steadying himself against the roll of the sea
with one hand, the other holding another mug of hot choco-

late, didn't respond, and in the faint wheelhouse light that had been rigged for red, Eleen didn't realize what had happened, until a sky-rending fork of lightning momentarily flooded the *Cloud* with light and he saw McBride had the thousand-yard stare. It was that eerie look of detachment, signaling the brain's inability to comprehend what was going on about him, the terror that had affected the bravest of the brave since Thermopylae through Omaha Beach to Vietnam. How long it would last could vary, from seconds, the ears ringing, eyes glazed, to the nightmares of post-traumatic stress syndrome.

How on earth had McBride escaped, if he wasn't even cognizant of where he was? Eleen wondered.

The wheelhouse door opened, a blast of sea air rushing in, hitting McBride like a slap in the face. He didn't move, though his free hand, like an automaton, grasped the roll bar. Entering the wheelhouse, Jubal said something to McBride, the youngster's voice drowned in another roll of window-shaking thunder that was followed by a sprinkle of rain.

"Oh, crap!" said the militiaman skippering the *Cloud*. "We're gonna get dumped on!"

"Don't knock it," Jubal said. "It's a gift from God. It'll hide us if the Feds are on our tail."

CHAPTER FORTY-FOUR

"I'M SURE YOU'LL find it nice and quiet," the Blue Jay Motel operator told Marte Price. Marte returned the night manager's assurances with a broad smile, her lips and eyes perfectly coordinated in a smile that ever since childhood had immediately won over almost everyone she met—except for the odd grumpy pilot. Together with her slightly husky voice, the winning smile had set her apart amid the press pack early in her career. Her courage had done the rest, establishing Marte Price as CNN's preeminent field reporter.

Within seconds of closing her motel room door she was on the phone, calling the local police, fire, and Coast Guard stations, giving them verification numbers in Atlanta should they doubt who she was and asking whether anything out of the ordinary had taken place on the island. Police and Fire were excited that she'd called, breaking the monotony of the midnight-to-dawn watch. But they had nothing to report. "Only thing goin' on hereabouts," reported the lone fireman on duty, "is a storm. Passed over us, heading south to the sound by now."

The policewoman was trying to sound nonchalant. In fact, she was already thinking about whom she could tell about that "CNN woman—what's her name—Rice? Price? Yeah, Price, I guess that's her name. Wanted to know if anything outta the ordinary was goin' down. Told her there's always drug shipments through the San Juans. 'Whale watchers,' I told her—natural cover for shipping whatever you like from the States to Canada—heroin, Chinese, terrorists, you name it." She had to admit to Marte Price, however, that right now there wasn't anything being reported.

The Coast Guard duty officer sounded nervous. The sinking of the *Orca* was not yet public knowledge, but trying to keep it under wraps until Washington, D.C., was ready to put its spin on Rats' Nest, pending the outcome of Freeman's mission, was straining everybody concerned.

Next, Marte rang the Washington State Ferries Corp. She got a recorded message, press this, press that, five minutes to reach a human being.

The human being knew nothing and, looking to rid herself of Marte's inquiries, asked, "Have you tried the private ferries in Anacortes? They service the San Juans. Maybe there was an accident or something?"

Marte was taking off her earrings, which some general during one of her overseas missions—possibly Freeman, or was it Rodgers?—had warned her not to wear in a war zone. "Ready-made shrapnel!" they'd told her. She dropped the two C-shaped earrings on the night table, sat on the bed and looked for complimentary mints. None. She could get only recorded messages from the private ferries in Anacortes, except for an outfit called Kingfisher Catamarans. The line was busy. At five A.M.? She put on her best frantic voice, telling the operator she had to get through, it was urgent.

A few seconds of white noise, then the operator. "Who are you, ma'am?"

"A relative," Marte said, an ancient reporter's ploy. "I *have* to speak to the owner!"

"He's not available, ma'am," but Marte could already smell that something was wrong.

"Look!" she told the operator, "I told you this is an emergency, and if I don't get to talk to someone I'm going to sue the pants off you people!"

Precisely who "you people" meant—the phone company, Kingfisher Ferries, or both—the operator didn't know, but she was sufficiently intimidated to put Marte through to a man who identified himself as Mark Aitken. Marte instantly recognized the voice as that of Police Chief Cordell's aide.

"Aitken?" Marte Price said.

There was a long pause. "Who is this?"

"CNN. Marte Price. What are you doing in Anacortes? Where's Chief Cordell?"

Aitken, tired, stunned by the disaster that had befallen his and Cordell's plan—well, it was mainly Cordell's, wasn't it?—hesitated.

"Look," Marte raced on, "Cordell told me something interesting might be happening in the San Juans, which means something's in it for him and *you*. You want me to get a Seattle camera crew up there?" It was a threat as much as a question. Marte gave him no time to think. "You don't want to be one of those bureaucrats on *Headline News*, do you? You know, denying whatever the hell's happening, only to retract it the next morning . . . ? Well?"

"On one condition," Aitken said. "You hold it till noon."

All of her senses alert now, Marte could smell the lavender deodorizer in the room trying to cover up ancient cigarette smoke and stale beer. "All right," she agreed, "but only if I have an exclusive. I'll tape it now. Anyone else gets it, I'll run it before you can change your shorts!"

"I can't control every news—"

"Sure you can—till noon. Besides, I'm the only one Cordell gave the bait to."

She could hear Aitken, his breathing labored. "There's this island southwest of Lopez, unnamed till we called it 'Rats' Nest.' "

"Who's *we*?"

"The Chief, Washington, D.C."

"The White House?"

"Yes. The President and—"

"Hold on." The pinpoint red light on her mini-recorder was flickering. Hurriedly, she took out the two AA batteries. Tearing open a new pack from her purse, she tore a nail. "Goddammit!"

"What's wrong?"

"Nothing," she said. "Go!"

"We sent in a force of National Guard and cops . . ."

Marte had no sooner thanked Aitken, telling him she'd repay the favor someday, than she was calling Grumpy, the pilot who, despite his previous unwillingness to communicate, struck her as a veteran of countless helo flights, a man who knew his job.

"Never heard of the place," Grumpy told her. " 'Sides, I'm in bed."

"How much would you normally charge to take me down there—if you weren't in beddy-bye?" That'd get his goat.

"Two hundred dollars. One way."

"One way. Wouldn't you want to come back to bed?"

"Depends who with!"

Oh my, Marte thought. Grumpy was quick.

"How about coming back with a few snapshots of Grover Cleveland?"

"A thousand, huh? It'd be rough. There's bad weather down there."

"Does it frighten you?"

"I know what you're doing, lady."

"Is it working?"

"No."

"I apologize for being a smartass bitch, but if I make it three grand, would that interest you? Plus I'd try to get the camera crew after to get a close-up of your helo. You can't *buy* advertising like that."

"You want to go now?"

"Yes."

"Quicker if I pick you up," he said. "I'm on Tucker Avenue."

She thought he'd said something else and smiled to herself, then wondered how he knew where she was. Maybe he'd suggested the motel to her, but she didn't remember him doing it. Maybe he'd followed her, and maybe this was reporters' paranoia.

After he picked her up, en route to the airport, he inadvertently hit a chipmunk momentarily transfixed in the headlights. "Stop!" she implored him.

He pulled over, walked back, and returned, his footsteps heavy on the gravel. "He's dead," he told her, and one of the toughest reporters at CNN began to cry. He handed her a Kleenex that reeked of aftershave.

She blew her nose hard. "How long will it take to the island?"

"Depends. We'll have the wind behind us going down, but I'll have to go east for a while, go around the back end of the storm. And coming back, the wind'll be against us. An hour—an hour and a half maybe."

Marte was surprised—she'd thought it would be much longer.

"There mightn't be a place to land," he told her.

"Aitken says there's two beaches. The island's quite small." She handed him the fax Aitken had sent to the motel.

"What d'you expect to find?"

"I don't know." Right now she wasn't thinking about the exclusive she wanted to get about the clash of the two legendary leaders and how such a coup—interviews with the main players, if they were still alive—would further boost her ratings. She was thinking about the chipmunk. It was silly, she told herself, primitive, anthropomorphic, but she was sad they hadn't dug a little grave.

Whether it was the onset of the torrential rain or the successive booms of thunder and flashes of lightning that affected McBride, Eleen didn't know. Perhaps it was the news from the wheelhouse that there was a blip on the radar—something to the west of them—or simply the fact that for the first time in hours of vicious combat, no one was shouting at him or trying to kill him. Whatever the reason, McBride had awoken from his torpor, asking, "How close are the other four boats?"

"Half a mile or so," the ad hoc skipper replied.

"That's no good," McBride said. "Get them to spread out. Not safe to clump together." He turned to Jubal. "Signal them by flashlight to spread out."

"I don't know how," Jubal said, embarrassed.

McBride turned to Eleen. "Get someone who can. No radio messages. Freeman'll be listening."

"Yes, sir," Eleen said, leaving the wheelhouse, crashing into Jubal as a rogue wave smacked the *Cloud* hard amidships, foam broaching the gunwales.

"Did Captain Eleen tell you that the egg's all set?" Jubal asked McBride. "It'd be tricky but—"

Now everything clicked for McBride. The militiaman shouting at him so loudly on the shore hadn't yelled, "Go on the *Cloud*," he'd said, "*ROE's* on the *Cloud*!"

"You're lucky, sir," Jubal continued, "that it was stowed in one of the boats that didn't get walloped."

"Lucky McBride!" the starboard lookout said, his tone shot through with envy. "Be nice if we all had one! Guess you'll reach the mainland before us?"

"Keep your eyes open," the skipper told the lookout. "And your yap shut."

"Can't see a thing in this shit!" the lookout retorted.

"Remember the guy," the skipper riposted, "who saw the Jap fleet through the tiny hole in the clouds? Near Midway?"

"Yeah, well, we're not near fucking Midway, are we?"

"Serenity now!" the skipper said, trying humor instead.

"Nothin' funny about this," the starboard lookout groused. "Those Feds catch us, they could sink us. We're carryin' too much weight!"

"You're right," Jubal chimed in. "But if the major escapes on the egg-breaker, that'll mean we'll be almost three hundred pounds lighter—give us a hefty increase in speed, eh?"

"Unless," the skipper told the lookout, "you want to jump over the side?"

"Yeah, well—"

"That's enough!" McBride said. The lookout had got it off his chest. Allowing any more would be to brook sheer insubordination. "Everyone does what they're told," McBride announced, "or I'll shoot them. Right now!" And everyone in the wheelhouse knew that this man who'd shot at his best friend in the room at Hayden Lake wouldn't hesitate do it. Next, McBride grabbed the wheelhouse's mike from its cradle above the fathometer and flipped the toggle switch to Deck. "Everyone off their ass. Lock and load and look alive!"

He glanced through the wheelhouse's rear glass, but couldn't detect any movement among the dark shapes of the men huddled against the wind and rain. "Jubal!" he ordered. "Go out there and stir them up. We're not finished with those Feds yet. Last thing they expect is a counterattack. They think we're running scared."

"Aren't we—*sir*?" the starboard lookout dared to say.

McBride knew the history of his nemesis, chapter and

verse. "*L'audace,* son," he told the lookout, "*l'audace, tou-jours l'audace.*"

"What's that?"

"It means," McBride said, "that we're going to give the general some of his own medicine. Skipper, how far away are they?"

"A mile."

"When will they reach us?"

"I don't know for sure. I—"

"Approximate, man, approximate."

"Fifteen, maybe twenty minutes."

McBride left the bridge, saw Jubal rousing the men, and added his own words of encouragement. "Come on, fellas. Everyone up. We're going to turn this around." It was a bad choice of words, some men thinking he meant literally turning the *Cloud* around. "I mean we're going to win this."

"How, Major?"

"Because," he shouted against the violence of the storm, "I'm *lucky*, dammit. Have I ever let you down?"

No, he hadn't, and men who had just passed from victory to defeat on the island now stirred, rejuvenated by McBride's uncompromising confidence. "Jubal!" McBride called out. "Over here." McBride put his arm around the young soldier. "Get three of the strongest men on the boat—"

"Yes, sir," Jubal cut in, immediately turning to his task.

"No no," McBride said. "Not yet. I haven't finished.

"No, sir, I mean, yes, sir."

"Calm down, son."

"Yes, sir."

"And listen carefully. We haven't much time."

The *Cloud* shuddered against crisscrossing waves, an enormous phosphorescent cloud of spray enveloping the boat. Eleen, having finished flashing his signal to the nearest two boats, telling them to scatter and pass the signal on to the other boat, made his way over to McBride and Jubal. "What next, Major?"

"Bowline knots," McBride said. "You know how to tie them?"

"Yes, sir. I was a Boy—"

"All right," McBride cut in. "Use the mooring lines if necessary. Then collect all HE grenades and take them below to Jubal." Back in the wheelhouse, gripping the roll bar as the *Cloud* smashed into an oncoming swell, he ordered the skipper to turn on the deck lights.

"They'll see us," the skipper objected.

"Even in this rain?" McBride asked.

"Yes."

"Good!"

CHAPTER FORTY-FIVE

ON THE WEST side of the narrow neck, Logan's men paused and brazenly offered the militia, about twenty of them, a chance to surrender. The militia's answer, delivered by Buzz Cut, was such a long burst from her M-60 that the barrel was in danger of overheating.

The return fire from the eight commandos wasn't as unrestrained, Logan and the Delta commander conserving their ammunition. "Pepper spray?" a Delta man asked through his lip mike.

"Negative," Logan replied. "Winds are still too helter-skelter. Besides, the rain wouldn't help it. We can wait 'em out. They're not goin' anywhere."

"Unless," the Delta leader posited, "they have a few more boats stashed. They might be buying time, then shove off under smoke. That'd put the general between 'em and the other militia boats."

Logan acknowledged the point. "Okay, we'll pop pepper and watch. If it seems to be working, we'll go in for CQB."

There was some cursing—no one, no matter how well-trained, wanted to go into Close Quarter Battle, the only mitigating factor in this case being that the fire that had ravaged the base of the island was dying, hissing like a thousand woks as the heavy rain came down. Ironically, though, the rain, in the process of dousing the fire, made the matter of moving in for CQB even more pressing for the commandos. Logan realized that the longer they put off an attack on the militia, the better chance the rebels had of returning to their Redoubt, which, while gutted by the fire, would nevertheless allow the remaining militia room to move—lots of cover still available in the form of blackened trees, stumps, and the wreckage strewn about the old soccer field. And what if some ammunition boxes had been buried?

"Fix bayonets!" Logan ordered, taking his own M-9 from its scabbard, fixing it to his M-16. The Ranger leader, surprised, as he always was, by how long it extended his weapon, recalled Aussie Lewis's comment during training: "Makes you feel like you're carrying a bloody lance." Bayonets, like mines, were out of date, not considered "sexy" by the Pentagon's procurers. But Logan, like the rest of Freeman's commandos, had a healthy respect for the M-9. In a pinch, the sapphire-sharpened bayonet, with its voltage tester and green-probe-light-equipped scabbard, could also double as a razor-wire cutter and screwdriver, and had saved more than one commando's life when his weapon had jammed or suddenly run out of ammo. Only Perez, at his own expense, had dispensed with the M-9, electing instead to carry the ten-inch-long Eickhorn-Solingen BMTK. The trigger-operated, spring-loaded Ballistic Military Throwing Knife attachment was loaded with a four-inch superhardened blade, and Perez's scabbard held two reserve blades.

"Pop canisters!" Logan ordered, and eight dull thumps could be heard above the sizzle of the dying fire and the sporadic crack of militia small arms fire. Logan instructed his men to hold their fire as they entered the smoke, which for once favored their advance rather than the militia's retreat. Then, suddenly, the militia ceased firing and a cold fear gripped Logan—perhaps Assmeir had been right: the militia rearguard, having bought time for their comrades to escape, were now following suit, gone, using boats undamaged by the fire?

Then he and his comrades, flash hoods and NVGs back on, heard the panicked coughing of pepper spray victims. Figures, barely visible through the rain-curtained firelight, were stumbling and cursing; others were clutching their chests, some holding their hands out in front of them like disoriented blind men. Most were yelling for water; others, more in control, though blinded by the grenades' spray, turned their heads skyward, letting the rain wash the irritant away. Though not publicly acknowledged by those law enforcement agencies that used it in riot control, that course of action could cause heart attacks, through the sheer breath-stopping panic it induced. Some militia, however, reflecting the wide range of human reaction to any one substance, recovered quickly from the spray, and half the militia were spared because of wind eddies. It was this group that now took up the most forward positions. Most of them, as McBride had trained them, were tearing up cloth, wetting handkerchiefs, anything that could

serve as protection from the residual spray, which thankfully
for them posed no threat, having been diluted and dispersed
relatively quickly by rain and wind.

The commandos, with the bloodcurdling yells employed
throughout the ages as much to pump up the warrior as to
instill terror in his enemies, were among the bayonetless
militia, a deficiency for which the militia paid a terrible price.
In conditions of wind-driven smoke and rain, the danger of
blue on blue was at its highest, and in the melee of screaming
and clash of metal on metal, the commandos' bayonets took
the night. Only two of Logan's men were wounded—one, his
nose smashed by a fist-sized rock, the other, to what would be
his eternal chagrin, blindsided by a hysterical young militiaman, knocked hard off balance and, falling and reaching
out with his left hand to break his fall, slicing his left wrist
open with his bayonet. Logan's medic ran to him, only to have
his neck broken by the powerful downward blow from a
shotgun's stock, the gun's ammoless owner out of his mind
with the frustration of being unable to fire his weapon.

Perez saw another World War Two helmet rushing at him,
what looked like a .45 in its owner's hand, and released his
third blade. He didn't see it flash, because of the gloom, but
instead heard it strike the figure, which crumpled to its knees
with a guttural grunt and, seeing no other militia in danger of
being hit, fired the .45. Its round slammed into Perez with
such force that he was thrown back into a spill of rocks, his
Fritz flying off his head as a second .45 bullet zinged above
him. By now the militiaman was dead, the blade having
passed through his jugular. Perez got up slowly, the wind
completely knocked out of him, despite the lifesaving protection the Kevlar had given him. The fighting suddenly ceased.
Logan looked down at the dead medic, felled despite his clear
red cross armband and the unmistakable marking on his
helmet. The first medic killed might have been an accident.

This one, however, was intentional. Drawing his HK pistol, Logan grabbed the sodden hair of a wounded rebel and forced the barrel into the prisoner's mouth.

"He can't talk with a gun in his mouth!" Assmeir said.

Logan stared at the Delta leader, withdrew the gun, and jammed it against the prisoner's head.

"Tell me where your boats are headed on the mainland. I mean exactly *where* on the mainland, or I'll blow your god-damned head off!" He pressed the gun in harder.

"I don't know." Logan was shocked. It was a woman's voice. "And even if I did," she continued, "I wouldn't tell you—you snot scum!" It was Buzz Cut.

Logan was still prepared to shoot her. Any SpecWar type with his experience had come across more than one bitch ter-rorist. He pulled the hammer back.

"Ease up, Rick!" Perez said. "She doesn't know."

"That doesn't help us," Logan retorted, releasing the hammer.

From Freeman's boat, Sal, still queasy, spotted a small, bobbing island of light in the darkness and checked the radar. "It's the last one we had on the radar screen."

"Then that's him," Freeman said.

"Why's he got all the lights on?"

Freeman steadied himself against a high, corkscrewing pitch. "A trap," he concluded.

"What kind of trap?" Salvini asked.

"Don't know. The wily prick."

The *Cloud*'s lights had been on only a second or two when McBride, in the wheelhouse, instructed the skipper to switch them off. "I want the Feds to think it was inadvertent—otherwise Freeman'll think I'm setting something up."

"They'll probably have us on radar anyway," the skipper said.

"*Probably*'s not good enough. Sea's picking up. Doesn't take much for wave scatter to fuzz out a radar set, and I want to be damn sure they saw us." McBride, hunger pangs assaulting him after his extraordinary expenditure of energy over the last few hours, called down to the galley to ask if there was any food.

"A few power bars," a voice replied.

For the first time in weeks McBride actually whined about something, power bars in his mind concomitant with his disdain of those he considered health Nazis. "No OHenrys?" he complained.

"No, Major." There was a pause. "Don't you remember you banned 'em 'cause a few of the guys had a peanut allergy? You said one bite and they'd—"

"Anaphylactic shock," McBride said. "Yeah, I forgot."

"Got a few apples. Bit spotty."

"They'll do. Thanks," and he smiled. Maybe it was his battle fatigue and the invasive cacophony of the storm directly overhead that had caused him to forget about the Canadian OHenry bar with its bilingual printing which he'd had Cope give to that helo pilot from Whidbey, to make her and the Feds think the Redoubt was over, or on, the Canada–U.S. border. Well hell, he mused, it had worked for a while. He was relieved that, despite the avalanche of worries that had descended upon him about whether he and his men would reach the mainland, his sense of humor apparently was intact.

Jubal called up from below to go over the instructions McBride had given him earlier on the deck, and McBride went down to the crowded galley. Jubal and three other men were carefully arranging twenty-four Frag grenades in two twelve-packs, each pack held tightly together by bands of duct tape. Jubal and his colleagues planned to use two eighteen-inch-long pieces of wire, which, when pulled sharply, would simultaneously arm a dozen grenades for what Jubal, in high expectation, predicted would be "one mother of a fragmentation bomb!"

"Have we any claymores aboard?" McBride asked.

He heard Jubal repeating his question, Eleen saying he'd go on deck to check whether anyone on *Cloud* had retained one in his kit during their humiliating withdrawal.

On deck, the rolling seemed much worse to Eleen, because his eyes had not yet adjusted to the rain-slashed night. He found it difficult to keep his balance and impossible to avoid stepping on men who, though roused for impending action by McBride, were still huddled beneath whatever cover they could get. Most of them had only their steel helmets to shield them, several having expressed concern that the cluster of metal on the open sea would sooner or later attract a lightning strike. Eleen assured them it wouldn't, though wondering the same thing himself.

Several minutes later, as the skipper, his voice pregnant with concern, informed McBride that the Feds must be no more than a quarter mile behind the *Cloud*, the militia leader's morale received a welcome boost. Eleen had found three men had claymores, snatched from what had proved to be the unnecessary second line of defense around the soccer field.

"Good stuff!" McBride said. "Eleen, rig the claymores, one on the bow, two astern."

"We have no electrical charges," Eleen answered.

"Hey!" McBride said. "Where are we here? Kindergarten? Rig 'em with trips, one man behind each. I'll have the skipper turn the tub around, head back into the wind—that'll cut the roll."

Eleen resented McBride's tone. He hadn't been spoken to like that in years, not since he'd been taken POW and shoved into Fairchild. In a moment his anger manifested itself in

hatred of Moorehead, who'd brought him to this. He was glad
the militiaman with the birthmark had shot the commandant
point-blank.

"C'mon." He pointed to three men. "We've got to rig these
claymores." They looked as tired as he felt. "Stay awake. No
mistakes. Whoever sets them up will be responsible for pulling
the trip."

Smart move, McBride thought as he approached the wheelhouse and overheard Eleen. That would wake them up. Last
thing they wanted to do was kill themselves.

"Someone grab that Beaufort raft up by the bow," McBride
called out, "and bring it astern with the clothes."

"I see the Feds on radar," the skipper told McBride. "Two
hundred and fifty yards. If that!"

Jubal called up to tell McBride the two grenade lines' release wires were in place.

"All right. Hold on a sec." McBride turned to the skipper.
"Bring her into the wind!" Then he asked Jubal, "Have you
got enough men to bring up the ROE?"

"No problem, sir."

"All right, son, let's do it."

The *Cloud*'s skipper turned the wheel by degrees, using
NVGs despite the rain-slashed background, because at least
the goggles gave him some warning of oncoming swells, en-
abling him to bring the boat more easily into the wind. The effect was dramatic—from what had been a stomach-churning
sea, the boat now entered a sea which, though by no means
calm, was noticeably less turbulent. It would make rigging
the claymores and bringing up the equipment from below less
onerous than Jubal or Eleen's men had anticipated.

But having come about, the skipper knew the boat was virtually stationary, the engine barely sufficient to hold the
boat's position against the allied forces of wind and current.

This also meant that the pursuing boat would close even more quickly on the *Cloud*.

"They'll be here in five minutes!" he shouted.

"See them?" Freeman shouted against the wind and rumble of the inboard's engine.

"Not yet," replied a sodden Aussie, stationed at the inboard's bow. "Rain's coming down in sheets."

"Choir?" Freeman hollered, alerting the Welshman positioned at the stern. He wanted his five-man squad ready, should the militia boat dead ahead try a sudden C-turn to sneak up behind them. Accidentally overshooting the militia boat was also a distinct possibility in the foul weather, now that the radar was acting up, its sweep revealing nothing but static.

As Jubal and four other men aboard *Cloud* manhandled the ROE to the stern deck, its shape through the skipper's NVGs appeared as a monstrously long and ugly folded umbrella. Its collapsible rotors had been lashed securely to its side, the gas tank, fold-down seat, and footrests obscured by Jubal and the others.

Ignoring Jubal's strenuous efforts to place the ROE upright against the wheelhouse, McBride focused his attention on collecting as many flashlights as he could. He had wanted to use the *Cloud*'s issue of life jackets—only six in all—but decided against it, since it was highly unlikely in such a downpour that the tiny salt-activated lights on the life jackets would be seen by the Feds. And so now he was piling the half-dozen flashlights he'd commandeered and switched on into the small six-man inflatable raft.

"Can we borrow your man to help us here?" McBride asked Eleen.

"Sorry, Major. We're about to set the trip."

"All right, men," McBride told his raft squad. "We'll drop it over the port side."

"Port side?" came a landlubber's voice.

"Left side!" another said.

"Heave!" McBride shouted, and as if on cue, a sky-rending streak of lightning lit up the sea around them. The skipper's NVGs, and those of Aussie Lewis, the militia's bow lookout only two hundred yards to the west, bloomed.

Aussie saw nothing but a whiteout. "Son of a—"

Before he'd finished cursing, McBride's men, having lifted the raft, now adroitly dropped it atop a swell. A second later the raft was twenty yards out.

"Ten o'clock!" Brentwood shouted. "About 250 yards." All he could ID through his single-tube night vision binocular was a watery blur of light and what looked like the figure of a militiaman—because of the World War Two helmet—appearing momentarily, then disappearing between the swells.

Freeman had also seen something momentarily illuminated through the hiss of rain, but Aussie hadn't reported anything. Besides, what Freeman had seen wasn't at ten o'clock, as Brentwood just reported, but more like one o'clock.

"Probably saw the same thing!" Choir asserted.

But the wide arc between eleven and one o'clock at such short range bothered the general. "No, I think there are two of 'em, Choir. Bastards are gonna come at us on either flank." With that, the general cautioned, "Hold on, boys!" spinning the wheel hard aport. "That smartass McBride. I'm coming up on *his* flank. Put one of his two boats between us and him. See how he likes them apples!"

"Give 'em shit, General!" Aussie shouted, and through his NVGs, now back to normal, he spotted a small but clearly winking hot spot that was the *Cloud*'s rotating radar arm.

"You're right, General. There's something at one o'clock."

"Right!" Freeman was jubilant. "Aussie, stay at the bow.

Sal, at the stern. David, you and Choir on the starboard side."
This way he knew he could bring four weapons on full automatic to bear. Snapping on the helm's "club" to hold the inboard steady, he walked over to the wheelhouse's starboard
window, the boat rolling heavily, and using its leather tongue,
pulled down the window so he could fire his weapon if he got
the chance.

The sharp electric crackle of lightning and the unnerving
claps of thunder increased, and in one spectacularly multi-
pronged display, the small rubber boat that McBride had
hoped would continue to confuse his pursuers was revealed
again to Freeman's lookouts, but this time for what it was—
an uninhabited raft, cast adrift and containing nothing more
than a jumble of flashlights and a strangely rigid figure,
which Brentwood through his NV binocular tube could see
was a militia uniform bound tightly to a stick or rifle, a World
War Two helmet fixed atop the hastily constructed mock-up.

But if Freeman's small five-man squad were no longer
fooled by McBride's ploy, the latter had succeeded in distracting the general's team long enough for them to have lost
sight of the *Cloud*.

In fact, the militia skipper, on McBride's orders and aided
by a strong local westward current, had taken the *Cloud*
though the sheets of rain, across wind, swinging it about and
coming up behind the Federals. The *Cloud*'s skipper was now
using the effervescent wake of the inboard's prop as a marker,
one that Eleen, now manning the *Cloud*'s bow-mounted claymore, took as Divine aid in their hour of need. The Federal
boat was not yet visible, but the *Cloud*'s radar indicated it was
no more than 150 yards away, the storm's north wind now
giving the *Cloud* such a push that the militiamen crowding
behind Eleen ready to start firing their weapons the moment
he detonated the claymore momentarily felt as if they were on
a huge surfboard.

"Slow us down!" McBride ordered the skipper. "Sound of our engine'll carry with the wind behind us. Don't want to tip them off before—"

The skipper heard it too, the faint but distinct sound of rotors chopping the air amid the howling of wind and the constant hiss of rain spattering the sea. Federals? Lucky McBride felt his stomach churn. Maybe his luck was running out? he thought. Eleen and the other men forward of the wheelhouse heard it too.

So did Freeman and the squad ahead of them, Aussie looking up vainly into the pelting rain, seeing nothing but a tiny red light, which he supposed was the helo's tail rotor blinker.

Then, as quickly as it had come, it was gone, and in that time, during which a flash of lightning miles to the north revealed a bug-shaped chopper heading in the direction of the island, the *Cloud* was closing on the Federals. Lightning threw the sea into stark relief, long streaks of spindrift everywhere, like some giant spiderweb over the heaving ocean. Both boats saw one another in the light, so bright it drained all color, each boat's complement seeing the other in sharply etched black and white, Salvini spotting the other's bow-mounted mine.

"Claymore!" he shouted.

"Full ahead!" McBride shouted. "Everything you've got."

Freeman did the same, neither wanting to expose his boat to a broadside of fire, red and green tracer now streaking through the rainy darkness.

The high, whistling sound of over six hundred ball bearings shot forward from the militia's boat, giving way to the sound of them striking the Federals' boat. Everyone on Freeman's vessel took cover, all hitting the deck except for Freeman, who had no option but to crouch low in the inboard's wheelhouse. Several of the steel bearings ricocheted off the boat's gunwales into the wheelhouse's windshield, a spray of small but razor-sharp glass lacerating Freeman's face before he could resume control of the wheel.

The *Cloud*'s skipper was dead, killed in a burst from Salvini that completely blew out the *Cloud*'s wheelhouse glass, wind and rain invading. The *Cloud* rolled hard astarboard, Lucky McBride having left the wheelhouse after giving his order to the skipper. A two-storied wave slammed into the *Cloud*, washing several men across the deck and over the port side, the huge, black wall of water continuing to push the *Cloud* through a thirty-degree arc before she righted herself, wallowing dangerously in succeeding troughs.

Eleen, now trying desperately to reach the helm, was fighting gravity as water was sucked rapidly back into the sea, creating a vortex that tore several more men away from the gunwales as if they were mere detritus in some enormous oceanic sink. Their cries were lost to the sound of wind-whipped sea and the tortuous creaking of the *Cloud*'s timbered and acrylic decking under enormous strain. Finally reaching the wheel, Eleen, though slipping in a mush sloshing to and fro on the wheelhouse floor, regained control. He brought the boat into the wind to steady her, McBride yelling down below for Jubal to bring the grenades. Jubal, however, was gone.

"You!" McBride yelled. "Go below—get the grenades!"

"Get 'em yourself."

"What's your name?"

"Mickey Mouse."

McBride, legs astride to counter the roll, drew his pistol and shot him, the dead militiaman thudding to the deck.

"You!" McBride ordered another. "Bring me the grenades. I have too much to do here!"

The man was already there, leaving McBride angry at

himself for having offered any explanation. Discipline was going to hell.

What he needed was a bit of his legendary luck.

Eleen, on the other hand, saw it as a time of trial—an unequivocal test of faith.

On Freeman's boat, now three hundred yards away, Aussie could hear the chopping sound of rotors again, confirmed by Ali, Brentwood, Choir Williams, and Salvini, though their eardrums were still recovering from the din of the storm and firefight.

For Mark Aitken in Anacortes, everything was coming apart, the query from Marte Price only the latest in a line of inquiries about what was going on, based upon an open radio report from a fisherman south of Lopez. While the fisherman was in the security zone imposed by Whidbey's jamming, all he could hear was static. But once out of it, en route to his home port on Lopez, he had called the Coast Guard to ask about a mysterious glow over one of the far islands. A Gulf War vet, he also reported what had looked to him like streaks of tracer beyond the island.

After that, a flood of calls came into the Coast Guard from others who had picked up the fisherman's inquiry on their shortwave. The Coast Guard officials struggled to keep the lid on by giving vague reassurances that nothing was wrong, one imaginative official near the Canadian–U.S. border absurdly suggesting to a caller that what the fisherman had seen was the "northern lights."

"In a *storm*?" came the tart reply.

And with the fisherman's report of tracer, a shaken Aitken called Brownlee. "What'll we do?" he asked.

Brownlee too could see the headlines: "Disaster Upon Disaster."

"All right, all right!" Brownlee said angrily. "Don't panic!"

his bad temper masking his own fright. "We'll have Whidbey cease the jamming and have the Coast Guard respond. Dammit! We have no way of knowing whether that bastard McBride is dead or alive."

As he hung up, Aitken noticed his hands were trembling, and he reflected upon the fact that Brownlee was concerned only about McBride, not the fate of Freeman—their only chance of mitigating the abysmal failure so far. He called Boeing Field and told the Osprey to go back.

"In this weather?"

"Yes, dammit. In this weather. And check the waters off the island." Next he called Whidbey and asked them to send out rescue choppers as well.

CHAPTER FORTY-SIX

FREEMAN FOUGHT THE inboard's wheel, the wind and rain blowing at gale force through the smashed bridge glass. Leaning hard against the helm, he called to his men, "Everyone cool?"

Ali, despite their dire situation, couldn't help but laugh. *"Cool?"* It just wasn't part of the general's vocabulary, but just as Freeman had kept himself upgraded with every advance in things military, he also tried to keep up with the lexicon of youth.

"Cool?" came Aussie's shouted reply, as spray drenched him at the bow. "It's as cold as a fish's tit."

The helo's rotors, having faded, were now audible again. Then, after another flash from the chain lightning, Choir Williams shouted, "Jap overhead!"

In the wheelhouse, Freeman couldn't see up, but he instinctively reacted by heeling the inboard hard aport as Brentwood, looking skyward, saw nothing in the darkness that enveloped them again. But he did hear a loud thump on the starboard gunwale. McBride, his ROE bucking the wind, was almost blinded by spray as he'd released the first series of taped grenades. Their explosion, after striking and bouncing off the gunwale, produced an enormous bluish-white flash astern. The force of the detonation perforated the inboard's hull, everyone except Freeman firing above the explosion. But they knew it was a crap shoot, the militiaman no doubt having veered off the second he'd fired his homemade bomb.

"Sal!" Freeman roared. "Check damage! Choir, Ali, ready with flares. He'll be back!"

"Unless we're already sinking," Brentwood called.

"What the—" They could hear rotors again, but this time they were much louder, like those of a larger chopper.

"Mightn't be him!" Brentwood cautioned.

"He's a fellow American!" Ali said out of the blue.

"So was Robert E. Lee. Get ready with that damn flare!"

The rotors were growing louder, then Aussie remembered seeing the winking tail rotor light of another chopper.

"Fire flares!" Freeman shouted.

There were two bangs, one a second after the first. Beneath the dazzling flare light, they plunged into a deep trough and rose to see the ROE, a black stick insect, its rotors a shining blur. McBride's body seemed to be grafted onto the stick; the rotors louder, they realized, because now he was coming in, this time with the wind behind him.

Firing erupted from every part of the boat, Freeman and company spraying the air above them with automatic fire while the flare lights, illuminating them as well as McBride, made them a clearly visible target for the *Cloud*. The militia boat, however, was over five hundred yards away, Eleen ordered by McBride to keep it well clear during his runs at the Federals. Meanwhile, the men aboard the *Cloud* had opened up on Freeman's boat, but given the state of the sea, wind, and rain, the militia's fire was wild and ineffective, only a few rounds striking the Federals' boat, wounding Ali in the left arm and knocking David Brentwood down. Losing his footing, the impact, despite his helmet, caused Brentwood to black out.

Though McBride could see how intense the fire was from the Federals' boat, he steeled himself as he closed with the second "bomb," his body numb with cold, but all his concentration centered on controlling the ROE. Unlike its smooth performance in the Cascades, it was now acting more like a Brahman bull than a helo, the grenade bomb dangling precariously from its quick-release bowline beneath his foot bar. He glimpsed the Federals below. Dropping to an altitude of a mere forty feet, he released, and rose to 120 feet, when the ROE suddenly began vibrating beyond control. The usual *wokka wokka* of the rotors had been replaced by a jerking, arthritic shrieking, the blades disintegrating in a burst of automatic fire. Knowing he had no more than three seconds before he'd crash, he punched his harness release and fell forward, twenty feet above the roiling ocean. He heard a heavy, rapid chopping sound nearby as the fractured blades, having sheared from the main shank, cartwheeled then sank, the rest of the ROE disappearing beneath the waves.

But McBride had been lucky with the second drop. The grenades detonated adjacent to the inboard's fuel tank, diesel vapor immediately exploding as Freeman yelled, "Abandon ship!" knowing they had only five to ten seconds at most before the heavy diesel liquid would be raised by the vapor burn to its flashpoint.

There was a roar of jubilation from the *Cloud*, whose men, unable to see McBride going down on the Feds' off side, had nevertheless seen the bomb go off. This was followed a few seconds later by the huge orange blossom of the vapor fire, and then the boom of the fuel tank itself. The only reason Freeman and company survived, at least for the moment, was the heavy seas, which threw up several walls of water between them and the doomed inboard. It didn't protect them from the effects of the concussion, however, which stunned them, especially Brentwood. Having barely regained consciousness following his fall on the deck, he was grabbed by Ali and tossed overboard. Salvini was throwing up on his life jacket, while trying unsuccessfully to use a sodden bandage from his helmet pack to put as a tourniquet on his left arm, which had been ripped open at the elbow by a piece of grenade shrapnel.

Looking around, treading water, gathering his wits, Freeman inflated his life jacket, then saw Salvini nearby, his head back, mouth open like a fish, sensibly getting what moisture he could from the rain. "Sal?" the general cried out. "You okay?"

Sal closed his mouth. "You still want that damage report, General?"

"Think they—" Ali began, his voice cut off by the next wave cresting. "Think the militia'll pick us up, sir?"

"Everyone in close!" Freeman yelled. "Tie up! Stay together!"

Aussie came in, like Sal and Choir, but David Brentwood couldn't be seen, and now Salvini could smell the oil.

"What are you doing?" a tall, thin militiaman bellowed at Eleen.

"Going to pick them up," Eleen said, raising his voice to be heard over the ice cold rain.

"Are you *insane*?"

"*Captain* to you," Eleen retorted.

"Are you insane?" the man repeated, his bullying tone receiving a guttural chorus of support from other menacing, dark figures gathering about Eleen. Curses were now directed at Eleen's "wacko" idea, as the big militiaman now described it, to attempt rescuing the Federals.

"We've been fightin' the bastards in this goddamn storm, and now you wanna pick 'em up?"

"He's a Jesus freak!" someone charged.

"They're men in the water," Eleen said.

"An' let 'em stay there!"

"They're Federals, for God's sake!" another enjoined.

"*God,*" Eleen shouted, "would want them picked up!"

"Then let *'im* pick 'em up," another said. "Our job is to get to the mainland under cover of the storm. That's what McBride wanted us to do."

"Yeah, *Captain*. That was his order."

"He might still be alive," Eleen said, his body pushed rudely about by the force of the wheel spinning under the impact of a fifteen-foot wave.

"Are you kidding?" growled the big militiaman who'd started the confrontation. "The major went down like a friggin' rock!"

"I didn't—see—him," Eleen retorted, fighting to regain control of the wheel, his eyes peeled for the life jacket lights that, God willing, would give him the positions of the men from the sunken vessel.

"I did," the malcontent lied. "I saw 'im. Still strapped to the fuckin' helo. Poor bastard!"

"Yeah," another said, as Eleen continued his fight to regain control of the wheel, and his men.

"You hear us, Captain?" a mortarman said. "We gotta get outta here."

Before Eleen could muster another reply, the big militiaman bellowed for everyone to shut up. "Listen!" he began,
but before he could continue, a raging torrent of foam-
greased water roared down from the *Cloud*'s bow, flooding
around the tiny island of the wheelhouse. One man lost his
grip, screaming for help, but was swept over the stern before
anyone could reach him. Seconds later someone shone a flashlight beam, looking for him, but all anyone could see was a
puny, pale beam of light on the heaving wildness of the sea.

"Put that out!" the big militiaman shouted. "You idiot—
you want 'em to see us?"

"Who?" a militia youngster asked.

"The Feds in that chopper!" the big militiaman said.

And now they could all hear the distinct *wokka wokka*
somewhere above.

"How do we know it's Feds?" the youngster pressed.

"Well, it sure as hell isn't McBride, is it?"

"Guess not," the youngster commented sullenly.

"Jesus!" someone hollered, watching the compass in its
gimbals mounting. "Eleen's still steering us toward where
those bastards—"

Eleen didn't hear the rest, his head exploding in a crazed
pattern of light, his body crumpling, blood running down his
neck where one of the mutinous militiamen had brought
down the AK-47's stock, splitting open his skull.

"Take 'im below," the lead mutineer barked. "I'll take the
wheel." With that, he swung hard away from the southern
course the *Cloud* had been on and turned due east, in the direction of the eighty-mile-long mass of Fidalgo and Whidbey
Islands, thirty miles away. Both islands were joined by the
famed bridge over the whirlpools of Deception Pass. Anywhere but the pass would do to land.

"We shouldn't have done that," said the militiaman who
had lied about seeing McBride go down.

"Now don't you go all Willy Dick on me!" the tall mutineer told him. "Willy," referring to Bill Clinton, was one of the favorite put-down words of the Northwest militia. "How many of our guys are dead?"

"I don't know—about four, five."

"Well, whatever the number, throw 'em overboard. We need all the speed we can get from this tub."

The young militiaman hesitated. "Just like that? Overboard?"

"Hey, the salt chuck was good enough for McBride. It's good enough for them. Right?"

"I—I guess so."

"Then get moving, and tell the others to toss over everything that isn't bolted down. Every pound counts."

Now they saw a bluish, narrow, cone-shaped light probing the darkness about a quarter mile to the west.

"You see?" the lead mutineer shouted. "We left just in time. Right? Or would you rather be picked up? Do like in Fairchild?"

There was no answer.

"Uh-huh," their leader said. "Just as I thought. Well, boys, we could do with an extra knot or so. Get to the mainland 'fore this storm blows itself out."

No one spoke, but after a while he could see a clump of them making their way slowly and laboriously against the swells to the starboard side, dumping something that made a heavy splash.

CHAPTER FORTY-SEVEN

FREEMAN'S HOPE THAT his five could all join together, or "tie up" with him, as he'd put it, had been thwarted by the wind and massive swells. As soon as either Aussie, Choir, or Sal appeared to be nearing him, they were swept away by another wave, disappearing into the deep troughs. He hadn't seen Brentwood or Ali at all, and soon, as the second flare spluttered out, he could only see Choir—or was it Sal?—coughing violently, none of them recognizable, hair plastered down from the spreading slick of oil.

At last he felt someone grab him. It looked like Salvini, and Freeman kept a grip on his collar, the diesel having made his clothing and life vest so slippery it was difficult to get a firm grip anywhere else. For a moment, as the two of them slid down into the next trough, Freeman had to release Sal in order to complete the tie-up, when the tumbling crest of another wave came crashing down on them with such power that, though the general reached out to grab Salvini's collar again, the New Yorker was gone.

"Sal? Sal?" But if Sal answered, Freeman couldn't hear him.

The rain eased, then stopped almost as suddenly as it had come. Moonlight appeared. It appeared to the general as a cruel joke, for while he could now see the blue search beam stabbing down at the sea in the distance, he could literally hear his teeth chattering and knew that all of them would very soon be in the clutches of hypothermia. He saw a wink of orange light, no bigger than a thimble to his eyes. "Sal?" The light disappeared, then a few seconds later reappeared. Or was it a different light? Whoever he or they were, possibly Ali and Brentwood, he wanted to tell them not to swim, the expenditure of effort in such conditions only depleting one's energy, when every bit was needed in the narrow margin between life and death.

For a moment he thought it was the militiaman who'd attacked them, then he thought it was David Brentwood, the man still wearing his helmet. Or was it a toque? Perhaps Ali? The general didn't know—he was becoming delirious, and now he saw all of them jumping out of a Herk, on one of their many HALO or HAHO jumps, a part of him shouting out to get control, another part of him watching himself and seeing a long white tunnel, a man beside him groaning in pain, his head lolling dangerously in the water, covered in oil and saying, though it took him a long time, "Damn! You're Freeman?" But was it real?

It wasn't a voice the general recognized, but fighting against the deepening stages of hypothermia, he thought it might be McBride, the man he'd been sent to kill. Even so, he said, "Hang on, you bastard," grabbing the man's oily hair, time and again lifting the man's head above the water. "Hang on!"

Sal was bleeding badly, his tourniquet having come unraveled. He was unable to grasp a floating plywood door that had been blown out of the boat amid the other debris, the door also greased by the storm-driven diesel slick around them. By the time Freeman saw the door, he could no longer speak, but with his left hand wrapped about the other man's neck, keeping the other's head up, he felt below his life vest and removed one of his two remaining grenades and felt it fall from his hand. Just barely managing to grasp the other grenade, a flash-bang, he freed it from the vest, and using his teeth to pull the pin, dropped it on purpose. The five seconds before it blew was enough time for him and his companion to be swept twenty or more feet away, the explosion barely visible as a fuss of effervescent bubbles in the plankton-rich sea, but bright enough for the chopper pilot to spot through NVGs. It was also sufficiently powerful for Choir and the others to feel the shockwave, its sound traveling in the water four times faster than in the air.

Sal called out, "Over here—" and Freeman could see him clinging to the door, its oil-slicked surface momentarily mirroring moonlight.

The general exhorting his companion, "Hold on!" trying to use his right arm as a paddle, his left arm still around the man's neck, holding his head up. Freeman's legs spread slowly, then pushed in breaststroke fashion. In fact, he was making no progress at all, the floating door, with the rest of the debris and oil slick, moving toward him in a trail of assorted flotsam from the inboard's explosion.

Though attracted to the general area where they'd seen the upwelling of phosphorus from the grenade, the helo's crew elected to attend first to two survivors who were without the benefit of anything like the door to hang onto.

"Deploy swimmer," came the pilot's voice, and the helo's air mechanic engaged the hoist gear. Within seconds the thin cable began lowering the wet-suited and Day-Glo-harnessed rescue swimmer. As the swimmer gyrated, the pilot and copilot fighting to keep the helo steady in the fiercely buffeting winds, they could see the bright white circle of the chopper's spotlight fifty feet below. It slid up and down the swells like a sodden sheet, tendrils of spindrift crisscrossing it as it moved toward the two survivors, bobbing like ebony-colored corks as the spotlight was reflected off their oil-slicked hair.

It was dangerous, nerve-wracking work, but the helo crew of four had done it before off this part of the wild West Coast where the vast Pacific rollers finally approach landfall after their unimpeded five-thousand-mile journey from the other side of the earth.

The rescue swimmer was in the water, the flattening down-blast from the rotors creating a minor storm within the storm, spray and wind swirling about. The swimmer moved the harness toward the first survivor as they were both swept up and down a big cross swell. The mechanic thought he saw the bright orange web harness attached on the survivor, and had his gloved hand on the hoist's gear. Nevertheless, he was waiting for the hoist-up signal from the swimmer. Unequipped with such dangerous impedimenta as throat mikes, the only trusted signal was a hand signal, a swimmer's voice unable to be heard, lost in the maelstrom of wind, prop wash, and raging ocean.

The mechanic saw the swimmer's arm moving in a circular motion above his head, and he immediately engaged the winch for slow lift, the swimmer staying behind with the second man.

The body of the man being lifted appeared as two-toned, jet-black from the top of his head to neck and upper chest, a sodden greenish khaki from there down to his feet. Water, silver in the spotlight, streamed from him as he rotated slowly, water spitting from the straining wire. The man's hands and arms hung stiffly by his side, too frozen to grasp the harness's swivel neck, telling the mechanic that despite all the technological wizardry of the twenty-first century, he'd still have to manhandle the survivor into the chopper.

"We see another three, possibly four," came the copilot's voice. "They're clinging to some kind of wreckage."

"Roger," the mechanic said, hurriedly strapping the rescued man into a seat and punching the heater to full blast, while lowering the harness at fifty feet a second, signaling the swimmer that there were more survivors sighted.

"How's it going?" the copilot asked, his query annoying the mechanic, who knew damn well that the copilot *knew* how it was going. All the fool had to do was glance through the helo's nose panel. But at the same time, the mechanic understood the copilot's concern. If they didn't reach the others quickly, hypothermia would kill them.

The moment they had the other man and swimmer aboard, the helo veered several hundred yards farther to the south, the swimmer, pushing back his Nomex hood, handing both men drip-top water bottles. "How you feelin'?"

David Brentwood nodded.

"What's your buddy's name?" he asked.

"Will—Will—" Brentwood began, but his tongue was already swollen from his exposure. "Choir, Choir Will—"

The swimmer smiled, patting the Medal of Honor winner's arm before turning to the Welshman with a heavy woolen blanket. "Hang in there, Mr. Choir."

The Welshman gave a hoarse reply, but now the chopper was shaking violently as the pilot again took it down, this time closer to the waves. In the continuing race against time, the rescue swimmer would have to jump in, hook and harness coming after.

Pulling the wet suit's hood back over his head, the swimmer took a deep breath, splashing down at the rim of the beam where the rotors' wash made it almost impossible for the men clinging to the door to see, their eyelids and eyebrows already encrusted with salt.

Freeman, his right arm on the door, still had his left around his companion's neck, and in a flash of lightning saw the man's face clearly. It *was* McBride. The general, holding his enemy's head out of the water, could tell the militiaman was drifting in and out of consciousness, probably as a result of his loss of blood from the injuries as he'd ejected from his one-man helo.

Ali, though guided over toward the door by the grenade's explosion, was clearly exhausted by the effort, having swallowed oil, which was now making him violently ill. To make matters worse, a long, diagonal crack in the door seemed to be widening.

Freeman, though aware that the flying glass that had lacerated his face had also punctured his life vest, insisted to the rescue swimmer that he take Ali and Sal up first, followed by him and McBride.

"I'm in charge here, General," the swimmer shouted, then proceeded to do exactly as Freeman had suggested. The swimmer tried to slip the harness onto Sal, missed as a rush of foam passed over them, then managed to snag him and go up with him. Ali kept losing his grip on the ad hoc raft, trying to reach for the blister pack of Gravol in his top pocket, but his fingers were too stiff to deal with it. It was as if he didn't realize that he'd soon be hoisted into the helo. Or perhaps he did.

The hook and harness were coming down again when the improvised raft was lifted high and fast by a rogue wave, one edge of the door jutting out of the water. As the wave passed, it came down on Freeman's elbow with such force that the general lost his grip on McBride, both of them disappearing into the dark, heaving world beyond the spotlight's beam.

"Shit!" the swimmer yelled, and quickly looked around, but saw no sign of them. He grabbed Ali, his attempts to get the big black man into harness his most difficult task that night. Even so, within forty seconds, a remarkable achievement for the swimmer in such outrageous seas, he had Ali "wrapped and away." The helo's spotlight shifted now, so that while Ali was still "in beam," he was no longer at its center, the pilot trying to move the light as far as he could in the direction in which the two other men had vanished.

"There they are!" the copilot announced, but it was the door, and only the door.

"Got 'em!" he said again excitedly. "Ten o'clock, hundred yards."

As soon as Ali had been "landed" and the swimmer was retracted high enough above the water, the helo moved toward Freeman and McBride. The swimmer hung onto the harness hook, suspended fifteen feet below the helo, the wind tearing at him. His face was numb and his eyes were tearing, the swimmer, like most of his ilk, disdaining goggles, which invariably fogged up precisely when you needed them.

As Freeman retrieved McBride, who had momentarily been torn away by the force of a wave, he saw what to his tired eyes looked like something surfing on the next swell. Then it disappeared. It wasn't until he saw the fin again that it dawned on his tired brain that it might be a dolphin. The third time it was closer, and there was no mistake. It was a shark, no doubt having been attracted by the blood pool from Ali and McBride. And Sal.

Don't panic, don't panic, Freeman thought. Wasn't that what he always told his SpecWar trainers? Think, man, think!

By now the pilot and copilot were receiving radio instructions from Port Angeles Coast Guard to be on the lookout for various Coast Guard cutters. Simultaneously, the USCG's smaller rescue hovercraft and some local boaters were converging on the area, and a tilt rotor Osprey was en route to the island to pick up Freeman's remaining commandos and the most seriously wounded militia. The helo crew were also asked to report any militia boat sightings. Ranger leader Rick Logan estimated from the information given him by cooperative militia prisoners that there were about four or five boats "on the run." The latter description amused the rescue helo crew—as if they could identify friend or foe in such conditions.

In fact the militia boats were now on the cutter's radar, those aboard the *Cloud* and the other boats recognizing the futility of trying to outrun the fast Coast Guard ships armed with formidable 76mm guns.

The rescue swimmer was now making his way toward Freeman and McBride. Freeman, with McBride in tow, desperately tried to reach what was now a badly splintered door on the verge of disintegrating.

"Kick!" Freeman told McBride, the general calling forth all his own resolve and remaining energy to stay afloat and drag McBride to what was left of the door, when Murphy's Law struck. The ply of the door was now so waterlogged it would no longer take the weight of the two men as they attempted to grasp its edges. Freeman saw the dorsal fin pass by into the blackness, only to reappear thirty seconds later, swimming about them in ever-decreasing circles.

His left arm still holding McBride's head to keep it from flopping down where the constant wash of water would quickly drown him, the general reached down until he could feel his holster and drew the Glock, the swimmer still an agonizing fifty feet away. As the shark rushed at them, riding an oncoming swell, illuminated by spotlight, the swell lifting the two men and the great white in unison, Freeman fired four shots, none of them hitting the predator as far as he could tell, but the noise of the supersonic rounds perhaps surprising it. The shark veered off, but not for long, the heat from the Glock meanwhile producing a minor miracle in Freeman— the firearm's warmth suddenly warming the general's hand, giving it much more flexibility.

McBride's head was up; four shots fired adjacent to an ear was better than espresso to rally even the semicomatose. "What the—" The militiaman's whole body jerked as he saw the nightmarish rows of white saw teeth in the huge pink mouth racing toward him from barely six feet away. McBride couldn't hear anything, swallowed in a hollow cone of silence, as Freeman fired another four shots, three of them smashing home—a silent implosion of crimson blood jetting from the roof of the great white's mouth, another round smashing a tooth, the last shot missing the mouth but boring into the would-be killer's left eye. There was a whack on Freeman's shoulder. He swung the Glock around.

"No! No!" the swimmer shouted, both hands thrust high above his life jacket.

A second later, one hand grasping the harness's swivel joint, he released Freeman's arm from about the militiaman's neck. "Give him to me!" the swimmer said, moving the harness toward McBride. "Can you go up with him?" the swimmer asked Freeman.

"Don't think I can hold!" Freeman admitted.

"All right, we'll make it a threesome. I'll—" His voice was lost in the roar of a cresting wave, the swimmer smelling the blood in the water. "I'll loop your vest to his harness."

It seemed to take forever, as Freeman still kept lookout for the shark. There was a warm sensation in his legs. It was something he would never admit to for the rest of his life: he'd involuntarily urinated from the sheer fright he'd experienced on seeing the mass of razor-sharp teeth coming at him, then wondering whether the shark would return.

The hoist was straining, precariously near its 600-pound limit. The mechanic could see the strain, the hoist's engine vibrating so violently he feared it would break free of its mountings. The pilot could also feel the extra pull, the twin rotors roaring above, the spray they whipped up now coming down on the greenhouse window above the cockpit so that it seemed as if it was raining anew. Meanwhile, the copilot, continuing to search the darkness with his NVGs, saw what he assumed

must be the approaching lights of Coast Guard vessels, before
he realized the pinpoints of light, visible one moment, gone
the next, were much closer than he thought to the helo. Ignoring the thumps and bumps behind him as the mechanic
hauled the swimmer aboard first, so they could grapple with
Freeman and McBride's harness, the copilot concluded that
what he was seeing was a boat. He was mistaken, but not by
much, the lights being those of the militia's sucker rubber raft,
its lone, helmeted dummy, clothes blown away, now having to
share the company of Aussie Lewis, whose grateful comment
upon being winched to safety was, "About fucking time!"

Eight miles east of the U.S.–Canada maritime boundary,
heading back east towards Whidbey, the long strings of
mussel farm lights coming into view, the pilot left the chopper's controls to the copilot, and went aft to check on the survivors. Aussie Lewis, though freezing, was in better shape
and more alert than the others, given the protection afforded
him by the raft. He was the first to realize that the pilot was a
woman, aware of her perfume before he saw her helmeted
face and figure in the chopper's dimly lit interior. "You look
okay, soldier!" she told Aussie, smiling as she squeezed past
the air mechanic, who was busy wiping the oil from Ali's face.

"Not really, Lieutenant," Aussie said. "I'm freezing. But I
read somewhere it's customary for rescuers to lie naked with
survivors. You know, help raise their core temperature. Otherwise they might *die*!"

"Well, maybe our air mechanic could assist?" she parried
with another smile, and checked on the others, pleased to see
that all were rallying. The life-saving heat blasting out of the
heater was so stifling that she was about to return to the
cockpit when she recognized McBride, the rescue swimmer
about to place a gauze patch on the militiaman's head wound.
They looked hard at each other.

"Lieutenant Frieth," he said finally.

She'd imagined so many times what she might say to the man who'd traumatized her and shot the policeman, throwing his body out of the helo; the militia rebel who'd scared even his accomplice witless. But now all she could think of was a banal, "So we meet again—McBride."

"Major," he said defensively, then grimaced hard as the swimmer doused the wound with iodine.

Then she thought of something better. "I guess it's back to Fairchild for you and the boys."

"I've never been there!" he responded defiantly.

"You will be now."

"We'll see."

She paused. "You should thank the general you're still alive."

McBride looked across at his nemesis. "Thanks," he said but his tone was ambiguous.

Freeman nodded but his eyes conveyed the same kind of ambiguity, the general wondering if his gallantry would come back to bite him and his men.

"Lieutenant?" It was the copilot, with a message from Whidbey. "Reporter from CNN's at the base. Old man says we're to say nothing. Let the general handle it—if he's up to it."

"Damn reporters," was all Freeman could manage at the moment, but in fact he was delighted. What was it Omar Bradley had said about Patton? "Give George a headline and he's good for another hundred miles!"

"General!" Aussie said. "Would you like a shot of whiskey?"

"You betcha!"

"So would I," Aussie said, guffawing—Choir still too cold to do anything more than grin, the others silent, luxuriating in the helo's warmth. Then the copilot saw an SOS flare.

"Boater in trouble!" came Robin Frieth's voice. "One o'clock—three hundred yards. On fire. Ready to deploy swimmer!"

"Busy night," Aussie said, but no one answered, the air mechanic quickly readying the hoist, the swimmer pulling his nomex hood forward, tucking in a few errant hairs from his forehead.

The chopper descended to fifty feet above the waves, the boat a sleek, fifteen-footer ablaze at its bow, the boater, man or woman—it was difficult to tell—struggling frantically into a survival suit. It looked like a woman, with long, flowing hair.

Caught in a wind shear, the helo dropped precipitously, the copilot sure they were going in. The helo stopped short barely ten feet above the crests, the chopper's windshield, despite its wipers working overtime, opaque from the spray blasted up by the rotors.

"Go!" Robin ordered, the swimmer splashing in two seconds later, harness smacking the water a second later.

"If we're too heavy," Aussie said loudly, looking across at McBride, "we'll throw you back in. Then you won't be so fucking *lucky*!"

McBride scoffed at him. "Your general would jump in to save me."

"You sure about that?" Freeman posed raspily, barely audible above the noise of hoist, rain, and rotors.

"Yeah," McBride answered, "I am. Beneath that 'clear the bridge' hide of yours, General, there's a hero trying to break out. Your ego'll keep pushing you till it pushes you over the edge. That's why we're gonna beat you."

"I'm no hero!" Aussie warned McBride.

"No. You're an asshole!"

Aussie, clenching his fist, tried to get up but couldn't. He was weaker than he'd thought.

"Knock it off!" the mechanic shouted, his eyes never leaving the swimmer and boater coming up.

Even when the survivor, the boat now burning from bow to stern in the storm-tossed sea, was dragged in, it was impossible for Aussie to tell whether it was a woman or man until the survival suit's hood was removed. It was a man who, though obviously not having liked the precarious haul-up, was in pretty good shape.

"You oughta buy a bloody lottery ticket, mate!" Aussie called out. "Another coupla minutes and you'd be sleeping with the fishes."

The man was nodding vigorously, obviously aware of his good fortune. "Thank you, guys," he told the mechanic and swimmer, shaking their hands. "Talk about the right place at the right time!"

"Make that the *wrong* place at the right time," the swimmer joshed.

"I guess," the man agreed. "I'd like to thank the captain and—"

The swimmer took him forward and tapped Robin Frieth on the shoulder, the man thanking her profusely.

"That's our job," she said, her tone not unfriendly but her concentration focused on her instruments.

Her copilot, more relaxed, took "five," before it was his turn to take over the controls. "It's what we get paid for," he told the rescued man amiably.

The man only now realized how many fellow survivors were on the chopper, and, as if something suddenly clicked in his brain, he looked back from them to the cockpit, asking the copilot. "Those guys back there militia terrorists?" he asked.

The copilot nodded, but added reassuringly, "Don't worry, though—all their arms are locked up. Standard procedure if we pick up anyone who's carrying."

"Good," the man said, clearly relieved, his left arm flashing out, grabbing the copilot in a headlock, his right hand jabbing a handgun into the copilot's neck. " 'Cause mine isn't locked up." He shot a fiery glance at the swimmer. "Get back with the others. Move!"

The swimmer obeyed.

Robin Frieth, fighting the wind gusts, her eyes off the instruments momentarily, asked angrily, "What do you want?"

"For you to do just what I tell you!" the man commanded. "Or I'll take his head off!"

"What do you want?" she demanded. "These men have to get to Whidbey. They've been in the water—"

"Shut your face! You've gonna do what I tell you."

Only now, the boater having lowered his voice, did McBride recognize the hijacker. Mike Ramsey, the "Beachcomber."

Nice work, Mike! Gutsy! McBride thought, but he stayed quiet. He was outnumbered—the others would get him before he could join Ramsey. He would say nothing until they landed wherever Mike was taking them. Better say something, though. "What the hell's going on?" he asked no one in particular.

"A crazy," the mechanic said. "Probably a runner." He meant one of the scores of drug runners who used small, fast boats to skip across the Canadian–U.S. maritime boundary.

"Calm down!" Robin told Ramsey, seeing she couldn't "rock and roll" the helo and try to dislodge him, because he was using her copilot as a stanchion. "Calm down. Where do you want to go?"

He told her the lat and long. *Déjà vu.* "That's over the Cascades," she told him. "We'll have to use the auxiliary tank."

"Then use it!" he snapped.

"All right, but I'm going to have to reach down by his foot, check the valve monitor, then toggle the floor switch. You'll have to move your foot an inch or so."

"I'm not moving shit! You think I was born yesterday, bitch? You do it, and slowly."

"But you won't be able to see my hand," she said, adding acidly, "I might undo your shoelaces!"

He flexed his gun hand, and she saw the copilot wince. "All right," she said. "Don't flip."

Her left hand on the control column, Robin leaned over and down, slowly. "Valve monitor says okay. I'm going to—" A gust hit them broadside, so powerful that she thought it might dislodge the hijacker. It didn't. He'd tightened his grip on the copilot, who was whey-faced, eyes bulging, staring at the wipers swishing madly to and fro.

"Toggling the switch," Robin informed Ramsey.

"Hurry up!"

"I thought you told me," she began, pulling on the control column with her left hand, her right coming up with the Ultra Carry. She fired three times, Ramsey slumping between the copilot's seat and the fuselage. Robin swiftly replaced the twenty-five-ounce gun in her ankle holster while fighting to regain control of the wildly yawing helo, her human cargo unappreciative of the violent gyrations but grateful for her quick thinking.

McBride, initially thinking it was Ramsey who was firing, had tried to leap up, but was thrown to the Huey's floor in a shuddering gust.

"Oh dear!" Aussie said, glancing from the bloody-headed hijacker down at the militia leader. "Must be your unlucky day!"

Up forward it was several minutes before the copilot regained his composure enough to laugh at Robin's inventiveness. *"Valve monitor! Toggle switch!"*

"Well, I had to think of something. It worked."

"Thank God!"

CHAPTER FORTY-EIGHT

AT WHIDBEY IT was a zoo, a throng of press and Naval Air Station officers trying to manage the scrum of radio, TV, and then the press. They were waiting anxiously for Freeman's arrival, for first bragging rights in celebrating the legendary general's return with the notorious militia leader McBride—"America's most wanted man," according to Chief Cordell. When he deplaned from the Osprey with his surviving SWAT team and a clutch of badly wounded militia prisoners, the chief was rushed to Whidbey's Oak Bay Memorial for observation.

Rick Logan and Freeman's six other commandos were still engaged in mop-up and containment duties on the devastated island, where they'd been interviewed by Marte Price. In fact, they were happy to avoid any of the hubbub on the mainland. The prospect of walking the gauntlet of microphones, flash-bulbs, and talk shows was more frightening to them than Freeman's fear of fading into obscurity. Marte Price had managed to get to Whidbey, however, ahead of the rescue chopper, and was among the throng waiting there.

In Washington, D.C., the President's aides were still walking on eggshells, knowing that they'd take an awful beating in the media for the National Guard/police failure. Brownlee, however, assured the President that the American people—the guy in the street—didn't bother with editorials and op-ed press. "They're written for armchair quarterbacks," he told him. "Most people are too busy making a buck to get beyond the headlines and sports."

"You don't think this'll be a headline?" the President shot back.

"Yes, but the screw-up was *yesterday*. Today it's Freeman, whom *you* sent in, Mr. President, and who's brought that bastard back in leg irons."

"Leg irons?" cut in Brownlee's junior aide, Ray Lawson.

"I'm speaking metaphorically," Brownlee replied.

The metaphor, however, was now a reality. Lucky McBride was shackled by sheriff's deputies the moment the rescue chopper touched down.

The press scrum was packed with every reporter from Seattle's KOMO-TV to CNN's Marte Price. The CNN reporter made her way around the periphery of the crowd with the local stringer in tow, camcorder held high.

"Ms. Price?" Whidbey's Search and Rescue PR office said, looking for an opportunity to turn over the floor to his SAR crew or Freeman.

"I'd like to ask General Freeman a question." Marte said.

"Over to you, General," the captain said.

Freeman, his battle uniform still wet, an SAR cap hastily put on to cover his oil-soaked hair, nevertheless evinced an aura of command. "Ms. Price?"

"General, given your success in defeating the militia, can you tell us why you weren't sent in first?"

Freeman was pleased with the question. It gave him the opportunity to criticize the President. But for once, the man who had offended every bureaucrat in what he called "the swamp," and had therefore assured his early retirement, decided to spare the Guard and police—fellow colleagues in the war—any embarrassment and gave what he truly believed was a diplomatic reply: "I have no idea, Ms. Price."

But what he assumed was quintessentially diplomatic turned out to be a firestorm that evening for the President, who was forced to sing Freeman's praises for his daring attack which had defeated the militia and captured "its murderous leader."

It was a long next day and night for the President and his advisors, stretching into the early hours of the morning, as they tried to put the best spin on Rice's and Cordell's failure, as more and more details kept coming on the train of Marte Price's scoop.

"But he did get McBride, sir," the CNO bravely pointed out, upon which the Commander in Chief strode angrily from the room, uttering a string of obscenities.

A half hour later the President returned, florid face matched by a violently red robe and pajamas. "Michael!" he snapped.

"Yes, sir," a startled Brownlee said.

"I want you to call him—right now! This minute! And you tell him—"

"Yes, sir, but, ah, it'll be midnight on the West Coast."

"I don't care. You call him. Find out where he is and wake the son of a bitch up!"

"Yes, sir. Ah, his number's in my office. I'll call him from there."

"Right away, Michael!"

"Yes, sir."

Alone in his corner office, deliberately delaying the call, Brownlee was going over the *Washington Post*'s mug shots of McBride's captured lieutenants, a mean-looking bunch that included one with a birthmark, a guy they said was a Mormon. There was a woman too. God, she looked tough.

He put the newspaper aside, took a deep breath, and punched in the numbers of Freeman's cell phone at twenty after midnight West Coast time. He expected to hear an operator informing him that "the cellular customer you have dialed is away from the phone or temporarily out of the service area. Please try your call later." Instead Freeman answered, the general's voice raspy, as labored as when Brownlee had originally contacted him about the possibility of using his commandos.

"General, Michael Brownlee here."

"Yes," came the reply, followed by a rush of air.

"Good God, General," Brownlee said. "You're not in the middle of another practice HALO jump, are you?"

"Not a HALO, HA*HO*. High altitude—" He paused. "—High opening. Can make this sucker—last—for over an hour."

His breathing was even more labored now, Brownlee amazed at Freeman's mental resilience and physical fitness when he was barely back from combat and almost being drowned.

"General, you did a magnificent job routing the militia."

"*Routing* them? Hell, we—whopped—" He paused again. "We whopped their ass."

"Yes, and got McBride. We'll lock up him and his boys where they belong. What's left of them."

"It's not the end of 'em—" The general was wheezing.

"You okay, General?"

"Yeah—think I might spiral this chute—cut my drop time."

"Uh-huh. What were you saying about it not being the end?"

"I mean those bastards like McBride and his sidekicks never give up. You boys might need me again."

"I don't think so, General. In fact that's what I want—"

"Gotta go, son!" the general said urgently. "Call you back." And the line went dead.

In the dimly lit hotel room that overlooked Seattle's Pike Market, Marte Price murmured softly, "Who was *that*?"

"White House. Congratulating me."

"Then I'll forgive you."

"Sorry," he told her. "Should've turned the damn thing off. Hate people who are always big-timing with their cells, but I thought this time o' night, might be an emergency. If I'd known—"

"Shh," she said, smiling, putting her finger to his lips. "All this talk. I thought you were a man of action?"

"I am."

"Make me believe it."

He did.

They've drawn the line—in blood.

BATTLE FRONT
USA vs. Militia

by Ian Slater

The militia movement is spreading like wildfire
—more violent, more organized, and more
committed than ever to an armed victory over
the United States.

Battle Front is the terrifying story of home-
grown terrorism on a grand scale.

Published by Ballantine Books.
Available in bookstores everywhere.

MANHUNT

USA vs. Militia

by Ian Slater

The United States Militia Corps, fighting for its life, pulls off a daring hospital breakout of two injured soldiers. An all-out chase across the desert leads to a showdown at the California state line, where transporting kidnapped hostages becomes a federal offense. And Federal General Douglas Freeman is waiting for the word to get back into the fight.

Manhunt is a wild ride into the heart of America's Second Civil War, but this time with high-tech modern weapons and tactics that threaten national annihilation.

WWIII:
WARSHOT

General Cheng is massing divisions on the Manchurian border while Siberia's Marshal Yesov readies his army on the western flank. If successful, this offensive will drive the American-led U.N. force into the sea.

WWIII:
ASIAN FRONT

At Manzhouli, near the border of China, Siberia, and Mongolia, the Chinese launch their charge into the woods. It's all-out war, and only the brave and ruthless will survive.

WWIII:
FORCE OF ARMS

Four sleek Tomahawk cruise missiles are headed for Beijing. It is Armageddon in Asia.

WWIII:
SOUTH CHINA SEA

On the South China Sea an oil rig erupts in flames as AK-47 tracer rounds stitch the night and men die in pools of blood. From Japan to Malaysia, the Pacific Rim is ablaze in a hell called WWIII.

The World War III series
by Ian Slater
Published by Fawcett Books.
Available in bookstores everywhere.

**Find an enemy. Choose a weapon.
Start the clock.**

FORCE 10

USA vs. Militia

by Ian Slater

Someone has hijacked one of America's most
important military secrets and it could mean
the destruction of the United States.

Force 10 is the gripping story of a deadly
conspiracy launched against America and the
elite soldiers who will risk their lives to stop it.